Fingers Of The Black Hand

He saw Phil. "Ya ain't goin' nowheres, punk!" he said in a harsh whisper. *The dumb-ass punk was gonna pay, more than Sammy Constantino. Maybe this was Sammy, trying to screw him? Huh? Naw!* Vito wasn't about to be tricked by a punk kid no more...

Ow! my legs hurt! Only one ting ta do! He reached for his pistol, brought it out butt up, lifted it high, ready to pound that hated face, so close, so close!

Guido stirred and blinked his eyes as if waking from a long dream. Color returned to his pallid face. He understood, and burst into life: "No, you miserable stupid turd!" he screamed at Vito, With a reckless courage he didn't know he had, he dived for Vito's gun, arms extended. He knocked the gun aside with both hands.

"Out the front! Go, Phil, run! I'll... hold him!" Guido gritted out the words. He grabbed Vito's gun hand and hung on with the tenacity of a bulldog.

Stung, angry, Vito flung Guido from side to side, intent on freeing his gun hand. Guido bit down on the hand, hard.

"Ow! ya little punk!" Out of his mind now, Vito wrenched free and thudded the gun butt against Guido's head. Guido's knees buckled. He fell to the floor, and lay still.

"Ya called me a turd again!" Vito cried at the prostrate figure. "Well, I showed ya, ya little prick!" He suddenly remembered that Guido was not his top priority. He swiveled his neck, an eerie glow in his eyes.

To Donna - From The Godfather! Joe,

Flavio Joseph Rosati.

Fingers Of The Black Hand

by

Flavio Joseph Rosati

Commonwealth
Publications

A Commonwealth Publications Paperback
FINGERS OF THE BLACK HAND

This edition published 1995
by Commonwealth Publications
9764 - 45th Avenue
Edmonton, AB, CANADA T6E 5C5
All rights reserved
Copyright © 1994

ISBN: 1-896329-46-2

Printed in Canada

Cover Illustration by:
Scott Taylor

To Suzabelle,
a great lady.

PART I

Chapter 1

Phil Martello looked up into the sky. Dark, threatening clouds promised unexpected relief from the unbearable hot, humid August heat. But Phil had lived in New England all his almost - sixteen years, and he knew that it hardly ever rained in August. At least that was so in Holly Hill, where he now lived. It hadn't rained last year, or the year before, or the year before that, just like Lofton Height, where he formerly lived. And there seemed no reason it would begin raining this year, 1935.

Phil came slowly up a gravel path bordered by high weeds and skunk cabbage. He nibbled a huge double-scoop strawberry ice cream cone, looked at the sky again, and gingerly lifted a triangle of sweat-drenched sport shirt off sticky skin, and shook it. He stopped at the top of the path, looked to his right at a long, oblong cinder-block building at the end of a rutted gravel court and forgot the heat. A shiny black car parked in front of the building caught his eye.

He sauntered towards it. Cadillac? LaSalle? Packard? he wondered. The car was parked under a red, white and green hand-painted sign that read: 'Italian-American World War Veterans Social Hall'. Two men, their backs turned to him, leaned indolently against the hood of the... the... It's a Packard, Phil told himself. Just as I thought.

Both men turned and looked at Phil from under broad-brimmed straw hats, their gaudy sport shirts and gabardine slacks a crude contrast against the elegant, sculptured lines of the black Packard. Their hard eyes locked on Phil, scrutinizing him. "Just a punk kid," one said. "Droolin' over the car, like all the rest of dem around here."

"Yeah, big hunk of salami though, ain't he?" the other laughed.

"So? The bigger dey are, the harda dey fall. Hey, you guys, hurry up and load da truck. We gotta get out a here." The urging was for the benefit of two muscular men, stripped to the waist, bodies glistening with sweat, who carried wooden crates out of the side door of the building, and manhandled them onto a canopied truck. The two cursed lustily, but moved faster.

Phil gulped, as the attention of the men at the Packard shifted away from him. But the deep chill that had taken hold of him when those hard eyes stared at him persisted. Young men, in their twenties, but deadly, he thought. His mother, Rosa, had told stories of men such as these, in the old Country, and what they had done to a terrified countryside. Why... Suddenly, the screen door under the sign opened. A calico cat ran out, howling, its back arched. A burly man ambled out, threw an empty bottle of Naragansett ale at the cat, missed, and as the cat skittered away, he kicked the screen door, breaking the wood frame.

What a nut, Phil thought! And what a slob! Crummy red sport shirt unbuttoned, half out of his pants over his big paunch. Yuck! The man jerked his head towards Phil. Small, deep-set eyes, surrounded by scar tissue, seemed to read Phil's thoughts.

"Hey, you!" He pointed a stubby finger at Phil. "Quit clownin' around, and c'mere. Yor gonna do me a favor."

"I am?" Phil asked, with a hint of sarcasm. "What do you want?"

"I wantcha ta go back ta Jimmy's store, where ya got da ice cream. Tell'im ta give ya two quarts packed tight. All chock'lit for Vito. Now go. An' don't let it melt on da way back."

"Sure! Without money. Huh!" Phil's scorn was evident, and Vito caught it this time.

"Da ice cream is for Vito, ya hear? For Vito! Now, on your way, and don't let dose two tings hangin' between your legs slow you down. Ha, ha!"

"Get the quarts yourself, you... you oaf!" Phil said, angrily. He turned, and began walking rapidly away, but his armpits wet with nervous sweat.

"Look out, behind you!" The warning shout came from somewhere ahead.

Phil bent low, swung around, and immediately dropped to his hands and knees. Charging like an enraged bull, Vito tripped over him. He went sailing over Phil's back.

"You son of–"

He hit belly first, a lump of soggy meat, and the hard, unyielding surface slammed the wind out of him with a rush of beer breath.

Terrified, Phil scrambled to his feet. Run! Now! But fingers, and then arms, curled around his legs, held him fast.

"Aw right Vito, dat's enough! Da fight's over."

"Yeah, leave da kid alone. He didn't do nuttin' ta you!"

The two Packard men pulled a groggy Vito to his knees, and dragged him back to the broken screen door. They looked back anxiously at a rapidly approaching dark-haired man dressed in a business suit and tie. The screen door, and then a solid door slammed behind the three.

"You all right, young fella?" the dark-haired man asked.

Phil nodded. The man who had warned him! "The nut was gonna brain me!" he said. He exhaled deeply. "Thanks!"

"Don't mention it. Now listen! That washed up pug, Vito, may have it in for you now. Never know with him. He was in the ring one fight too many. So, stay away from him and his boys. They're no damn good, just a peck of trouble. Understand?"

As Phil nodded, the man gave the building a long, narrow-eyed look, then walked away down the gravel path towards the main street.

Phil took a deep breath. Slowly, he walked to the opposite end of the court and through a narrow gravel driveway. It opened into another, smaller court. At the back end, its entire breadth was taken up by a huge, wooden eight-plex brown tenement house. Phil began climbing the concrete steps of the landing leading to the steep central wooden steps that served both sides of the tenement. Hot! Unhappy! That's how he felt. He frowned. He had to talk to his father... ask questions. Could they be here... so close?

"Ss-ta," a voice intruded. It belonged to a slender boy with black curly hair. "Hi! My name is Vic. Did you ss-ta... just move in?" He tried hard not to stutter.

"Huh? Oh, yeah, we moved in yesterday," Phil answered. He stood two steps below Vic, and eyed him closely. About my own age, he thought. Could Vic be a friend, for a change?

"Hey, don't look so glum! You'll like it here. Ss-ta, what's your name?"

"Phil." He looked at the cinder-block building, whistled, and shook his head.

"I know," Vic said. "I saw what happened. Good thing Sam was around."

"Sam?"

"Uh huh, Sam Pizzuta, the guy that helped you. He grew up around here, knows all the boys. But they don't like him much. See, he's a detective."

"Oh!" But... but who the heck are 'the boys'?"

Loud, shrill voices cut the conversation off. A group of boys, returning from morning baseball practice, gloves hanging limply, bats dragging, jockeyed and shoved for the most shaded spots under a big elm tree near the entrance to the court. Shouts of victory, taunts, and jeers, nudged up through the still air, as each boy claimed his precious turf.

And then it happened.

"Ah, for Christ sakes, Mi-fi-lay, next time I'll trow you a beach ball!"

"Shut up, Nick! Yor not that great a hitter, neither. I sawr you strike out. And don't call me Mi-fi-lay. I don't like it."

"Awright! How about Straight-up-and-down?" Nick taunted, sticking his puffy face out in derision. The tormented boy, thin but wiry, uttered an angry "Oo, you!" and leaped at Nick, his fists flailing. Dust and gravel flew as the other baseball stars, the sultry heat forgotten, gleefully jumped into the fracas.

Phil watched, entranced. What a neighborhood! He didn't notice the arm curving gracefully over Vic's shoulder, until a girl's face appeared over it. She had big brown eyes and a broad smile.

"So you're the new guy," she said, tilting her head just so.

Phil gulped, nodded.

"I like your wavy hair," she said, reaching over and running her hand through Phil's light brown hair. "And blue eyes, uh huh! I'll see ya, real soon, handsome!" she said, rotating her hand, palm out, in hep-cat style. Then she bounced down the steps into the courtyard, giving the battling players a disgusted look. Swinging her hips, she paraded down the sloping gravel road leading to the main street. A heavy, canopied truck rolled past slowly in the opposite direction, heading for the cinder-block building. The truck creaked and groaned as tired thudded into ruts; and gravel flew as the driver meshed noisy gears. The truck bucked and swayed.

"Hey, Mona, does yor mudda know yor out?" The driver, his black hair pasted down with greasy pomade, leaned out and leered. Mona wiggled her behind and shot him a hateful look. Sticking out her tongue, she gave him an Italian salute, a hand gesture whose meaning was clear to all who saw it.

"Monica! -you be a gooda girl, capeesh? Don' you pay attensh to dat man. Heesa no good." Monica's mamma, watching her high-spirited daughter from the third floor back porch, poured out admonishment in the language of the tenement, a mixture of fractured English and Italian dialects. Monica flounced away, not looking back.

"Animale!" Italo-American invectives, in a screechy female voice, cascaded down from the fourth floor where a fat woman hurriedly gathered in laundry from a rotating clothesline anchored to the porch.

Vic pointed. A sooty cloud, coming from the railroad yards in the valley below, approached. Phil could hear the engines hissing, puffing, and spewing.

"Sometimes the wind is just right," Vic sighed, and shrugged.

"Yeah, so I see," Phil said, lamely. Such noise, such naked emotion!

"Doin' anything right now?" Vic suddenly asked.

"Just helpin' my folks unpack, I guess. Why?"

"Let's go to the Majestic. Jerry-next-door is an usher and he'll let us skip in. We'll see a great cowboy show. And hey, we'll be cool! They just put in a new air-conditioning gizmo. Okay?" Vic didn't stutter.

"Uh..." Phil hesitated. But, he wanted acceptance-even by the gang below. And gee, 'skipping in' sounded exciting. He had never done that before! The questions he had for his father... about them... could be asked later.

"Okay, let's go!" Phil said.

As they went round the scuffling players, a shrill blast of broken English split the air. "You boysa, stoppa dat fight, righta now! Nicky, you shut appa you face, an' acta you age!" Grace Noce, Nick and Mona's mother, leaned over the third floor porch railing and shook her finger vigorously, her round, mobile face contorted.

Laundry now safe, the fat woman joined in, hurling verbal bolts at Nick. "Don't touch Ferruccio! I tella you fadda!" She leaned over the iron railing, and glared at Nick. She was angry – she was Mi-fi-lay's mother, Amalfia. She frowned down on Grace Noce, who mumbled "Strega!" (Witch!) – and huffed back into the house. The water was boiling in the pot. Time to pour in the daily two pounds of homemade pasta!

The scuffle ended; the boys melted away. Baseball, again, tomorrow!

On Columbus Street now, heading downtown, Vic watched a flash of lightning and cocked his head. Moments later, thunder rumbled.

"We'll make the show before it rains," he said. "But we gotta move."

"What happened at the tenement today," Phil asked, pensively, "is it always like that?"

"No. This was a quiet day. Say, how old are you? I'm fourteen. Most of the guys are about that, too... except Nick... he's seventeen, and not very bright." Vic grinned, continuing with a twinkle in his eye. "Mona is fifteen. Boy, she goes for you!" His face turned grave; he leaned in. "Some of the guys say she has hot pants? You think so?"

Hot pants? Phil had never heard that expression in Lofton Height, but he knew what it meant right away. He was almost sixteen and the sweet mystery of girls was beginning to become unraveled.

"I... I don't know," he replied. "Mona seems wild though, so... maybe... but gee, you can't tell about those things by just looking. You gotta–"

"Look!" Vic interrupted. "That's the railroad yard."

He pointed to his left, across Columbus Street. "Someday our neighborhood will have enough clout to stop the soot. And oh, that's the Union Station, across from the old railroad steeple with the big clock face on top."

The station, a granite monolith with cracked steps, was covered with a thick layer of soot. Filth that covered everything. Phil felt a wave of uneasiness.

Soon, they crossed Jefferson square and walked under a foul-smelling, rusting railroad bridge. to the east end of Front Street, the beginning of the city's downtown area. Rain, in fat droplets, began splattering the gum-stained sidewalk.

"Never expected this," Vic said, wiping his face. "C'mon, we can duck from doorway to doorway." He ran under the metal awning of Handelman's market, slipped into doorways of shoe stores, pawn shops, and old office buildings owned by the New England yankee landed gentry. Phil hurried to catch up. His uneasiness evaporated. This was fun!

Vic had zipped by the old brick Williams Hotel, when a revolving door leading to the lobby abruptly swung open. A thick-necked, stocky man in a bright sport shirt pushed through. Shoulders hunched, he trudged over uneven cobblestones towards the granite curb, where a black La Salle sedan was parked, its back door open.

Phil, at full speed, eyes fixed on Vic, ran into the man's right side. "Gee, I'm sorry, sir!" he said, reaching out with a steadying hand. It was brushed away with an elbow, and it hurt.

"Damn it, punk, open your fucking eyes!" That voice! Phil looked up. Vito!

"You!" Vito said. He grabbed Phil's arm in a tourniquet hold and raised his other arm, ready to deliver a vicious back-handed slap.

"Vito! No! *Stupido!*" The words hissed out of the La Salle. Vito froze, and jerked his head around. A smooth hand with long fingers vigorously beckoned to him from the darkness of the back seat. Vito managed a quick snarl at Phil, lumbered to the car, and the car door slammed behind him. The La Salle roared regally away, followed by two other black sedans.

Phil sagged. He flexed his cold hands, worked his

slack jaw. He swallowed and licked raindrops. He felt a tug at his sleeve.

"He... he was going to hit me! The lousy bastard! Even though I apologized. Just who does he think he is?" Phil pushed Vic's hand away.

"Hey, take it easy!" Vic said. "Vito? He's just one of the boys." Vic cracked a wan grin. "Don't worry," he added, "it didn't mean a thing!" He tapped his head, bobbed and weaved, imitating a boxer; then he grunted and belched. "He'll forget. He's punchy, okay?"

"You can say that! You weren't going to get hit – I was! And what does 'one of the boys' mean? You never told me."

"You don't know? Really? Oh, I forgot; you just moved in." Vic looked over his shoulder. The black cars were gone. He expelled a deep breath.

"'The boys' run the rackets. You know, horse race fixes, graft, gambling... all kinds." He giggled- "and whorehouses. Honest to God! They work for a guy named Di Anello. They meet here at the hotel and take off to the horse races in their big cars, like they own the town. I know! I've been watching and listening around since I was eight years old." Vic grimaced. "At the rate they're going, they will own a good part of the town. Gee, you know, the word in the neighborhood is that Di Anello even has the mayor in his hip pocket."

"No!"

"Oo-fa, you're a real greenhorn, Phil, fresh off the boat! Yes, the mayor. He was around last week, the big Irish potato, shaking hands, promising to fill the pot holes in the streets. Some smart aleck asked him if he could hear the race results from the back of the religious article store. He said, 'My boy, you have quite an imagination' in his brogue. And you know what? He went right on shaking hands."

Phil said nothing and dodged a stream of water from a roof downspout. Vic slithered past two old women opening umbrellas. "So the mayor doesn't know or hear a thing from the setup Di Anello has back there. Why should he? He's getting his payoff, the crook. Shit, City Hall is full of crooks. Come on, we'll make it before the heavy rain starts."

Phil forced a wry smile and nodded. "Okay... sure," he murmured.

"What's the matter? You look terrible. Did I say something wrong?"

"Naw," Phil said. He thought fast. "But, does Nick make up those crazy nicknames for everyone? I don't want him to make fun of me that way!"

"Oh, I got it! For a while I thought you were worried about that crumb Vito. Nick? Oo-fa!" Vic eyed Phil's broad shoulders, developing muscles. "You look tougher than him, the slob! He won't bother you." He brightened. "We call Ferruccio 'Rusty.' His name means 'little piece of iron' in Italian." He fought back a stutter. "If Nick ever calls you 'Mi-fi-lay', bust him in the mouth! Okay?"

Phil smiled. "Okay!" he replied.

A moment later, they sidled into the narrow entrance of the Majestic. Jerry-next-door, a small sixteen-year old with a big nose and rotten teeth, caught Vic's signal and turned his back to study a coming attractions poster of Tim McCoy in his ten-gallon white hat. Heart thumping, Phil followed Vic past the ticket collection booth and walked serenely into the welcome darkness of the theater. Phil sighed and told himself he wouldn't even think of *them* for the next few shoot'em up hours.

Chapter 2

Sergeant Sam Pizzuta stopped at the bottom of the gravel path. He stepped onto the cobblestone sidewalk and stamped his feet. A fine film of dust fell from his black wing-tip shoes. He leaned over and wiped the remaining grit from the rich leather with a white handkerchief. Satisfied, he glanced back at the tenement with amused tolerance, his rancor reduced somewhat by the antics of the battling ball players and their excitable mothers. His gaze hardened as it moved to the cinder block building. He snorted. *Social Hall for veterans, my left nut, he thought. Smoke, that's what it is! Oh sure, the vets played cards there, at tables set up for them, shot pool, ate club sandwiches and drank of vino... and all free.*

We pay off our great debt to our unemployed neighborhood war heroes! Are not these tough times, eh?

Pizzuta grimaced. Smart! Very smart! The vets had a fine time and kept their mouths shut. Well, all the vets, but one. Pizzuta's face lit up briefly at that thought, and a shrewd evanescent smile cracked his tight lips...

And the warehouse side of the building – filled with cases of olive oil, crates, and boxes of canned goods – was a great cover, and good business too, for it supplied all the neighborhood grocery stores without exception.

The Social Hall and the warehouse served as working fronts for the reigning head of the neighborhood mob, Massimo Di Anello. 'Da boys' played cards and pool here too. Instructions were received and passed on, warnings and tips acknowledged, bribes and payoffs (and maybe worse) planned. The building, Pizzuta knew, was one of the satellites Di Anello used in running his rackets. As he regarded the set-up with grudging admiration, the clash of metal on metal, slashed through his ruminations.

At the canopied truck the two bare-chested loaders slammed the tailgate shut, closed the wide sliding door of the building, and locked it. They turned, jumped into the truck, cursed the heat, and the truck jerked forward with the gnash of gears.

Moments later Pizzuta muttered, "Damn hoods," as

Vito now came out, escorted by the two young men in straw-hats who had pulled him away from Phil. They looked furtively about, jumped into the Packard, and drove off down the court, staring straight ahead.

Fine, thought Pizzuta. They calmed him down, and now they're off to meet the local intelligentsia – at the horse races! He snorted. His vile mood returned. He unbuttoned his shirt, loosened his collar and tie, and leaned against a maple tree thrust up from a ragged hole in the sidewalk. He looked at the tenacious roots of the tree.

Sergeant Pizzuta should be Lieutenant Pizzuta by now! he fumed. Earlier in the day Captain Hennessey, decent and clean, whose long face had seemed to lengthen to his knees, informed Pizzuta, that "Upstairs had decided to promote someone else, sorry Sam. You know I recommended you."

Oh! How he wanted that promotion. He had earned it – worked his ass off for it! "Why, Captain?"

"Don't know, Sam. You can probably figure it out better than I can."

And Sam had, Di Anello, the mayor. He was being given a message. 'Lay the fuck off the neighborhood! Quit prying into things that don't concern you. For now no promotion, so back off, Sergeant!'

Sam had gone too far to back off now; not that he wanted to. A little break here and there, and he'd nail Di Anello, clean up the neighborhood, and damn it, he would be a lieutenant, and a captain after that! No one could stop him! *But... what if you get no breaks,* the little voice inside his skull whispered? *You could find yourself pounding a beat in – the boondocks, or planted... deeper than the maple tree you're staring at.*

He'd take his chances with Di Anello's flashily dressed apes. Yes, crude apes! No class! Wish we had more clean-cut young guys like that new big fella in the neighborhood. The way he took on Vito was something, Pizzuta mused. He admired guts. Wonder who he is? He'd find out, when he had time.

Pizzuta now walked down Columbus Street, the steel taps of his leather heels clanking on the baking cobblestones, echoing oddly in the stillness. He passed the religious article store and smiled dourly at a red-robed, crowned statue of the Infant of Prague in a window display. A few steps later, he was enveloped by the cloying, ripe redolence of the Old Country market, with its garlic necklaces, cheeses, and open tins of salted anchovies. He quickened his pace, swallowing.

A few doorways away he stepped down, opened a creaking screen door, and walked into an alcove-like basement store. He stood under a slow-circling ceiling fan, and ran his finger along the cold top of the ice cream showcase.

"Hello Sam! Hot enough for ya?" Jimmy was slicing cold cuts, and his body swayed back and forth with the rhythm and hum of the machine. A drop of sweat hung from his thin nose, and his bushy eyebrows were wet. His mouth opened, displaying several yellowed teeth.

"Yeah, it is," Sam answered. He saw no customers, so he told Jimmy how a 'new young fella' had just bested Vito. Quite a sight!

Jimmy, his eyes deep in dark hollows, said nothing as he continued to slice, more rapidly now. "I sold the kid the ice cream cone. Guess I'll have to give him a free cone when he shows up again. Right?"

"Right! Did he tell you his name?" Pizzuta asked.

"Nope." Jimmy selected three slices of boiled ham, two of mortadella.

"No, Jimmy, no sandwich today. Too hot. But I'll have a strawberry ice cream cone. Damn, that young fella got to me!"

"Sure," Jimmy said. And in a low voice he added, "Nothing new. Some talk of hi-jacking liquor trucks, City Hall payoffs, but I got nothing definite. Look, I'm going to the Veterans Social Hall tonight after I close. Maybe I'll pick up something." He limped behind the ice cream showcase, slid the glass door open, worked a scoop, looked up, and handed Sergeant Pizzuta an icy tower of a strawberry ice cream cone.

"Thanks," Pizzuta said mechanically. "Damn it, Jimmy, we need solid evidence – something that can't be fixed. You know, if we can't work it," he pointed his ice cream cone, "this town will be a Di Anello cesspool, just like Chicago was ten years ago when Capone was the *Capo Grosso*. Time is running out on us!" He took an angry bite.

"Sam, I know that, but I gotta go slow. If they find out I work for you–" Jimmy swatted a fat fly with the palm of his hand, "I'm gone!" He paused, shut of the slicing machine, and exploded, "Why the fuck don't you get married? Raise kids, yeah! Forget about this dangerous shit! Lots of nice girls in the neighborhood, you know. Go after'em, lay'em. Better for your health!"

Pizzuta chuckled at Jimmy's outburst. "Thanks for the good advice, friend, but not for me, not yet. But–" he scratched his head, and his eyes twinkled, "there is one beautiful dish I'd like to check out when I have have time–"

"Yeah?"

"Yeah. I saw her in the Den of Thieves couple of weeks ago. She was walking down a corridor, kind of slow, a pencil in her teeth, thumbing through a bunch of papers she was holding."

"Den of thieves?" Jimmy cocked his head.

"That's what I call our corrupt City Hall."

"What the heck were you doing there?"

Pizzuta held up a staying hand. "Okay, okay! Calm down! I wasn't there to brown-nose. I took a short cut through the joint; had to see someone at the Waldorf. You know, the cafeteria across the street."

Jimmy nodded, but his body had stiffened.

"So she hears my shoes clicking and looks up," Pizzuta picked up his story. "She stops, gives me a quick, warm look, and walks away. Fast. I stare at her back and behind. Down the end of the corridor she looks over her shoulder at me. You know, like this." Sam tried to demonstrate a graceful turn of the head. It didn't work.

Jimmy nodded impatiently. "I get the idea. And?"

Pizzuta shrugged. "She turned and left. Jimmy, that is some woman!"

"Sure. And probably married."

"I'm a detective, remember. She wasn't wearing any rings."

"Uh huh. By the way, where in City Hall did you see her?"

"Where? Let's see. Near some of the mayor's conference rooms. Hey, I gotta go. Duty calls. See you soon.

Sandwich next time." Pizzuta went to the door. "Good luck tonight! You know, I just might find the time to take your advice on women." He smiled, ducked, and was gone.

Jimmy understood what Pizzuta meant by 'women'. The City Hall woman! *Mess around, Sam, mess around,* Jimmy said to himself as his war wound started to throb, *and you'll find yourself pushing up daisies.* Absently, he picked up a long slicing knife with his right hand, and a salami with his left. The ceiling fan whirred monotonously, adding to his daze. He placed the salami on the solid butcher block before him, trembled, and began slicing. He muttered to himself, in a disjointed way, "Got to keep Sam away... away... from her... if it is her... oh! but if it is! – *Mano Nera*... will kill... destroy him... never be found! Gotta find out–"

Jimmy, oblivious of his surroundings, continued to slice. The fan spun in soporific circles; a dull peal of thunder; raindrops... hissed on the sidewalk.

Suddenly, a look of horror twisted his face. His bleary eyes bulged. Transfixed, he studied the red blood filling the crevices in the chopping block. It seemed like an eternity, but was really only a split second.

"Santa Maria Immaculata!" Jimmy cried. And then the pain slammed into him, wrenching his gut. Moaning, slobbering, he wrapped the bottom fold of his butcher's apron around the deeply cut index finger of his left hand and pressed hard, as if he were gluing two pieces of wood together. He plunged out of his store, a marionette in jerky motion.

"Sam! Sam!" he choked, to a surprised Doctor Caradonna, three doors away.

Chapter 3

Phil plunked himself into the hard wooden seat of the Majestic theater, and sighed. He liked his new neighborhood; it would be better for his family. Vito? Stay away from him! He looked at the Coming Attractions, but he thought of the grimness and poverty of Lofton Height, and his father's decision to move back downtown to the neighborhood, The little corner grocery store he owned, near the city line, hadn't done well. The Depression, the growing list of unpaid accounts he kept in his penciled ledger: "I'll pay you something next week," or the young widow, Mae Mello: "Sebastiano, I'm out of milk for the kids. Can you trust me some more?"

Phil knew his father did, until he couldn't pay his own bills. And Old Man Barney, the senescent Yankee who held the mortgage on the store, would drive up in his sleek, black, curtained Pierce-Arrow, and cry, actually cry, when Sebastiano said he couldn't make the payment this month. Barney would wipe his bony hands and scold Sebastiano for voting for Franklin D. Roosevelt. That devil in the White House! He is bankrupting the country!

Barney would sob, shake his head and demand payment, or, he said in a quavering voice, "I will have to foreclose."

Sebastiano paid, from a little 'going-back-to-visit-the-old country' bundle buried in the store's cellar.

"Lagrime di cocodrillo!" (Crocodile tears!) Phil recalled his father's exasperation with Barney, and he sold out to the Atlantic gas station owner next door, Karl. Karl wanted to convert the store into a weekend retreat for his brown-shirted German-American friends, who had formed a society called the Bund.

"We follow in Mussolini's footsteps," Karl had said proudly when he showed Sebastiano and Phil swastika armbands his friends would wear at their meetings. But Sebastiano was apolitical, though he disliked *'quello mafioso'* in Rome, and cared little for swastika-wearers playing children's games. In 1920 he had crossed the Atlantic with wife Rosa to start a new life in America, and with God's help and hard work, he would succeed. He did, until the Great Depression struck. After years of hopeless struggle, Sebastiano told his family he had found a way to live well again. Phil recalled the joy on hearing the good news.

Giovannino, a fellow member of his father's Italian mutual benefit society, offered him a job in a big Italian grocery store located on the busiest section of Columbus Street, crowded with immigrants in cold water tenements. He told Sebastiano that the business would soon expand, and he could use Sebastiano's know-how. If war broke out, as seemed likely, imports would be cut off, and he meant to be ready. Obviously he didn't want his beloved countrymen deprived of the necessities of life- olive oil, provolone, macaroni. Is it not so?

"Our *paesanos* will buy, at our prices, *naturalmente!*"

A well-paying, steady job! -with a growing company! -is what Sebastiano heard, and passed on to his family. And best of all, he would be free of the heartless Yankee, Barney! And how nice... to be in a slice of Italy! Sebastiano accepted the offer, and the city line experiment was over.

Back to the neighborhood he and Rosa moved, with fifteen-year old Phil and eleven-year old Albert. They had moved to Lofton Height when Phil was eight. Left behind was little Maria, in a flower-covered grave.

She had died years ago of a strange fever; she would of been thirteen years old...

"Hey Phil, for cryin' out loud, you asleep?" Vic's piercing, nasal voice jolted Phil back from his reverie.

"Huh? Nah, I was resting my eyes, just getting used to the dark."

"Oh-Heyyyy look! Here comes Tom Mix!"

Vic could hardly be heard over the yelling and stomping of the smaller kids. Tom Mix was some special cowboy!

The crowd of young people came surging out of the Majestic, pushing and shoving, anxious to stretch and run after four mesmerizing hours of cartoons and cowboys.

It was dusk now, the long summer day ending. The streets, swept clean by a just-ended heavy rain, sparkled, and the sharp smell of ozone was still in the air. Tomorrow was Monday but school was still out. The summer had been long, and everyone exulted.

Phil was still in sage brush country. He grinned at Vic, who grinned back. Breaking into a dog trot, they put distance between themselves and a group of loud boys. They sped by Handleman's market, and had just passed under the dark shadow of the railroad bridge.

"Hey, you guys! Vic... you too, handsome! Wait up for me!" A girl's voice, self-assured and commanding. Mona! Vic and Phil stopped.

"Mona, what the heck are you doing here?" Vic asked, surprised.

"Don't you know what's going on? I work at Handleman's, part-time. I have the butter tubs and cheese counter. You come see me–" she gazed into Phil's eyes, a finger on her chin–" and I'll give you at least a pat of butter." She ran the fingers of her other hand over the back of Phil's hand, her nails lightly scratching his skin. He gulped, stayed intact. His hands didn't become chunks of awkward flesh, and his feet didn't get in each other's way. It had been that way once, when girls came near to give him demure but meaningful glances. Now he felt a surge of disturbing pleasure. So! girls could be regular... almost like guys. But... not quite. There was always the question of... 'hot pants'.

"Sure," Phil heard a voice, "I'll drop by Handleman's for the butter." It must have been his voice, for Vic just stood there, mouth open, gawking.

"Good!" Mona said. "See ya! Oh, before I go, me and my girlfriends are goin' swimming at the lake tomorrow afternoon. You both come with us. Oo! I gotta go! My mother will kill me!" She sprinted away, the soles of her brown leather saddle shoes squeegeeing the pavement.

"Does she mean it? Should we go?" Phil turned to a recovering Vic.

"Sure," Vic said. "She wants to show you off." He smirked at Phil, and gave him an eyes-lowered look. "Oo! you're so handsome!" he mimicked, scratching the air with the fingers of both hands.

"Aw, cut it out!" Say... will her brother Nick be there?"

"That cement head? Heck no! He likes to hang

around the lower end of Columbus Street with other dumb clucks. They never even graduated from Miss Doyle's special class of dunderheads. A bunch of strangers to the eighth grade! I'll bet that ex-pug Vito was one of them, way back when."

Phil looked at Vic with a puzzled expression on his face.

"Don't look so funny. Where do you think Di Anello gets the muscle to do his dirty work? Ha! From these tough, dumb shits, that's where. Boy, and are they grateful! They follow orders; they don't ask questions."

In the distance thunder boomed. The wind whistled through the leaves of the elm trees, and whipped the puddles in the sunken, crumbling pavement into Lilliputian storms. Phil, running and dodging the larger puddles, his sneakers slapping and spraying water, didn't feel the dampness.

* * * *

Phil walked jauntily into the kitchen. His father sat at the kitchen table, the Evening Post spread before him. Little brother Al, sweaty and dirty from a day of playing kick the can, cast a wary eye towards the pantry where Mama Rosa rattled pots and pans, readying the evening meal.

"Hi Phil! Played ball yet? Hit any homers?" Al, smaller and darker than Phil, gazed with delight at his big brother, his hazel eyes shining.

"No, I haven't played yet... But when I do, I'll stretch a triple into a homer for you."

Sebastiano Martello raised his head from the newspaper, sighed helplessly, and fingered his thick mustache, the tips of which tilted up in the fashion of *Alpini*, the Italian mountain soldiers. Baseball jargon was incomprehensible to him. His deep blue eyes settled on Phil.

"You enjoying your new home, Filippo?" he asked, in Italian.

Phil nodded.

"Since we moved in, I have hardly seen you. Too much to do here, and in my new job. But it is going well.

Giovannino has been good to me." He wiped his brow up to the receding line of reddish-brown hair.

Phil studied his father. He too, spoke in Italian. "Papa, did any *Mano Nera* gang members come to America?"

"Now, *figlio caro* (dear son), how am I supposed to know that, eh? You haven't mentioned that name in eight years. Nightmares come back?"

"Heck, no!" Phil said, in English. "That was little kid stuff." Sound from the pantry ceased, as if cut off by the hand of an invisible maestro. Sebastiano tapped an Old Gold cigarette out of a pack, lit it, took one puff, eyed the pantry door, and cocked his head towards it.

"Pop?" Phil saw his father turn to him. "Tell me about the *Mano Nera* – You never have, you know."

"Yes, I know. All right!" Sebastiano seemed relieved to get his attention away from the silence of the pantry. He took three quick puffs, put his cigarette down. "Italians are flamboyant, with a sense for the dramatic in life," he began. "This flair is perverted by the underworld, and in the old days particularly by the *Mano Nera*. Conditions in Italy were bad, before your mother and I left. Lawless gangs of ruffians were everywhere, one group adopted the practice of leaving the imprint of a *mano nera* – in English, a 'black hand' – correct?" Phil nodded. "...on the doorstep of those they wanted to terrorize or intimidate," his father picked up. "If this failed, property was destroyed, reputations ruined by gossip and innuendo, and sometimes–" Sebastiano drew a finger across his throat, and rocked back and forth, wreathed in blue cigarette smoke.

"You said 'in the old days'," Phil prompted, ignoring the theatrics.

Sebastiano arched an eyebrow. "So I did, Filippo. You see, the brigands of the *Mano Nera* were local villagers, and not organized. When some became ambitious, they trespassed on the territory of rival thieves and scoundrels who were smarter, and better organized-the *Camorra*, the *Mafia*, not to mention the Reds, Fascists, and the rest of the scum strangling a prostrate Italy, ravaged by the world war. The *Mano Nera* gangs ceased to exist."

"Ah! But not before poor cousin Lucia was destroyed by them!" The throaty, emotional voice of Rosa erupted from the pantry, and she appeared, carrying a big pot of minestrone.

"Si!" exclaimed Sebastiano. "We have heard that *canzone* many times." He sighed, a deep resigned sound, and glanced at Phil.

Yes, Phil had heard the 'song' many times from his mother up until he was ten years old, and his father, in a foul mood, had commanded her to stop it. Phil's periodic nightmares then ceased, whether because of his father's admonition or because he was growing up and scare stories didn't bother him any more, he didn't know...

In the Old Country, a ruffian of the *Mano Nera* had sought cousin Lucia's hand. She had rebuffed him, for she was enamored of a young *carabiniere* from a nearby town. The ruffian was incensed. The young policeman subsequently disappeared, and soon malicious lies about Lucia and the young man spread throughout the village. Dishonored, she entered a convent where, the legend according to Rosa Martello went, she died of a broken heart, for she knew her intended had been murdered in his sleep by the ruffian.

Phil recalled how, at age four, he had bravely waved little fists in the air and promised to tear the hearts out of any *Mano Nera* members he met when he grew up. A true vendetta! How his mother had beamed at him. Then his nightmare had begun... a big black hand creeping over his bed covers towards him! And he would scream...

"Look," Sebastiano now said, also switching to English, "August here soon. I buy good grapes from California. We make plenty wine. Okay?"

"Can I help?" Al piped up. He sat on the floor, legs crossed.

"Of course, *piccolino*," Sebastiano patted Al affectionately on the head.

Pans clanged and rattled in the pantry where Rosa Martello had returned to fetch thick slices of home-baked bread and an arugula and dandelion greens salad. She emerged, tight-lipped, carrying a platter and a bowl of each. Down on the table they came with a resounding thud. Sebastiano flinched and then peered at the glass salad bowl with an exaggerated roll of his head. "*Non è rotto*," he said. "It is not broken." He stroked his mustache.

Rosa Martello's lips parted. She pouted and hot steam hissed from deep within her, or at least so Phil imagined. oh shit! he thought, here it comes, and he gripped the edges of the oak kitchen table with both hands.

"*Ciarla, ciarla, ciarla!*" she said in her rich contralto. (Talk, talk, talk!) She accompanied the words with a shake of her head, and strands of dark brown hair shook loose from her black hair net. "*Che cosa è questo?*" (What is this?) And her Italian descended in a crescendo on Sebastiano Martello's head: "*Mano Nera, Camorra*, California grapes, *vino*. Signor Martello! Did you not tell me that grapes would cost eighty cents a crate this year? Who is going to pay? Eh? You... you..." she choked, recovered, "...haven't even received your first pay. And look," Rosa's tongue moved and lashed, "we need a modern gas stove and a refrigerator to replace this leaky ice box." She kicked it. Water seeped from the ice compartment, trickled down the oak frame, and formed a thin, guilty line in the kitchen.

Rosa, eyes teary, bosom heaving, knelt on both knees and dabbed at the water with her apron, then wiped back and forth... back and forth.

A little voice broke the palpable silence, "And we need a new radio too!" Al pulled his neck into his shoulders, expecting paternal wrath. None came.

"*Dio mio!* (Such a family!)" Sebastiano Martello said. "So quick to draw and shoot, as the American cowboys say. All right! Rosa, the refrigerator is yours this very week! And next week, you shall have your new stove. And you, Alberto," his voice dropped, "will be taken, by me... to the radio store... where you can pick out your radio, one with many tubes, eh?" Sebastiano's voice smiled, and he chuckled. Phil saw why; Al... was beaming.

But Mama didn't seem amused. Her smooth brow was furrowed, and the corners of her expressive mouth curved downward. She got up and dried her hands on an apron corner. When she spoke, in English, her voice matched her visage, "You sick? You have a fever?" She approached her husband cautiously, her hand held out as if to touch his forehead.

"I no sick," Sebastiano replied, also in English. "I am healthy as a... *a cavallo*... a hoss! I tell you now Rosa, Sebastiano Martello," he thumped his chest with a finger, "he make forty dollars a week."

"*Quaranta dollari la settimana!*" Rosa shrieked, reverting back to the language she knew best.

"Quieto!" the master of the house cautioned, and continued in Italian. "The walls have ears. Nothing escapes that one." He nodded towards the adjoining flat, where Amalfia reigned supreme. He said his new job was going well, and Nino had hinted that soon... there would be an even bigger job for him. But Phil could tell that his mother and brother had quit listening at 'forty dollars a week'. Why, that was more than twice what ordinary mortals earned if they had a job. His mother, Phil thought, already polished her new white enamel stove, and Al turned the knobs of a big Grunow radio console. The meal was a happy one.

Later that evening in his room, Phil thought of his new neighborhood, and gazed out his fourth-floor window at the dark silhouette of the cinderblock building. He thought of the heavily-laden canopied truck he had seen there (wonder what was in it?), of Detective Sergeant Pizzuta, of Vito, of his father's good fortune to land such a good-paying job, and of Mona, and the intriguing question about her hot pants. He felt a warm tingle.

And then excitement and warmth of another kind rippled through him. The local mob! It's boss, Di Anello! Could he have been a member of the *Mano Nera*, the Black Hand, in the Old Country? You've been reading too many pulp magazines, Phil told himself. Or, was it the influence of his mother's sad story about cousin Lucia? Whatever it was, Phil's curiosity was sky-high. He realized he just had to find out more about the mob. Examine it, see what made it tick. Danger? Sure. He gulped. But he knew his course was set and couldn't be checked. Not now, not anymore!

But how to start? He lived in the tenement, of course. From his room he had a clear view of the so-called Italian American World War Veterans Social Hall (what a misnomer!). Vito and the hard-faced young hoods that grabbed him off me weren't veterans! And the way Sergeant Pizzuta looked at the place, and warned me!

Phil's churning thoughts were interrupted by the sight of a black car coming up the gravel road. It passed by the hand-painted sign and went to the side of the building. It stopped, a sliding door creaked open, and the car went in. The door closed.

Phil sucked in his breath. He knew what he must do! Tomorrow he would check the area, and every evening he would watch for the black car.

Chapter 4

"Yuk!" Mona said the next morning. The clouds were low, the drizzle heavy. Swimming at the lake, she realized, would have to be postponed until tomorrow, Tuesday, when the sun would surely shine.

Phil found himself polishing furniture and unpacking boxes, supervised by his mother, who saw the advantage of a dreary day and took it...

But that night from his room Phil watched a La Salle roll slowly up the gravel road. The pebbles crackled under the wheels, the sound amplified by the still, steamy night. Near the cinderblock building a dog barked. The big car stopped its slow climb; its driver sat motionless, his fear betrayed by his tight grip on the wheel. From the passenger side of the front seat a head popped out the open window. As it pivoted, the pale light of a nearby street lamp washed over a flattened nose.

Phil shuddered. Vito! Nevertheless, he quickly descended the dark tenement steps, crouched behind a stout elm, and heard Vito's hoarse voice:

"I tink da mutt is yappin' at us boss. Want me to..."

"Just chase him away, Vito. We don't wanna wake da neighbors."

"Sure, Boss!" Vito smiled and walked away, his fists clenched. Behind him, through the wet blackness of weeds and brush edging the court, Phil followed. A few moments later Phil heard a high-pitched "Yelp!" nothing more. Then the La Salle curved past the tenement hulk and disappeared in the shadows of the cinderblock building. Phil crept closer. Vito, in the glare of headlights, unlocked a large sliding door; he cursed and slapped the air wildly... Mosquitoes! highlighted with him in a bizarre dance.

"Come on, come on, open the damn door!" A voice from the car.

Muttering and sweating, Vito obeyed, looked into the headlights, squinted, and stepped aside as the car purred into the building.

"Now hurry up, close the door! We don't want any mosquitoes in here."

Vito turned and blinked at the darkness. He rubbed his eyes, cursing under his breath. He groped for the door, still blinded. It creaked and groaned as he found it, his eyes still not adjusted to the sudden darkness. Swearing lustily, he stooped and pushed several stones out of the garage door's travel path with his foot. Phil made his move. Bent almost double he scooted by Vito's clumsy form, almost touching him. Glancing quickly over his shoulder he saw Vito hurriedly straighten up – Oh my God! He lunged at the door, and slammed it shut.

The crash of the closing door coincided with the rattle of cans inside as Phil dove for cover...

It seemed to be a window-less warehouse, with crates and boxes stacked nearly to the ceiling. Up ahead, long, manicured fingers grasped the door post of the La Salle. A thin, dark man with an angular face and thick black hair beginning to gray, leisurely stepped out. Two other men got out; one short and swarthy with dark eyes that darted about the warehouse; the other of medium height had a wide smile on his cherubic face. Mid-thirties, all of them.

"Have you made arrangements for all this?" he of the manicured hands asked in Italian. He swept the stacked goods with an elegant hand motion.

"Si," replied the one with the angel face. "He is honest and trustworthy. This is all he will see and work with – goods for a large legitimate business." His smile grew wider.

"What is his name, Nino?" the swarthy one asked, with a leer.

"Sebastiano Martello, a friend of mine," Nino said, his smile wide.

"Martello? I do not know him. So... he is a friend of yours... Then, of course... I must conclude he is not a Sicilian, or even a Neapolitan." The swarthy man spoke in a formal but sarcastic tone of voice.

"No Oreste, you have not met him and you are quite right, he is neither Sicilian nor Neapolitan. But then, neither am I... Eh?" Nino smiled, but his voice was cold and biting. And his eyes glinted dangerously.

"All right you two, enough!" The voice, soft and controlled, in accented English, commanded attention. Its owner brusquely motioned Oreste and Nino to follow him, and they did, meekly, their verbal sparring abruptly coming to an end. Phil's heart leaped. *That man! He's... he's gotta be – Di Anello! – the Big Boss!* Phil felt a swirl of panic. The man spoke:

"Vito, go in the meeting room and turn on the lights. After, go back to the car and wait with the driver. Understand?"

"Yeah, sure."

"And don't forget, you take Guido to fly his airplane tomorrow. Are you listening?"

"Yeah. Of course I am." Vito hurried to the rear of the warehouse, went into the room, and turned on the lights. Then, head down, he shuffled back past the three men and headed towards the parked La Salle.

"Shit," he said, muttering at a stack of boxes, "now I gotta be a nursemaid to his lousy kid. I got better tings ta do wit my time."

The men, out of earshot, didn't hear the grumbling, but Phil, crouched behind the boxes, did. A few moments later, he heard the slam of a car door behind him.

Now! Slowly he threaded his shadowy way from behind one stack of boxes to another until he was close to the meeting room. What now? The door was slightly ajar. Phil heard the murmur of voices. *Quit while you're ahead! Get out now!* a feverish voice inside him pleaded. *How?* he asked himself. Foolishly he had blundered into the warehouse, and now he was trapped inside. But they'll have to leave sometime! And I can get out then... somehow! Meantime? He glanced back to where the La Salle was parked. He couldn't see it behind all the clutter. He listened intently. Not a sound. He gritted his teeth, quieted his panic. He had to know more, for the "Nino" his father worked for was this Nino... a Di Anello lieutenant! That truth hit him hard now. Did his father know? Agitated, he involuntarily pushed against a stack of boxes. He gasped, and circled the tilting tower with both arms. It steadied, held fast. Trembling, a moist clamminess gripping him, he sat quietly, breathing slowly. He knew he must go on! He had to! He was onto something big. He thought a moment. It would be risky. Nevertheless, he moved from his hiding place, a silent wraith...

Flat on his stomach, Phil angled himself behind the inches of open door. If anyone got up to leave he'd be behind the boxes in a moment. Safe. And from his ant's eye view on the concrete floor, he'd see Vito first, or even before that, hear the loud clack of fancy leather shoes... he hoped.

Barely breathing, Phil propped himself on his elbows and peered inside. The thin dark man – Di Anello, Phil thought – the mob head, whom Oreste and Nino had obeyed instantly, *why he could even be one of the–*

He spoke, breaking into Phil's bouncing-ball thoughts: "All right you two, sit down. Good! Now, Oreste, you first. Talk! What's da big problem bodderin' you?" He produced a long, black Di Nobile stogie, cut it in half with the knife he produced, and lit one half with a solid silver lighter. He offered the other half to Oreste, who took it and accepted a light. Nino lit a cigarette, and puffed into the reek of the stogies, as if to neutralize their stench.

"The little lame guy down on Columbus Street owns da hole-in-da-wall store across from da diner," Oreste said slowly, "he's gotta be straightened out... real good."

"Jimmy? *Madonna mia!* Next you'll be pickin' on da old ladies in da tenement over dere." Nino waved his hand, puffed vigorously, and smiled.

"Yeah? Den why does he hang around Pizzuta so much? And a coupla times, afta dey talked, our crap games were hit. Why, Smiley? Answer dat for me, will ya? Oh, he's gotta be straightened out! Maybe even more dan dat, ta keep his trap shut." Oreste looked malevolently at Nino.

"Pizzuta hangs around everybody!" Nino snapped back. "He gets his eats at Jimmy's, or the diner. Even has coffee half and half dere wid da boys; even wit you, Sicilians! I seen you passin' da time of day wit him!"

"Are you accusing me of being a traitor?" The words, spoken in Italian, were pure menace, and Oreste's face a dark, threatening storm.

"*Zitto! Tutte due!*" (Be still, both of you!) It continued, "I know all about Sergeant Pizzuta. He is a good detective, and soon he will be on other assignments where he can be more productive. You see, he hasn't been able to come up with a thing on neighborhood crime, or the *Mano Nera*, whatever that is. So Massimo Di Anello has spoken to the mayor. *Capite?*"

Oreste and Nino chuckled and rolled their eyes. "We understand," Nino said.

"Just the same," Oreste said, "about Jimmy..."

"All right, all right!" Di Anello cut Oreste off. "I leave it to you. Set something up. Let the word get to Jimmy. Nothing too big, nor anything that can be traced to us." He shrugged. "We'll see what happens."

"Consider it done!" Oreste said.

"Now, we catch up on business," Di Anello said.

They talked of horse races, politicians, the need to up the numbers take, and Oreste's godson, Gennaro, soon to arrive from Catania. Phil listened, mesmerized, to the brains of the neighborhood *Mano Nera*, for that's who these conspirators were! Oh! but it is a dream! That's it, he thought, a bizarre change from the nightmare of the creeping hand on his bed, many years ago...

The noise of scraping chairs jarred Phil back to reality. He was awake all right-wide awake! Inside the room the three stood up, stretched, and started for the door.

Jolted, terrified, Phil crawled a few feet to the shelter of a wall of boxes. Flattened against them, he tiptoed back towards the La Salle and knelt behind the same olive oil cans he had rattled coming into the warehouse.

"Vito," a voice reverberated in the cavernous maw, "we're coming out. Douse the warehouse lights, start the car, and open the sliding door."

Phil cautiously looked around the cans. He sweated heavily. His clothing dripped moisture. In the car Vito mumbled to the sleepy driver. Then, slowly, his body swaying like some primitive being, he got out, grunted, placed one hand on the metal sliding door handle, and reached for the light switch with the other. Phil heard the clatter of heels on concrete behind him getting steadily louder. Oh shit! Di Anello and his henchmen! Soon there would be no escape!

Come on, come on! Phil implored Vito silently. Adrenaline pumped through him, his rubber-soled sneakers pressed the concrete floor, his body tensed and his leg and arm muscles hardened, as if by a burst of compressed air.

"As soon as I flip da light switch, put on yor parkin' lights," Vito instructed the driver, who stirred, mumbled.

The lights went out. Vito pushed the heavy door open a foot, cursed, lowered his shoulder, pushed it open another two feet. The La Salle's parking lights switched on. Suddenly, Phil erupted. With a jack-rabbit spring and head-first slide he was outside, prostrate and still in the weeds and skunk cabbage, just as Vito opened the door all the way. Di Anello strode around the pile of olive oil cans, the stub of his stogie glowing red.

...In the weeds, next to him... What?-something soft? A hairy hind leg? Phil peered into the darkness and stifled a scream. A small dog! A dead small dog, its broken neck lolling grotesquely on a rock.

Phil pressed his body down hard on the leg as the light of the La Salle passed over him. Its occupants, grim-faced, looked straight ahead. Phil began sobbing. He couldn't help it. What he had seen! What he had heard! His narrow escape! He bit his lower lip and stood up slowly and warily.

The creeps are gone! A huge weight seem to lift from him.

He was cold and miserable though the drizzle had stopped and the night was balmy...

Sergeant Pizzuta! Jimmy! Gotta warn them! Just gotta! He ran back home to the tenement and slipped undetected into his room, barely getting his clothes off before dropping into bed, exhausted.

Chapter 5

Tuesday morning. The sun broke through the haze and Mona smiled. She picked up the living room phone and called her girlfriends. The message was the same, ending with "...about an hour and a half... in the court. See ya!"

She heard the loud sound of a truck; curious, she went out to the back porch. The truck, minus canopy, ground up the gravel road. But the driver wasn't the lecher with the slick black hair who loved to ogle her. No, it was a younger man of about eighteen, and he was angling the truck towards an outdoor water faucet by the warehouse. Mona laughed and hurried downstairs. The day was hot, and riding to the lake would be much better than walking!

"Hi, Little Angelo," she said, coming up close. "How about taking me and a couple of friends to the lake? It's only a mile away. I'll sit in the front seat with ya!"

Later, back upstairs in her room, Mona smiled smugly and tried on her new blue bathing suit. Her mother looked in and exploded:

"You not gonna wear dat ting out a dis house, Monica! I can see you in da funny places! Imagine wat people will say when dey see you. How dey will talk and move da eyes. *Che vergogna*, what a shame!"

"Oh Mama, there's nothing to be ashamed of. This is the latest style – and from Italy, too. The girls are modern there. They have fun and they don't live in convents either, like you say. So don't be so old-fashioned!"

As a concession to her frowning mother, Mona tugged the bottom of the blue two-piece creation up so it would cover her navel, and adjusted the top decollete. Then she changed quickly into a skirt and blouse, shoved the bathing suit into a small bag, and zoomed by her mother, kissing her on the cheek as she rocketed past.

"See ya, Mamma. I'll be back late this afternoon. And don't worry, I'll be okay." She ran out the door, stopped at the wooden landing, and whistled for Vic and Phil. Mama Grace Noci had had little time to react, but now, she positioned herself behind a curtain overlooking the court. She wasn't about to miss a thing. Neither were any of the other sentinels in the tenement, as shades, curtains or draperies rustled, raised, or opened. Accustomed places were taken; tongues clucked; heads wagged hypocritically.

In the court the truck, now washed and swept out, idled. Little Angelo's leg shook, and Mona, sitting next to him, giggled. Two girls and Vic, standing in the back and holding on to the sides stakes, kept glancing at the tenement. Finally Phil appeared, walking slowly, a pre-occupied look on his face.

"Gee, Phil," Mona said, "you look like you lost your last friend. What's the matter? I know! You miss your country girlfriend!"

"Naw, nothing like that. I'm okay." Phil smiled wanly. He hadn't slept well, and the events of last night tormented him. As soon as he could break away he had to warn Sergeant Pizzuta and Jimmy. No, Phil thought, not Jimmy! He'd have to tell Jimmy how he got his information. If Jimmy got scared he could throw suspicion off himself by squealing to *them* about me! So, uh-uh! Phil had seen enough movie serials and dime action magazines to know that a double cross was possible. He was leery; he would put his trust only in Sergeant Pizzuta.

"Phil?" Mona took his arm, and led him to the back of the truck. "Meet my girlfriends, Carmela Martucci, and Marjorie Fleming... Marjorie! No, Marjorie – let him go! He's sitting up front with me!"

Mona, as promised, sat in the cab. Little Angelo couldn't paw her, for between him and Mona sat a guy bigger than he was – Phil. Mona... was no dummy!

"Where's Slick?" she asked, innocently. "Doesn't he drive this truck?"

Gears shifted slowly in Little Angelo's brain: "Oh... him. He's gotta do sumting special for da boss, Nino. So dey ast me ta clean da truck. I mostly work at da relijuss ahticle store down da street. I sell Madonnas. Guess you know dat, I bet." He nodded, importantly.

"No, I didn't know!" Mona said, her eyes wide, a hand dramatically moving to her cheek. "But I could have guessed it! You look real smart!"

Little Angelo squirmed with delight, his glands somewhat appeased.

"C'mon Phil, I'll race ya to the float. " Mona had taken her time in the ladies' dressing room, and now she made what she knew was a spectacular stage entrance. Her girlfriends, already on the float with Vic, gasped with admiration touched with a bit of envy. The near-noon sunlight, breaking through wispy clouds, caressed Mona's ample curves and contours – expertly on display.

"Huh? Oh, sure," Phil answered, tearing his eyes away from a flat clearing on the hill above them. A guy about his own age held a high-wing contest-type rubber-powered model airplane above his head. Phil had built a few himself, but this one, with a narrow body and big wing, looked as if it could soar and glide forever. He was enthralled at the sight.

"I'm gonna beat ya, slow poke!" Mona high-stepped into the water, made a flat dive, and began thrashing her hands and legs.

"No you're not!" Phil plunged after her, reaching the float a hand-length ahead of Mona. Close! But no matter. No girl was going to beat him.

The terror of the previous night was temporarily forgotten and the terrible consequences he had conjured... for everyone touched by the fingers of the dread *Mano Nera*, bane of his childhood dreams.

* * * *

On the hill, at the edge of the clearing, Vito (Vito Amorusi) gazed hungrily at Mona's soft, tanned flesh. He ran the thumb of his right hand down his nose several times, rotated his thick shoulders, snorted, and gave his undivided attention to her hijinks with the little group of stupid kids on the float.

Head moving slowly from side to side, Vito started down the slope...

* * * *

The young people on the drum-supported planks of the float dived or pushed each other off the swaying surface. They screamed and splashed, laughed and giggled, and became acquainted. Phil learned that Marjorie Fleming wasn't from the neighborhood, but from the Irish section of town, perched high on a massive granite ledge above the neighborhood. She was Irish-Italian, and she moved easily between both volatile groups.

"You sure are a hit with Mona's friends," Vic said, as he pulled himself onto the float. "Watch out! They'll get you! Ha–" he began to stutter.

"Phil, how tall are you?" Marjorie asked, coming up behind them.

"Me? Oh, about five-ten, I guess."

"Gee, by the time you're sixteen or seventeen, bet you'll be over six feet tall. I like tall men. I'm five-six you know, and just a few months older than you." She tossed her wet red hair, smiled at him.

So she's been asking questions about me Phil thought. He liked that! He lowered his head, glanced at Vic, who avoided eye contact...

Marjorie continued, "I'll bet we'd look good together on the dance..."

Now Mona's eyes narrowed. "C'mon," she said, "let's go ashore; we'll need more tan. You too, Skinny." She glared at Marjorie and said, "We don't have all day, you know."

Carmela, well – endowed herself, tittered and jumped into the water, taking Phil and Vic with her. A few strokes later they all stretched out on the grassy slope at water's edge, and soon the soothing warmth of the sun on wet skin and the sweet scent of green grass had them in a torpid state. All but Phil. He got up slowly and sauntered to the top of the hill where he had seen the guy and his plane.

The guy, about his own age it seemed to Phil, stood in the middle of the clearing. He was squeezing drops of glue from a small tube of Comet cement onto a thin piece of balsa wood, the cracked left elevator of the model plane.

"Hi!" Phil looked closely at the model. "Boy, that's a real flyer! I've never built one this big... but I built a Spad 13, a Fokker D-7 and a few other World War models... past few years." He paused. "My name is Phil. What's yours?"

"Guido," the boy said. "You like model building a

lot?"

Phil nodded.

"So do I!"

And the discussion began: the merits of the Comet and Megow scale model kits; the extra cement, banana oil, and tissue that had to be bought to finish the model, and the expensive super-detailed kits the Iver-Johnson store on Main Street sold.

"If you want a real flyer though, get one of these non-scale models," Guido said. He liked this tall, unpretentious, husky boy with the deep blue eyes and a ready smile.

The attraction was mutual. Phil liked Guido, for he was soft-spoken and intelligent – unlike some other guys he had run into! Guido was slender, of angular face with dark, piercing eyes, and a head of thick, black hair that contrasted sharply with his expensive-looking white shirt and spotless red sneakers. His fingers, the longest Phil had ever seen, worked the balsa wood and glue expertly. Obviously, Phil thought, a great model builder!

"Ever build a gas model plane?" Guido asked.

"No." *Never had the five or ten bucks for the engine!* Phil thought.

"I just bought a Class B job. Would you like to see it?"

"Yeah! Say, what's your last name? And.. and... where do you live?"

"My last name? Its Di Anello... and let's see, I live up on..." His face tightened. "Where do you live?" Guido countered.

"Holly Hill, in a big green tenement near a warehouse," Phil answered.

"There's a big sign over the door–"

Guido's sharp exhalation, of relief Phil thought, intruded.

"The place belongs to my father! Tell you what! Meet me in the court tomorrow. I'll bring the gas model."

Vito Amorusi had taken his eyes off Mona to watch the big kid in the swim suit come up the slope towards Guido. He was suspicious but then, watching from behind tall lilac bushes on the edge of the clearing, he let loose a thick stream of spittle, and crammed a fresh wad of bubble gum into his mouth.

"Stupid kids and dere toy airplanes!" he mumbled, and took his hand off the pistol in his waistband. Somehow the big kid looked familiar, but he couldn't figure out why. He wiped the sweat from his scarred face with the sleeve of the shirt and picked his way down the slope, staying close to the heavy vegetation at its border. His cold predator's eyes locked on the nubile female body lying face up at the water's edge.

Mona stretched deliciously. The heat felt good on her naked belly and near-naked breasts. To get a decent tan, and for other reasons she knew, she had adjusted her two-piece suit, and she was satisfied with the result. Little beads of sweat bubbled up on her, so she turned on a hip, propped herself up on an elbow, sighed, closed her eyes, rubbed them, opened them... and found herself looking squarely into Marjorie Fleming's unimpressed face. Mona's eyes swung back and forth. "Where is–"

"He's up there," Marjorie cut in, pointing. There he was, talking animatedly with another guy, oblivious to the world around him.

"Oh!" Mona said, rising and stamping her feet. She put the little finger of each hand in the corners of her mouth, ready to rend the heavens with a piercing whistle. *He couldn't do this to her!*

"At least Carmela is having a good time," Marjorie said, pointing again. Carmela, at the opposite end of the small lake, was running through a copse of young elm, oak and brush, in hot pursuit of Vic. She was gaining on him.

"I know what that vampire wants!" Mona said, momentarily distracted.

"So do I! Wait till she catches him. He thinks she's playing a kid's game. Gee! He doesn't know much..."

Both girls watched and waited. Marjorie ran nervous hands over her waist and down her hips. Mona pouted.

But Vic and Carmela did not emerge from the humid stillness of the woods...

Mona sighed, turned, and faced the slope. She took a deep breath and lifted a shrill whistle into the azure sky. Marjorie put both of her hands over her ears, closed her eyes, and grimaced.

The whistle caught Phil and Guido high above the clouds. The two land-of-dreams pursuit pilots came down to earth with less than a perfect three-point landing. Mona beckoned Phil with a 'come here' hand flip, pointed to the dressing room, and ran towards it. Marjorie, motionless, hands on hips, just stared.

Phil grinned at Vito and said, "We can talk some more. It'll take her a while to get dressed."

But Mona came out quickly. She tugged at her skirt and looked at Marjorie, then up the slope. Phil chuckled and then something alien caught his eye. His heart banged against his chest and his throat constricted in spasms.

"That guy coming out of the bushes near the water," he wheezed, "he's a goon! He tried to smack me down twice! What's he doing here?"

The magic spell of the day was shattered. Phil sweated, trembled, his mind raced. He hadn't wanted to connect Guido Di Anello with the *Mano Nera* head – after all, many people have the same last name and are unrelated.

Right?

He wasn't so sure now with Vito skulking around.

"Relax!" Guido said. "You got the wrong guy! He's just my driver." Phil sensed worry in Guido's voice, and he didn't relax. His eyes darted to the side of the road and there it was – a shiny, blue 1935 Buick sedan, its chrome naked Flying Lady hood ornament sparkling. No one in the neighborhood can afford a car like that! Ah, but a few can! Guido's last name? – Di Anello! Though the day was steamy hot, a chill wave of fear swept through Phil.

"Your father," Phil began, haltingly, "your father–"

"My father," Guido cut in, "is a good businessman. No cheap politician screws him, and none of those westside Yankee bastards own him. He helps a lot of our people, and gives more money to the church than anyone. That's it, Phil... Look, I like you; we're still gonna get together, aren't we?"

"Yes, but keep your driver away from me. I don't like his looks."

"Aw, he wouldn't hurt no one. He's just an old, washed-up pug. But sure, I'll keep him away from you. I'd better call him. We gotta go."

But the "washed-up pug" had other ideas. He'd liven up an otherwise dull day. He popped his bubble gum and thought of the fun he was soon to have. He kept walking. Dose big tits! Dat curvy behind! Pop! Another bubble burst, and covered his face with goo. He swaggered up to Mona, who was picking up a towel.

"Hi dere, doll! I was watchin' ya. Ya swim good for a broad, know dat?" He sidled closer, grinning through the gum film. Serenely confident, he patted Mona's behind three times... fast.

With a look of surprise and disgust, Mona swung her right arm and smacked him on the mouth with her open palm. The sharp sound alarmed two foraging ducks, who flapped away, quacking loudly.

"Just who do you think you are?... You... you clown, you mistake of nature!

"Lemme alone! I don't know you! Get lost before I let you have it again." Mona balled a little fist, her eyes blazed, and her bosom surged with emotion.

Vito wiped the trickle of blood and stringy gum from his lips with a swipe of his thick fingers. Sammy Constantino had slugged him like that... in the tenth round at Mechanics Hall. And, toe to toe with Sammy, he had bashed Sammy good until the bell sounded... and he had won. But his head did funny things to him after that, and his manager said he couldn't fight no more. But he'd fight again, only different... with this broad! It was the tenth round again and his head... and crotch... felt funny...

"Youse," he snarled at Marjorie Fleming, "get lost!" He patted the bulge in his waistband. Marjorie needed no prompting. Terrified, she whirled and ran towards the woods, where Carmela and Vic had disappeared. Long legs pumping, she glanced over her shoulder, not at Mona and the thug, but up the slope, where Phil had been.

God! Hope he's safe! she thought.

Vito looked at Mona's angry face. "So ya wanna fight? Oh! I'm scared shitless!" he mocked, and he dug a fist into her belly. She doubled over. Then he rabbit-punched her and dragged her, open-mouthed and gagging, towards the concealment of the bushes. He pushed his crotch against her buttocks

Mona struggled fiercely through her mantle of pain. Vito pushed harder. Why, this was better than lambasting Sammy Constantinto, or snapping that dumb dog's neck!

Almost at the bushes now, Vito snuffled hard, the sound harsh. His chest heaved, and his head clogged with unbearable heat and buzzing noises...

Now... the knockout!

Chapter 6

Phil tried to yell; nothing came. His knees shook and terror touched him, shouted at him: Run! Run! Away from here, from Vito, from the curse of the Di Anello's! But Mona was in big trouble! He couldn't leave her with crazy Vito! Someone had to do something.

He scanned the water's edge. No one! And Mona was about to be... Suddenly, Phil knew. Though his heart pounded, and he smelled the stink of his terror, he... was that someone.

And so the cowboy hero of the Majestic spurred his white steed and closed in on the villain... The intrepid flyer of the dawn patrol, hunched in his Spad, high above the trenches of no-man's-land, spotted the Fokkers below, and dived... Phil charged on!

Guido watched, open-mouthed, and understood. Vito, there! wrapped around a limp Mona.

"No, Vito, no!" Guido screamed, his arms waving impotently.

But Vito didn't hear. The crowd roared, floodlights glared, and the bell rang incessantly. The cringing form he had tied up on the ropes needed one more hit. He clenched his fist, and his face contorted.

Vito never delivered the blow. For the essence of the cowboy, the flyer, compressed into a 155 pound young body of strong bone and growing muscle hurtled down the slope, its goal clear.

Out of the corner of his eye Vito saw a blur just before the sky opened and a thunderbolt hit his right side. He staggered back, took two little steps, and fell face down on the canvas. But it was wet! And little... What? Pebbles! stung his face, his eyes, his hands. He lay dazed.

Phil, in a burst of clarity, realized how crazy his action had been.

"Come on, Mona!" he shouted, "He's got a gun! Run! Run."

Mona needed no urging. She had seen Phil running down the slope, shoulder inclined like a battering ram, and she had pulled away from Vito at the moment of impact. She had fallen hard, scratched arms and legs, and tore her skirt and blouse. But now she grasped Phil's offered hand. He lunged away, dragging her behind him, swaying and stumbling.

"I can't... keep up," she panted piteously. "Oh... Mama will kill me!"

Phil supported her, half-carried her, and headed for the woods at the far end of the little lake as clouds gathered and a strong wind blew.

"Phil! In here!" Marjorie! behind a thicket of blueberry bushes and birch saplings. Phil pulled Mona, sobbing quietly, down beside Marjorie.

"Look!" Marjorie, said. She extended a sunburned arm, tossed her wild tangle of red hair. For the briefest moment, she was a slender wood nymph...

Phil blinked, coming back to 1935, Marjorie's extended arm, and Vito.

"See, he's not getting up!" Marjorie said, highly excited.

True! Vito's lay still in sand, water, and pebbles. Guido stood over him, screaming in the wind: "You dumbbell, you turd! What's wrong with you? I yelled at you to leave the girl alone!" He grabbed a handful of wet shirt and pulled. Vito got up unsteadily.

"Take me home, turd!" Guido yelled.

Vito snarled, "Don't call me dat!" But he calmed down and said, "Which way did da guys dat hit me go? Dey was afta you, know dat? Good ting I was here to protek ya. Dere was tree a dem, right?"

"Huh? Uh, yes, three of them!" Guido answered tersely. "Now, not a word of this shit to my father. Got it? You were supposed to be watching me, remember? What do you think my father would do to you if he found out you left me to go after a broad? Got it, *strunzo?*"

Vito did. Again, he had been called a turd, in peasant dialect. He seethed! He would get even! His hands twitched at the thought of ripping this stinking kid's tongue out and pissing on it. For now, he'd wait. If he didn't he could find himself in cement shoes staring at fish, or with six slugs in his head...

"Aw shit, Guido," he sniveled, "she upset me, dat's all. Dose big tits were lookin' right at me... Geez! what could I do?" He kicked at a pebble.

"All right, forget it! You just tripped and fell. Got it?"

"Sure, I got it!" Vito grunted with relief.

They walked up to the Buick. Vito got behind the wheel and Guido slid over the whipcord upholstery next to him, placing his plane carefully on the wide back seat. The car pulled away.

The drama over, Marjorie, with a slim arm around Phil's shoulders, expelled her breath in a moist gush. She and Phil watched the car disappear and Phil whispered, "Thanks, Guido, thanks! You didn't squeal on me! Phew!"

Hot tears blurred his vision, and the tight invisible band around his head loosened. Then, for the first time, he felt Marjorie's protective arm and heard a whimper behind him.

He turned. He had been so engrossed that he had forgotten about Mona. There she sat, dishevelled and Carmela, her face flushed, and her eyes wide, knelt by her. Vic, a bewildered look on his face, stood over them. Blades of grass clung to his hair, curled into ringlets by the humidity. He scratched his head, and cracked a silly grin at Carmela. She said nothing, but adjusted a dangling bra strap and vigorously brushed Mona's hair.

Mona moaned, "Mama will kill me! And those nosy busybodies-how am I ever gonna get by them-ohhhh... ohhhhhh!"

"I'll get you home," Marjorie said, calmly. "The snoops won't see you."

Silence... palpable and thunderous! All eyes locked on Marjorie. "How, Marj, how?" Mona finally said. "Those old ladies are glued behind their curtains!"

"Vic and Phil will go ahead of us," Marjorie replied. "They'll come up the gravel road into the court, yelling and screaming."

"That'll get the curtains out back moving," Mona mumbled, "but-"

"Vic goes up the back steps," Marjorie cut Mona off. "Phil stays in the court, like he's waiting for someone. Vic goes in the house, comes down the front steps, and opens the front hallway door – wide." Marjorie snapped her fingers. "That's when us girls run in, quick like a bunny!"

"Oh yeah? From where?" Besides, we'll be seen."
Carmela came to life.

"No we won't, we'll be behind the stone wall of the
grammar school across the street. Remember, no one
uses the front hallway door except on Sunday. Anyway,
the snoops will be out back, peeking at Phil. It'll work!"

Marjorie paused and took a deep breath. "We'd better start; it's gonna rain pretty soon." Thunder lent ur-
gency to her words.

Rapt faces glowed. Heads nodded; Mona sighed.
Marjorie got up, her white swim suit standing out sharply
against the darkening sky.

"I can't go yet" Phil blurted. "Neither can you, Marj!
My pants and shirt; your shorts and blouse-are still
across there-on the grass. I'll get them." In all the excitement he had forgotten, and so had she.

"Wait for me!" he said, and ran off at full speed.

Marjorie followed Phil's fast-moving body with glistening eyes. Her lips moved, but there was no sound.
Vic also watched, and made a decision.

"Wait up for me!" he shouted, and sprinted to Phil's
side.

"You're either brave or dumb, I don't know which –
the way you took on that big ox. Cripes! he could have...
could have... killed you." Vic stammered. "Why'd you do
it? Hey, don't run so fast, no one's gonna steal your
clothes!"

"Why? I don't know why... Guess someone had to. I
don't know. I just did... because I did, that's all." And
Phil couldn't exactly explain his dangerous deed to himself, either. Deed? The word brought up his fantasies,
his mythical heroes. Had they urged him on? Maybe.
But Vic wouldn't believe him – or think him nuts! It was
more than that, though. What was going on inside him
anyway? He gave it up and shivered at the thought of
what could have happened to him.

"Did Vito see you?" Vic asked, in a high-pitched voice.
"And what if that kid tells Vito who you are, where you
live? Gee!"

"Guido won't tell! And no, I don't think Vito saw me."
Phil reached down on the grass now, picked up and put

on his pants and shirt, then retrieved Marjorie's things. But Vic had planted seeds of doubt within him. He swallowed hard and said, "We'd better hurry back." He had to quit thinking of that crazy sadist, even for a little while, and give his confused mind a rest. He turned to Vic: "What happened between you and and Carmela... in the woods?"

Vic frowned, picked up a smooth, round stone, and skimmed it across the water. It bounced twice, lost velocity, and sank.

"We ran, had fun. I told her I was gonna be fifteen tomorrow. She jumped on me, then pushed me down, kissed me, and said she wanted to see my birthday suit. Carmela said she would show me hers." Vic picked up another stone, and threw it. It sank immediately.

"She almost did, but I got up and said we should head back. My mother told me about girls! They get boys in trouble. But now that I think of it, I don't know if she's right anymore. Girls can be nice! Carmela... she... she... wouldn't get me in trouble, would she?"

"No, Vic... She's a really nice girl." And I thought I was naive, Phil thought.

They arrived at the path in the woods where the girls waited. Marjorie dressed, and close together they all started out. Marjorie took Phil's hand, and in silence the little group trekked through the woods. At last, they ducked behind the grammar school wall.

Phil and Vic, after wishing the girls good luck, left the wall and followed their instructions with military precision.

The curtain sentinels were indeed bamboozled! Once inside the house, Carmela cornered Mama Grace Noci in her pantry, talking excitedly. Mona, led by Marjorie, slipped into her bedroom and collapsed on her bed.

"Get up, Mona!" Marjorie urged. "Your messy clothes! Take them off!" Mona did. Marjorie handed her a clean sweater and skirt. Mona put them on.

"Fine. Now go to the bathroom and get cleaned up. I'll tell your mother you had to go to the toilet real bad." Marjorie pushed Mona out of the room and ran to the pantry. "Oh, Mrs. Noci, guess what? The lake didn't agree with Mona. She's got the runs!"

From behind the closed door of the bathroom Mona heard Marjorie, and a giggle broke through her fear. I made it! I made it! she told herself. And nobody saw me!

But someone had! Her brother, Nicola Amadeo Noci – Nick. Slumped in the front seat of a green 1934 Ford coupe, bleary-eyed, enveloped in sweet-smelling smoke, a thin cigarette dangled from his lips. Next to him sat nineteen-year old Gaetano Montegrande, nicknamed Longcoat for the black topcoat he wore both winter and summer. He was a runner for Di Anello, picking up gambling bets from an assigned shoe factory and turning in the money to the religious article store on Columbus Street. He skimmed a few dollars for himself, and he was lucky. No one's horse had come in, nor anyone's numbers, except once. He quickly paid off with his own twenty-five dollars.

Longcoat played drums on the side, and a fellow musician gave him a new kind of smoke – said it did wonders for musicians. The smoke came from a plant called marijuana.

Nick first met Longcoat at Sforza's Diner, a mob gathering place for meatball and sausage sandwiches, coffee half and half, and hanging around. Nick tagged along when some of the boys, full of sausage, waddled and burped their way to nearby Amerigo Vespucci Park to play a game of bocce. Nick complimented Longcoat on his strong play, and Longcoat, who had never been fawned over by anyone, not even his mother, offered Nick a smoke. With that, a friendship – of sorts – began.

Nick now took a heady pull from the reefer, and it jacked up his courage. He wanted to ask Longcoat if he could help with the numbers collections; not because he wanted to help Longcoat, but because he wanted to help himself. After he turned Longcoat in for skimming (the crud!) and he was straightened out, Nick saw himself getting the route, then a promotion to board-boy, chalking in racing odds, and when the ponies came in, the results. After that – who knew? Bodyguard, maybe? His own bookie joint?

He didn't ask, for just over the hood of the car, around a slight bend in the road, he glimpsed his sister, smudged with dirt, clothes torn. She looked around, panic-stricken it seemed, and ran into the open front hallway door, led and pushed by two other girls. One was... was Marjorie! Momentarily, Nick almost drooled.

Then, he snapped back, cackled, and said, "Ah! now I'll get even wit her fa razzin' me! Bet she was pumpin' some wise guy in da grass." He turned to Longcoat, "My sister – she bugs me all da time."

"What?" asked Longcoat, struggling to crank his eyelids up from their half-mast position over his vacuous eyes.

"Nothing. I gotta go." Nick opened the car door and gingerly stepped up to the curb. It was very, very high today! But he felt good! Just wait till he got a hold a her! She'd better tell Nick everything... or else –

Phil waited in the court. He looked at the tenement, at the warehouse, and at the gravel road. Nothing. Marjorie had probably gone back out the front door with Carmela – smart move! And both were hurrying home to beat the rain. Vic? Behind a closed door in his room by now, sweating. No sense in trying to see him...

Now what? He couldn't even go swimming with his friends without running into them! But he knew who they were now – Di Anello, Oreste, Nino, and Vito.

Unlike his old nightmares of the creeping hand, he had seen... and yes, even been roughly grabbed (damn Vito!) by the real *Mano Nera*! And he was in a position to retaliate, given his scary night in the warehouse, listening and peeking. Wouldn't his mother be pleased if he could somehow destroy *them*! Phil's little four-year old fists danced behind his eyes, and a vision of poor dead cousin Lucia flickered, said 'Vendetta', and was gone. Isn't that what his mother wanted, even today? Could he ease the years of bitter hate in her heart for them? He didn't know. But he knew he had to see Sergeant Pizzuta, and tell him what he knew.

Hold your horses! an insistent voice within him challenged. What of your own father? He works for *them*! Phil thought a moment, perplexed. No, he decided, his father was in a legitimate business, a cover for Di Anello, sure, but legitimate just the same. Yet... Phil was troubled. He didn't want his father hurt. But the voice was unrelenting. Okay, how about Guido? He's your friend – saved you from Vito! That stumped Phil. *Why can't I be like all the other guys?* he thought ruefully. *Why me? Shit, I'm not even sixteen yet. Yeah, and almost a man, too!* he couldn't help adding... *The unreality of it all!*

Without realizing it Phil had walked down the gravel path, through the weeds and skunk cabbage, and had pressed his forehead against the stout maple tree in the cracked sidewalk. His father, dazzled by his new job – and now, the complication of Guido! He groaned and looked at the black sky through the swaying branches of the tree. Vic's words seemed to float down to him: "At the rate they're going, they will own a good part of the town. And... Di Anello even has the mayor in his hip pocket."

So... soon, its would be worse, for everyone. And only he, Phil realized, had the inside dope that could nail the *Mano Nera*. Isn't that what he had decided before thoughts of his father and Guido intervened? He nodded absently. What he must do was risky, but he had to do it..

A distant rattle of thunder. Humidity, heat, sweat! A storm approaching. Phil, though uncomfortable, murmured "Great!" He glanced around furtively, and began running down Columbus Street. As he had figured it was deserted, and an eerie pre-storm glow hung in the still air. He arrived at Jimmy's store, and pushed through the screen door as a gust of wind whipped the street and rain fell in slashing sheets.

"Jimmy," Phil blurted, "Sergeant Pizzuta... he lives around here somewhere – Vic told me. Can you tell me where? I gotta see him! It's important!"

"Yeah? who are you, kid? Why do you come to me?" Jimmy limped to the screen door and looked out, trying to pierce the rain with a frightened look. His unbandaged hand grasped the open main entrance door.

"You gave me a big ice-cream cone day before yesterday. Remember? I saw Sergeant Pizzuta right after that. He... he helped me. Now I gotta see him. Honest! Can you help me? He might have even walked by your store yesterday."

Phil's pleading did not move Jimmy. He pointed at Phil, then at the door. "Out!" he said.

"I did see Sergeant Pizzuta! And afterwards he told me to stay away from the warehouse up there at the end of the court."

"Why? What do you mean by 'afterwards'?"

Phil sighed. He had to take a bold chance. With that, he told Jimmy about his run-in with Vito at the court, and of Sergeant Pizzuta's intervention. "I want to thank him," he lied.

Jimmy's memory clicked back. Sure! Now he remembered. Sam had mentioned a 'new young fella' shortly before he had almost hacked his finger off.

"Didn't you thank him already? Why again today, in all this rain? Can't it wait?" Jimmy's survival instincts told him there was more to this.

"No it can't wait, damn it!" Desperate now, Phil told army of Vito's attack on Mona at the lake. He held back on his warehouse eavesdropping.

Jimmy's eyes brightened. "Hey, we just might have something! Come on out back; get into my jalopy." He slammed the entry door shut with his right hand, locked it, and hurried to the rear of the store, beckoning Phil to follow him.

"Sam is home. He's getting ready to see his captain about a new assignment. Somebody with clout wants to get rid of him, get him out of the way." Jimmy skidded his old Chevy into a right turn from Columbus Street onto a steep, narrow street, shifted into second, then first, the engine laboring and coughing. Almost with human relief, it seemed to Phil, the car stopped wheezing as it turned onto a level stretch of Holly Hill. The tenement loomed ahead, all of its curtains, drawn or lowered. Slanting rain lashed in from a low-hanging black cloud. Wind whipped up sand from the gutters, creating dancing ghost-like forms. A bolt of lightning hit somewhere nearby.

Jimmy stepped on the accelerator. The wheels spun, caught. "*Madonna mia! il mal' occhio!*" he said, "the evil eye!"

But Phil wasn't listening. He fought hard to overcome a wave of sudden fear and melancholy. He gripped the door handle and gritted his teeth. He began to press down on the handle, slowly, slowly–

"Okay kid, here we are. By the way, what's your name?"

"Huh? What?" Jimmy's sharp voice cut through Phil's self-pity. His hand dropped from the door handle. "Oh," Phil answered, shocked at what he had almost done, "my name is Phil... Phil Martello."

The car slowed and stopped at a brown two-story house. A small hand-painted wooden sign nailed to the front door read: "Mama Cipra's Room and Board."

Upstairs Jimmy knocked twice on a door at the end of a long hallway. The door opened. "Come in," Sergeant Pizzuta said. He seemed surprised to see Phil, but said nothing. He led them through a small kitchen, past a bedroom door, and into a small living room. "Sit down," he said, nodding towards a brown leather couch.

"Phil here has something for you," Jimmy said, with an excited lilt that Sam Pizzuta didn't miss.

Without sitting down, looking straight at Pizzuta, Phil told him of the lake incident.

"Told your parents. Anyone else?" Pizzuta asked, lighting a Camel. His hand trembled ever so slightly.

"No... except Jimmy."

"That's okay," Pizzuta said with a sly grin, "he works for me."

Phil's shoulders sagged. "Phew!" he said, puffing his cheeks, and blowing out a noisy breath of relief.

"What did you think? that Jimmy was one of 'da boys'?" Pizzuta chuckled, and formed exquisite smoke rings. They floated leisurely towards the ceiling, watched closely by Sergeant Pizzuta.

"I... I don't think so." Phil looked sheepish. "Say," he quickly asked, "how come you know my last name?"

"I'm a detective, remember? Besides, how can the name of a new family moving into the neighborhood – and your tenement – be kept a secret? Even the cockroaches know the names of everyone in your family."

Phil thought that funny and smiled, but then a frightened look twisted his face. "Sergeant Pizzuta," he said, "there is something else, something I didn't tell Jimmy.

After you helped me at the court... Well, that night... I... I... sneaked into the warehouse behind a La Salle... Vito... I hid behind some boxes, and–"

"You what?" Jimmy asked, his voice cracking.

"Let him finish!"

"–and I heard everything Di Anello, Nino, and Oreste said!" The words tumbled out with a rush.

Both men tensed, their lips pursed, their eyes widened. Pizzuta dropped his cigarette; Jimmy forgot about his bandaged hand, thumped it with his right hand. He felt no pain.

"Okay," said Pizzuta, in a controlled whisper, "what did you hear?"

Phil gulped, and relived that awful night. He left out nothing: the hiring of his father to manage the warehouse, the fix to move Sergeant Pizzuta to 'other assignments', the setting of some sort of trap for Jimmy because he hung around Pizzuta and had to be 'straightened out', and of the other 'business' Di Anello and his cohorts had touched on. When Phil finished, Jimmy's face was cadaver gray, Sergeant Pizzuta's was flushed. The storm's violence outside was the only sound.

"I've changed my mind," Pizzuta finally said. "I'm not going to bring Vito in. Too much risk for the girls and you, Phil... Got a better idea."

"But the girls will blab," Jimmy said, alarmed... "fuck everything up."

"No, they won't say a word," Pizzuta said, knocking another Camel out of his pack. "You see, men," Phil liked that – Pizzuta lit and puffed, "the girls' parents would beat the shit out of them for being in that kind of a fix. This is a neighborhood, with Old Country ways, remember? On top of that, who would dare squeal on Vito, Di Anello's joy?"

"I wouldn't be afraid to speak up," Phil said.

"I don't mean you," Pizzuta said, with a wry grin. "Now both of you listen to what I want to do. First, I've got to convince my captain to ease the pressure on getting me transferred. Could be hard, but when I tell him what Phil heard – Damn! This is the break us honest cops have waited for.

"Meantime Jimmy, you're not going to take Oreste's

bait. Oh, he'll try again, believe me. He'll panic a bit when we don't raid his first setup, so he'll throw something juicer at you after that. When it's over and you haven't nibbled you'll be a hero and Oreste will lose face – maybe more. 'Da boys' will trust you, won't clam up when you're around. Then you tell me what's happening, and when the time is right we move in, big!" He paused. A slow grin split his face. "Who knows? Oreste might even come in chirping like a canary!"

Phil was elated. What he had done! What he had seen! brought on the big detective's strategy to snare the *Mano Nera* in its own trap. Great! And he wanted to be there when it all happened... He'd better ask Sergeant Pizzuta about that. But before he said a word–

"All right, take Phil home," Pizzuta said, nodding to Jimmy. He turned to Phil. "It's still raining; no one will see you when Jimmy let's you off. And oh, Phil, don't worry about your father. Not yet, anyway... And, a few more things: Keep away from the lake." A kind smile, followed by, "you'll have time for girls in white bathing suits soon enough." Then sternly, "Stay close to home. No heroics, and promise me our conversation today stays with us three until I say otherwise. Agreed?"

Phil nodded lamely and said, "Yes sir!"

"Fine! Get yourself an ice cream cone or a tonic at Jimmy's, starting tomorrow. On the house. Right, Jimmy?"

Jimmy rolled his eyes, "There go my profits," he said, trying but failing to be jovial.

"And Phil! Thanks!" Sergeant Pizzuta smiled. Jimmy led Phil out. He didn't smile. He thought of Orestes vengeance if Pizzuta's plan got screwed up, and the Evil Eye he was sure he had seen in the storm's black cloud. *Madonna mia!*

Phil had thoughts of his own. He'd keep his mouth shut all right – he had promised that, but nothing else. No way, he told himself, was he going to be excluded from the coming action. He was going to be in on it... all the way!

"Ready to go, Jimmy?"

Chapter 7

Wednesday morning dawned cool and gray, with a fine drizzle, the aftermath of yesterday's heavy rain. The Holly Hill baseball players sat on the steps of the tenement, tossed friction – taped baseballs back and forth into worn mitts, tapped hand-me-down Louisville Slugger bats on the landing, and looked hopefully at the sky.

When the heck was that sun coming out? The ball field needs to dry out a little bit before we can play! Looks, murmurs, gestures...

Ferruccio – Rusty – tired of waiting, went upstairs and came down with a basketball. He bounced it back and forth with Vic.

Phil, leaning over the back porch railing of the fourth-floor shouted to Vic, "I'll be right down." He scanned the warehouse court, hoping. No Guido with his gas model kit. After yesterday, Phil really didn't think Guido would be around, not for awhile...

"Here, catch and shoot." Rusty tossed the basketball to Phil. It was intercepted by Nick, who had been at his bedroom window, staring. Then he had followed Phil down the tenement steps, on his way to Sforza's Diner for hanging on."

"That's my ball, give it back!" Rusty shouted.

"Oo-fa, Mi-fi-lay!" Nick replied, and tossed the ball through the hoop on the metal post at the edge of the tenement court.

"Don't call me that! My name is Fer-ah, Rusty, R-u-s-t-y. Understand?" Ferruccio spelled out his nickname, emphasizing each letter.

"Hey Nick, this is Phil Martello." Vic interceded, wishing to avoid another fight.

"Yeah, sure," Nick said. He hadn't met Phil, but he knew who he was. "Watch this, kid," he said. He leaped with the ball; it swished in. He retrieved it, and dribbled it around Phil, his face jiggling with exertion.

Big belly, and an even bigger fat ass, Phil thought. He looks like a slob, but he is older than me... I don't know...

"All new kids have ta guard me. If I get tree baskets

first, I win, and I'm the boss afta dat. I tell ya when ya can play and what position. Got it... Mi-fi-lay?" Nick leered and snickered, at Phil.

"Okay, Big Ass!" Phil could not let that challenge pass!

Nick's mouth slammed shut, his anger evident. His eyes narrowed.

"Oh, ss-ta... shit!" Vic cried. "Watch out for him, Phil. LOOK OUT!"

Vic's shriek brought the boys out into the drizzle, the day's baseball game forgotten. They sensed a battle for king of the hill.

Nick came at Phil, feinted left, and dug an elbow into Phil's side. Phil winced; Nick's big rump battered him in the crotch and sent him reeling backwards, down onto the gravel. Then Nick scored easily with a lay-up shot.

"Two points for me" he said. "Get up, Big Mouth," he taunted. "Tell ya what... new rules. We fight for da ball under da basket." He waited.

"Come on, Phil, get up! You can take Big Ass – you can, you can!" Rusty retreated behind Vic, his Adam's apple bobbing like a yo-yo.

Phil got up. His elbows and arms were scraped and droplets of blood congealed on the broken skin on the palms of his hand. He felt a cold fury grip him...

"You're on, Big Ass," Phil said. Rusty screamed, stamped his feet, and punched Vic in the stomach. Vic grunted, balled his fists... and smiled.

Phil had played an occasional game of pick-up basketball at Lofton Height, and he could tell Nick was a better player. But then, this wasn't going to be basketball, but degradation – his! Well, he'd see about that! While basketball wasn't played often at Lofton Height, other activities built muscle and stamina: Felling trees, splitting logs for winter fires, and lots of swimming and hiking... Phil eyed Nick's flabby body...

"Bet ya like da girls... right, Big Mouth?" Nick tossed the ball up. It teetered on the rim and dropped slowly over it, like a slow leak. Phil leaped for it, a split-second after Nick. They both grasped the ball, but Nick wrenched it away, and tried to lay it up. Phil blocked the shot.

"Did Carmela let you mou' on it, Big Mouth?" Nick, upset, leered. He breathed hard now, his exertion evident. Phil had never heard such gutter language before, but he knew what it meant... Dirty mind! That's what that hunk of suet has! Phil didn't answer Nick.

As the white heat of the sun burst through the mist, the ball went up, hit the backboard and caromed down. Again both grasped it. Phil tried to tear it away. But Nick, mouth open, gasping, held on, swaying from side to side. Phil spun around, taking the ball – Nick attached – with him. Nick's heels left the ground, and his toes scraped a perfect circle in the gravel. His hands slipped off the ball as centrifugal force tugged at him. His eyes widened as he lost his grip, and he went crashing into the tenement's empty-can bin. It was overflowing. Collection day was tomorrow...

The jolt caused assorted cans that had contained anchovies, olive oil, tomatoes, and other juicy contents to cascade onto a dazed Nick, who sat waist deep in the rancid mess. For a moment he was framed in the rising steam of what promised to be a very muggy day.

"Ah'll get even wid ya, you'll see!" Nick shouted, pushing cans away, and shaking a grimy fist at Phil. Head down, humiliated, he ran up the tenement steps, taking them two and three at a time.

"Come on, come with us, quick, before the mothers come out!" someone said. "Play ball with us at the bug yard!" Phil needed no urging. He followed everyone down the gravel road.

Vic tugged Phil's elbow. "Gee," he said, his voice awestruck "another fight and another enemy. You've hardly even moved in yet!"

Phil, calm now, felt regret. "I shouldn't have mixed it up. I should have ignored the big slob. I don't know what gets into me some..."

A strange joyous whooping sound erupted behind him. He turned. Rusty, his feet alternately pounding the ground, danced an Indian dance. A million-dollar-smile was on his upturned face, its rapture bathed by bright sunlight.

* * * *

"Hey, open up, Jimmy! It's wet out here!"

"I see him; he's coming," another voice piped up.

Jimmy unlocked the door of his store and the little knot of men pushed in. On their way to work at tanneries, foundries, wire mills or construction jobs, they had waited to buy Jimmy's club sandwiches, one of which was enough lunch for two men in more sedentary occupations.

"Half price today," Jimmy said. "You guys have to help me make 'em." He held up his bandaged left hand. "And my striker isn't gonna show up to help today, the lazy bum!"

True enough, but not the whole truth, Jimmy knew. Last night at the IAWWV Social Hall Jimmy had told *Senza Sang'* – No Blood – a pale, stringy AEF veteran who had been gassed in the war to end all wars, that he didn't have to show up at the store in the morning to make sandwiches. They had been made up ahead of time, and so *Senza Sang's* help wasn't needed. A couple of beers and several bottles of wine, poured by Jimmy, assuaged *Senza-Sang*, and washed away any bruised feelings he may have had.

..."C'mon, Jimmy, we gotta get to work. You kin work faster dan dat!"

"Sure, sure," Jimmy said. He grinned, wiped his good hand on his white apron, and slapped cold cuts and tangy provolone cheese into waiting buns and thick slices of Italian bread...

An hour later Jimmy locked the front door and turned a sign in his plate glass window from 'Open' to 'Closed'. He scratched in 'Back in two hours'. Maybe by then the sun would break through the drizzle and his ice cream business would pick up. "Bullshit, Jimmy!" he told himself. That's how long you hope it'll take you to case City Hall and find out if Oreste was right or just shooting off his big trap. Oreste did have a hair trigger temper, and sometimes it got in the way of his judgment.

Jimmy got in his beat-up car and chugged downtown. He recalled that strange night after he had closed his store about a month ago, when he sat in a corner stool of Sforza's Diner...

He was sipping coffee when Oreste came in, took in the near-empty diner with a sour glance, and glared at him. Jimmy's insides turned ice-cold.

"Hello Oreste," he said jovially, somehow. "Can I buy you a cup of Joe?" Oreste hesitated and said, "Go ahead. Glad to see dat even you still got some respect." He twitched, tightened his sport coat around his shoulders.

"Hey, Marco, coffee here for the gentleman," Jimmy said, hoping no one heard his pounding heart. He turned to Oreste, "Jelly doughnut?"

"Why not? You know, Jimmy, you're a smart fuck! Single, a nice small business, no worries. Dat's da way to be, yes sir!" Oreste gulped hot coffee Marco had served, and grabbed the accompanying fat jelly doughnut.

"I had a wife once, Oreste," Jimmy said. "She died – influenza – back in '18. I was in France then with the AEF. Couldn't do a thing about it."

"Yeah, I remember da influenza; lots of good people died. No disrespect, Jimmy, see, but now you're better off. Believe me." Oreste's eyes clouded.

"What's the matter? Some dame give you trouble?" Jimmy goaded. He pointed to both mugs. Marco scuttled over to refill them. His hand shook.

"No, not me!" Oreste exploded, and slammed a fist on the counter. "But some people who should know better, they mess around. Broads... are nothin' but trouble!" Oreste's voice rose in a menacing wave.

"You bet!" Jimmy encouraged. "Look what happened to John Dillinger... A broad double-crossed him, got him shot full of lead."

"*Sì, assolutamente! Bisogna guardarsi!*" (Yes, absolutely! One needs to look out for himself!) Oreste slid off his stool with a sudden jerk, his face flushed with anger. He turned towards the door.

Raw nerve, that's what I've hit, thought Jimmy. Make the most of it!

"Yeah," Jimmy echoed, "you're right, broads are nothin' but trouble." And he went fishing, "No matter who they are or where they are."

"*Sì,*" Oreste said, in Italian, "they are particularly dangerous when they are close to the power in City Hall. Some people can't see that. Some day–"he passed a hand across his throat,"it will happen!" He stormed out. Marco dropped a tray. Jimmy hunched over his coffee, blew in it.

And Sforza himself, who had come out of the kitchen on hands and knees when he heard Oreste's loud accusation and placed himself under the counter opposite Oreste, now got up and walked nonchalantly back to the kitchen.

The real owner of the diner, Massimo Di Anello, had to be informed of Oreste's strange behavior. Jimmy saw Sforza's forced nonchalance, and chortled deep in his mug...

Now, as he parked on Main Street across from the soiled granite and tall campanile – like clock steeple of City Hall, Jimmy considered his options. He would start at the top. His Honor The Mayor's Office. Could it be, Jimmy thought, that Di Anello is messing around with a babe close to the mayor and Oreste is angry... and frightened? *Madonna mia!* How Pizzuta could exploit that gem! The drizzle slackened as Jimmy got out of his car.

The girl at the outer reception desk was young, blue-eyed, and of high school age. She wore a bright pink dress. Not her, Jimmy thought... she's just a kid. Behind her he saw bold, black lettering on a closed door. It read: Timothy Hoyt, Esquire; Executive Assistant to the Mayor.

Inside! – got to see who and what's inside. Jimmy thought hard.

"Excuse me, Miss," he said, straightening his best tie. "I was told to see Miss... Miss... I can't remember her name now..." He snapped his fingers, pursed his lips.

"Oh," the young girl said, "you must mean Mrs. Coyne... you know, she's Mr. Hoyt's secretary?" Her voice rose in a helpful interrogative.

"Hmmm, no," Jimmy said, brow furrowed, as if deep in thought. He took a wild shot: "The other one."

"Mrs. Fleming? But Mrs. Coyne is Mr. Hoyt's secretary. Mrs. Fleming is just a clerk." The girl looked puzzled.

Irish women, and married! Not Di Anello's style, Jimmy told himself. Still, he'd like to see for himself. Damn! how his leg hurt.

"I think maybe I got the wrong office. Thank you, Miss," Jimmy said. *Now where do I go?* He looked at the long marbled corridors and closed doors. Make a decision, for God's sake! You ain't got much time. Go left... no, right! His leg shook, his shoe tapped the floor... and stopped. A door behind the girl opened and a woman came out, pushing a limp blond curl away from her eyes. She had a body that had seen better days, but she must have been a beauty at one time, Jimmy concluded, appraising her with interest.

"Sally," the woman said, "go to the small conference room. Be sure it is properly set up. Mr. Hoyt's meeting is on in thirty minutes."

"Yes, Mrs. Coyne."

"Call me Mary," she said, smiling, blinking puffy eyes, and revealing yellow, nicotine-stained teeth. "Don't worry about your desk," she added, "Fully will be here in a minute to watch it for you."

Jimmy watched as Mary Coyne hiccuped and went back inside. Not her! Geez! ...But the door opened again.

"Oh! Hi Mrs. Fleming," the young girl said. "Ready to hold down the fort for me?"

"But of course," Mrs. Fleming said. "And Sally, my name is Fulvia, okay? Don't be so formal. Not necessary."

"Oh, its just that I'm so new. This is my first job... Fulvia!"

At the precise moment that Nick Noci careened into the empty-can bin, Jimmy felt a giant force (twin lightning bolts?) crash into his head, race through his body, and transfix him to the marble floor. Immobilized, he stared, unable to take his eyes off the beautiful lady with the dark hair and the husky, accented voice.

Her name – Fulvia! As Italian as the Bay of Naples! But 'Fleming'? His mind whirled and he remembered. *Fulvia's married name was Fleming.* The newspapers printed it and radios blared it, years ago, for her husband (can't remember his name), a city trolley car conductor was killed when his car jumped the tracks. Tipped over. Talk about lack of maintenance! Shoddy roadbed; corruption, big civil suit. Then silence, and the years passed, the incident forgotten until now.

It's her! Got to be! Di Anello's woman, close to the power, spying for him. Oreste is scared shitless and jealous of her, all at the same time! And, oh my God! Sam Pizzuta! the 'beautiful dish' he wants to 'check out'. It's her, too! The ceiling lights flickered and dimmed, and a gloomy half-light enveloped the two women. Raw fear gripped Jimmy, snapping him out of his wild reverie. He turned and stumbled, recovered, then hurried away as fast as his pain-racked body could go.

"Do you know that odd little man?" Sally asked Fulvia, wide-eyed. "He gave me the creeps – the way he was staring at you."

"No, he is a stranger to me," Fulvia said. But easily identified; bandaged hand, heavy limp, thin nose, bushy eyebrows, and mismatched clothes.

"Wonder what that clown wanted?" Sally asked. She shrugged, and left.

Fulvia Fleming wondered too. If she did as she was told she would report the odd occurrence to Massimo Di Anello. She wasn't going to though, for she was determined to break his hold on her. Why, oh why, had she let herself fall into such a terrible trap? Because, she told herself, at the time it didn't seem to be a trap. Di Anello had helped her family, and she had been grateful...

When her husband was killed, the city promised her a lifetime position if she didn't sue, and offered her a small sum of money. She accepted, and became a file clerk in the mayor's office.

Her family, sickened by ancient vendettas, had left Sicily generations ago and lived peaceful lives in Brindisi, on the heel of the Italian boot facing the Adriatic Sea, vendettas forgotten. But one hard-headed, tradition bound *signore*, still in Sicily, had not forgotten and sought bloody redress. The townspeople knew of his obsession, as did the local *Mano Nera*. No one paid attention to this old *Signore* – the townspeople called him Mad Salvatore – until he whispered to two young town toughs that he would pay them handsomely if they would eliminate a certain Avellini family he had tracked down in the city of Brindisi.

To get to Brindisi the men knew they would have to

sail across the Strait of Messina, then continue on by cart, horseback, and perhaps by boat again across the instep of the Italian peninsula. A dangerous undertaking, given the chaos in the southern provinces. Cutthroats were everywhere, and so was the *Camorra*. No self-respecting member of a *Mano Nera* gang could tolerate being fleeced by a sharpie *Camorrista*, least of all the two young toughs who had promised their fealty to Don Pietro, the local *Mano Nera* chieftan, and sealed their vows with their sacred oath and blood.

The two young men went to Don Pietro, told him of Mad Salvatore's scheme, and asked the avuncular gentleman for his advice.

"Accept Salvatore's lire and travel to Brindisi," he said. "But we must make a few changes in his plan."

One month later, the two young men were in Brindisi, and as instructed by Mad Salvatore, met his informer who pointed out the stone house of the family to be butchered.

The family wasn't – the informer was – and minus a tongue, his body was pushed out to sea in a leaky boat. Late that night, as prearranged, Olga Avellini opened the door after the fourth sharp knock. She was surrounded by a trembling old man, a sobbing crone, and two crying children.

A young smiling Massimo Di Anello bowed graciously, and with considerable panache said, "I am a Don Pietro's ambassador of good news. Your family is safe, forever. *La vendetta... non esiste più!*, the vendetta... no longer exists!"

The Avellini family cried for joy. Don Pietro had sent a messenger ahead to warn them and await the special knock on their door from his trusted *ambasciatore*.

Don Pietro had worked out the sequence of events very carefully. The eldest surviving Avellini, the old man, was a godson of Don Pietro's long dead, sainted grandfather. Mad Salvatore... did not know this and never would. On his way across the Strait of Messina the following day to conduct 'pressing business' in Naples, he somehow, when a ground swell rolled under the boat he had hired, fell over the side and disappeared. The two fishermen who owned the boat-honest townsmen, everyone agreed-swore that the wave was thirty feet high! They searched for Mad Salvatore in vain. They were believed. of course, Don Pietro was the first to gravely announce to all that the men had done all they could.

Olga Avellini, deeply grateful, said her family was indebted to young Massimo Di Anello, and that included her adventuresome younger sister, Fulvia, who was in America and promised to a rich American who owned a transportation company in a city near Boston.

Shortly thereafter Di Anello left Sicily with the national police – *the Carabinieri* – and a *Mafia* executioner, hard on his heels. Some years later, in America, he paid his respects to Fulvia, now a widow. Some day, he said, he would call on her for a little favor. He had but to ask! – she said.

He did not associate with her publicly. Instead, there were occasional social phone calls, messages delivered, and discreet evening rides in Di Anello's black sedans... "Away from telephone party lines," Di Anello said, "so you can freely talk to me about the rotten potato eaters at City Hall."

She provided valuable information as to what went on in the mayor's office. She realized too late that he wanted more than that. Afraid for herself and her young daughter, for his flowery prose contained veiled threats, she reluctantly submitted her voluptuous body to his amorous advances.

* * * *

Jimmy, out of City Hall now, breathed with a heavy rasp, a cold knot twisting his insides. Tile omens were all around him! – his injured finger... the bolt of lightning striking close by on the way to Pizzuta's flat, and worst of all, the eerie glow above Fulvia's head in the City Hall. The powers of darkness warned him, and instilled the fear of hell in him! They protected one of theirs-Di Anello! *Santa Maria Immaculata!*

He must find a way out! Abandon Pizzuta to his fate? That's it! And what of Fulvia? He shuddered. What horrible fate awaited her? God help her! Jimmy mentally flogged himself for believing Phil Martello's line and taking him to Pizzuta's place. But then he wouldn't have known of Oreste's scheme to trap him... And Jimmy, decorated for valor by Blackjack Pershing himself for his fighting at Belleau Wood, cringed and sweated, unable to overcome ingrained centuries-old peasant terrors and lore.

Chapter 8

Mona tossed and squirmed, stifling a scream as she awoke. The nightmare tonight had been horrible. Her wet body stuck to the sheets as she now forced herself to lie still, her heart pounding in her ears, her eyes searching the darkened room. No one lurked in the shadows. Hesitantly she touched the headboard of her bed, felt the comforting gloss of hard-rock maple, and then she heard the soft whistle of her father's snores in the next room.

See! It was only a dream! Forget it Mona, fight it off! Think of other things: clothes... how nice boys they like me... the cheese counter... of Phil... yuk Slick... reefers... Nick... love... Marjorie... Slowly she dozed off and finally, fell into a restless, light sleep.

Darkness turned to a gray, dull dawn. The soft rumble and aroma of perking coffee... the murmur of voices... familiar voices... lulled her, soothed her as she half-awoke. Dawn and security! Mona drifted off into a sweet dreamless sleep. Her father Saverio, preparing to leave for his highway construction job, had whispered to Grace that he had overheard two Irish potato foremen talking about some really big jobs coming up and that they would need a few gang bosses who could speak "Eye-talian." Saverio left for work earlier than usual. Mona slept on until...

"Mona, wake up! What's this?" Her ten-year old brother, Izzy, dangled a handkerchief close to her nose. Something soft was wrapped in it.

Mona groaned, stretched, opened the proffered handkerchief. She focused her eyes and she sniffed. "Izzy!- where did you get this?" she asked. She kept her voice low as she leaped out of bed and grabbed him by the hair.

"It ain't mine! It's Nick's!" Izzy whined. "He dropped it on his way out. Listen, can'tcha still hear him goin' down the back steps?"

Mona nodded. "Where's Mama?" she asked.

"In the pantry, makin' bread."

She nodded again. "Okay! Forget about this, understand? We don't want to get Nick in trouble. I'll take care of things. Here's a dime; go play with the other kids, then get yourself a real big ice cream cone and an orange tonic at Jimmy's. Go Izzy, go!"

Delighted and relieved, Izzy scampered out the back door.

Still in her light nightgown, Mona surprised her mother by saying she would help with the bread. The phone rang. Mona rushed into the living room and answered it. It was Carmela. Mona listened, talked quietly. At one point she held back a giggle. When she hung up she took a deep breath and licked her lips. She went back into her bedroom and tuned out the excited yelling of boys in the court. She glanced out a side window. Sunshine struggled to break through the thick mist.

Wow! It's gonna be another scorcher. Mona selected a light jersey top and a pair of striped shorts. She posed in front of a full-length mirror; she pouted prettily.

"Monica! "

"I'm coming, Mama!" Mona came out into the kitchen.

Suddenly the back door opened and slammed, shaking the small entryway. Brother Nick, wet and angry, stormed by Mona and into his bedroom.

"Oh! Yuk! You smell like a sewer. What did you run into, Genius? And why don'tcha change your underwear once in a while, huh?"

Nick's door opened. He curled out a puffy, tomato-paste smeared face. "At least I stay out a da tall grass, and my underwear ain't ripped. Ha ha!" He slammed the door shut. Color drained from Mona's face. The lake incident! She gasped, and then remembered her phone conversation with Carmela. What a friend! Now she had to confront Nick; see and hear for herself. And she had a surprise for him!

Grace Noci took her eyes briefly off the bread dough she was hand-kneading, and glanced around the pantry door. Such noise! And she so busy!

"It's okay, Mama. I gotta talk to Nick," Mona said in a sweet voice.

"Go, go! And don't you forget, you help me afta!" These modern kids!

With Nick's handkerchief behind her back, Mona slid into his room.

"What a ya want? I'm changing up. Get out a here and..."

Mona held the handkerchief over her head. Nick saw, recognized, and gagged. Mona closed the door, and with exaggerated daintiness unfolded the handkerchief.

"Where... where didja get dat?"

Mona told him.

"I'll kill Izzy! He should keep his stinkin' hands off a..."

Mona cut Nick off. "You leave Izzy alone! What if Mama or Papa had found this junk instead? Ever think of that, Genius?" She held the dry leaves and roll-your-own paper in front of Nick's sweat-soaked face.

Nick fought back. "I wasn't gonna tell on you Mona, honest. I just happened ta be in Longcoat's car when I saw ya comin' home messed up da other day, honest. Now gimme dat stuff. I gotta give it back to Longcoat." Nick held out his hand.

"No, Nicola Noci! This stuff is marijuana, isn't it? You make reefers... and smoke them, don't you?" She pulled open the bottom of the window screen, and let the stuff float gently away.

"You ain't gonna squeal on me, are ya? Remember, I ain't sayin' nuttin about you." Nick pleaded, but with a subtle threat.

"I'm staying quiet," Mona said, sticking to her own agenda, "if you quit using that junk and stay away from that drip, Longcoat. He's a case!"

"Mind yor own business! What I do wit my own time is up ta me!"

"Then you'll never make Marjorie Fleming!" Bam! The moment had arrived.

"She don't mean nuttin' ta me! No siree! Who... who da hell gave you dat... nutty... bullshit?"

Mona knew she had scored. "Never mind! Besides, Marj goes for Phil." She pivoted, tossed her head, brushed her brown hair away from her eyes, and, nose in the air, walked to the door.

She stopped, looking triumphantly over her shoulder: "I slipped and fell in some brambles on the way home from the lake. Carmela and Marjorie helped me up. If you had listened to Carmela when you saw her near the diner last night she would have told you. Instead, you kept bugging her about Marjorie, and who she was with, and smoking that... that junk. You're as subtle as... as a bull in a china shop, Nicola Noci!" Mona wiggled away, closing the door with an exaggerated sweep of her hand, mentally thanking Carmela over and over again for her phone call.

"Ready, Mama," she said. But her euphoria evaporated. Marj wasn't the only girl with a crush on Phil. How about herself? Now that was a problem! But a bigger problem was gonna be Nick, now that he knew how Marj felt. Aw Mona, she told herself, forget it. There are a lot more fish in the ocean besides Phil. And, huh! Nick! Would he try anything funny against Phil? Oo-fa! he's a jerk, and a coward. Still...

"I tot you said you were ready?"

"I am, Mama, I am." Mona began kneading bread, back and forth, back and forth... slowly, lackadaisically.

"Whasa matter? Too hot for you? You sick?"

"Nooooo!" Mona slammed her slab of dough down on the bread board. Tears welling in her eyes, she ran to her room and banged the door shut with her foot.

"You should be in da opera!" Mama Noci said. "Modern kids!" Mona heard bread dough heavily being slapped, "they have too much. Now in the Old Country..."

Mona flung herself onto her bed and buried her head in her pillow. She heard Nick's heavy footsteps, a "Where you go now?" from her mother, and the front door open and close. She rolled off the bed and walked into the kitchen. She shook her hands up and down, as if she were shedding water.

"I need some fresh air, Mama. I think I'll walk over to Marjorie's."

"Now dat da bread is bakin', you feel better, *ma chè*! Go! Go Marjorie."

Mona needed no urging. She headed for the front door.

"You and Nick! The back door no good anymore? What? You afraid of some-a-ting out dere?"

Mona cringed. Oh Mama, she thought, if you only knew half my troubles!

* * * *

The baseball game at the bug yard, so called because at one time an insane asylum was located there, didn't last long. The white heat of the sun burned, the humidity suffocated. The gang headed for the lake, except Phil who headed home. He felt he had to play it safe until he heard from Guido. He heard from him sooner than expected.

"Hi," Guido said, running out of the court warehouse. "I looked for you earlier, but didn't see you. What do you think of her?" The corners of his mouth stretched in a wide smile, threatening to touch behind his neck. He held out a solid balsa wood model of a Martin B-10 bomber.

"Great job!" Phil ran a hand over the olive drab body, the twin engines, the front gun turret, and gazed appreciatively at the star insignia on the yellow single wing and the bar insignia on the tail. "I just got back from the bug yard..." He paused and looked at Guido. "Say," he suddenly said, "how about you? We don't have a regular team yet, but we will next year. Jerry-next-door's brother promised to coach us next spring. Come out and practice with us. You'll have fun, and be ready for the season too."

Soot from the railroad yards drifted overhead. It didn't bother Guido's electric-light grin. "It'll be okay? I mean, I haven't played much. The private school I go to..."

"Don't worry! We don't have Lou Gherigs on the team. Anyway, I bet by next summer you'll be a semi-pro star." Guido swelled before Phil's eyes.

"I'd like to practice with you!" Guido swallowed. "I can bring new balls and a couple of bats and gloves... and everything!" He was excited, and so was Phil. What a change it would be from taped balls, repaired bats!

"Phil," Guido said, his voice bouncing, "come home with me. I'll show you the gas model kit, and a Boeing P-26 pursuit I'm building. Little Angelo can drive us. He'll

be here soon. He loves to come by here." Guido jerked
his head towards the tenement.

"Oh, I get it!" Phil said. "He's stuck on Mona, huh?"

"Yeah. He says she's nuts about him. Says she told
him so when he dropped you all off at the lake. Kind of
dumb, right?"

"Guess so." Phil's heart fluttered. The lake incident!
Pizzuta's plan and now Guido's invitation. God! what a
chance to poke around. But what about Guido? He trusts
me! Phil shuddered, and his face paled.

"Hey, you all right? You look kinda funny. C'mon,
let's get under a tree." Guido sounded worried.

"No, it's not the heat!" Phil thought quickly. "It's...
it's... Vito! Is he gonna be around?" Well, he hadn't really lied, had he?

"Heck no! He's making some rounds with my father.
But even if he showed up he wouldn't know you from
Adam. Honest! He's so punchy even the bats in his bel-
fry get lost. Cripes..."

"Yeah? Then why doesn't your father tell him to get
lost?"

"Why? Because he's been with my father a long time
– back when he was in the fight ring, and afterwards.
See, my father backed him in the old days, and he won
lots of fights, made plenty of money. But he stayed in
the ring too long. It wasn't my father's fault, though. He
wanted Vito to quit long before he did. Other backers
were greedy, and they talked Vito into more fights, then
they disappeared when he was washed up. My father
gave Vito a job driving for him, and running little errands. Not a bad egg, right?" Guido elbowed Phil gently
in the ribs.

Phil nodded absently, and wondered what 'running
little errands' meant.

"Hey! Here comes Little Angelo. Gonna tell your
mother where you'll be?"

"Naw. She knows I'll be out all day." Anyway, Phil
thought, she might object if she knew where he was going.

Little Angelo sighed wistfully as he turned the truck
around at Guido's signal.

At about the same time Little Angelo drove slowly

out of the court, oblivious to Phil and Guido's snickers, Jimmy returned to his store. Little kids milled and fussed at the entrance. Jimmy smiled, City Hall and all it represented shunted aside for now. These kids knew where to get the best two for a nickel ice cream cones – Jimmy's! He opened the door.

Shortly after the last chattering kid left Jimmy mopped his brow, settled himself under the ceiling fan, and took two aspirins. He really should take it easy for a few days as Doc Caradonna had advised...

"Hi dere, Jimmy. Hot, ain't it?"

Jimmy's head jerked up. "Oh, hi Skinny. No horse races today?"

"Naw, ah'm takin' da day off. Tell ya what. Fix me up a nice, big cold cut sandwich. Ah'll go to da pahk and watch da bocce games from unda a tree." Skinny fanned himself with a broad-brimmed straw hat, barely missing a Pinocchio-sized nose.

"Sure. Glad to." *This guy is up to something!* Jimmy thought. "No meatball and sausage sandwich at the diner today?" Smooth and easy! Jimmy retreated behind his showcase.

"Naw. Told ya, it's too hot. Besides, I wanna rest up for a crap game tonight." Skinny took a sample slice of mortadella.

"Yeah?" Jimmy kept filling the sandwich.

"Yeah. Some wise guys a comin' in from Providence wid lotsa moolah." Skinny chomped and smacked his lips. "Good stuff. Yeah... real interestin' deal tonight. Hey, yor a friend, why don't ya come. Ah'll let ya in."

"I do all right in this business, but I'm not big time." Jimmy shook his head. "Here's your sandwich, Skinny. It's a winner."

"Yeah, tanks. Tell ya what. If ya change ya mind, come ta Egan's barn near Lofton Height at the city line. Know where dat is?"

"Sure do." Jimmy knew it was an old supposedly abandoned barn near a Di Aneilo warehouse that 'da boys' used from time to time for crap games, poker, and what-not.

A few minutes later Jimmy had Sergeant Sam Pizzuta

on the phone.

"They just threw me the first bait," Jimmy said, and explained.

"Fine, fine," said a jubilant Pizzuta. "It'll still be on the hook when they pull the line up." He hung up, spit in his hands, and rubbed them brisky together. His promotion to lieutenant no longer seemed a distant dream.∴.

Hell, he might even do something to please Jimmy – start thinking about settling down, and look for a good woman. He figured he knew exactly where to begin the process: the marbled corridors of City Hall!

Chapter 9

The truck wound slowly up steep, wooded East Hawthorne Road. It stopped before an iron gate moored between two somber seven-foot stone lions guarding the entrance to a big, gabled white house on the western upper lip of Holly Hill. A tall stone wall extended some distance on both sides of the lions, curved gracefully, and disappeared behind the house. To the east, beyond Vespucci Park below, rose a granite ledge, its steep mass the boundary line between the Irish and Italian neighborhoods that Marjorie traversed so easily.

Guido got out of the truck, inserted a key in the gate's lock, pulled the gate open, and waved Little Angelo in. The truck crunched fifty feet up a gravel driveway and jerked to a stop.

"Okay, Guido? I hafta go now. Ya see, I gotta make more deliveries, den I gotta turn da truck in. Afta dat, I gotta see a couple of guys—"

"Sure, take off," Guido interrupted Little Angelo. He turned to Phil: "I can get someone to drive you home later."

"Heck, no thanks, I can trot home in less than half an hour." No way, Phil thought, would he go with Vito, if that's what Guido meant by 'someone'.

Inside, Phil followed Guido downstairs to the basement into a fully-equipped kitchen. Angling off to the left a pine den, complete with radio, Victrola, heaps of books and pulp magazines, a black leather couch against the far wall, and... model airplanes everywhere, including the promised gas model kit. Phil felt transported to a dream world, and barely heard Guido say, "This is my own den. Like it?"

Phil did. For an hour he touched, examined, and 'Gee-whizzed' with an eager Guido at his elbow, explaining, showing, demonstrating. But slowly, Phil realized he was in the Di Anello mansion, and he knew he had to probe...

"Is the rest of the house like this?" he asked, thumbing casually through a Lone Eagle pulp magazine.

"Don't I wish," Guido said. "Naw, just a regular first

floor, and on the top floor, bedrooms and my father's office." Guido's eyes lighted up. "I'll show you the office. I have a key. I use it when my father calls and wants something. It's also for an emergency, whatever that means. C'mon, let's go! My mother isn't home, but even if she was she wouldn't go near the office." He shrugged. "But she does keep asking me about girls. Phil, do you have a girl?"

"No," Phil fidgeted, "just friends."

"Like Mona? And that tall redhead at the lake? Boy, can she run."

"Uh huh. Her name is Marjorie. Haven't seen her since... You know why."

"Vito? Aw, Phil! He wouldn't know you from Adam. Remember? He's too busy with the bats in his belfry. Okay, here we are." Guido unlocked the door to his father's office.

Phil walked to a window under a gable. "What a view," he said, admiring the rugged procession of trees and vegetation that swept down in a wild tangle to the edge of Vespucci Park.

"Look." Guido pointed. "Down there – Sforza's Diner. And up there on the ledge is where the *mangia palate* politicians live. Crooks, all of them!" Phil turned and stared at Guido. His lips parted, but he said nothing.

Guido paid no heed. "Know what's in here?" he asked, tapping a big oak cabinet behind an oak desk. Carved lions adorned each of the two cabinet doors. The detail was fine and pronounced, and each lion had a set of unfurled wings held upright against its sinewy body.

"No, I don't know," Phil said, staring at the intricate intaglio. "They're lions with the wings of eagles," Guido said, noticing Phil's fascination with them. "My father saw something 'like that in Venice, and he brought over a craftsman to carve his cabinet. The eagles stand for power, strength, and freedom. How about that? But, hey, wait till you see what's inside!" Guido's voice dropped to an excited whisper.

With a second key, Guido unlocked the heavy doors, and swung them open.

Phil sucked in his breath. He had never seen anything like this! – except maybe in an Edward G. Robinson gangster movie. On a smooth rack, against the cabinet wall, were several rifles with polished stocks. In an open walnut container were two telescopic sights, and on each side of the row of rifles lay a drum-fed sub-machine gun.

"Souvenir rifles from the war," Guido said. "My father's got a Springfield, an Enfield, a German Mauser, and some other foreign guns."

But it was the Tommy guns that mesmerized Phil. He heard the rattle of their fire and he saw thugs leaning out of long-hooded old cars, ripping up a rival gang's hide-out with a wall of hot slugs.

The distant murmur Phil heard was Guido's voice: "Souvenirs from the old bootlegging days. My father said he happened to come across them."

Phil recovered. "I see..." And, his voice quavering, "Does he have ammunition for all this?" He waved his hand across the cabinet. His armpit felt wet and sticky.

"Uh huh, for the rifles, locked in his desk. He target shoots, uses the scopes. I'll show you." Guido lifted out the Springfield, and with a delicate movement of his long fingers attached a telescopic sight. "Take a look," he said, handing the rifle to Phil.

Phil gingerly tucked the stock into his right shoulder, swung the barrel towards the window, closed his left eye, and peeped through the sight with his right eye. "This is great! I can see things all the way to the diner. And," he swung his body around, "even on that ledge. Bet I could pick off a bad guy near the fence around that big house... if I wanted to." For some reason he couldn't understand, his throat tightened. He swallowed saliva. His heart beat faster than it should.

Guido laughed. "Fun, isn't it? I move the rifle around too, when my parents aren't home." He cocked his head, as if listening. "I think we'd better go now. I'm not supposed to have a key to the cabinet." He winked. "But I have! You're my buddy now, so this will be our secret, right? No one will know what we know. Blood brothers?"

"Blood brothers!" Phil answered, without thinking. He grasped Guido's extended hand. Guido seemed about to say something else when the sound of a car coming up the driveway intruded.

"My mother! Coming home from her church meeting."

Guido hastily closed and locked the cabinet, and both quickly ran down a long hallway, took the flight of stairs down two at a time, and were in the den when Julia Di Anello came in.

"Mama, this is my friend, Phil Martello," Guido said.

She was made up like a movie star, Phil thought, and wore lots of jewellery. She put down an engraved silver cigarette case and studied Phil.

"Sebastiano Martello's son. Hello! So Guido likes you. How nice."

Moments later, Phil was on his way home. He stayed close to the side of the road, and walked rapidly. He didn't want a ride home, he had said in response to Guido's offer. It was just as well, for Mrs. Di Anello didn't seem much inclined to give him a ride. She just looked at him, her gaze cutting through him...

Was she trying to figure out whether I had been in the secret inner sanctum? The way she looked at me! Holy smoke! If so, strange... for someone. who '...never goes near my father's office' ...Or, maybe she doesn't want Guido to have Holly Hill friends. But then, she does know my father. And he works for Nino, who works for – oh shit! I don't know! Maybe she's just suspicious of everything and everybody...

Phil quickened his step. Soon he saw the hulk of the tenement. Drawn shades against the heat, Phil thought, gave it a bleak, inhospitable appearance.

But Guido and I are not really blood brothers! Phil suddenly told himself. *We never exchanged blood. Maybe that's what Guido was ready to do when his mother returned.*

Phil felt as though he were being swept away, and had no control over his destiny. But he knew it was his own fault. Hadn't he flaunted fate by starting the whole process in motion?

He was hot and sweaty. Jimmy's! That's where he would go. Get his free ice cream cone and tonic, pump Jimmy, find out if Pizzuta's plan was working, and then... he would go home for dinner. With Sergeant Pizzuta on his side, he thought, his confidence returning, things would work out.

Do you really believe that? the little voice inside him asked. Phil brushed the negative thought aside.

Jimmy's long face didn't help. He answered Phil's questions with noncommittal grunts. Phil said, "See you later," and left, ice cream cone in hand. Jimmy looked worried, and Phil wanted to know why. Somehow he had to keep an eye on Jimmy's store. Something had to be done!

"Something" turned out to be Dom De Prospo's Old Country Market. As Phil walked by Dom stood on the sidewalk, cursing the East Side Export-Import Company, Little Angelo, and all the truck drivers of the world.

"Look at this!" Dom said, waving his hand at a stack of boxes and crates. "He just dump them and he leave. No help take them in, even though he come late. Slick never do dat to me. No sir!" He spat in the gutter.

Phil stopped, looked, and it came to him! "Where do you want the stuff, Mr. De Prospo?" he said, lifting a box filled with tins of anchovies.

Thirty minutes later Dom De Prospo's anger was gone. In fact, he seemed pleased. "You come back in da morning. I crank down da awning, make shade. Den, you help me put da boxes outside, and open dem. You do it, for me?"

Phil nodded, trying not to gag from the smell of wet sawdust and garlic.

Dom beamed and put both hands on a huge belly. "Den later, come back again when the sun she go down, and we put everyting back in da store. No worry, I pay you."

"Sure Mr. De Prospo, I'll help." Phil tingled. Only a few doorways away from Jimmy's store. Ideal! He could see who went in and who came out, particularly at closing time. So if 'da boys' tried anything he would call Sergeant Pizzuta. And then – until Pizzuta arrived – what? No answer came to him, but the pulse in his wrist threatened to break skin.

"See ya in the morning, Mr. De Prospo." Phil smiled and sauntered away; nice and easy, he hoped. He saw Dom scratch his head, a surprised look on his florid face. Phil thought he knew why: He hadn't stuck out his hand when Dom said he would pay him. A wry smile formed... He felt chilled.

Shit! He could be sticking out more than his hand... His precious neck!

Chapter 10

Massimo Di Anello leaned back in the rear seat and luxuriated in the exotic perfume of paint, leather, and rubber that his brand new Cadillac sedan exuded. The car would get much of its early breaking-in miles out of the way today, he mused, rubbing his chin slowly and sensuously against the black leather.

"Vito," he said, addressing the back of the thick neck in the driver's seat, "Egan's barn."

"Yeah, yeah. Sure, Boss."

Vito, about to leave for the horse races at Suffolk Downs from the lobby of the Williams Hotel, didn't go. Di Anello summoned him. Change of plans! Vito, who thought he had a free day, sat hunched behind the wheel, grouchy and disgruntled.

Di Anello wanted to observe Vito closely today. He saw things he didn't like happening to his old fighter and bodyguard. It could be the hot weather, he reasoned. Like the *scirocco*, the hot south-east wind in the Old country, New England summer heat did strange things to people's brains, and in Vito's case... Enough! *Vedremo!* We shall see! Much had to be done this day...

Not that he didn't trust Oreste, but as a man of caution, Di Anello left nothing to chance. The rush of country air into the open windows of the Cadillac was suddenly curtailed as the car approached the barn and slowed. Another day of *sole a leone* (sun with the strength of a lion) he thought, irritably. The mist was clearing, but not a maple leaf nor an oak leak stirred. Soggy stillness... except now for the harsh sound of Di Anello's oxfords stepping on the crushed granite walk near the barn door.

Later, the sun glinted on the chrome of the car as Di Anello, with a satisfied smile, said, "Let's go, Vito. Take me to our Front Street business. Natale and I need to talk."

He settled back, eyes narrowed, hands clasped; index fingers up and touching, forming a steeple. Natale managed Di Anello's big bookie and gambling joint behind Handleman's Market, and now Natale wanted to talk about the mayor's son-in-law, Timothy Hoyt, who had been spending more and more time at the place, drinking free booze, gambling... and losing heavily. Di Aneilo thought he knew what was on Natale's mind, for Fulvia, until recently, had kept him informed on what went on at City Hall. Fulvia... now she could be a problem. *Peccato* (too bad) if she thought she could break away from him. Time enough to deal with her – if his suspicions proved to be true. For now, first things first.

And 'first' was to be Sergeant Pizzuta's raid on Egan's barn – TONIGHT! If Oreste was right about Jimmy being a snitch. If so, the cops, when they came, would find Egan's barn to be just that – a barn, old and decayed surrounded by bits and pieces of rusting farm machinery and acres of weeds. No tables, no games, no Di Anello men running the show, and no out of town wise guys.

In time Jimmy would be taken care of... Again, if Oreste was right. Regardless of how that turned out, Di Anello was pleased with himself. Soon he would be invincible! No cops, no insidious Mafiosi, no one... could touch him.

Screech! The car suddenly swung from side to side as locked wheels skidded on gravel and packed dirt. Vito fought the wheel. Di Anello, legs braced against the back of the front seat, slid back and forth on the leather, cursing mightily.

"Sorry, Boss," Vito said, as he muscled the big car back into its lane. "We just squashed a couple a lousy squirrels." He smiled incongruously. The words 'You idiot!' formed and died on Di Anello's lips. He said nothing, but his long fingers clawed and scratched the rich leather of the back seat.

That night Massimo Di Aneilo stood motionless at a window in his study, his hands folded behind him. He looked at the distant, blinking lights of Columbus Street. They seemed to dance through a sudden downpour, sweeping the hillside like a giant brush. After a while he sighed, glanced over his shoulder, and scowled at his oak table and the straight-backed chairs used by Oreste and Nino. His lips curled into a cunning smile. Again he looked out at the darkness and the majesty of the storm.

It pleased him. Below, in Vespucci Park, the bocce court was deserted.

Slowly he turned his gaze eastward and upward. He couldn't see it in the rain, but he knew the ledge was there, and on its uppermost granite ridge sat Timothy Hoyt's pseudo-New England colonial aerie, secure and serene. The back of his lot abutted the edge of the ledge. A high cyclone fence protected against a fall to certain death, but didn't block the marvelous panoramic view of the gently rolling, wooded hills and ridges in the distance. A combination of flagstone and grass graced the entire back lot. Dahlias, tiger lilies, and hedge bordered both sides of the property. An ideal place for entertaining! Timothy Hoyt did just that – on a grand scale, for he was the mayor's son-in-law and chief confidant.

Massimo Di Anello had never been invited, but he had been there... *Ma sì!*... through his binoculars. Disturbed by what and who he saw, he asked Fulvia to intensify her spying for him. She had complied, and she covered more and more for Mary Coyne, Hoyt's secretary. Mary Coyne liked booze, before and after holidays and anytime in between. Encouraged by Fulvia, she spent much time in the ladies' room, suffering from women's problems, she said. She was a lush. Fulvia knew. Others too. But she was the mayor's sister; she had to work somewhere, didn't she? Besides, everyone at the City Hall took a nip now and then!

So Fulvia Fleming, as Mary Coyne's 'women's problems' got worse, did more secretarial work for Hoyt. She even served coffee in his private office where he wheeled and dealed, and blamed all city problems on Dagos, Frogs, and Polacks who "even now are thinking of running for office in this fair city of ours." Guffaws all around.

Mary Coyne, grateful for what she thought was Fulvia's loyalty, blabbered constantly, adding to Fulvia's storehouse of information. The more Fulvia learned the more she grew to despise Hoyt and his cabal of City Hall crooks. Why it was all – how did one of her cynical friends from the neighborhood put it? Oh yes! "Hurray for me and fuck you."

Di Anello confirmed much of what Fulvia told him by noting through his binoculars, and invariably recognizing the invited guests at Hoyt's cook-outs and bleary-eyed bacchanalian binges. With that information, and the whispers of his well-paid network of spies, Di Anello charted a lucrative course for his varied business ventures. He would show the *mangia patate* – how a *signore* of respect and honor could outsmart them! A few broken heads along the way? Worse? *Così è la vita!*. Such is life. Lots of bad people in this world. *Davvero!* In truth! For sure!

The storm continued to rage. A strong wind shook the gables. The window in front of Di Anello rattled. Then bringgg! The phone, harsh and insistent. Di Anello moistened his lips, worked his jaw, once, twice-the tightness diminished. He picked up the phone on his desk.

"Yes?" Cautious, tentative.

"Boss, it's me, Oreste. Uh, nothing happen tonight. Nobody show up. The fuckin storm, ya know? So I wanna set it up again. Dat Jimmy is–"

"No names! All right, go ahead. I give you one more chance. And hurry up, we got important things we gotta do. *Hai capito?*"

"*Sì! Grazie* – thanks! I understand perfect! You'll see! I know I am right. I am not a capo di legno (wooden head), like Nino. When this storm ends..."

Di Anello hung up. He cast a withering look at the straight-backed chairs and thought of cement and dark watery depths, not wood. Quarreling underlings could screw up his grand plan, maybe worse than that meddler, Sergeant Pizzuta. Well, it wouldn't happen! No one could stop him now. He had come a long way since his early days of huddling in the cold hallways of the few Columbus Street buildings, and following the horse-drawn trolley line, picking up horse shit for a few cents a day. He thought of the Avellini adventure in Brindisi and how Oreste had enjoyed slashing and cutting out the informer's tongue...

And now, as Sforza had informed him, Oreste had shot off his mouth at the diner when he drank coffee with Jimmy, and lashed out belligerently at 'some people' who 'mess around' with 'broads' who are 'close to the power in City Hall'. Oh! how Sforza had loved mimicking Oreste, with exaggerated gestures and facial expressions. Di Anello flexed his long fingers and regarded his immaculate hands. *How much did the volatile Oreste really know... about Fulvia? And wasn't it Jimmy, who had egged him on?* Di Anello pondered that for a short time, with wrinkled brow...

No matter. Since his talk with Natale at the bookie joint earlier in the day, Di Anello knew he must – how did the potato eaters put it? Reorganize. But with a *Mano Nera* twist! A giant gust of wind shook the house. Lights flickered and dimmed. Heavy raindrops, interspersed with hail, beat a sharp drumbeat against the old clapboard siding.

Di Anello paid little heed to the cloudburst. He paced slowly, hands clasped behind his back, deep in thought. And what of Nino, his other partner in the Brindisi affair? *How far can he be trusted? He is a good businessman, smart, ambitious. Too smart? Too ambitious? Does he look out for his own pagnotta first? His round loaf, his interest?*

And Fulvia? Why didn't she tell me about Jimmy's visit to the City Hall? It took that high school girl on her break at the Waldorf cafeteria with young Luke Peris to mention the strange behavior of 'the little man with the bandaged hand' when he saw Fulvia. I wouldn't have known, otherwise.

Di Anello promised himself to thank Natale for having Luke hang around nursing coffee at the Waldorf as much as he could even though he worked in the Parks and Recreation office-keep his eyes and ears open, and report what looked promising to Natale.

The Waldorf sat on Main Street at Harrington corner, across the street from the City Hall. A perfect observation post. Luke had seen Jimmy rush out of City Hall, limp to his car, and rattle away. He thought nothing of it, he told Natale, and still didn't, but Sally's story was funny. "What the hell do you think got into the little bastard?" he had asked Natale.

Di Anello thanked Natale, and told him to thank Luke and give him twenty bucks. "Who knows what gets into Jimmy," Di Anello said, rhetorically. "My guess is his leg bugged him. He got hit bad in da war. Yeah! By the way, Natale, we never had dis little talk. *Hai capito?*"

Natale swore on his mother's grave that his lips were sealed.

Minutes later, standing pensive at the window, Di Anello noticed that the storm had passed. Another storm, a man-made storm, one of his making, was about to begin. Though he knew he was a man of great patience, some things he could not tolerate: Disloyalty, disobedience, disrespect! His reorganization was about to begin. He pivoted, picked up the phone, dialed, and spoke quietly for a few minutes. Then he said in a soft low voice, "Yes a Packard, it will be a Packard." His voice rose suddenly as he said, "Agreed! Do it!"

He hung up, gazed at his long fingers, touched a miniscule hangnail. "Must take care of that tomorrow morning at Tony's," he murmured.

Chapter 11

Morning, 7 A.M. Phil walked slowly to the old Country Market. He skirted muddy puddles in the cracked sidewalk and sneaked a look over his shoulder. No one. Aw, shit, relax! he urged himself. *That dumb pug would never connect you with the licking he took at the lake. Why, even the bats in his belfry get lost. Remember?* Thus bolstered, Phil walked faster and soon saw Dom De Prospo unlocking the front door of his market.

"Filippo, very good! You right on time." Dom peered pompously at his gold Waltham pocket watch. "I open up now, crank down da awning." He looked at the scudding clouds and shrugged. "Don't know what dis crazy weather gonna do. Not like August last year. Anyway, we get busy! You go in da store, bring out da boxes we put in dere last night. After you left, I went down da cellar and I take up a few more. Bring dose out, too."

Phil heard Dom as if from a distance, for his eyes were locked on Jimmy's store entrance. Nothing unusual. Just the familiar working stiffs, getting their thrill of the day, Jimmy's well-filled sandwiches, as they exchanged small talk, toted up their numbers game losses, and trudged away. Phil turned down the collar of his light jacket, and began working...

Finished, with two new quarters in his pocket, Phil loitered. No one he could identify as one of 'da boys' showed up at Jimmy's. Maybe he should feel relieved. He wasn't. He had poked his head under the flap of the *Mano Nera* tent, and now he wanted to be in on the main event, no matter what...

He shivered, though the humidity was rising. Throwing his jacket over his shoulder in a gesture of bravado, he stalked home.

But one of 'da boys' – Skinny, under his trademark straw hat, had already been to see Jimmy as he opened his store, shortly before 5:30 A.M.

"Hey, Jimmy, sorry about last night. Da weather fucked everything up. We had to cancel da crap game. You didn't go, didja?"

"Are you kidding? In that miserable storm? Forget

it! Jimmy controlled his shaking hands as he put on his white butcher's apron.

"Yeah, too bad. But hey! it's on for tonight. Same place, rain or shine dis time. Yor still invited, as my friend." Skinny's face smiled, but his eyes were cold.

"Cut it, Skinny!" Jimmy warned. "Here come my customers." Then under his breath, "We'll see. Anyway, thanks for the invite. I appreciate it."

"Anytime! Dat's what friends are for, right? Mmm, Jimmy, gimme a sangwich before I go, will ya? Put lots of provolone in it."

After Skinny left, and before Phil arrived at Dom De Prospo's market, Jimmy phoned Sergeant Pizzuta.

"They won't let me alone! Skinny came back! He invited me—"

"Take it easy, Jimmy," Pizzuta interrupted. "It's going as we planned, remember? We didn't raid Egan's barn last night, Oreste comes up empty, and he's plenty worried. So he puts his stooge Skinny on you again. The storm shit? Don't you believe it! Somebody was watching the barn last night – believe it! Maybe even *lu Siciliano*, Oreste. Tell me, did Skinny's nose lengthen a couple of inches when he threw those crappy lies at you?"

"Huh?"

"Forget it! After tonight you should be in solid with Di Anello's boys. A man to be trusted. Damn! We'll send 'em all up the river yet!"

"Yeah, but what if I really go to Egan's tonight, and nothing's there?"

"Jimmy, for Christ sakes! You're not going. You're not expected to. What Oreste expects is that you sing to me! I raid Egan's, and I get egg on my face, and—"

"Sure! And I get wrapped in a burlap bag and dumped someplace."

"But you won't be! Moretti's Florist shop'll be doing funeral wreaths all right, but not for you, not for you..."

* * * *

Ah'll get even wid ya, you'll see!
Nick Noce, silently smoldering, looked out his bed-

room window, and remembered the threat he had flung at Phil. Now he had to do something about it. 'Da boys' never went back on that kind of a promise, and he considered himself one of them... almost. And suddenly, there he was – Phil Martello – so early in the morning, mending his way down through the skunk cabbage, and turning left on Columbus Street. *What is he up to now?* Nick asked himself, rubbing his puffy bloodshot suspicious eyes. *Marjorie? Can't be! It ain't even 7:00 A.M. yet!*

Marjorie. His broad! She didn't know it yet, of course; he'd make his move real soon, and... But shit! Mona, his own sister had given him a hard time, told him that Marjorie had a crush on Phil. Well, no young punk was gonna muscle in on his territory, for he was still king of the hill around here. Yeah, but he had to make things happen – quick. Why, that big Shinola is gonna be over six feet tall soon. Nick cracked his knuckles, suppressed his envy. *It would be nice*, he thought, *to break one of his arms, or two, and maybe a leg. Oo-fa! Maybe even cut up his face a little bit, zig it and zag it. That would fix Romeo's hot wagon real good!*

Nick sucked his lips, drawing saliva. *But how?* He stared out the window, trying to think. What a ya know! There was Phil, swinging back to the tenement, flipping what looked like coins in the air and then catching them. In a few moments, Nick heard Phil's footsteps on the wood stairway, and the back door above open and shut.

"He couldn't a met Marjorie," Nick assured himself with a liquid mutter, "and a been back so soon." Could he?

He had it! The flying coins reminded him of Longcoat and how high he flew of his reefers! He listened carefully. No sound. The tenement still yawned. Dressing hastily he scooted out the front door and headed for Columbus Street, and Sforza's Diner. Longcoat, after a night of poker and hanging around, was just leaving...

He saw Nick, produced a wilted, bent cigarette butt, lit it, took a big drag, laughed hysterically, and handed the butt to Nick, who faked a drag. He gave the wet remains back to Longcoat.

The two had drifted away from the diner, Longcoat

patting his pocket and winking at Nick. Now, hunched over in a secluded edge of the four-lane bocce court at Vespucci Park, he puffed long and deep.

Nick waited and watched. *Shit!* he thought, *now's a good time to ask Longcoat about going with him to collect numbers bets.* He knew that Longcoat still wasn't turning in all the cash he collected, either... Nick had kept his mouth shut about that! *So the miserable fake owed him! Besides,* Nick reasoned, *he kept Longcoat company. Everyone else avoided him,* kind of like he had lice in his hair, or worse. *So, he needs me!* Nick thought, sure of himself.

Smiling fatuously, he asked Longcoat if he could accompany him on his next factory rounds. Longcoat said nothing and looked fixedly at the ground.

"And I want a favor too, between us friends," Nick continued, and waving at the sky, he said it would be tough on Longcoat if Natale found out he was skimming. "But ya know me! I'm yor friend! I'd never snitch!"

"What's da favor?" asked a rapidly sobering Longcoat.

The favor was the maiming of Phil Martello.

"Hey, dat's a big order, Nick, know dat?" But very interestin'... yeah!"

What a flake! Nick thought. He said, "Well, can ya do it?"

Strange sounds came out of Longcoat – sinister cackles that rose and fell, rose and fell, and ended in a deep hiss. He took two mighty puffs. His eyes bulged and he seemed to writhe under his topcoat. *Geez!* Nick thought, watching the transformation in frightened fascination, *the crum bum looks like a freekin' slimy snake!*

Longcoat's gaze steadied. "I gotta go ta New York fa a few days. Ya see, I gotta huddle wid relatives a mine. No big ting. When I get back, we kin talk more. But ya gotta promise me dat you'll do a nice favor for me, too. Okay?"

"Sure! Just ask me." *The dumb fuck is out a his skull,* Nick thought. *Gotta string him along.* "Shake," he said. They did.

Longcoat imagined Nick hanging by his balls. *So, the fat slob thinks he's got me screwed? The sneaky pick!* He smiled as his mind raced. *I got him where the hair is short, he ain't got me! I know what I gotta do, and I'll be on my way into da big time... by myself, without him!*

"Be seein' ya, I gotta get some sleep. Big tings comint up," he said, running an index finger straight down between Nick's shoulder blades. Involuntarily, Nick flinched.

Chapter 12

Phil sat at the kitchen table, the two quarters Dom had given him lined up by his toast. He sipped his cup of cocoa and played with his soft-boiled egg. He was restless, jumpy. Should he go to Jimmy's, get an ice cream cone, and ask questions? No. Jimmy wouldn't talk, and Sergeant Pizzuta wouldn't like it, when Jimmy told him, which he would. So... now what? Phil folded his arms in frustration.

Laughter floated breezily up from the tenement court. He gulped his breakfast. Baseball! At the bug yard! "Bye, Mama!" he said to his bewildered mother, and tore out the back door. He bounded down a flight of stairs and bumped into Mona, who had a basket of clothes ready for the clothes line.

"Thanks for what you did for me!" Mona whispered, feigning a stumble. Phil caught her arm then held her. Mona smiled and shook her head. "Not yet," she said. Phil understood. He nodded. A tacit agreement. The girls, Carmela and Marjorie, would not be by to collect Mona, or anyone else. They would stay apart until certain the Vito lake incident blew over.

Phil stepped into the court, to cheers. Puzzled, he walked towards the baseball players and realized the cheers were for him. Rusty had seen to that, for he had embellished Phil's tussle with Nick until it sounded like a Joe Louis fight. No contest! Nick's big ass buried in putrid cans. When he got up he smelled like a cesspool and cried like a baby...

Phil accepted the accolades with aplomb. Then, as if on cue, everyone headed for the bug yard; slapping, teasing, yelling, tossing baseballs in the air – and looking at the uncertain sky. Rain? Gee, hope not!

The day turned out hot and humid, but it didn't rain. Nor did rain fall the next day, Friday, again baseball-filled. After supper Friday Phil and Vic sat under a big sugar maple tree on Holly Hill near the tenement. They looked wistfully at each other, chewing the ends of bitter grass stems. Crickets chirped and fireflies pricked the gathering dusk with their evanescent light until the night dampness and mosquitoes forced them to head for home.

"Will we ever go to the lake again?" Vic asked, with an unhappy frown. "Or is... everything... all over?" He raised his sad eyes to Phil.

"Heck no, Vic! I'll bet this is just the calm before the storm." He started up the stairs, not sure he wanted to win the bet.

Phil slammed the back door and walked into the kitchen. His mother peered at him from the pantry. "So, you make uppa you mind to come home, eh, *piedi lunghi*?"

"Oh, Mama, I didn't go nowhere. I was just sitting outside with Vic, that's all." Phil knew what was bothering his mother, and it wasn't his 'long feet'. She was worried about his father, who hadn't come home for supper, a rare occurrence. Phil's words to Vic echoed in his mind and he went to his room... "I'll bet... the calm before the storm." Holy shit! what the hell was going on around the neighborhood...?

* * * *

Nino detained Sebastiano at the big Columbus Street market because he wanted to drive Sebastiano out to see a new warehouse.

"Before we go," he said, "look there." He pointed to a long showcase at the far end of the market. Sebastiano saw a display of veal chops with attached kidney portions, ground meat for meatballs, fresh rabbit...

"Look to the right," Nino directed, as Sebastiano salivated. "There." Nino jabbed his stogie at a separate showcase, full of cut-up chicken parts.

Answering Sebastiano's surprised stare, Nino said, "My friend, the *yadinaro's* days are over. Our women are working now... here, in department stores, in factories. Times change! We can't be old-fashioned anymore."

Sebastiano grimaced. He heard 'old-fashioned' more and more at home, but he saw the logic of what Nino said, insofar as the *Yardinaro* – dialect for chicken-man – was concerned. The custom was to buy chicken live from the chicken-man, who would kill and dress the bird for a quarter; or the women could take it home and do the job themselves. Fresh, tasty meat! But these?

"I know what you are thinking. Come!" Nino led Sebastiano through a doorway behind the showcase. Two women and a man, in blood-stained aprons, dressed freshly-killed chickens in a steamy room.

"We hafta charge customers more now," Nino said in broken English, "but just you tink of da time dey save, and da dirty work." He went back to Italian, "We work tonight, and the chicken is fresh in the morning."

Sebastiano had to agree. Nino beckoned. Both left the room, leaving the stench of wet plucked feathers and chicken shit behind. Sebastiano breathed freely again, though his stomach felt queasy.

Soon the night breeze whistling through the open front window of Nino's new black Chevrolet did wonders for Sebastiano, and he no longer felt like vomiting. He took several more deep breaths and began recognizing landmarks. Surprised, he realized that Nino's warehouse, a grim, windowless concrete and brick building, was near the city line, not far from his old Lofton Height home.

It was situated on a wooded hill next to a small pond and surrounded on three sides by oak, maple and brush. Access was a mile-long deserted gravel road. A small dairy and chicken farm were situated half-way up the road. The barn, old and weather-beaten, leaned next to a ramshackle tar-paper covered shack. An old stone wall crumbled in a tortured curve around shack and barn. *Not an idyllic – what's that American painter's name? Norman Rockwell –* setting for his paintings, Sebastiano mused.

A men coming out a side door shocked him back to the moment, for he carried a rifle – no, a shotgun! He peered into the car, smiled, said, "Hi, Nino. No problems." He nodded at Sebastiano. The patent-leather hair, the wise guy demeanor – Danny "Slick" Bastone. *So! he has other duties besides driving a delivery truck!* Another man, whom Sebastiano did not recognize, slid the warehouse door open, and Nino drove the car in.

Nino eyed Sebastiano closely. "Do not be alarmed, he said. "Precautions, my friend." He waved both hands in the air, as if greatly exasperated.

"*Ladri, qui?*" (Robbers, here?) Sebastiano asked, feeling uncomfortable. His brow creased. The new guard, Slick's partner, reminded him...

"Eh, why not?" Nino asked. "We can't take chances," he continued, "even in this wilderness. A fortune is stored here. And more is on the way. It will be your job, Sebastiano, to run this business. Come, look around."

Sebastiano did, under the watchful eye of Slick's partner, who was a short, heavy-jowled young man with an oily complexion and two moles on his face. Sebastiano's skin crawled as he glanced at the mountain of goods, but instead saw the guard's face and faces like it emblazoned in his mind's eye... Faces he thought he had left behind years ago in Old Country. Faces of the *Mano Nera*. But that was only a bad memory, brought back by this... honest man.

Could he help how he looked? Sebastiano dismissed a nagging thought. Hadn't he told his son Filippo that the Mano Nera no longer existed? And it suited him to believe likewise, didn't it?

"And so, Sebastiano," said Nino's voice, "you will spend a few days at the big market, helping me. Then you will spend time here. This space will be yours to fill as shipments arrive. Specially chosen men will work for you under Slick. We will build up our reserve supply for the coming months, years maybe. And... oh, fill neighborhood store orders from the court warehouse near your home. The building... is ours."

Sebastiano raised an eyebrow. What did Nino mean by 'ours'?

"The whiskey... there," Sebastians nodded his head from floor to ceiling several times, "the Canadian and Irish... is it also 'ours'?"

"Ah, you are as sharp as a Milanese moneylender! I knew you were the man for this job! Dear friend, I have a business partner. Sometimes... we get shipments like this whiskey at very reasonable prices. When the time is right we sell at a good profit. *Benissimo, no?*"

Yes, great, Sebastiano thought. *Stolen merchandise!* his inner voice screamed at him. *Why not? Armed men? This remote location. Nino must be in league with ex-*

bootleggers and hi-jackers who have found new ways to use their skills.

"And may I ask who your business partner is?" Sebastiano asked.

"Of course," Nino replied. "He is a respected resident of our neighborhood. Why in a few days, for the Feast of the Assumption he will give many food baskets to the poor. We will distribute them from our Columbus Street market."

"That is a great act of charity. Do I know this benefactor?"

"You may have heard his name."

"I see." Sebastiano paused, searched Nino's face.

"The business man... is Massimo Di Anello. But you work for me, not him, Sebastiano. You must understand that." Nino coaxed a tight smile. "I think he is Sicilian, if I am not mistaken."

"*Per l'amor di Dio!* So he is Sicilian! Many are... in our neighborhood. They are respected people, devoted to their families." Nino seemed flustered, then quickly rubbed his hands together. "But we talk too much. Ah! I almost forgot. As my honored assistant, and now warehouse manager... I must raise your salary to one hundred dollars a week."

Sebastiano was suddenly very dizzy. *One hundred dollars a week!* Four times (or more) than what other immigrants and most potato eaters earned. He hadn't even collected his first week's salary of forty dollars yet, which he thought was a fortune. The tenement rent was only twenty-two dollars a month. Soon he could move to a bigger house, maybe even buy one in the country... His nagging doubts vanished in a wave of euphoria.

Dazed, he looked at Nino, who suddenly seemed very serious. "You must remain in the tenement, Sebastiano. Eat and drink well, buy better clothes for yourself and your family, but do not move away. I am sorry, but that is the way it must be. Some time in the future perhaps – but for now – and for business reasons I cannot divulge, employees must live in the neighborhood. And one other small favor. The money you surely will save – deposit it in the *Banca* Di Anello on Columbus Street. Agreed?"

"Agreed!" Sebastiano shouted. The brightly lighted

marquee in his mind was covered with huge letters, and they trumpeted: ONE HUNDRED DOLLARS A WEEK!

The blood thundered through his head, filling his ears and throat. He would have agreed to almost anything his good friend proposed for one hundred dollars a week! *Madre di Dio, che fortune!* (Mother of God, what a fortune!)

Nino cut through Sebastiano's mental blubbering. "Sebastiano, you must be formally introduced. Slick! Luccio! Come here, meet your new boss."

Nino introduced the two to Sebastiano.

"Glad ta meet ya, Boss," Slick said, "I tink I saw ya once at da tenement." He backed away, nodding and smiling deferentially.

Luccio, short for Bartoluccio Sebastiano knew, bowed as if to nobility and said, "*Signoria!*"

Sebastiano's pride soared. Such respect! And why not? He was not a coarse peasant *cafone*, but of a higher social order! And yet, he wondered, a pang of – fear – stabbed his gut. *True, he worked for Nino, but Nino... was Di Anello's partner. And what of Di Anello? A Mano Nera capo? No one knows. No one accuses.*

So, truly! Nino accommodates to a splendid business arrangement, and so shall Sebastiano Martello. All else is someone else's affair. *Ah, Sebastiano, Sebastiano, your head is going soft!* – a small voice inside him stirred... *What of your noble principles? Sacrificed at the altar of gold? Do not be misled!*

Sebastiano assured himself he would not be. He would ferret out the truth and if Di Anello and Nino were of the underworld, why he would quit his job in a minute! But why rush? He wanted many bulging pay envelopes first. ONE HUNDRED DOLLARS A WEEK!

"Come, Slick, Luccio, show me the rest of the warehouse," Sebastiano said. He glanced at Nino, who nodded. Sebastiano's confidence soared.

Chapter 13

Oreste Straniero's confidence, like Sebastiano's at the warehouse, came back as the big Packard chewed up the miles on lonely Route 9, near Pittsfield, many miles away from the neighborhood. He thought clearly now. Yes, he had lost face over the Jimmy fiasco for the expected raid on Egan's barn, led by Sergeant Pizzuta, didn't occur. Oreste wanted to try again, but Di Anello said no, and Oreste knew it. But Oreste knew he was angrier at that little fart Jimmy for putting him on. And the brains running him belonged to Sergeant Sam Pizzuta. Of that he was convinced. While he didn't dare fuck with Pizzuta, Jimmy was another matter. When he got back from this trip – what a you know! Jimmy's store would be robbed and Jimmy worked over. Goodby, out of town journeymen. Jimmy would get the message and drop his cop. No one makes a fool of Oreste!

But for now arrangements had to be made to greet godson Gennaro in a house south of Albany. In a few days Gennaro would work for him, and after that Oreste would make his move. First that smiling bastard Nino and his ass wiper, that sniveling new guy, Sebastiano Martello. Then... ah! *Sangu di la Madonna!* (Blood of the madonna!) His eyes gleamed maniacally at the thought of what he would do, and when it was over, his triumphant ascendancy to the throne of–

"*Bestia!*" he screamed, as a car he couldn't identify snaked past him on a long curve, forcing him onto a gravel shoulder. Calming down, he wondered: *Second car tonight! First the Cadillac, now this lousy wise guy.* He speeded up, swaying dangerously around curves, often on the wrong side of the road. Below him were drops of steep embankments and ravines choked with wild vines and brush.

The Packard's headlights pierced the inky night. Oreste strained, looking, looking, for what he did not know. Around a blind curve, the Packard skidded and Oreste slammed on the brakes. The Cadillac and the other car were slanted together across the road, trunk to hood. An accident? Two men, arguing it seemed to Oreste, jumped out of the way as the Packard screeched to a halt behind the Cadillac.

"What the hell's the matter with you guys? Can't you see you're blocking the road?" Oreste approached the men cautiously, hand under his coat.

The two, in dark suits and fedoras, slowly walked towards him. One grinned, and his face and teeth glowed in the Packard's headlights.

Sforza! From the Columbus Street diner!

"What the fuck are you doing here?" Oreste asked. He knew as soon as the words spilled out of his mouth. He pulled his gun. It didn't matter, for men he did not see behind him knocked it away, and something exploded behind his left ear. Through the whir and dizzy dance of the star showers somewhere above him, he thought he smelled whiskey! A wave of pain hit. The stars showers disappeared.

"He's out like a light," Sforza said. "Let's go! We gotta work fast!"

* * * *

Five A.M. Jimmy shivered in the cool damp grayness of the morning as he stepped into the alley behind the three-decker boarding house where he lived. *Rheumatism weather, bad for my leg and my hand.* He touched both. *Another stinker of a hot day though, as soon as the sun comes up.* Jimmy's glum thoughts were shoved aside by a swell of panic as a firm hand grasped his shoulder and a big body pushed him back into the deep shadows of the alley. Fight! Kick! But Jimmy's body would not respond. His eyes and brain did. He recognized Sergeant Sam Pizzuta, who held a finger to his lips.

"Jimmy! Easy for Christ sakes! It's me. Sorry! I didn't mean to scare the hell out of you." Sergeant Sam released his hold.

"I thought... I thought... Aw hell, Sam, You shouldn't have come up on me like that."

"I called to you. You didn't hear me. I had to do something before you got into that heap you call a car."

"Hey! I got lot's on my mind! Say, what are you doing here so..."

"All right. Listen! We got a call from the state police a while ago. Looks like something unraveled for Di Anello, and he decided to do something about it. Oreste... Oreste Straniero, the number two boy–"

"Yeah... Yeah?" Jimmy began to sweat. His leg shook.

"–was found dead in a burned out Packard last night. Word is he lost control on a curve in the Berkshires, the car bounced down a steep ravine and exploded. The state boys found broken glass from a whiskey bottle. They told us Oreste must have been drunk and speeding... the road was dark, narrow, and Beano! – Oreste gets his cement shoes, so to speak."

"You mean...?"

"Maybe, Jimmy, maybe. It's all too pat, too simple, but we can't prove otherwise. That's why I'm here. You, Jimmy..."

"Oh no!" Jimmy's mien was that of a whipped dog. "I've had it Sam! I ain't gonna do no more! You want me killed, or something?"

"Sh!" Pizzuta warned. "You've got them by the balls, tight! Oreste tries to set you up, but you come out clean as a fuckin' lily. So now you can move around easy, play cards and pool at the social club, have coffee half and half at the diner, and listen. Now that Oreste is gone the boys will really open up to you. God, Jimmy! we've got ourselves a gold mine."

"Sam, I can't, honest to God!"

"Bullshit, Jimmy! This is our big chance. Di Anello is on the way down, I can feel it. A little shove is all, and we clean up the neighborhood for good! You gotta come through for me. What do you say?"

"I say I'm scared shitless! No more, Sam, no more." Jimmy shook his head. Sweat dripped from the tip of his nose.

"I see," Pizzuta said. "Okay." He shrugged and turned to go. "Oh, by the way," he said, a finger on his chin. "What are those two decorations you got in the war called? You know, the ones Pershing himself gave you? You keep them in your cash register in your store, right?"

Jimmy straightened, smiled. "Yeah, I do. You're talking about the Purple Heart and the Silver Star. Yep! Old

Blackjack pinned them on me!"

"And let's see," Pizzuta said, knitting his brow, "You got the Silver Star for wiping out a heavy machine gun nest – a Spandau – I believe you told me it was." Jimmy nodded, his eyes dancing. "And though hit yourself, you dragged back two more badly wounded buddies through rifle fire."

"Yeah, something came over me that day. Hell, Sam, I was just a kid then, twenty-two years old. I'm old now, almost forty."

"Jimmy, you took on the whole damn German army and you came out on top. And now, shit!-you're running away from punks you can beat easy, have beat! What the hell, you volunteered to help clean up the neighborhood, guess you can pull out when you want to... The whole German army – *Madonna!*"

The two stood looking at each other in the silver dawn. Two statues.

"So long, Jimmy." Sam Pizzuta padded slowly away.

"Wait!" Shame? Courage? Bravery? Stupidity? Jimmy didn't know. "Damn you, Sam Pizutta, damn you all to hell!" he cried. "Count me in."

Sam Pizzuta grinned. He kept walking, faster now.

* * * *

Later in the morning, Nino arrived at the court warehouse and looked at his watch. He had overslept. No matter. Last night he had accomplished much with Sebastiano. He got out of his car, opened the front screen door of the warehouse, and walked inside. Grim-faced men glanced at him and buried their heads in playing cards or newspapers, or hurried back into the recesses of the warehouse. One young man, Little Angelo, head down, shouldered past and headed towards his parked truck.

Nino, puzzled, called out, "Hey... you, wait a minute. I want–"

"Forget it, Nino!" a raspy voice interrupted. A strong hand gripped his shoulder. "Da boss said fa you ta see him right away when ya got in."

"Take your hand off me!" Nino said, whirling, and

faced... Vito.

Vito grinned through his scar lumps. "Sure, sure, Nino," he said, lowering his hand. "Read dis, will ya!" He opened a folded newspaper, swept it flat on a card table with the back of his hand, pointed to a front page column, and sat down with a grunt, his eyes fixed on Nino.

Nino read the column in the early edition of the Post slowly. When finished, he showed no emotion, turned his back to Vito, and walked rapidly through the rest of the warehouse. Vito was disappointed. He wouldn't have been had he seen the look of horror that Nino fought to overcome.

Nino straightened his jacket and knocked on Di Anello's meeting room door. "Boss, it's me, Nino!" he said in a cracked, strained voice.

A buzzer sounded, Nino pushed open the door, and entered. Di Anello, seated at the table, folded the Post, got up, loosened his tie, unbuttoned the top button of his white shirt, and motioned Nino to a chair. He went to a rear window, stroked his chin, and looked out. He said nothing. The silence gnawed at Nino. Panic welled within him.

Di Anello looked over his shoulder and jerked his head in a 'join me' gesture. Nino did, and a glimmer of hope washed away some of the panic.

"You have seen the news in the paper?" Di Anello asked.

Nino could only nod.

"Oreste was corrupted, and his brain hopelessly scrambled," Di Anello said, choosing his words carefully, his face impassive. "He met Timothy Hoyt – you know who he is – married to one of the mayor's daughters. Runs City Hall."

Again, Nino nodded.

Di Anello selected the darker of the two stogies in his shirt pocket, examined it and lit it leisurely with a silver lighter. The pungent smoke curled slowly towards the high ceiling. Di Anello turned to face Nino. Di Anello continued: "Hoyt likes to drink – and gamble – at our Front Street business behind Handleman's Market." He shrugged eloquently, opened his hands as if in prayer, long fingers tightly pressed together and said, "Over time

Hoyt lost much money and couldn't pay. Our manager, Natale, pressed him, and so Hoyt asked to meet with the owner. To humor the drunken *mangia patate*, Natale introduced him to Oreste, who was there. And it began!" Di Anello smiled sardonically, then sat down. Nino sat opposite him, on the edge of his chair, tight as an eight-day clock, newly wound.

"*Peccato, peccato!*" Di Anello said. It was too bad Oreste had transgressed. He went on to say Oreste had been taken in by Hoyt's siren song of a partnership. Hoyt would permit expansion of the rackets beyond Columbus Street to forbidden sections of the city, and offer protection from the law to Oreste – for a price. First, he wanted his gambling debts canceled; second; he wanted access to the immigrant dump truck and construction equipment owners he saw roaming around Columbus Street. A road-building boom was imminent, and money to be made by smart people.

Di Anello now affected an Irish brogue, "Who says that concrete has to have so much cement in it? And why does asphalt have to be so many inches thick, when less would do? And wouldn't the poor *paesanos*, many of whom cannot read and write Italian–let alone English-jump at the chance to do business with City Hall? A handshake and a promise will do!"

Nino got the picture as he listened to the caustic, controlled voice of Massimo Di Arello; he of the long deadly fingers – the *Pezzo Grosso*, the Big Gun of the Black Hand. Vast power and wealth for Oreste only! But such thoughts had truly scrambled *Lu Siciliano's* brain, Nino thought. If sane, he would have realized Di Anello would learn of the treachery from his informers, perhaps even his 'City Hall mystery woman'. And Nino trembled anew. *What are my enemies saying to him, about me?*

"But you are still in danger," Nino said, screwing up his courage, and looking concerned. "And so am I," he blurted, unable to stop himself.

The trace of a smile cut across Di Anello's lips. "No, Nino, neither of us is in danger. You see, to the *Americani mangia patate* I am an honest Columbus Street business man who contributes generously to their political campaigns. As a result they do not bother me. As to other matters," he shrugged, "perhaps some suspect, but the neighborhood is large. We have others who have prospered; bankers, jewelers, real estate sharpies, smug doctors, all of whom cast large shadows. Let it be that way to outsiders. Within the neighborhood? We all know each other well, do we not?" He held up a hand as Nino's mouth opened. "So I am safe, Nino, and so are you as long as I remain in the background... and you and other members of our family conduct business with honor and respect, as I know you will. Is it not so?" Mouth agape, Nino nodded. His chin sank into the folds of fat beneath it.

"For you see, Nino," Di Anello turned away, and then whirled back, pointing the glowing stogie at Nino's heart, "Oreste's unfortunate accident is our opportunity. The profits of the road-building projects Hoyt speaks of must be *una cosa nostra* (our business alone). Natale will introduce you to Hoyt as the new owner of our Front Street business. Talk to Hoyt, tell him that you and Oreste were business associates. Say you know about his arrangement with the esteemed Mr. Hoyt, but now that Oreste is dead you are anxious to take his place. Assure him that no one else knows of the partnership, and that you know the Columbus Street *paisanos* as well as, no! – better than Oreste did." He paused, smiling sardonically.

"Drink with Hoyt – whiskey, not wine – and when he gambles, see that he wins a pot or two. Understand me, Hoyt is smart. He will know that Oreste has been silenced, that someone who was over him is in charge. He will go along, of that I am sure. His greed will see to it. Leave the rest... to me!

Overcome with relief and emotion, Nino sank to his knees, and pounded the gray woolen carpet on the hard concrete floor with both fists. He looked at Di Anello, his face contorted, "I will not fail you, Don Massimo, I swear it! And I will never betray you! This is our business, for-ever!"

"Please," Di Anello said, "get up." He helped Nino to his feet. Nino had called him 'Don Massimo'. He liked that! And why not? With the addition of the city road construction fraud and kickback schemes to his other lucrative businesses, he would no longer be an unimportant neighborhood businessman. He would grow in power and strength, a man of great respect. No sneers from the New York boys anymore over his 'crummy small town operation'. And, in time, he meant to control them – maybe even Chicago! So 'Don Massimo!' suited him fine. The *Mano Nera* is not dead! The sound of a truck cranking up outside excited him. It was an exclamation point to his soaring thoughts of power and conquest... on the wings of a fabled lion.

"Sì," he said to Nino, in perfect King's Italian, "*Veramente, sarà una cosa nostra, per sempre!*"

Nino nodded gravely. "*Sì, una cosa nostra, per sempre!*" he echoed. (Yes, our business, our thing, forever!)

A few minutes later Nino strode through and out of the warehouse, no longer afraid for his life. He squared his shoulders and smiled his cherubic smile.

Vito, leaning on a tower of olive oil cans, watched closely and gave Nino a terrible look. Why hadn't he, Vito, been promoted to take Oreste's place? He could handle the job. Hadn't he handled Sammy Constantino? Of course! Boiling inside, he lurched forward, towards Nino, and caught himself, but not in time...

Nino, happily blinded by his new commission and Di Anello's apparent trust in him, never noticed, nor did he hear the crash of olive oil cans behind him, and Vito's virulent curses.

Chapter 14

Phil, up early and ready for another day of baseball, saw Di Anello's Cadillac come up the gravel road to the court warehouse and purr into the open side delivery door, which then slid closed with a loud clank. Why so early, Phil thought? The car had turned away from him, so he couldn't see who was driving. Vito? Well, what if it were the crazy pug? He doesn't even know whether the sun is shining, the nut!

Phil looked down to the empty-can bin and saw Vic and one of the neighborhood boys thumping taped baseballs into worn gloves. Vic looked up and caught Phil's eye. "Comin' down?" he asked. "We're going to the bug yard."

Phil pressed his head against the window screen, cupped his hands and said, "Yeah. But I'll go out the front way. Meet you at the field." Vic nodded knowingly and glanced at the court warehouse. He knew that by going out the front way Phil wouldn't have to pass by the warehouse, and a chance meeting with Vito. "Poor Phil," Vic muttered, and sped off.

Later, after a long muggy day of baseball practice, Phil returned home alone, the long way around. He rang his front doorbell; once, twice, and waited. Finally his mother, wiping soapy hands on a dish towel, leaned over the front porch, looked down on him, wagged her head in disapproval (but came down nonetheless) and unlocked the front door.

"So who you think you are? Fancy company coming for Sunday dinner?"

"Aw, Ma!" Phil thought she was unusually cranky and agitated.

On the kitchen table, under a cold cup of coffee, he saw the stained reason for her ill-humor: The Post, folded to a sharp edge along a column. Curious, Phil picked up the paper, and read; key words jumped at him:

...Oreste Straniero... East Side Export-Import Company... a fiery death... speeding... drinking... Berkshires... on way to meet godson... Mr. Massimo Di Anello, company president, expressed shock... told Straniero...

shouldn't drink so much... will be missed... didn't listen... Straniero lived at...

Phil felt his insides churn and gurgle. He wanted to run to Jimmy's, better yet... rocket to Sergeant Sam Pizzuta's apartment, wait for him and ask him if Oreste had really had an accident. Or was it the work of the Black Hand, ordered by Di Anello? Maybe because Oreste's plan to trap Jimmy hadn't worked? Phil had to know! He was entitled to the truth! For hadn't he started it all – the unraveling of the Black Hand – with his eavesdropping at the warehouse? And hadn't Sergeant Pizzuta and Jimmy acted on his information? Yes but... the big detective had told him to stay close to home... Reluctantly he went to his room, clenched his teeth, and lay on his bed, arms folded behind his neck. He thought hard... and made up his mind.

The next morning, Phil again heard the ritual song of baseball. This time he bounded downstairs and told the gang he would be at the bug yard in an hour or so. He had an important errand to run first.

"Can't it wait?" Vic asked, urgently. "We got a game lined up and we need all our heavy hitters – like you, Phil."

Phil shook his head. "I'll be back before you start. Honest. And thanks for the compliment!"

Vic watched open-mouthed, as down through the skunk cabbage path Phil walked. He didn't see Phil sneak nervous glances at the warehouse, nor did he know that Phil's heart was in his throat.

It seemed as if forever, but was only a few minutes before Phil turned safely onto Columbus Street. He breathed deeply. No one from the court warehouse pursued him. *See!* he told himself – *you have nothing to worry about.* Whistling an improvised tune he passed quickly by Dom De Prospo's market, and a few strides later stepped down into Jimmy's place.

Jimmy finished wrapping a club sandwich for a customer, rang up the ten cents, wiped his good hand on his white apron, and said, "Well, I thought you got lost or something. What kind of ice cream you want?"

"Naw, Jimmy, too early. And I didn't get lost. Just

doing what Sergeant Pizzuta said to do – staying home. I saw the papers though, about Oreste." He paused, saying, "Guess you're in the clear now, right?"

"Yeah, maybe. Look Phil, you did good keeping quiet about our plan." He looked at his door and saw no customers coming. "We got you-know-who running scared now. Just a little bit more, and–" He snapped his fingers. "But you gotta still keep out of it. If you do, look!" He opened the cash register drawer, pulled out his Silver Star. "I'll give you this, for keeps."

Phil's eyes widened. The red, white and blue ribbon; the gleaming five pointed silver star suspended from it; the center device of wreath and smaller star within it radiating glory! Phil held the decoration up. The star swung back and forth, and Phil was in the trenches, hunting Huns, wiping out Spandau machine gun nests, though severely wounded and bleeding...

"Well, Phil, we got a deal?"

Jimmy's voice brought Phil back from his trench warfare.

"Thanks a lot, Jimmy, but I couldn't keep it. Maybe I can borrow it for a while though, show it to my pals..." Phil, seeing it, seized a very unexpected opportunity. Clear-eyed and calculating, he added, "I know! I'll show it to my friend Guido first. He builds model airplanes with me, lives in a big white house on East Hawthorne Road – you know up there, top of Holly Hill." Phil waved a hand, languidly.

Top of Holly Hill? Big white house? Jimmy licked his lips.

"Guido... Guido?" he asked, as if thinking hard.

"Di Anello... Guido Di Anello," Phil said. "He's a real good guy! Told me his father is a businessman who gives to the Church and takes care of the poor. Guido showed me his whole house – even a cabinet full of guns. And oh! what a view of the park, the diner, Hoyt's place... from Di Anello's study. Anyway," Phil nodded, "I'll see Guido in a day or two. We gotta finish covering some models with tissue." He took a short, quick breath, stepped forward, and seemed to examine the ice cream showcase carefully. He watched Jimmy's reflection shining back at him. It seemed carved in glass, it was so still. But suddenly it disappeared.

Phil turned quickly, Jimmy was at the front door, locking it and now putting up a 'Closed' sign. Hunched over, mouth tight, eyes gleaming, he limped back to Phil.

"Step in the back with me! I got a great idea!" Jimmy pushed Phil hard. He was sweating heavily from his face and armpits. He looked, thought Phil with a sly smile, like the cat that just ate the canary, and he knew that what he had tried to do was working. Jimmy had bitten... hard!

Phil worked himself up. "Hey, Jimmy, take it easy! I can't spy for you up there! Guido is... is... my friend!" His voice modulated up and down, and his hands fluttered.

"Now you take it easy! It'll just be between you and me," Jimmy said, wiping his brow. "I won't tell Pizzuta, honest! Check in with me every couple of days, around closing time; come in the back door. If you got something juicy, I'll tell Sam I found out my own way. See, you'll be out of it. So if Di Anello is really an honest business man," Jimmy made a choking sound and a wry face, "fine. If not, and we both know he's not... well, you don't want your own father mixed up with a crook, do you?"

Phil hadn't thought of that angle, and he had a new, higher appreciation of Jimmy. Smart. And no fool.

"Deal!" Phil stuck out his hand. "I'll take the ice cream now."

As Phil left the store, biting hard into a triple chocolate ice cream cone and fingering the Silver Star, Jimmy smiled. *This way*, he thought, *Phil works for me, and he won't talk to anyone else. Not that I wouldn't trust him staying out of this mess the way Sam wanted, but he's young, could get excited, yap away, and get Pizzuta and me... and himself, in deep trouble. Yeah, maybe six feet deep of trouble... But – Madonna Mia! He's friends with Guido Di Anello! Lucked out, that's what I did!*

Jimmy mused. His mastery of Phil, his nearly forgotten war decorations and what they stood for (thanks to Pizzuta) had stiffened his spine with pride and re-. solve. He stood quietly, and savored old memories of gallant deeds.

"Screw the Evil Eye!" he said suddenly. "Shit! I took on the whole German army and won, didn't I?" He nodded, reassuring himself and went to the door. He tore up his 'Closed' sign then unlocked and swung open the door with a flourish.

Phil also smiled as he jauntily walked away. So! Sergeant Pizzuta wasn't about to cut him out of fracturing the Black Hand! And when the showdown came Phil Martello would be there! Through Jimmy he'd know what Pizzuta was up to, of course, he had to string Jimmy along somehow, feed him inconsequential shit observed at the Di Anello household, and keep Jimmy drooling for more.

Guido? Phil was sure he'd see him again, as soon as the Oreste killing, er, accident, was ancient history. Knowing the fractiousness and turbulence of the neighborhood now, Phil guessed that would be two days, as other events of daily living occupied the minds of excitable people. So he and Guido were what? Blood brothers? He blinked then let that portentous thought pass quickly and quietly.

What of his father? Well, like the cowboys meandering over the silver screen of the Majestic, no crook would lasso him or brand him. He would wear no despicable *Mano Nera* collar! Or would he?

Phil didn't dwell on that thought either, and forced himself to think of the baseball game. He looked at the dull, somber sky. Another muggy day! Well, he thought, *we should be through playing ball before it gets too hot.* And he himself planned to be 'hot' today; the heavy hitter his team longed for. After that – a pleasant warmth coursed through him – check with Mona if he saw her; about going to the lake again with Carmela and of course, Marjorie...

Phil began to run, and forced himself to think of his morning's work with Jimmy. He threw a backward glance at Jimmy's receding store.

Satisfied with himself he grinned and tossed the almost finished ice cream cone over his shoulder. He heard no noise of its fall, and turned to look. He saw a thin film of chocolate on the grate of a storm drain.

The cone had gone down below, almost without touching metal...

What a shot! he told himself. *How can I miss, huh? How can I miss?*

The baseball field was bordered by tenements on two sides (east and north) and on the third side (south) by the cyclone – fenced back entrances of small business structures and a Buick dealership. Mulberry Street framed the rectangular field on the west end.

Two baseball diamonds, one at the east end the other at the west end, had been carved out of the weeds that grew luxuriantly in the humid heat and summer rains. Phil joined the tenement players – at the west field. The game that Vic said was 'lined up', didn't materialize. Several players from both sides had opted for a day at the lake. The remaining ball players milled about, some eyeing Phil's developing frame and then flexing their own muscles in a furtive comparison. Most, like Phil and Vic, wore old pants, T-shirts, and sneakers. A few were in short-sleeve sport shirts and baseball caps. One lad, Oopesh-dialect for The Fish – wore a much repaired and oversize hand-me-down baseball uniform. On the other hand, Jerry-next-door's ragged uniform seemed several sizes too small. Phil observed the melange with amusement, but also a twang of pity. The neighborhood!

"I know! Let's choose up sides and have a pick-up game," Rusty said. "Here, Vic, ketch my bat."

Vic caught it in his left hand, halfway up the taped handle. He held the bat out to Rusty and the time-horrored ritual began. Alternately each grasped the bat over the other's grip, hand over hand, until the top of the bat was reached by one of them. The winner! He chose first.

"I pick first," chortled Vic. "Phil, come stand next to me."

Finally, all thirteen players were chosen; five short for two complete teams. Vic had a bright idea. "Hey you guys," he called to boys tossing balls around on the east diamond, "wanna play? We need more men."

"Sure!" And the four Irish lads from ledge country joined the Holly Hill tenement gang.

"Hey, Brother, you wanna play too? We need another man." This time it was Rusty, calling to a husky boy sitting on a bank nearby. He had an old baseball glove, and watched the formation of the teams with interest.

"Ah guess so." Brother, Heywood Hampton, got up slowly and ambled over to the group. This had never happened before. Heywood Hampton came from a cluster of old brick apartments on the north side of the neighborhood. Rusty knew he was a very good ball player, having seen him play with his own kind at the bug yard. He was Negro. The game began...

Guido had a hunch. "Vito," he said, "don't stay on Columbus Street. Turn the car down Mulberry Street. I wanna go by the bug yard."

Vito grumbled. He didn't like this smart-ass kid. He still owed him big for the insults at the lake. He thought of the shiv in his pocket... But, he did as Guido ordered. They were returning from a shopping trip to Iver Johnson's, where Guido had bought several new baseballs, two outfield mitts, and three Louisville Slugger bats of different lengths and weight. Guido was going to be ready! He had promised Phil that!

"Now turn right onto Ford Street," Guido said, "and slow down." Vito did, sliding down into the seat, his mouth working furiously.

Guido craned his neck out the right front window of the car. He was right! A ball game was in progress. And the guys were his age! He looked more closely. There – at the plate – batting!

Crack! A mighty swing. The ball sailed high and long, curving foul.

"Vito!" Guido shrieked, "stop the car'"

Vito tensed, like when the bell rang for his last round with Sammy Constantino. "What the fuck's da mattah wid you?" he said, looking at Guido angrily, his teeth bared and clenched.

"Nothing! I just want to watch this game."

"We can't, fa Christ sakes! I gotta pick up da boss, remembah? He'll get tear-ass at me if I don't show up on time."

"All right, calm down! I'll stay here. Go! Drop off the

baseball equipment at the house, except for this ball. Shit, Vito, just tell my father it's what I wanted to do. I'll go to the court warehouse after the game; someone there will take me home. What are you waiting for?"

"Three and two!" the umpire yelled. Guido heard, and got out of the car. Vito was interested in the three and two pitch, but he started the La Salle's motor, nonetheless.

The pitch came. Crack! A line drive into deep left field. The batter took off, and the left fielder back-pedaled. Guido yelled and stomped. The runner rounded second base and legged for third. The left fielder had picked up the bouncing ball with a graceful sweep of his glove, dug it out with his right hand, and thrown a perfect strike into third base. The third baseman caught and dropped the ball as the runner slid into him. Safe!

"Great throw," Guido shouted back at Vito. But he had rooted for the base runner, who now stood up and dusted himself off. Phil!

"Yeah," Vito admitted grudgingly, "not too bad a trow." He shifted gears, and started to pull away, He leaned across the steering wheel. "But, didja see who trew da ball in? A niggah, a coon! He should stay wid his own kind! Dis ain't his territory!" Vito jammed down on the accelerator, roaring away.

Guido shook his head. Gee, he thought, doesn't he realize times are changing? Heck, this is 1935!

As he drove, Vito thought of the base runner sliding into third base, very hard. That blur of motion, the smooth movements. The way he had knocked the third baseman on his keister. Had he seen him before? He shook his head in dismay. Nothing came, no connection with anything. Damn it!

Chapter 15

Guido leaned back on the black couch in his den, both hands clasped around one knee. He basked in the after-glow of happy thoughts.

"You made a big hit with the guys this morning," Phil said. "Cripes, they went bananas when you showed them that new big league ball. Real cowhide, tight lacing. Phew!"

"Yeah, and how about when I told 'em I had more equipment for next year?"

"They all shit, that's what!"

"Do you think the name Nightingale Juniors is a good name for the team?"

"Sure! We all voted for it. You chose a good name for us, Guido."

"Wow!"

Phil went back to poring over the intricacies of the plans for the gas model kit spread out before him on the den floor. After an early supper, they had hiked up East Hawthorne Road to the big white house. Guido had met him outside the gate, and solemnly said that the house was theirs for several hours. His father was very busy cleaning up after Oreste, and his mother was at a church sodality meeting. Thus assured, Phil relaxed and eagerly joined Guido in talking about next year's baseball team and its equipment, gas model planes, and... girls. Guido didn't see why they couldn't all go to the lake again. He'd see about transportation. Phil said he'd check with Mona. He still had qualms, despite Guido's 'Don't worry about Vito'. But Phil knew he too wanted a lake trip... badly.

As Phil examined the model plans, Massimo Di Anello relaxed in the back seat of the Cadillac. With Vito at the wheel it had just turned into East Hawthorne Road. The car windows were wide open, and the woodsy smells distracted him from the sultry heat. Today Di Anello had dressed informally, blue short-sleeve sport shirt, pleated gray slacks, and patent leather shoes. If the rich *mangia patate* dressed this way in hot weather while they went about reorganizing their businesses, so could he.

He had visited most of his key businesses and people today, except his two houses of prostitution and the madam who ran them. As long as earnings poured into the Banca Di Anello there was nothing to fear, though Di Anello planned to phone her later in the evening, just in case.

He sighed now, and lifted his head to catch the rush of air streaming into the back seat. *All is well! The death of Oreste caused hardly a ripple in my organization. He shouldn't have boozed it up, right? Right!*

He had talked to Nino during the day. Timothy Hoyt, after a night of big winnings at Natale's, had listened to Nino and agreed to think about the proposition offered by the late Oreste's 'senior business partner'. Di Anello chuckled at that. Somewhat suspicious, Hoyt had said that before he would commit himself he wanted to see if Nino could put his money where his mouth was by providing 'reasonably priced labor'. Nino assured him that he could. Di Anello lit a long stogie and took a puff. Arrangements... were complete.

The warehouses? Managed well! That new man Nino hired, Sebastiano Martello, works hard, has things under control. Good! More time for Nino to spend on construction and road projects, and for me to control... and pull strings. In time, this Martello... who know? We shall see.

"Vito."

"Yeah, yeah."

"I just remembered. I have to go back to the court warehouse. Look, don't leave, wait for me at the house. When I get back we will have a talk."

Routine. No problem. The boss often took off alone to do this or that. At the big house on the hill Vito would get into his own little Chevy and wave to the boss as he drove away in the La Salle, and now, the Cadillac. Vito would drive back to his room in a house on Columbus Street, after first stopping off at the diner to chew the rag, have coffee half and half. Or the boss would ask him to stay in the room over the detached two-car garage for an early morning trip, a couple of times as far as New York.

But this time, something... didn't quite fit. Struggling hard, he tried to figure out what it was. Di Anello had never asked him to wait for a 'talk'. Why? The worry bug in his brain kept chewing.

They were at the house now, and Vito watched Di Anello drive away in the Cadillac. Chrome flashed bright under a street lamp.

"The crummy kid Guido! He squealed on me – da lake!" Vito said out loud, panic and burning anger overcoming him. In a half-daze he trudged to the front door. He'd go into the kitchen, have a cup of coffee from the pot that was always on the stove... and wait. Maybe he'd be taking Oreste's place.

"Geez! Dat what da talk could be about... yeah!"

In Guido's den the gas model kit had been set aside, and Phil was helping Guido re-tissue the wing of an old flying model plane, using banana oil as the adhesive. When they had both carefully stretched and smoothed the tissue as best they could Guido murmured, preoccupied with a stubborn fold in a section of the wing's leading edge.

"Phil, will you get me a glass of water? I'll spray the wing with this little spray tube... Wing should be as smooth and tight as a baby's ass when it dries."

"Sure, Guido," Phil chuckled. Guido was coming out of his shell, that's for sure! Phil got up, rubbed his knees, stretched then massaged his thighs. Gad! He hadn't realized the cramped position he had been in for the past few hours. He walked slowly into the kitchen, selected a tall glass, opened the faucet slightly, and watched the water slowly rise.

The tinkle of water mesmerized Phil, but even so he heard the knob on the side door turn, and then – huh? the door creaked open. Guido said we had lots of time to ourselves! Instinct, foul thoughts of *them!* spun Phil around towards the door as it slammed, and Phil spilled a full glass of water. There, looking at him, a dumb gorilla look on his face... was Vito!

Compartments opened and closed in Vito's punch – damaged brain. He blinked at Phil, who stood before him in frozen silence. But Phil's quick turn had jolted loose blocked memory channels, and bits and pieces of information floated free and banged together behind Vito's eyes, forming patterns that began to coalesce: The big kid that had run into him as he came out of the Williams Hotel on the way to the racetrack – and how the boss had stopped him from pasting the kid with a backhand. The blur that slammed into him at the lake... just as he had that broad ready for action... The slide into third base...

A slow, terrible smile creased Vito's face. His years in the fight game had paid off. If there was one thing he knew, it was an opponent's style, how he moved–

"I've been lookin' for ya, punk! I owe ya dis!" He lunged forward to grab Phil's T-shirt, and his other arm cocked back to deliver a brutal closed-fist haymaker. And he would follow up with many more. The kid had to pay... like Sammy Constantino. No mercy, no bell to save him...

In addition to Vito, Di Anello's business this night included Fulvia. He meant to phone her, arrange a visit. It had been a long time, and he would tell her when he met her that disloyalty – by anyone close to him – merited severe punishment. He would casually mention Oreste, and ask how her daughter was doing. He chuckled, puffing on his stogie. Then he planned to make another call, to Florida, and arrange a place on the beach for Vito. It was time to retire him. He had earned it. Too bad he is slipping more and more into a shadow world, and he isn't there anymore. Di Anello tapped his head. So... after the Florida call he would return home, talk to Vito, tell him that it was time, and that he–

No! You will talk to him now, Di Anello suddenly told himself. The need – imperative! Why, he didn't know. But he had had such a feeling before, a feeling of impending disaster. All else he had to do he would brush aside until later. With a powerful tug of the wheel he spun the car around on the narrow road. His foot hit the accelerator. The tires kicked up gravel, grabbed, and roared back up towards his house. He must get home fast! The feeling, honed over hundreds of years in peasant genes passed on to him protected him – many times – and now pervaded his being as never before.

Chapter 16

Vito's voice! A peal of doom. Phil snapped back, eyes swinging wildly about. Trapped! Vito's bulk blocked the side door by the kitchen. The front door – a long way off. A bullet in the back if he tried for it.

Suddenly, a second later, or was it an eternity? Vito's grasping left hand shot forward and closed viciously. His haymaker, thrown hard with his right hand, whistled forward, aimed for Phil's jaw. Phil avoided the hand by quickly stepping back, and he ducked to avoid Vito's telegraphed punch. The fingers of Vito's left hand dug painfully into the palm of his own hand, drawing blood. His haymaker sailed harmlessly over Phil's head.

Phil crouched low, leaped to one side of an off-balance Vito, and thrust a hard maple kitchen chair at him. Vito stumbled over it, cursing, bellowing, snuffling through his flat nose. Phil curved to his right, out of the kitchen and into the den where Guido now stood with a dazed, uncomprehending look on his lean face.

"Get the hell out of the way!" Phil shouted. He scrambled onto the black couch and fumbled to unhook the latch of the double-hung window behind it. Sweating heavily, his eyes burning and rivulets of fear sour in his mouth, he unhooked the latch and yanked at the window. Stuck! It was stuck!

Vito turned the corner into the den, staggering, his eyes glazed and hard, his mouth curled down, his face contorted. In his haste to untangle himself from the chair he had cracked both shins, and they now stung and throbbed.

He saw Phil. "Ya ain't goin' nowheres, punk!" he said in a harsh whisper. *The dumb-ass punk was gonna pay, more than Sammy Constantino. Maybe this was Sammy, trying to screw him? Huh? Naw!* Vito wasn't about to be tricked by a punk kid no more...

Ow! my legs hurt! Only one ting ta do! He reached for his pistol, brought it out butt up, lifted it high, ready to pound that hated face, so close, so close!

Guido stirred and blinked his eyes as if waking from a long dream. Color returned to his pallid face. He understood, and burst into life: "No, you miserable stupid turd!" he screamed at Vito. With a reckless courage he didn't know he had, he dived for Vito's gun, arms extended. He knocked the gun aside with both hands.

"Out the front! Go, Phil, run! I'll... hold him!" Guido gritted out the words. He grabbed Vito's gun hand and hung on with the tenacity of a bulldog.

Stung, angry, Vito flung Guido from side to side, intent on freeing his gun hand. Guido bit down on the hand, hard.

"Ow! ya little punk!" Out of his mind now, Vito wrenched free and thudded the gun butt against Guido's head. Guido's knees buckled. He fell to the floor, and lay still.

"Ya called me a turd again!" Vito cried at the prostrate figure. "Well, I showed ya, ya little prick!" He suddenly remembered that Guido was not his top priority. He swiveled his neck, an eerie glow in his eyes.

Phil had heeded Guido, for he was now at the solid oak front door. He pulled it open with all his strength and cast a quick glance over his shoulder. A stream of adrenaline surged through him, and without hesitation he flung himself headlong onto the gravel driveway just as a thunderous shot rang out behind him. A bullet kicked up dust a few feet from his head. The shadows of the night, his leap (or car noise on East Hawthorne Road?), had saved him from a bullet in the brain. But there could be more shots! He's flipped his lid... he's a madman! Another shot, wild this time, followed by a guttural "Gonna getcha! Commin' aftah ya!" and wild gibberish and cackling.

Phil rolled into the shadows of the stone wall and some shrubs to the right of the house. Move, move! Where? How? If he sprinted out the driveway for East Hawthorne Road, Vito standing in the front doorway, neck swiveling like a snake, eyes searching the darkness, would spot him and shoot him dead! And now Vito stepped down from the doorway. He leaned forward, staring left. Now right. Close, closer to Phil's cover.

The roar of a car! Tires screeched and a car slid into the driveway, a distraction! Now! Phil sprang to his feet, took the one escape route he thought offered him safety.

He might break a leg, or his neck, but he had to try – get away from Vito – and what could be his buddies in that car! Phil began running in long zig-zag strides towards the back of the house, towards the wall and the steep grade behind it. Coils of thick New England mist rising from dense woods and ponds screened him as they battled for supremacy with an insistent new moon. He glanced over his shoulder. Vito, bathed in the headlights of the car, uttered a wail – straight from the depths of the damned in hell, Phil thought, his spine tingling with the horror of it.

Crouching low, he turned to move behind the house. Vito began running... towards him? A shot sliced a chunk of wood from the corner of the house. Yes! He's seen me! And he's coming! Get moving! Phil ran to the rear of the house, and with a powerful leap, he grasped the wall with both hands, pulled himself over, and pushed hard. Airborne, Phil glimpsed below him a tangle of old tree trimmings and decaying grass clippings. He landed flat, arms spread. Brittle branches cracked and snapped, the noise loud. Oh shit! How could Vito not hear? Around the house he'd come, and head for the well, followed by his buddies piling out of that car in the driveway. The nightmares of his childhood now a flesh and blood reality!

The car in the driveway stopped in a swirl of dust and gravel.

"*Figlio di puttana!*" Di Anello cried, as he lurched out of the car. (Son of a whore!)

Di Anello's gnawing fear had unfolded its wings into fact. He had heard a pistol shot and as he slowed to turn into his driveway, a second shot. Vito! Vito! his brain told him. On the doorsill, wailing at the sky, Vito waved his gun. Di Anello watched, the knuckles of a clenched fist in his mouth as Vito lumbered away towards the back of the house, screaming wildly. He disappeared, as if pushed around the dark side of the house by an unseen black hand.

Another shot! from behind the house. Di Anello leaned back in the car, pulled out a gun from its padded pocket under the front seat, and took three steps towards the back of the house.

"No!" he screamed. The front door-open! A demented Vito! He turned and ran into the house, his leather heels echoing on the polished marble of the entryway. He lunged into the kitchen. His wife and son! Where–?

Horror-struck, his eyes swept the scene. Chairs over-turned. A table upended. A lamp broken. He felt nailed to the floor, his blood draining from him. His eyes darted about, glazed and uncomprehending.

"Oh, oh!" Low moans. From where?... From the den. Licking his lips, Di Anello snapped out of his funk and hurtled over the kitchen jumble into the den, steeling himself for the carnage he was sure to see.

"*Sangu di la Madonna!*" he blurted, his impeccable Italian deserting him. "Guido! Guido! My son! Are you all right? Here, let me see. Oh, your head... the blood! I'll get a doctor. Who did this to you? Where is your mother?" The Italian poured out, passionate and in torrents.

"I... I think I'm okay," Guido responded in English, rising up slowly to one elbow and gingerly touching the broken skin on the side of his head. "It was Vito. He–"

"Ah! I thought so," replied Di Anello also in English, his face hardening into stone. "First, a doctor for you. Then–"

"No! First help my friend Phil. Vito will kill him. Papa, you gotta stop Vito!" Guido gulped. His father seemed puzzled. Quickly Guido recounted the incident at the lake, and how he thought Vito had forgotten about it.

"You should have told your father," Di Anello said, with just a hint of reproach in his voice. "But then for some time now I have known about Vito's condition. So, my son, the fault is mine." He shook his head. "No matter," he continued, "your father will take care of things. But we haven't much time. I'm sure your friend Phil is heading for the park. Vito may be close behind him." He held up his hand to stop Guido's question. "Later, Guido, later. I must make two pressing telephone calls." Bending low, Di Anello bounded up the stairs to his office. In less than two minutes, he was back. "The family doctor is coming to tend to you, Guido. Rest quietly until he comes. Now, you had a question or two?"

"Yes! About my friend Phil, and that turd Vito! What..."

Di Anello put a finger on Guido's lips. "*Calmati!* Help is on the way to Phil. Pray that it is in time. But, from the way you describe Phil, he is too swift and smart to be caught by Vito. As for Vito, do not concern yourself. Now, I must go. Your mother should be home soon. Talk to her. But not a word of this to anyone, understand? This is now a family matter, and must remain so."

"Phil, and his own family–"

"I have thought of that. His family will be proud of him. I shall see to it. They too will say nothing to any-one, for you see the Martello family... is now very close to our family." With a long sigh of relief, he embraced Guido, turned, and left. A few moments later Guido heard the throaty roar of the Cadillac as it zoomed away. He sat still on the floor, open-mouthed. He didn't recall when his father had last embraced him.

The third shot Di Anello had heard, when he watched Vito disappear behind the house, was aimed in the general direction of the sound of snapping branches and twigs caused by Phil's fall. Firing wildly over the wall, Vito moved forward, his gait jerky and labored.

Ping! The bullet tore a chunk of bark from a young oak near Phil.

"I know ya in dere, ya punk. Yor dead!" The voice hollow, sepulchral... The sound of scrabbling, heavy panting, and Vito's head appeared, lit by the thin bright-ness of a veiled moon.

"He's a zombie!" Phil uttered, terrified. Up in sprint position now, he threw himself into the darkness be-hind him, and slammed into a tree. His shoulder! He felt light-headed, and panic gripped him. He wanted to run, cry, scream, dig a deep hole with his bare hands and crawl in. His heart pounded... the stink of sweat... ripped clothes... lungs taxed...

A sticky, warm trickle on his neck. He touched blood. His blood! He took a deep breath and gingerly felt the back of his head.

"Ouch!" he said. The gash was above his right ear. How bad? He couldn't tell. And then his shoulder throbbed, and it began. A creeping tide of anger boiled in him, shoved panic aside and possessed him. With the anger his mind became clear and crisp. Cold reasoning emerged. He knew what he had to do. No lout tied to *them* would do him in. Lips tight, he began a slow, steady, noiseless descent down the steep slope. Behind him he heard the sound of a heavy body crashing through brush.

"Hope you get poison ivy in your crotch!" Phil yelled. The sound of his voice, loud and clear, shocked him and thrilled him too. He felt he could swoop through the woods as easily and quickly as a wraith, or at least like the heroes of the pulps; the Lone Eagle, G-8, Doc Savage! Lay off the kid stuff, something inside his head warned him. Maybe you're hurt more than you know, Phil told himself, soberly. He slowed down and saw the fissure in the ground; in time. It was granite-faced, and about fifteen feet deep. At his brisk pace, he would have fallen in and been hurt badly... perhaps killed...

Now his eyes burned. He realized that he limped – his right ankle! – and he felt so tired. The trees were thinning now, and soon he saw tiny dots of light. The park! And Columbus Street off to the right, with people, lots of people! Vito wouldn't dare! Maybe he's lost, or fallen and broken his neck. Great thought!

Out of the woods Phil came. Behind him, nothing. Almost at the bocce court, he saw the dim shapes of three men, huddled together at one end, away from the single park lamp.

Suddenly, Phil felt himself flying forward, off balance. *You tripped!* his mind flashed. Taking bigger and bigger steps, Phil tried to stay upright but didn't succeed. Arms braced he fell forward, sliding and scraping on grass and gravel.

"You all right?" someone asked. Phil had heard that voice... somewhere. Then, "Dis is the guy I mean! Let's fix his wagon, now!"

Nick shouting to his dark friends, his harsh voice piercing through the pain of pebbles embedded in the broken skin of Phil's palms! The sting of abrasions on his arms and knees. His head pounded, his ankle ached, and he winced. His eyes filled with tears. He struggled to his feet to meet his fat-faced assailant. And, through the agony, Phil knew he had to get away or be maimed by Nick and his ugly dregs-of-Columbus Street creeps.

Phil remembered Nick's words vividly: "Ah'll get even wid ya yet," as he got up shakily from the pile of empty cans where Phil had flung him during their melee with the basketball. He had been plotting how to get even, Phil thought, ever since. Now he felt his arms being pinned. Nick leered at him.

"Break 'em, break 'em!" Nick cried, over his shoulder.

One creep, a skinny bum in a too-big black coat grabbed an arm, ready to twist. Longcoat! Then Nick's other partner stumbled up and looked Phil straight in the eyes. A look of terror wiped the stupid grin from Little Angelo's face as he recognized Phil...

"Leave him alone!" he yelled. What's da matter wid you guys? Don't ya know who he is?" With that, Little Angelo hurled himself at Longcoat, clawing at his hands. He bumped a surprised Nick away with a hip twist.

"Fuck you!" Longcoat snarled, his less than nimble mind numbed by the effects of the happy leaf he smoked. But now he wasn't happy. He was jarred by Little Angelo's attack and he turned, angry and vicious. Out came a knife, and with an enraged shriek, he slashed at Little Angelo, nicking his right forearm.

"Why you dumb basted!" Little Angelo grabbed his bleeding arm with his left hand. His big foot flew up and caught Longcoat in the belly. Longcoat's cheeks puffed. He blew out his lungs, doubled over, and the knife flew from his hand.

"Dat guy is Phil, you dumb jerks! He is—"

Little Angelo didn't finish his sentence, for Nick jumped on his back, pummeling and screaming: "Stop it! Cut it out! He'll get away! Don't let him – get him, get him!"

Little Angelo had other things on his mind, namely, the screaming lunatic on his back, and Longcoat, moaning (but nevertheless) reaching down for his knife. Shaking off Nick, Little Angelo, tired of trying to explain that Phil was Guido Di Anello's friend, went for Longcoat. He had his own skin to save now. But Nick jumped him again, and the three rolled on the ground, grunting, groaning and throwing punches.

Phil didn't stay to see the outcome of the battle. When

Little Angelo's foot found Longcoat's gut he took several steps back. No one paid attention. *Go!* his mind urged him. And he did, towards Columbus Street, walking, running, limping, grimacing with pain. But... what is that? He stopped, dropping to one knee. Several excited men running towards him, their flashlights bobbing and dancing, their beams probing the night like fingers of doom. Fingers? His nightmares? A yellow moon broke the shackles of the mist, bathing the park in its wan light. Instinctively, Phil looked back.

By the park lamp, near the bocce court, stood Vito. He swayed, waved his gun, apparently saw the fighting trio on the ground, and headed in their direction, seeming to float through light and shadows. The wavering sight gave Phil chills. A disheveled flapping demon, on the loose!

Come on, come on! Phil touched his sweat-soaked body. Its only Vito! Only Vito? Shit! In a moment, Phil knew he would be seen by the crazy savage, and by the onrushing men, who were less than a hundred yards away now. Trapped! So! you wanted to penetrate the *Mano Nera*, put one over on Jimmy, did you? Oo-fa! you can't even handle Vito, and he isn't even a little finger of the Black Hand. Phil's mind raced, reproaching him for his foolishness. He couldn't permit himself to be caught, by anyone. He saw himself on the brink of a deep abyss from which there was no escape. There must be a way, there must be—

The ledge! That's it! If he could force himself – one big sprint – to safety, oh, so far away! He had to escape, had to, had to! So pop the cork, get the hell out of here...

The ledge-yes, the ledge. *Go, Phil, go!* the insistent voice inside him urged, with a growing unease, and Phil, with a compulsion born of desperation, got up and ran; away from the shouting men, away from Vito. He knew he was naked, in full view, running across the park, but oh! – how he prayed for a few minutes of invisibility, to get into the shadows, away from the moonlight – into the cloak of tall grass at the edge of the park.

Almost at the grass, nausea engulfed him, and a stab of pain shot up his leg. He crumpled to the ground, panting, and sobbing. He felt he could go no further.

End of the line. Finis! In agony, he waited for the goons with the flashlights-from Sforza's diner he was sure-somehow alerted by Vito, or maybe Vito himself would appear (he's not so stupid after all), gun in hand. Phil shuddered and managed to pull himself into a clump of grass. Rocks under him, rolling. He gathered several large chunks. If he went it wouldn't be like cousin Lucia! He'd break as many skulls as he could. As if in answer to his thoughts he saw a large granite boulder and crawled behind it. He waited, and listened. Nothing...

Slowly his nausea subsided, and while his ankle hurt, the unbearable stab was gone. Puzzled, he got up on one knee and peered across the dimness of the expanse of park he had crossed.

"Wonder what that's all about?" he asked, in a soft whisper. In the distance, near the bocce court, he saw the headlights of two cars. But they were too far away, and it was too dark to make anything else out. No goons, no Vito! But the cars, with Vito in them, could veer across the park and disgorge their vermin to search for him. He had to get to the safety of the ledge. But how? He doubted he could cross the expanse of grass he hid in fast enough to evade determined pursuers. Even if he got to the ledge and tried to climb it his ankle could give way, and he'd make the morning papers... Another foolhardy kid killed scaling the ledge. He visualized Nick's victorious strut as he laid into the tenement gang, Rusty in particular. And Vito – ugh!

But Vito suddenly had big problems of his own. After inspecting the thrashing trio he backed away, disappointed, for he had wanted Phil to be one of them. Then he saw the flashlights, the men behind them, two cars, and he dropped to the ground, whining, for an instinct greater than his urge to 'get dat young bum' now controlled him.

Everything that had gone wrong for Vito Amorusi was Phil's fault. He nodded in self-pity. From that time at the court warehouse when he had been tripped by 'dat bum' – when he was minding his own business – he had experienced only bad luck. Geez! He was even in dutch with the big boss and his kid Guido now. But he would get Phil – Guido had called him that – break his ass, and his head. And all would be right again for Vito Amorusi. Da boss would understand... or would he?

Dose guys are lookin' fa me, Vito Amorusi! For an instant, the channels of his mind cleared, and he knew what fate awaited him if he were caught. He recalled what he had done to Guido, the Cadillac spinning into the driveway and Di Anello coming out of it. Oh! how the curses must have flowed from him when he found his big-mouthed kid cold-cocked. *And da boss had phoned Sforza's Diner! Get Vito!*

Oo-wa! A hunted animal now, Vito backtracked to the edge of the wooded slope, dropped flat, and watched. The men with the flashlights stopped and slanted towards the three bodies rolling on the ground. Lights probed, men cursed, bleeding bodies were pried apart, and one shouted, his disappointment clear: "Oh shit! He's not one of 'em!"

Vito heard, and saw the men (his friends!) mill about uncertainly. *Gotta get the fuck out a here!* He snapped glances around him. His mind, a single pulsing channel now, guided him. Crouched low in the darkness, he headed towards Columbus Street, putting distance between himself, the searchers, and Phil. He reached the edge of the underbrush, and ran into a dark alley between the two rows of three-decker houses, angling back towards him from Columbus Street. He crouched behind a stack of garbage cans and listened to the occasional hum and swish of a passing car. No shouts, no sound of pursuing feet. He moved quickly behind a house fronting Columbus Street, two hundred feet across from the diner. No one seemed to be inside. No shootin' the shit tonight! Empty! Everyone in the park, looking for Vito Amorusi.

"But I ain't gonna be dere," he cackled, hyena-like. He dashed across the street and toppled into another alley between sagging tenements. His breath came with a hard rasp, a hot fire scalded his chest. He hacked, spit up, and looked dumbly at the phlegm. One hell of a lunger! Stooping, he dipped his finger in it then held it towards the dim stream of light coming from a street lamp. The goo was thick and greenish-yellow. *Afta I get dat punk kid, I'll have Doc Priore check me out. Yeah, it's gettin' worse.* Satisfied with his analysis, he plunged on.

Through the closely-packed tenements he went, hugging walls, picking up accumulated soot in the process. Finally he skulked past the last street lamp, the only light now visible being dim railroad signals in the distance. He pushed out weather-beaten boards from a tired wooden fence and squeezed into the railroad yard. Safe! It would be his temporary home... when Nino wasn't in town. He chuckled at the thought and ran to the opposite side of the yard. Out quickly, he headed up a dark, wooded road. At the top Nino lived alone in a white frame house, away from the prevailing wind carrying train soot. He was a bachelor, Vito knew, and he had a wine cellar. Vito had been there before, when he helped Nino make wine. He knew Nino worked seven days a week; at the market, the warehouses, on buying trips, or collecting the do-re-mi from the rackets. So Vito Amorusi had it all figured out – what he had to do, and how to do it. Stealthily, he approached Nino's darkened house.

* * * *

Jimmy dialed, mouthing the numbers silently. He heard the phone ring at the other end, and then a quiet "Hello."

"Oh, Sam! Guess you're not out."

"You guessed right. What's up, Jimmy?"

"A hell of a lot!"

"Yeah?" A spark of interest from Sergeant Sam Pizzuta.

"You bet. I was closing up and was gonna go across to the diner for a cup of coffee and nose around, like you said. But I saw a bunch of the boys leave in a hurry, and after that, a couple of cars. Nobody, but nobody was left in the diner. So I hung around the store and waited. Pretty soon they all wander back, looking mad. I go over, sit at the counter, order coffee, see Skinny, and ask what the fuck's goin' on. He gives Sforza a look from under his hat, and Sforza nods. Guess I'm in good. Right?"

"Right, right!" Pizzuta sounded impatient.

"They were looking for Vito!" And Jimmy told Sam why. Vito had attacked Guido trying to get to Guido's friend.

"Phil!" Sergeant Pizzuta shouted.

"Had to be," Jimmy answered. "Skinny didn't know the name."

"Damn! I should have brought Vito in. Phil, how about Phil?"

"Don't know. He must be okay. He started to run towards the ledge, Little Angelo said. The dummy was fighting with Longcoat and a kid from the tenement when the boys came up. It's all coming apart Sam, what a mess!"

"Vito, what about Vito?"

"Dunno. Little Angelo thinks he headed back towards the slope."

"Yeah, and he's probably across Columbus Street now, holed up in that rat's nest of tenements. He's got to come out sometime."

"Gonna go after him?"

"Hell, no! Nobody supposed to know about tonight, remember? Keep your eyes and ears open. The boys'll begin searching the tenements. You let me know how they're doing. When they've got it down to a couple of places I'll be ready. And be careful, Jimmy. They still could be testing you."

"Gotcha! What are you going to do about that big teen-ager?"

"Phil? Let me think about that a while. Anyhow, good work Jimmy. I'll be by in the morning." Pizzuta hung up.

What the hell, Jimmy thought, sighing deeply. *Phil wouldn't have made a good spy for me. Gets into too much trouble, much too much...*

Chapter 17

Behind the granite boulder, Phil didn't feel much like a spy. He lay quietly, listening. Nothing. A gentle breeze cooled his flushed face, rustled the grass and trees, came around, and seemed to push him. His hand closed around the broken branch of a young tree. He'd use it as a cane! The breeze again. He looked around the boulder, his gaze embracing the hardness of the ledge, above to his right. He glanced ahead, at waving grass and swaying trees. There! An old rock-strewn path, barely visible, leading upwards through trees and grass, on a hillside below the ledge's rim. Too narrow and steep for cars! Hard to find by anyone on foot...

Presto, Filippo, presto! The breeze spoke to him now, a sweet feminine voice. Or, was it cousin Lucia? Phil trembled, shook his head, and obeyed. Up the path he walked, leaning on his makeshift cane. He stopped, he listened, he pushed on. No sound, save the moan of a night breeze and the flutter of disturbed birds. Hope replaced the fear that had shackled his mind. He searched the hillside above him, eyes straining to pierce the darkness beyond the reach of moonlight. Shadows zoomed and swirled before him. He rubbed his eyes, blinked, and swept the landscape, not looking directly at any one object. That helped, he thought. And suddenly the apparitions were forgotten, and he gasped, a gasp of hope.

At the top of the hill, silhouetted in deep black against the sky, a line of dark trees crossed in front of him, forming a straight line to the left and right.

"There's gotta be a back road up there!" Phil mumbled. He wiped sweat and a trickle of blood from his face. If the road came out of Holly Hill somewhere... The trees swooped down in that direction! He'd be safe! on his way home! He raced up the hill, ignoring the pain, his mind filled with but one thought: A road, a beautiful road. *Please, God!* He burst out of the grass and brush into a clearing, his chest heaving, his eyes darting about desperately. The moon, playful now, skipped between passing dark clouds. But then the last clouds vanished. Phil gulped then whooped with joy. The gravel road, with high shoulders, ran straight and true downhill, towards the neighborhood! Uphill, a few hundred feet from where Phil stood spellbound, it disappeared around a curve.

A low growl, and a challenging "Woof!" broke through to Phil. He peered across the road, frightened but curious. The dog, a big German Shepherd, raised its hind leg and established its territory against a tree. He looked at Phil suspiciously, growled, and scraped his hind legs back and forth in the dirt. He sniffed the air then took two cautious stiff-legged steps towards Phil, his shoulder hairs bristling.

Oh shit! Not this! After all I've been through...

"Come here, boy. Good dog!" Phil held out a hand, palm up, and took two tentative steps towards the wary animal. "Easy, boy, easy, good–"

The dog leaped into the air! Phil fell to his knees, and both his hands tightened around his walking cane, ready to ward off a vicious attack from the monster dog.

Yelping with joy? Phil thought crazily, the dog swung its large tail in a wide arc, turned, lowered its body, and raced away up the hill, howling.

Leery, Phil got up, and cocked his head. He heard a distant whistle and a voice calling. He let out a sigh of relief. The owner of the dog! Obviously the dog's keen hearing had picked up a previous call. Phil wanted to be seen, helped, but then, this could be an enemy. Maybe even Nick and his gang of freaks! Relax, he told himself, it couldn't be.

"Oh no, oh no!" Phil cried. He rose to his feet, staggered to the center of the road, dropped his cane, and ran towards the figure with the streaming hair, coming closer and closer.

"Fritz, you naughty dog! You shouldn't run away like that!" The pale moonlight reflected off the gray gravel and waving treetops and cast dancing shadows on the scolding face. Suddenly the look changed to one of surprise, and then alarm.

"Phil? Phil! It is you. Oh, Phil! What happened to you? You... you look awful. You're hurt! Get away, Fritz! He's still young and playful, Phil, he won't hurt you. Oh! you're scratched all over, and your head! Here, let me help you." She came to him.

"Th-thanks, Marjorie." It was his voice all right. Unreal.

Marjorie? Here? Crazy!

He would wake up soon, still in Guido's den where he had dozed off. He felt dizzy, his breath labored, and he hurt all over. The dog licked his hand, and Marjorie suddenly seemed terrified. She held him tightly around the waist and pulled him to a soft bank by the side of the road. No dream this! He felt her heart thumping against him, and his returning beats. She helped him sit down and said nothing, but seemed apprehensive.

"What are you doing here, Marjorie?" Phil knew he sounded dumb. In response two trucks burst around the bend, heading downhill fast. Marjorie screamed and knocked Phil flat, protecting him with her own body.

* * * *

Earlier in the day at City Hall, Mary Coyne, private secretary, swiveled out of Tim Hoyt's office, nose in the air, affecting an air of cool nonchalance though a curl of an expensive permanent wave drooped.

Sober?

Abruptly an ankle turned and the side of a high-style sling pump scraped the tile floor. "Oops!" Mary Coyne said.

Not sober! Too much to ask, thought Fulvia. But she's coming out of the boss's office, and she wasn't that bad when she went in. Hmmm! Fulvia shrugged and turned her attention back to the morning's mail.

Mary Coyne straightened, carefully put the curl back in place, scratched an armpit, minced carefully over to Fulvia's desk, and leaned heavily on it, bracing herself with both hands.

"Fully?" It was a question, and Fulvia knew what it meant: I want to talk!

"Sure, Mary." Fulvia put the mail down. She saw two puffy red-rimmed eyes, and oval face, a slightly up-tilted small nose; red cheeks, cigarette-stained teeth, and a body that had seen better days. Mary must have been a beauty Fulvia thought. With that blonde hair of hers, she still could be, if only...

"The boss offered me a straight whiskey... double. He said just this once was all right. My, he seemed happy. He had two doubles himself. Said ordinarily he wouldn't drink in the office."

"Of course," Fulvia said. "Anything interesting?" She yawned.

"Oh, you don't get excited about anything, Fully. We're going to be rich! Tim told me that we're now in the construction business, and that he has a deal lined up." She paused, leaning closer. "With an Eye-talian from Columbus Street. A real oily, dumb type."

"Fine, fine." Fulvia turned back to the mail.

"Oh, oh!" Mary Coyne hiccuped, put a hand to her lips.

"You okay?" The letter opener kept slitting away, expertly.

"I don't know! Hold the fort, Fleming, I'm going to the ladies' room."

"Don't worry, Mary, I'll handle things. Take your time."

Mary Coyne looked gratefully at her faithful Fully. "One more thing, Fleming." She tried a secret wink and sly look, but failed, as both eyes closed. She staggered slightly, and said, "The shillelaghs are going to swing. The boss wants to serve notice," another hiccup, "that... oh! I feel awful – that the Eye-talian doesn't double cross..."

Mary Coyne retched, and lunged for the ladies' room.

It was after supper of the same day, and Fulvia was tired... She had put in a full day covering for Mary Coyne, and wasn't at all sure how long Coyne could continue working. She seemed on the verge. Fulvia dried the last of the supper dishes, and nervously looked at the wooden mantel clock on a shelf above the sink as it chimed the hour. Nine o'clock! This was the night for his call... anytime now.

Nine-fifteen. No call. *This has never happened*, Fulvia thought. *So you call him! You've done so in the past when you've had important information, and you have some now. You'll have the initiative, and can use the occasion to finish it with him.* But Fulvia wasn't quite sure how.

Ma, lo faccio (But, I'll do it) she thought bravely. *Basta!* (Enough!)

But first: "Marjorie," she said, "the dog wants to go out. Why don't you take him for a walk. Be back in fifteen minutes, and we will drive to the ice cream store before it closes for banana splits. All right?"

"Okay, Mama! Sounds great! I'll be back... in about twenty minutes."

Fulvia looked quizzically at her daughter. She's so willing tonight! Who can understand the young girls of today? Fulvia smiled, but the smile vanished as she walked into her little living room towards her phone.

The back screen door banged. Ah! Marjorie is gone. Fulvia dialed the private number.

"Hello?" A cautious, tired-sounding voice answered.

"Fulvia."

"Ah, *cara mia.*" Di Anello said, without emotion. "Look, I am busy. Some things need my attention. I will call you back when–"

"No! Now, Massimo! Listen." I do not know what this means, but it may interest you." She recounted what Mary Coyne had blabbed to her, knowing full well that Di Anello would be interested, for she assumed Hoyt intended to 'serve notice' on the head of the Mano Nera, Massimo Di Anello.

"And one more thing, Massimo, I will not be able to..."

Several minutes of quiet listening.

"Yes, Massimo, I'm glad I was able to help. But Massimo–"

Marjorie pulled away from the kitchen wall, her senses reeling, her mother's voice cut off. Only one 'Massimo' in town – Massimo Di Anello! Marjorie knew her mother had been a widow for fourteen years, and deserved a man's love. But Massimo Di Anello is married! Worse, he is a very shady person, maybe a criminal, maybe even (if the whispers on the ledge are correct) head of a gang called the Black Hand! Marjorie shuddered.

Slowly, on feet of cotton, she backed out the screen door, which she had propped open when she came back into the house to eavesdrop. At age thirteen she began wondering why her mother wanted her out of the house, always around nine o'clock. Well, now she knew why... and she also suspected she knew the reason for her mother coming home late from work, or leaving home after supper for 'rush typing' at City Hall that couldn't wait until the next day.

With tears in her eyes and a lump in her throat, Marjorie sped out the door, the young dog Fritz, at her heels. His leash remained in her hand. Suddenly free, the nine-month old pup loped away, tongue lolling happily. Marjorie's mind was on other matters. When she got back, her mother would make distracting conversation, maybe even ask her about the boy she always talked about... Humph! She looked at the leash, absently, and cried, "Fritz! Fritz! Where are you?" Marjorie became frantic. She had to find Fritz! *Oh! Why oh why didn't I put the leash on him?* She knew the answer to that, and she began running, her red hair flying out behind her, almost parallel to the ground.

Back at the house Fulvia hung up her phone, bemused. She had told Di Anello she could no longer spy for him, "You see, Mary Coyne is sick, and is leaving soon, so there is no need for phone calls or our seeing each other any more." He had not threatened, he had not raised his voice. He breathed hard but then hadn't he been doing that when he answered the phone? All he did was wish her well, in a strange voice, and hung up. *So other matters are on his mind. Good, he won't think of me!*

Di Anello did think of Fulvia as he replaced the phone in its cradle. He smiled cynically. Fulvia had been useful in many ways. But now it was time to reorganize, and beautiful Fulvia wasn't on his new organization chart. And, if she now has a suitor how troublesome and unfortunate, for him! But, first things first. He picked up the phone, and dialed long distance – New York. Finished, he again called New York, but a different number. He put in a call to Miami. He spoke briefly and tersely, as in the other calls. At last he leaned back, the grim, tight lines around his mouth relaxing. Arrangements for Oreste's godchild, Gennaro, were now complete. He drummed his long fingers on the table, a pensive but satisfied look on his face. The diner! Do not forget the diner! Picking up the phone, he dialed Sforza's number. By now Vito has surely been caught. If so, a long journey awaits him. One from which he will never return...

Di Anello lit a long stogie, took a big puff, and sighed. He had a new appreciation for the problems of the *mangia palate* when their big corporations reorganized. Not easy! No, not easy at all... moving people around, making new assignments, letting others go... employment terminated. He shook his head sadly. Such is the life of a corporation chief executive!

On the eighth ring, Di Anello heard Sforza's phone being picked up. About time! "Hello, Sforza? Di Anello."

Chapter 18

Phil groaned as his body crashed and rolled into the underbrush, propelled by the force of Marjorie's soft weight. He looked up at her and she clasped a firm hand on his mouth, muffling his question.

"Sh-sh," she whispered, "don't say a word. Don't move!" The alarm and fear in her voice convinced Phil. He obeyed instantly.

The two trucks spun past, picking up speed. From his face-up position Phil caught a glimpse of men on the bed of the first truck, pinned in the glare of the second truck's beams. Were they being jostled by the bumps or were they drunk? The truck flashed past; then the second roared past. Phil heard shouts and curses. Marjorie pushed herself off Phil, got up, and listened intently. She waved a hand at Phil. STAY DOWN! She ran down the road, Fritz romping behind her. She stopped, and again listened. Satisfied, she ran back to a still prostrate and very puzzled Phil.

"Come on, Phil, hurry! I'll help you. Oh! You're so pale. Don't pass out on me, please!"

"I... I won't," Phil said, and he managed a tight, thin grin. "What... was that all about?" he asked. His head whirled, the gash was bleeding again, and his ankle... and now his shoulder, ached.

No wonder she thinks I'm going to pass out!

"Those men work for Tim Hoyt, the mayor's son-in-law. You know," she coaxed, "he runs City Hall."

Phil shook his head, but he recalled his court warehouse nightmarish eavesdropping, and Di Anello's sarcasm when he talked about the 'crooked Politicians' feasting on the good people of the neighborhood.

Marjorie put an arm around Phil's waist, he an elbow on her shoulder. Slowly they walked up the hill, Fritz jumping, licking, and jealous.

"Those two drivers probably delivered booze and stuff," Marjorie said, "and the men there,"she sniffed, her voice low, "sampled the merchandise. Hoyt's got a huge house you know – has big bashes for his cronies. Lots of his men..."

"Marjorie," Phil interrupted, grimacing, "you almost killed me!"

"You could have been," she said crisply, "by the cruds in those trucks."

"Cruds?" They neared the top of the bend, a long, slow S, and in the distance beyond it, Phil saw what looked like a porch light.

"Yes, cruds. Hoyt's tough guys... they guard his house, have soft city jobs, come here once in a while... to get orders, I think. And when they get drunk, they are real nasty."

"But..."

"But nothing. Oh, Phil! You don't live around here, up in the ledge. They would know that. And they don't like–"

"Wops!" Phil finished the sentence for Marjorie.

"Yes! And if they had seen you, you would have been taunted, told you stink of garlic, ordered to run home to... Ginzo land, maybe even beaten up, more than you are. I know those... those–"

"Ignorant bastards! Sorry, Marjorie, it just came out."

"It's all right, Phil. Get it out of your system. Yes, bastards! Like the maniac at the lake! They're all around us, Phil, don't you see? On the ledge and below it. One of these days something terrible will happen. You'll see! Maybe they cooked up something nasty tonight – Phil? Phil! Ohhhhhh!"

"Mama, come quick, help me, help me!"

Phil sagged against Marjorie, who, afraid he would drop to the ground, tenaciously held onto him with both hands, pulling him forward.

Through a buzzing dark blanket that tried to settle over his head, Phil thought he saw two dark-haired, handsome women running towards him. Then the two became one, then two again, as if on the ends of a rubber band. They merged once more. It's only one lady, he told himself, and forced a smile at his foolishness. The blanket closed over his head, and it was cold, very cold. Warm, strong hands grasped him, and he was being dragged. Or, was it carried? He really had to figure that one out. Voices murmured. He passed out..

Phil opened his eyes and tried to bring the blurry

mass above him into focus. Hair... red hair. And wide, big green eyes, set in a young, lightly freckled face, worried, leaning over him. His forehead felt cool, good. He touched it, saw the tip of a damp cloth, and she took his hand in hers.

"Marjorie?" he asked, beginning to remember the trucks, the road...

"Yes, it's me!" Marjorie said, her face lighting up. She ran her fingers over his face, and gently through his hair. "You're going to be fine Phil, fine. I know it!" She came closer to him.

Another female voice, accented and melodious: "Good! Your color is coming back, Filippo, and – Marjorie, *per piacere!* – Please! Let him rest, at least until Guido gets here."

Bewildered, Phil raised his aching head and felt the bandage over his cut. He saw he was on a richly textured couch in a living room. Marjorie had backed away from him, but a strikingly attractive woman with dark hair knelt at the couch, and carefully placed pieces of ice, wrapped in a dish cloth, on his ankle.

"I am Fulvia Fleming, Marjorie's mother," she said. Phil was familiar with the accent, and he remembered that Marjorie was half Italian.

"I'm sorry for all the trouble I caused, Mrs. Fleming. But I just had to get away from the park, and–"

"No trouble at all, young man. I very happy to help you, Marjorie's friend–"she smiled, hesitated, frowned slightly, took a deep breath, and said in soft voice, "and a friend of Guido's."

Not comprehending, Phil heard the sound of a car pulling up to the house.

"When you came out of your faint you asked about Guido. You see, Marjorie told me what happened at the Di Anello house, after we took you in and laid you down." She swallowed, and with a trace of a smile continued, "You are big... and heavy, Filippo. I did not know that Marjorie was so strong."

"Oh, Mama!"

Phil missed the subtle exchange between mother and daughter. "Guido... here?" he asked. "How... how–?"

"Easy, Filippo! I assumed he still at home, no? So,

after we put you down, I phone Di Anello's, and Guido answer. He said he all right, and would be right over with family doctor who fix him up."

"And here I am!" Guido heard Fulvia's last sentence as he came into the living room. On his heels was a bustling little man in a dark, rumpled business suit. He wore pince-nez glasses, had a pencil-thin mustache, and a big mole on the side of his nose. He carried a black bag, and seemed impatient.

"Sit there," he commanded, motioning Guido to a chair, away from Phil, "and be still." Guido did as he was told, but he winked at Phil.

"I am Doctor Rocco Priore," the doctor said in a booming baritone voice. So much noise from such a little man, Phil thought. "Now, let me see what's wrong, young man." Doctor Priore approached Phil, opening his black bag. Thirty minutes later Doctor Priore straightened, coughed, wiped his brow, and dabbed at his lips with a huge bandanna.

"You are as healthy as a young bull," he said. "But even a bull gets exhausted in heat and fright. And the stumbling through the woods–" He shook his head, and began closing his black bag.

"Two sutures, ah, stitches, in your head, like Guido. Some cleaning, antiseptic, and... your ankle... will heal." A knowledgeable nod. "You have sprained it, Filippo. Stay off the foot as much as you can, eh? Here, take two of these now and two more in the morning. Call me, tell me how you feel. Guido has my number. No," he seemed to be speaking to himself now, "there is no concussion. A young bull! Well, Guido, satisfied? Come, I must take you home now and go home myself. You must rest too, my headstrong fellow. Your father may be waiting for us."

Guido grinned from ear to ear. "I don't know about that. I phoned him at the court warehouse, Phil, after Mrs. Fleming called me about you. I told my father I was okay, and that you needed a doctor. He said Doctor Priore should check you after he took care of me. I wasn't supposed to go with him, but I did. You're my best friend! Anyway, my father won't be home. When he goes back out at night he's busy a long time."

Marjorie thought she saw her mother fidget and blush slightly.

The sound of another car squealing to a halt distracted Marjorie. A car door slammed; footsteps on the front porch; a loud knock, and Fulvia went to the door. "Yes?" Her voice quavered.

"Is dere a guy named Phil Martello here? I'm supposed to drive him home. Da boss told me to. I drive for him now, once in a while." He was young, crew cut, and his white teeth contrasted sharply against a deep summer tan. His smile was meant for Marjorie, who had come up next to her mother. The young man sized her up, his eyes lingered and probed and left no doubt... Marjorie didn't like it. She stepped behind Fulvia. *What coarse nerve!* she thought. *And we're supposed to know who 'da boss' is. Oo-fa!*

Guido knew. "Hey," he said, "great! My father thinks of everything. Wow! But... I've never seen you before. What's your name?"

"I'm Luke Peris – Guido?" Guido nodded. Luke's macho deflated. "Glad ta meet ya, Mr. Di Anello."

"Guido, call me Guido. Where do you work?"

"Oh yeah, in Parks and Rec, in da office, though I'm outside a lot. But I'll probably work all da time for da – I mean, your father, pretty soon. Dat's what Natale tells me. Know him?"

Guido waved a hand. "Hmm, so the East Side Export-Import Company is hiring people?" He raised his voice in rhetorical question.

"I dunno. Guess so," Luke responded anyway, rather lamely.

"Well," Doctor Priore said, relieved that he wouldn't have to drive Phil home, "coming Guido? Lots to do, lots to do." He bustled to the front door, opened it, and waited.

"No thanks, Doc. I'll go with Phil."

"So will I!" Marjorie said. She darted an imploring look at Fulvia.

"And so must I, then," Fulvia said, in a resigned voice. "You will come with me Marjorie, in our car. Is that understood? No room for debate!"

"Hey dat's good Mrs. Fleming, cuz I couldn't drive ya back. See, I gotta return da limo ta Natale's ah, business place, after I dump Phil, and den I'm off work. Dere are tings I gotta do." Luke Peris blew on his nails, polished them on his purple sport shirt.

"How about that, Phil?" Guido beamed, "you get a royal escort home. Oh, Luke, after you dump Phil and me off, I think you better wait a while in the car for me. I'll need a ride home, and I don't want to take Mrs. Fleming out of the way. Whatever you gotta do... she can wait. Right?"

"Huh? Oh sure, sure... Guido. 'She', ha ha! Yeah, a course! Let'er wait, I always say!" Luke didn't seem at all upset by Guido's command. Doctor Priore had heard and seen enough. He shook his head back and forth slowly, and left the house alone, muttering under his breath, "*Ma, sono tutti imbecilli!* (But they are all imbeciles!)"

The black limo crunched up the gravel road, turned left into the tenement court, and stopped beneath the basketball hoop near the empty-can bin. Magically, though the hour was late, heads popped out of windows, back doors opened, people came out, gawked, and the tenement erupted in a babble of voices.

"Look, there's Filippo," shrieked Amalfia, unable to keep her voice down to a reasonable level. "He's hurt! And oh! all the people with him! *È una parada!* (It's a parade!)"

Upstairs, in Phil's flat, Sebastiano had just hung up the phone, his talk with Di Anello over. When Di Anello identified himself, Sebastiano was both thrilled and shocked. Then, as Di Anello calmly recited the events of the evening, Sebastiano broke out in a cold sweat and his hands trembled. He was relieved to hear that Phil was all right, and would soon be home in one of Di Anello's limos... "the ones we use for the races."

"Our sons are heroes," Di Anello had said. "Family heroes. And the unfortunate incidents, as they are family matters, will of course be resolved by the family, and only the family. Understood?"

Sebastiano understood. He agreed to say nothing, and wait for his son indoors. No need to disturb the tenement.

Both Di Anello and Sebastiano had much on their minds, and neither one gave the tenement a second thought. If they had, they would have realized that the tenement was never totally asleep. It was a living, pulsing organism, whose many eyes and ears missed nothing, no matter what the time of day or night.

And so, when Amalfia's piercing voice ruptured the quiet, humid night, Sebastiano and Rosa bounded out of the house and down the stairs. Little Al, having trouble falling asleep in the heat, followed, rubbing his eyes.

Phil sat quietly in a kitchen chair, exhausted. Doctor Priore's pills worked! The moist heat of the excited bodies around him on this sticky night added to his discomfort. Even the ceiling light bulb radiated heat at him.

He retold his strange evening adventure to the increasing number of tenement dwellers surrounding him, among which was Amalfia, in a flowery housecoat, and Grace Noci, fingering and apron, her hair now loose around her shoulders (strange, she looks different without a bun on her head). His own parents looked drawn and concerned. Little brother Al sat cross-legged at his feet, mouth open, eyes brilliant stars. Vic, who had bolted out of the house at Amalfia's fist screech, stood close, talking to Guido. And Guido; insisted that Phil tell his story, when Sebastiano said Phil was 'too tired'. Phil wondered about his father's reticence, but Guido prevailed, and how Guido smiled and his lips moved in synch with Phil, when Phil told of the grim tussle with Vito in the den!

"And then he smacked me, right here," Guido interrupted Phil. "And I blacked out... But Phil got away." He looked around the kitchen, saw admiring faces, and got a 'Bravo, Guido' from someone. He acknowledged the praise with a modest shrug. What a ham! Phil thought. No wonder he wanted me to talk! But was he saying too much?

How different Marjorie and her mother reacted when Phil mentioned how they had helped him – eyes modestly downcast, hands clasped in front of them. Someone urged them to say something. Fulvia shook her head, bowed and lifted a hand towards Phil, the gesture understood.

And Mona (was he too tired to see straight?), sneering at Marjorie and getting a toss of the head and a nose-in-the-air rebuff. Mrs. Fleming looked at them both, an amused expression on her face. Still in her office clothes, too. No time to change, Phil guessed. Neat lady! And the other ladies, how they stare at Mrs. Fleming! Bet they wished they looked and dressed like her!

"Come on, Phil, don't stop. Tell us... ss-ta... about the fight in the park again. You didn't say who they were. Didn't you recognize them?"

Phil snapped back. "Not again, Vic!" And cautiously, "No, I didn't recognize them. It was dark. One guy grabbed me from behind, and as I said before they began fighting among themselves. I broke loose when they knocked each other down and began rolling around. Heck!" Phil swallowed and licked his lips–" I wanted to get the heck out of there – make it to the ledge. Anyway, those guys were probably hoboes, drunk on cheap booze." Phil searched Grace Noci's placid face – no reaction, he was glad he had left out a few important details. So Nick had not come home yet! And Longcoat and Little Angelo? None of his concern. He glanced at Guido, who seemed to read his mind. Guido examined the plaster ceiling with rapt interest, and he frowned as if he had discovered a rat hole. The message to Phil was clear. He had said enough.

"Hey," Guido spoke up, "I have to go! My driver is downstairs, waiting. So good night everybody! And Phil... thanks, for everything. See you!"

"*Un momento*," Sebastiano said, working his mustache nervously, "those men running in the park, Filippo, were sent for Vito, not you." He paused, breathed heavily, looked at Guido. "I know because your father phoned me a short while ago. You see... Vito was not caught. The fight Filippo mentioned distracted the men, and Vito melted away in the darkness."

There wasn't a sound in the steamy kitchen.

"*Un altra cosa, molto importante* (One more very important thing)." Everyone seemed to lean forward, for Sebastiano had the confidence of...

"What has been said in this room tonight must remain in this room, for many reasons I am not at liberty to disclose. *Avete capito?* (Have you understood?)"

The tenement denizens assured Sebastiano their lips were sealed. Fulvia Fleming said nothing, her face impassive. Then awkward silence, broken by: "Gee whiz! Who knows what evil lurks in the hearts of men? The Shadow knows! Hahahahaha!" Little Al Martello looked proud, for what he thought was a great moment for his imitation of the weekly Blue Coal radio program.

No one laughed. To Al that was worse than the half-hearted backhand slap which his father administered. It was an unspoken signal, and Guido left quickly, in a sober mood now. Others shuffled away, heads bowed. Fulvia looked at Marjorie, and nodded towards the door. Marjorie glanced at Mona, who made no move to leave. Marjorie pouted and said, "Phil, I hope—"

The back door burst inwards, and a loud hoarse voice cut her short, "Grace, you come down quick. Someting bad he happen!" In came Saverio Noci, preceded by the fetid odor of stale sweat and sour wine. He staggered into the kitchen, bleary eyed. His underwear, a stained union suit which he wore winter and summer, protruded over an old pair of baggy pants with no belt.

Grace Noci looked at her husband, and flushed. "Saverio, wake up! Whasa matta wid you, eh?" She turned to Sebastiano and gasped apologetically, "He work hard now... get up early. Got no time..."

"*Mugliere*, you listen to me! " He waved his right hand in circles around his right ear. "Nicola, he eesa hurt. He come home, say he go fast and he fall off a *bicicletta*... How you say, eh?"

"Bike!" prompted Al.

"Sì, *biciletta*!" Exasperated, Saverio switched to his native tongue. "He is cut, bruises everywhere. He may have lost a tooth, One eye is closed. Come, wife, come, he needs your help. You too, Mona."

Grace left hurriedly, emitting a low cry. Mona turned her back on him, and looked Phil straight in the eyes. She smiled ever so slightly, and with a swing of a hip at Marjorie, left. Fulvia restrained a seething Marjorie, and they too left, but not before a flowery speech of thanks from Sebastiano and an offer of food from Rosa. Marjorie's hand was held out to Phil, which he squeezed, twice.

An hour later, Phil lay on his bed, uncovered, his hands clasped behind his head. He was sweating though he was wearing only his boxer shorts. Thoughts passed through his mind with kaleidoscopic quickness until, dozing, they became a dark, undulating sticky mass, with neither shape nor form. Why did he let himself get so tangled up with *them*? Whether he wanted to or not he had been touched by their long fingers, a touch of the damned! And now his family too, and Marjorie, lovely Marjorie! It seemed that no matter what he did – *Gee! maybe there is something to the superstition of the Evil Eye! Where is it all going to end?* And he realized, with a pang of regret, that he should have listened to Sergeant Sam Pizzuta... He tossed drunkenly, then fell asleep...

About the time Phil thought of him Sergeant Sam Pizzuta was royally pissed. He was standing next to the bandstand under a sugar maple tree in Institute Park, three solid miles away from the neighborhood, on the west side of town. Yankee country. A good place for a clandestine meeting, but it didn't look as though there was going to be such a meeting this night, if that's what Pizzuta was hoping for. Muttering to himself he left the shadow of the maple, then took four steps towards his car parked on a nearby gravel lane. Maybe, he thought, he had made a mistake to trust the bugger!

"Hey, Sergeant, wait up! It's me!"

Sergeant Pizzuta stiffened, then turned slowly... "Damn you! Where the fuck have you been? You're over an hour late. When I tell you to meet me..."

"Hey, hold on Sam! I got real good reasons fa bein' late, and dat's no shit! Wait till I tell ya what happened and why!"

Luke Peris, now-and-then driver for Di Anello, and a promising young mobster, was late. Only his impressive credentials had kept Pizzuta waiting so long, and Pizzuta thought of them as he fretted. Luke Peris, incorrigible in grade school, finally attacked two teachers with a janitor's coal shovel, inflicting much bodily harm, and ended up in reform school. Let go, he sampled petty thefts and later graduated to stealing expensive cars. Caught he got a stern lecture, and thirty days in the county jail. His basic training completed, he gravitated, like a moth flirting with flame, to the feckless lower Columbus Street crowd, and soon to Sforza's Diner, where his talents were known. Di Anello's net of informers had a few holes, so Luke was referred to Natale, who made the necessary financial arrangements for Luke's it employment in the city's Parks and Recreation Department.

But Luke, restless with his cushy job, one fine night went along with two slope-browed companions for a 'little fun' near the city line. He didn't like the drift of the conversation, wondered, got scared, and asked to be let out of the car. The hoods did so, not very gently, calling him very colorful names involving his private parts and his ancestry. This was fine with Luke. He didn't like guns, and the night's entertainment would most likely involve them, it seemed. Why would the crums have toted them? Happy with his decision Luke tried to hitch a ride and he got one from a city police car, the occupants of which were not friendly. He was frisked and cuffed.

Luke was walking a few blocks from where there had been an attempted payroll robbery at a small garter manufacturing company. The owner, who kept guns handy at payroll time, was killed, along with one robber. The other one got away, minus the payroll. It remained clutched tightly in the dead owner's hand.

Later, Sergeant Pizzuta had been delighted to meet Luke, a product of the neighborhood like himself, and he had made the most of it. He sat down next to Luke on his jail cell cot.

"You see, Luke," Pizzuta said, "it's murder – in cold blood."

"But I wasn't wid dem jerks!" Luke protested.

"You were in the vicinity, Luke. And one of the cops recognized you. You're small time, but this once you really screwed up. With a record like yours," Pizzuta shook his head, and held up a folder, "two and two makes four, and you get twenty years. Who knows? Maybe even the electric chair." Pizzuta puffed his cheeks and blew out a breath. The bluff worked. Sam saw Luke's face tighten and blanche... "There's a way out for you, Luke. Listen!"

Luke did. He wasn't fond of electrical shocks. And, being a prudent young man, he took Pizzuta's 'way out'. He became Sam Pizzuta's man inside Di Anello's mob for up to two years, time enough for Luke to progress and give Pizzuta information to help put Di Anello and his thugs away for good.

It's an awful long time, and stool pigeons get killed!

No sweat. You'll make it, Luke. Remember though, no one comes back alive once they sit in the state's real stool, the one connected to all the electricity. No exceptions! Luke forgot his objections. He was released... 'Insufficient evidence'. The diner boys crowed! Great guy, Luke!

Now, Luke told Pizzuta why he was late. Pizzuta smiled. Jimmy and Luke together, helping him penetrate Di Anello's wall of secrecy. And Sam Pizzuta would be right there when the wall crumbled. *But Phil Martello is in danger, and could be hurt, bad. So, what the hell can be done about it?*

PART II

Chapter 19

More than a week passed, and as Sergeant Pizzuta had predicted the tenements across from the railroad yard were searched, leisurely, cautiously, so as not to arouse the cop on the beat's suspicion. The word went out to the neighborhood stores (Jimmy's included) for any change in customer buying patterns. More wine? Beer? Gobs of cold cuts? Nothing. Sforza's boys were now down to the last few tenements, and all looked grim. Jimmy volunteered to help in the search at night, and Sforza accepted. Hell, he had hunted Huns during the war, hadn't he? We can use the help. Besides, with the changes coming up we want his store as another outlet... He'll go along – money is music!

Pizzuta, well-hidden with two other detectives he had convinced to donate their free time, watched and waited. The soot-encrusted tenements, over a period of three nights, were thoroughly searched. Again... nothing.

"Hey," Jimmy said on the third night, hunched over a cup of coffee black at the diner with his discouraged squad, "maybe he's hiding out in the railroad yard. It's worth a quick look-see."

Sforza looked up from behind the counter. "I don't tink so, Jimmy. Vito likes his comfort too much ta stay dere dis long. But I bet he hopped a freight with a couple of hoboes and is off out west someplace. Maybe even Los Angeles. I heard he got friends dere. Yeah, we'll send out da word. We'll get the fat fuck yet. Anyway, tanks for ya help. Say, Jimmy, c'mere and listen. I got a proposition for ya. I tink you'll like it."

Vito wasn't in the railroad yard, nor had he hopped a freight out of town. He sat on a low bench in Nino's wine cellar, chewing on a piece of bread wrapped around a hunk of provolone cheese. A gallon jug of red wine, half-empty, nestled close to his right foot. From here, or the empty boxcar, where he hid from time to time, he would do what he had to do – get that lousy Punk Phil! Then the world would be right for him! He lifted the jug and looked at it. Its contents came from the remaining oak barrel. Last year's wine. Shit, hadn't he helped Nino make it, pulling the long solid metal bar of the wine press, squeezing the must, extracting every ounce of juice? A course!

He glanced at two upright barrels and staggered over to them. He sniffed the fragrance of the fermenting Zinfandel liquid, looked at the bubbles, then grunted with satisfaction. This year too he had helped Nino make new wine. So Nino owed him, and Vito Amorusi was here to collect...

Days ago, he didn't remember how many, after crawling out the opposite end of the railroad yard, he had headed up a dark, wooded road. Nino lived in a white frame house at the top, away from the prevailing wind that carried the train soot. He lived alone, for he was a bachelor – and he had that wine cellar. He worked seven days a week, went on buying trips, was gone a hell of a lot. Great! Vito had found the house locked. He dimly remembered cellar windows. He struggled hard, and it came to him. Nino had said he planned to install bars on his cellar windows, which protruded half-way above the foundation. Nino had laughed about protecting his wine, and his cache of hoarded food.

The two side cellar windows were barred. Dismayed, Vito had crept to the back of the house, behind which lay a field used for sandlot baseball. Near the last cellar window he had turned his ankle on a beat-up baseball, its string innards dangling loosely. He had been about to angrily throw it as far as he could, when he saw the sheen of glass. No bars! Nino had not finished the job! Carefully he had broken the glass with a rock, reached in, unlatched the window, and squeezed himself through.

Grunting and leaning back outside, he had placed the baseball in front of the broken window. Should Nino look, and Vito hoped he wouldn't – at least not until Phil had been wiped out – Nino would figure that kids had busted the window with a fly ball or a hot grounder. Smiling, Vito had gone upstairs, cleaned up, smeared himself with iodine and swallowed several glasses of wine to soothe the fire in his chest.

Later, he had glanced around the cellar. He could

easily hide-even if Nino were home – behind the stacked cases of olive oil, tins of ham, breads, anchovies, and even behind the row of hanging cheeses in their mesh nets, side by side in a cool corner with salami, capocollo, and other prepared meats. The reason for all this hoarding, Vito recalled vaguely, was Nino's concern about a second world war; Italy's coming war with Abyssinia was just a skirmish, he had assured Vito during the recent winemaking.

"I tot da Wops are supposed ta fight da Ethiopians," Vito had said to that, rather puzzled.

"Abyssinia is just an ancient name for Ethiopia," Nino had replied indulgently. But then he shook his head, looked at Vito, and tittered.

Vito had grunted, not comprehending, but he didn't like Nino's insult, for he figured that's what it was, and the sidelong glance he shot at Nino was decidedly unfriendly. Yes, Nino owed him all right!

Comfortable and confident in his cellar hide-out, Nino stayed hidden during the day, his bruises and cuts healing, his body satiated with Nino's food and wine. But he was alert for a sucker punch – Nino's car crunching up the gravel path beside the house during the day. It had happened once, when Nino came stomping down the stairs to the cellar, scooped up a jug of wine, and hurried back upstairs. Vito barely had time to hide, and gave Nino's back a baleful look as Nino left. Vito knew when he would have the run of the house. On days Nino left for overnight trips he would throw a suitcase on the bed and stack clothing in it. Coming home in the late afternoon Nino would pack and leave in less than an hour, suitcase in hand. Vito, creeping upstairs, watched and grinned; then he inspected every room for traps. He found none.

But when Nino was home at night Vito didn't press his luck. A loud snore, a broken jug, and he would be discovered. So when darkness fell he left quietly from the cellar window, lugged along food and a blanket, and headed for the railroad yard. And yet! a longing. One night he chanced going to his own room on Columbus Street. Familiar figures skulked about, poking flashlights into tenements, talking softly. At his tenement, Skinny and someone he didn't know, looking about, caught in the silver-black of moonlight, caused him to slink back to the yard, hiding as he went. Old friends who didn't look friendly anymore passed by him.

"Da heat's still on, gotta wait some more, and figure some way to get the fuck out a here," he told himself, unhappily.

Chapter 20

Sunday, September 15. A balloon sun, low in the hazy afternoon sky, cast a Venusian glow on the earth below. Indian summer, the quiet omen of change, had arrived.

The soft swish of little waves at the shoreline of the lake added a somnolent effect, and birds rose and circled and basked in warm thermal currents. Phil, flat on his stomach, toes dug into the cool sand at the lake's edge, looked up, yawned, and grinned. Next to him, Marjorie was on her side facing him, dozing... her red-topped head cradled in both arms.

"You're going to be well-done on one side, Marjorie," he said.

Marjorie sighed, turned onto her other side, mumbled, and continued dozing.

Next to her, toes-to-head, was Carmela. And in order, next to Carmela, Vic, Lucy (friend of Marjorie) and Guido, in echelon formation, so that Guido's feet and knees were in the water. All were relaxed and stock still, their languor brought on, Phil thought, by the spell of the day.

It had been Marjorie's idea to work on tans one more time before the gaudily covered leaves fell and cold weather arrived. She had phoned Guido first, innocently asking if he thought the idea good. If he got Phil to go, and Vic too, she knew she could convince Carmela to come along, and by the way, a friend of hers, Lucy Burns, blonde and pretty, would love to join in the fun. Guido bit... Great idea! Matter of fact, he would ask Little Angelo, who now drove for his father, to drop them off at the lake and pick them up later, if that sounded okay with Marjorie. It did. But... when could Little Angelo be available? She held her breath.

"Today and tomorrow. After that, he's gonna be busy."

"Oh, fine, let's go tomorrow," she had replied, in a matter-of-fact voice. When she hung up the phone she cried, "Yippee!"

Mona would not be invited. She had to work late Saturday at Handelman's, for the Italo-Ethiopian war seemed to be days away and the inhabitants of the neighborhood were buying up all imported Italian goods. And maybe Mona would have to go in Sunday to restock shelves or something. Anyway, Marjorie had already asked Lucy, and... she realized, she didn't care for Mona's company anymore. For some reason... Marjorie's conscience... was clear.

Now Phil pushed closer to the water's edge, wiggled his toes in the tiny waves, the cold wash sending pleasant tingles coursing through his body. The soft mound in the white bathing suit next to him moved. Drowsy, he saw Marjorie jiggling and rotating her hips slowly, carving a more comfortable indentation in the sand for her bottom.

Why, she isn't skinny at all! Phil mused. But then, he had never really looked before. He took her hand. She murmured, but continued dozing. He looked at her, all curves in the sand, sighed, and turned over on his back. He blinked at the strange cast of the sky, and little transparent bubbles flitted across his eyes like so many minnows. He closed his eyes, thought of Marjorie, his friends, the past few weeks. Maybe, just maybe, as summer turned into fall, his luck would change for the better, his ordeals... over.

Phil had remained home after the park and ledge incidents, sleeping late and regaining his strength, his injuries healing. He had spent much time with Vic, listening to the radio, jazz records, and dabbling with Vic's model airplane building, which didn't interest him much. Strange! Guido had come by a few times, and they talked of Vito, baseball, Jimmy's Silver Star, pulp heroes... and girls. Marjorie kept the talk of girls going by phoning several times. Phil even phoned her once. And Mona... continued to be Mona. Bubbly, in perpetual motion, she worked long hours at Handleman's.

"School's open soon, and I want all new clothes," she had told Phil. "Lots of new boys to meet." She had sighed wistfully, giving him a look that asked, "What-are-you-going-to-do-about-it?"

"How's your brother doing?" Phil recalled asking, countering her ploy.

"He's in worse shape than you are," she had said, that knowing smile playing about her full mouth. "Must have been some bicycle crash, huh Phil?" Her eyes sparkled. Somehow she knew, Phil thought. Western Union had much to learn from this neighborhood!

Vito? Whisked away into outer space, Mars or Venus maybe, or so it seemed to Phil. He had disappeared, but if he were still around, and alive, Guido had informed Phil, nodding sagely, he would very definitely be caught. Phil had been relieved, and his fear of the kill-crazed ex-pug lessened.

Phil's thoughts now seemed to hover high above his prostrate body. Marjorie and the rest slept or dozed on, although Guido and Lucy seemed to have moved closer. Phil smiled. A cold wave splashed him, and he thought of Little Angelo and Longcoat. He recalled how Guido had vividly described Little Angelo's tearful pleading before Natale, who sat grim-faced in the rear of the religious article store when Longcoat and Little Angelo were brought in by Sforza's men after the fruitless search for Vito.

Little Angelo's story had been believed when, later that night, Di Anello returned Natale's phone call and confirmed that indeed Little Angelo told the truth about trying to help Phil escape from Longcoat and that tenement knucklehead, Nick Noci. Little Angelo knew Phil was Guido's friend so, "he would not have done other than what he tells you, eh Natale?"

Natale readily agreed, and Little Angelo, counseled not to stray from family business, was promoted to drive to the racetracks and on occasion, for Di Anello himself. Nick? The young plotter had been told by Skinny to "get lost and stay the hell away from the grownups around here, or else."

Phil chuckled as he recalled Guido's wide smile and gesticulating hands with their long musician's fingers, acting out the warning.

And what of Longcoat? What a name! He hadn't fared well at the hands of his judge, jury, and almost executioner, hollow-eyed Natale.

"You want to make your next birthday?" Natale had

rumbled at Longcoat.

Longcoat had assured Natale that he did.

"Den pay attention to your job and business. And stay da fuck away from Nick and other strangers. You ought a be ashamed; aced by a punk like dat. Aw right, you got one more chance. Don't muff it. *Capito*?"

Longcoat swore on all his sainted ancestors' graves that he understood.

Guido pulled no punches. He told the stories straight. Everything out in the open, between friends. Nice. And nice to be protected. *But look where it is coming from!* The little voice inside him hammered. And so, though he liked Guido, what of his vow to get *them*, and his deal with Jimmy? Mixed feelings about what was happening to him! Well, he'd pull out of the deal with Jimmy. That was in line with Pizzuta's advice, but he couldn't quit completely, for no one knew as much as he did about *them*, first hand!

And their influence had changed his family! His father; three new suits, an expensive Dobbs felt and two straw hats, and now the barber trimmed and waxed his mustache and he had his shoes shined by the urchins of Columbus Street. They delighted to see him coming out of the big market. He always paid more than the going rate. He talked expansively of a new car 'by the end of the year'. And how he strutted when he walked, smoking a big Havana cigar taken from the stores of warehouses packed with scarce goods. And more streamed in. With Nino busy, or out of town, Sebastiano Martello waved the baton!

And little brother Al, mesmerized before a new twelve-tube console radio; turning dials, changing bands, and squealing with delight at new discoveries.

And his mother, polishing her new refrigerator and enamel stove, as white as... as Marjorie's bathing suit there. And Mama set the tenement buzzing when she came home one day with her light brown hair done up in a marcel hair-do-with many waves. A movie star she thinks she is – *Madonna!*

Phil accepted his family's prosperity to an extent. His father had always worked hard, and his mother had always scrimped and done without. Was there a catch?

He wondered, and he suddenly felt his arms itch. Images that he'd rather forget surfaced, and a faceless fear gripped him...

He had woken early, for a long slow walk to the local public high school with Vic. The other guys would leave later, but would catch up. Phil's ankle, almost healed, required his earlier departure. As he dressed he heard a truck come to a stop out front.

His father, not quite ready to leave, said, "Filippo, go on the front porch. Ask the driver to come upstairs for a minute."

"Sure, Pa, what's his name?"

"Luccio. He works for me at the warehouse near Lofton Height."

But it wasn't the heavy jowls, the face moles, nor the heavy-lidded expressionless eyes that brought Luccio sharply into focus. It was... that damned introduction–

"Luccio," Pa said, coming out of the bathroom, "meet my son, Filippo. *Signor* Di Anello considers him a hero, and he is Guido's good friend." He pursed his lips, shrugged, and nodded dramatically.

An electrifying response from Luccio. He snapped to attention, as if pulled taut by a puppeteer.

"It gives me great pleasure to meet you," he had said, bowing. Actually bowing, and speaking correct Italian, no dialect! "I must tell Slick of this great honor when I see him later today."

"Sure. Glad to meet you, too," Phil remembered he had said in English. And then, hastily, his father and Luccio had left, Luccio walking backwards, bowing, cap in hand.

And Phil, now recalling the icy band around his head and the sinking weight in his gut, knew why he had felt that way. It was obvious. No spoken word was necessary. His father was considered a member, or at least a close ally. And as for himself... closer yet! Hadn't Guido said they should prick fingers and exchange blood to seal their friendship? An innocent gesture? Perhaps. Anyway, it hadn't happened... yet. If it did, wouldn't he be a young crown prince, one to be respected, a blood brother to Guido, to them, the hated *Mano Nera*... the Black Hand?

Holy mackerel! It just couldn't be! No way! He'd talk to Guido. He turned convulsively and saw Marjorie, head tilted, looking at him. She sat facing him, legs drawn up to her chest, arms clasped around her knees. A large white towel, draped around her shoulders, contrasted with the freckles multiplying on and around her nose.

"Does thinking of Mona bother you that much?" Soft, pungent... hurt.

"Huh?" Phil slid back from his somber reverie, pulled himself up onto the grass next to Marjorie, and shaded his eyes. She's prettier than the girls on the calendars in Jimmy's store, he told himself.

"Well?"

"No, Marjorie. But... I was daydreaming. I got carried away, I guess."

"Oh, I see. Say," – as if she had just thought of it- "did you ever see Mona at Handleman's? You know, for that pat of butter, and things?"

"Uh, yeah, sort of – when I was able to walk there." Oo-wa! How did she know about that?

"You know how Mona talks," Marjorie hadn't missed Phil's startled expression. "She called me to tell me you had gone to see her."

"And... and... there were no 'things'," he said uncomfortably.

"Phil, just how old are you, anyway? Mona likes older boys, you know."

"I know. A couple were at the butter counter when I was there."

"Oh my!" Marjorie looked thoughtfully at her twitching toes.

"I'll be seventeen in less than a year," Phil blurted. *Wi-i-se guy!* he heard his inner voice reprove. But he had not lied, he assured himself. He turned sixteen last week. So there! He felt as if he were sticking his tongue out... at himself. And then he felt confused, ill-at-ease, as if he were a small child again. God, he'd rather be fighting Nick!

"Gee, we're very close, in... in age I mean, just a few months apart." Marjorie got up, stretched luxuriously. Phil got up too, and for the first time noticed that they were alone. His eyes darted across the lake and he saw only the shadows of the trees on the water, lengthening, coming closer as the orange sun sank in the western sky.

"Phil, our sister school is having a fall dance." She paused, ran a hand nervously over her hair. Her eyes and voice softened, and out it came, a modulated caress of pubescent desire, "Phil, I want you... to take me to that dance. Will you?"

The tendrils of a long, flat cloud drifted and caught fire above the blaze of the low sun. Phil looked, and saw figures coming out of the edge of the woods across the lake, holding hands, and someone whistling. They came towards him, laughing, ignoring the few people nearby. It seemed all in slow motion, in harmony with the brilliant cloud wisps above and the shadows below. The scene would vaporize and disappear, like so much gossamer! Beautiful!

"Phil?"

"Sorry, Marjorie. I was... ah, distracted by our happy group coming back. Marjorie, your school is up on the ledge. Those creeps we met in the two trucks near your house – and their friends. You said that..."

"They'll be off celebrating," Marjorie interrupted, "at a Tim Hoyt clambake. Anyway, they wouldn't dare do anything to upset Sister Agnes. She can be a terror. Besides," she hesitated, "my mother will drive us. She's going to be a chaperone. Guido and Lucy will already be in the car when we pick you up." Marjorie took a deep breath, looked away...

"But... but, your mother's car is too small for..."

Marjorie turned abruptly and cut in, "We'll use Guido's car."

"Guido? He's... he's going to the dance?"

"Oh yes. Lucy asked him when they were walking in the woods." Marjorie smiled sweetly and continued, "Carmela asked Vic... in the woods. Vic said yes. So, both guys are going."

"Yeah, I guess so," Phil agreed. The whistler, now closer, was Guido. Vic had his arm around Carmela. A done thing!

"Uh, Marj? You know, I can't..."

"Dance?"

"Yah." Sheepishly.

"All arranged. Neither can your friends. We'll practice in Guido's den."

"Gee! You are quite an arranger!"

"Oh, I don't know," Marjorie said, "I'm not sure I
have a date for the dance." She ran a foot through the
grass.

"Yes, you have... me!" Phil's fervor surprised both of
them.

"Thanks Phil. You'll love the dance, I promise,"
Marjorie said. She kissed him on the cheek, her smile
wide.

"Marjorie," Phil took both her hands in his, "how
did you know..." Lucy and Camela tugged Marjorie away,
and heads together, they whispered and giggled. A tall
red head, and two smaller girls, a blonde, a brunette.
Nice picture, Phil thought.

"Say," he said to Vic, who was at his side, grinning,
"How come you all went off to the woods without letting
me know?"

"Aw, you and Marj were so cozy, and we didn't want
to disturb you. Besides, Lucy and Carmela said they
wanted to ask us something, and I wanted to show Guido
where we were hiding that time after you had knocked
Vito woozy and you and Mona ran like crazy to meet
us."

"Uh huh. Yah... I'm sure that's why you went into
the woods."

"Vic's dark eyes flashed. "Well, ss-ta, ss-ta- know
what?"

"No, what?"

"Carmela found an old metal screw and gave it to
me. I showed it to Lucy, and boy," he came close to Phil,
cupped his hand to his mouth, and whispered, "she told
me why Carmela gave it to me, and that Carmela..."

He didn't have time to unravel the sweet mystery.

"Look!" Guido yelled.

Young heads snapped up towards the road on the
hill above the lake. A big blue Buick screeched and
swerved to a stop on the shoulder of the road. A figure
leaped out, and raced towards them, beckoning frantically.

"That looks like the Buick Little Angelo drove us here in. Is he late taking it to the races?" Guido asked, frowning. "But that guy can't be Little Angelo. He doesn't move that fast. Come on, let's see what the big hurry is all about." They walked leisurely towards the galloping figure of Little Angelo!

He breathed in short gasps, and the late afternoon shadows grooved his frightened face.

"Come on Guido, quick," he managed to wheeze. "We gotta get the fuck out a here, fast. Da boss tole me ta take you all ta da house. It's guarded good by now."

The three girls screamed, and everyone tumbled into the car.

"We got big trouble," Little Angelo said, gunning the engine. He swept them all with a wild stare. "It's Vito!"

The big car lurched forward, engine roaring, wheels spinning.

Chapter 21

"Jimmy, you may have something there," Sergeant Sam Pizzuta said, nodding. "Vito could have holed up in the railroad yard. But, as Sforza said, he would be long gone by now. He probably knew his luck couldn't last."

"You gonna check it out anyway?" Jimmy, standing in the shadow of his boarding house, squinted at his wrist watch in the dark of the early dawn.

"Already have. Zilch. But I'll be going back again. I just have a feeling, an odd thing Jimmy, a cop thing, you know?"

"No, I don't know, and I ain't sure I want to know."

Pizzuta ignored Jimmy's comment. "You know Luke Peris?"

"The lazy bum hangs around downtown. Yeah, I know him. Seen him a couple of times there, and in the diner. Why?"

Pizzuta smiled; let the question pass. "He knows you too, Jimmy. I saw him a while back. He says your club sandwiches are the best in town. He wanted to keep talking, about you and your sandwiches, I suppose, but I stopped him and said I had something to tell him about you."

Jimmy stiffened noticeably. "*Madonna mia!*" He struck his forehead with the palm of his hand. "Don't you know the jerk is on Di Anello's payroll? Shit! I could be rubbed out! What are you trying to do to me? What did you want to tell him about me? Did you?"

"Jimmy, for chrissake, shut up! Listen good! You're with me against Di Anello, right?" Jimmy nodded. "That's what I told Luke." Jimmy rolled his eyes, and his knees buckled. Pizzuta grasped Jimmy's shoulders, put his face against Jimmy's. "So is Luke Peris, Jimmy, so is Luke Peris! Right inside Di Anello's gut, for almost a year now. I can play the spy game too!"

Jimmy flowed back like an incoming tide. "No shit!"

"Right. No shit! I want you two to meet. It's gotta be teamwork now. As I said – that cop feeling! That's why I wanted to see you this morning."

"And that's all? I mean – he didn't say anything more

about me?" Jimmy knew where Luke Peris hung out-
the Waldorf Cafeteria, and–

"No. Why should he? When he found out you work
for me he seemed surprised, like you are, and said he'd
be glad to work and talk with you."

"Fine!" Jimmy said, forcing a smile, but his mind
raced.

*Did Luke see me coming out of City Hall that day I
saw Mrs. Fleming... Fulvia? Maybe not. But if he did, and
Di Anello knows about it, so what? Lots of people go in
and out of City Hall. He wouldn't know why I was there.
Sam Pizzuta? Maybe-I dunno-maybe, if Luke saw me, he
was gonna tell Pizzuta about it when they got talking about
me, but he clamed up when Sam said I work for him.
None of his business! Besides, lots of people, me included,
go in and out of City Hall, pay bills, complain – you name
it. But hey! I gotta talk to Luke, find out for sure what he
knows, if anything. If something needs straightening out,
I'll do it. Anyway, my nose tells me there's muck in the
air. God! This is France, and trench warfare, all over again!*

"...and you can wipe that silly smile off your face.
Look, I gotta go, duty calls. I'll get you and Luke together next few days. Nights... I'll be crawling around
the railroad yard. Maybe Vito's always been there Jimmy,
right under our fat noses. So long, partner. We'll get this
neighborhood cleaned up yet for smart young fellas like
Phil Martello."

Half-dazed, Jimmy muttered, "Sure!" and watched
Pizzuta glide away.

* * * *

Three men squatted on a blanket in an empty boxcar and stuffed chunks of ham into soiled faces.

"Great ham, Champ. I'm gonna miss ya."

"Yeah, me too."

Hoboes. Products of the Depression and many broken dreams.

Vito looked at his companions on this September
night. Ex-pugs, like himself. He grunted, enjoying their
flattery, given generously when he brought food and wine.
He had been with them for – he thought hard – quite a

while. They had swung in on him one night as he drank wine from a gallon jug in an empty freight car near the hill leading up to Nino's place. They had eyed each other with caution, Vito fairly clean in one of Nino's sport shirts; the two, showing signs of the road-baggy old clothes, gray with dirt, filthy caps, scuffed Army shoes with broken laces, and beard stubble.

But Vito paid more attention to their scarred lumpy faces, their flattened noses, the way they both walked, and their hungry, darting eyes.

"You guys do any fightin'?" Vito had asked, his right hand inching to his waistband, the movement noticed.

"Yeah, we were in the ring – middleweights – around Chicago, Champ." The voice of the light-haired one was friendly, if perhaps a bit strained.

"Can you spare some of that?" the younger one with the broken front teeth and the really flat nose had said, pointing to Vito's ham and jug.

"Sure. Who did you guys fight?" Vito had said, expansively. Champ!

The days passed, the food and wine continued, and the two hoboes kept postponing their trip west, although it was to be 'any day now'. Vito didn't mind. They spoke his language, and when together, the stories of ring victories and crooked managers were juicy and wild. They would be in the big time now, if it had not been for those thieves. And dames. Yeah!

But now, around mid-September he thought, Vito was worried and restless. One of the hoboes, tongue loose with drink, said that he had seen a railroad dick talking to a big guy in a dark suit and tie, and that the guy had later been seen snooping around the freight cars. Vito's mental cobwebs melted. Someone – looking for him! That neighborhood detective? Vito decided he'd get lost, but first he had to finish something. After, he could head out west, to Arizona, for his chest pain and a new life. Maybe even a comeback!

"I'll be leavin' tomorrow morning," Vito said, "alone." He tensed.

The two hoboes exchanged quick glances, nodded and kept eating ham.

"I'm gonna miss ya, champ," one said.

"Yeah, me too," the other one said, on cue. "Ya see, Champ, we gotta leave tonight. Big freight goin' our way." He swallowed hard.

"Yah, well good luck," Vito said, his voice dry, his eyes alert.

"Maybe we'll run into each other soon."

"Maybe sometime, but not soon." Vito's smile wasn't friendly.

One last gulp of wine, and the two hoboes, Frankie 'Killer' Sandiewicz and Carlo 'Billy the Kid' Stracco, picked up their bedrolls and headed for the main switching area. Then, running low, sticking to the shadows, they left the railroad yard through a broken fence, and headed for the concealment of the woods on the side of the road leading up to Nino's house.

Next morning, Vito headed for his cellar hide-out, hugging the side of the road. He leaped into the brush as a taxi came down the hill. The passenger was Nino. Vito shrugged. So what? Now he knew the house was safe.

Suddenly, a long shadow, different from the trees, appeared before him, moving, and it was crowned by a round blackness. Trees don't move like that! Vito instinctively whipped around, bobbing and quick-stepping to his left. His right hand flashed up in uppercut fashion. He fired one shot from the gun in his fist.

The bullet shattered young Stracco's broken teeth. Blood gushed from several holes in his face as shrapnel-like fragments tore at flesh and bone. The bullet angled into his brain, exploding out the top of his head, taking skull, gray matter, and hair with it. He doubled over, the large rock he held overhead fell harmlessly to the ground and he fell on it, face down, hands frozen on what was left of his face, rump shoved high by the rock.

In the woods he heard the sound of cracking underbrush and a heavy body pushing, feet tromping. This was accompanied by loud snorts and short cries, a mixture of rage and terror.

"Damn you, Sammy Constantino!" Vito shouted, and he pumped two shots at the retreating sounds. "Yor friend won't be comin' out fa da next round," he added, smiling maniacally. But quickly his pathological hatred evaporated and he crouched, and listened intently. Self-preservation took hold.

No sounds except of trains and frightened birds. The road was deserted, the woods thick and muffling. Too early for kids to come streaming across the tracks on their way up to the empty field behind Nino's house for baseball or football games. At least he hoped so, for it was Sunday morning, and no kid wanted to get up early after a tough week of school. A long time ago he didn't, before he threw a full ink well at Miss Horne when he was in the special grade for three straight years. He was expelled.

Relieved, Vito pulled Stracco into the woods, covered him with branches and a tombstone of detritus, dropped to one knee and cocked his head. All quiet! He took a look in the direction of where Sandiewicz had fled then hacked, and spat contemptuously.

"We ran inta each udder sooner dan ya tot, eh? Ya second-rate bum! Go, go, run away ta Chicago! Ya don't cheat on da champ! Me!" Vito thumped his chest defiantly, and he hooted derisively into the birch, oak and brush.

Quickly, he calmed down, his eyes cold and hard, his lips screwed tight into a sullen, swollen snarl. The reason for his predicament flashed brightly in his mind. Slowly he headed up the deserted road to Nino's house, and had delicious thoughts of crunching Phil. He would be at the lake, Vito was sure. After he had 'strupiad' da big kid (disfigured him) Vito would disappear. No one would ever think of searching for him in a boxcar, not Vito of the soft life! Those dumb hoboes had really helped him. He was glad they were either dead or gone.

In Nino's cellar now, Vito prepared to leave. Gun reloaded, a burlap sack of provisions, a little of this, a little of that. Good! It was all working out better than he had planned. Nino is a dumb shit, just like da rest of dem, leaving his car here.

Suddenly, Vito's tortured thoughts were interrupted by the sound of car engines and the squeal of brakes. He peered out the cellar window, blew out a low frightened whistle, and lurched backwards into the gloom of the cellar.

A truck! Two men, stepping out of it, and Nino behind them, opening the door of a taxi.

"Here, dis one." Nino's voice. "Finish da job good dis time!" "Sure, Nino, sure," someone grumbled. Metal clanged against metal.

And it hit Vito, like a hard left hook to the jaw. His vision blurred. The men, about to install bars on his cellar window. Trapped, like a rat! He sweated; he trembled. His head and chest hurt, and he felt himself buffeted about in a silent vortex of terrible shapes and shadows. He covered his face, slumped behind stacked boxes, and was still.

A loud voice finally cut through his misery: "Okay Nino, come on out and take a look. The job is done." One of the workmen spoke.

"Sure." Nino's muffled voice, and the sound of footsteps above Vito's head were heard. Then, a few moments later there were hands on the new bars, tugging...

"Eesa good job, Cozzi. Don Worry! I pay you good. I tell Natale how you help me, eh? So, I gotta go, my taxi he come for me. *Ci vedremo.*"

"Yeah, so long... and thanks. See ya on Front Street some time."

The sound of departing vehicles was music to Vito's ears. Cautiously he uncoiled, rubbed his arms and legs, and wrapped a thick palm around his mouth to stifle a cough. He started up the cellar steps, treading softly. At the top of the staircase he stopped, apprehensive. Sweat dripped from thick eyebrows into his eyes, and his armpits leaked rivers down his ribs.

Silence! He crept into the kitchen, neck thrust forward, rasped out a breath, and looked out the kitchen window. He yelped with joy, "Everything in place – great! Now! First ting, look fa dat punk kid, Phil..."

Feeling no need for caution he pivoted and ran to the cellar stairs, taking the steps down two at a time. In his haste, he tripped and fell heavily on the concrete floor. He rose, paying no heed to the pain in his ribs. The thought of mangling Phil intoxicated him with savage pleasure.

Chortling, he turned his back to the staircase and reached down to gather up his sack. He would be on his way, and he wouldn't look around to steal a car neither!

"Appa you hands! Move and you dead man!"

Vito recoiled and staggered as the words slammed into him, the drumbeat in his temples terrible, the raw pain in his gut a hot knife thrust.

The black Colt .45 Nino pointed at his heart didn't help one bit.

Nino sputtered, his face a red mask, the cords in his neck and head swollen. He switched to his native tongue, and the words gushed, a torrent through a broken dam: "*Imbecille! Stupido!* Know that I am no fool! Don't you realize that I have a count of my wine and food stores? No, you are too crazy! And you insulted me more by wearing my clothes, hiding out in my house, dirtying my towels. Such filth! Isabella asked if I plucked chickens, and then came home to clean up. Eh, I didn't suspect. But she, good housekeeper that she is, alerted me, and I began checking. *Ignorante!* You could have gotten away with it, but you got too greedy, didn't you? Now–"

"No, Nino, no!" Vito cringed and screamed. The .45 stopped its thrust.

"Why not, Vito Amorusi? You have broken your oath, brought shame on us all." Nino, calmer now, sneered his advantage. "You fell into my trap. My leaving home in a taxi, coming back the same way to bar the cellar window. And leaving again by taxi, my car left behind with the keys under the mat. I thought you might catch on and spoil everything, but you didn't, and I couldn't wait any longer. Better this way than at the car. *Sei finito!*"

Vito didn't think he was finished. He bent over, sobbed, "Lemme go, Nino! See, I jus' wanted to borrow yor cah, ta get a punk dat got me inta all dis trouble. I was gonna take him ta da lake where he hit me from behind, and–" He glanced at Nino with shrewd eyes, looking for an opening.

"Finish!" Nino commanded, waving the .45, his hand relaxing just a trifle. "–and," Vito repeated, "I was gonna powder da punk by da lake shore, den I was gonna return yor cah, and tings would a been fine again. See?"

"No, I don't see! *Carogna!* You belong in a mad-house, that I see!

Vito boiled, but stalled: "How didja know it was me in yor house?"

"How? Oh what a dolt! Who else but you? You helped me make wine, knew where I lived, knew about the cellar window. And you had disappeared." Nino puffed importantly, enjoying himself.

"And ya told everybody how ya was gonna get me," Vito prompted.

"Of course not. Capturing you was going to be my surprise for the boss."

The powerful voice inside Vito's head increased in volume, echoing from the joists, possessing him, commanding him. Now Vito, now!

Vito doubled over in a paroxysm of coughing. He moaned and pawed at his chest where blood had seeped through his shirt. He retched, and up came a thick globule of foulness which he deposited at Nino's feet. Startled, Nino stepped back, the reflex causing the barrel of the .45 to point down. He recovered, his face purple with rage, and raised the gun with both hands.

He didn't move fast enough.

Vito smashed into him, tilting the .45 up. It boomed; the slug shattered the cellar light, and flattened itself in a thick floor joist. Vito chopped to the face and landed four quick one-two's to the belly. Screaming, Nino toppled backwards and dropped his gun, but drew a hidden knife.

In the gloom the battle raged, with fists, knife, teeth, feet, and thumbs. They were evenly matched: Vito, ex-pug; Nino, former Black Hand street-fighter. Nino slashed with his knife; Vito deftly backed away, and threw a jug of wine. Nino ducked. The jug sailed into a wine barrel. The .45! There, by the wine barrel, where it had clattered to a stop!

Nino lunged forward, slipped, and slid forward on his stomach. Vito saw, reached, slipped, tumbled, and landed on his back, feet up. Nino, unimpeded now, grasped the weapon, got to his knees, and raised the gun... But Vito rolled back up – into Nino – and the moist thwack of bodies crumping against each other filled the cellar, reeking now of sweat and wine mixed with a malodorous mix of broken cheeses, olive oil from cracked tins and smashed bottles, garlic necklaces, and anchovy paste.

Puffing, snorting, cursing, going round and round in a macabre death dance, each struggled for the gun.

Fire and smoke from the .45!

One shot, then another; and yet one more, the sound of each shot building on the previous one, echoing, deafening. Then, a shroud of silence. Shortly afterwards, a nattily dressed man – yellow sport shirt, light blue sport coat, navy blue pants – emerged from the house. On his head he wore a broad – brimmed straw hat, low over his eyes.

Isabella, trudging slowly up the hill for her bi-weekly house-cleaning, saw the man. Look at him, dressed like a Mafioso! She rubbed her back. I must talk to him, she told herself. He must drive me here, and afterwards, take me home. No... better I ask my lazy grandson to come for me. Together we can take a salami or two from the hoard the stingy one has in his cellar. He will never miss it! After all, it will be just payment for my work. She nodded wisely, adjusted the knot of the black kerchief covering her head, and tugged at the folds of her black dress that the humidity had caused to stick in the cracks of her sparse buttocks. Isabella always wore black. She was in mourning for her husband who had died twenty years ago...

Isabella waved at the man, now only a few hundred feet away. He seemed to be in a hurry to get into his car. He glanced at Isabella, didn't wave back, and pulled the brim of his hat lower over his eyes. He got into the car, started the engine, and without warming it up sputtered past Isabella without so much as a look or a smile in her direction.

"Spacimi! Fidenti!" she hurled after him, her insults graphic peasant vernacular.

* * * *

Killer Sandiewicz didn't feel much like a killer. Eyes wide with horror he watched the choreography of Billy the Kid Stracco's death. He ran, thrashing though the woods, away from there! as fast as he could. Vito's two shots snapped branches above, and Sandiewicz's feet dug in and pumped harder. He shouldn't have listened to that idiot Stracco! So simple, he had said. He had followed Champ before, knew where he hid out and got loot. It would be all theirs... after taking care of Champ. Then they'd be gone, all set for many, many months. Simple. Right?

Wrong! They hadn't reckoned on Champ-punch-drunk, but a sly bastard! – figuring things out. Now Stracco was dead, gunned down like the wild west outlaw whose nick-name he had adopted. Sandiewicz shuddered, looked over his shoulder then stumbled and fell, branches whipping his face, brambles, digging at his flesh. He winced and looked up, at a clearing just ahead.

Sandiewicz got up, took several steps, and looked around wildly. The yards were off to his left. In his frenzy, he had veered down to the right, and was now in the open space of a railroad crossing. Champ could spot him here, shoot him! He whirled, slobbering, bleeding from many cuts, and started to move to his left.

"You! Stop! Where do you think you're going now?" Low, with a brogue.

"Hold it right there! Turn around, slow." A second voice, harsh, nasal.

Sandiewicz obeyed. He saw an old cop in the faded blue uniform of the local police. The cop's hand held a gun. The other man-large, florid, young, cruel looking-a railroad dick!-raised a huge ham of a hand, and motioned Sandiewicz to come forward.

"Lemmee go! He'll kill me, like he did my buddy! I gotta leave! I'll hop a fast freight! I ain't done nothing, honest!" Sandiewicz backed away. Massive hands closed over his wrists. "No more freights for you, bum."

"Who's after you?" the old cop said, his pistol held limply.

"He is! Calls himself Champ – never mentioned his real name. He's the one killed my friend; now, he's after me." Sandiewicz whimpered, and cowered behind the big man.

"Take him in, will you O'Day? Something mighty wrong here. This bum is either crazy or something happened up there." The big dick waved towards the woods.

Officer Terrence Patrick O'Day nodded. "Watch him," he said. "I'll call in, bring out the wagon."

Terry O'Day was elated. This was the first time in twenty-five years he had drawn his gun. And if his friend, Denny O'Rourke was right, a criminal had been caught. Terry O'Day would retire with honor... and a medal. He would show those fat desk slobs downtown that he could still do good police work. Thank you, Lord, for letting me wait for Denny this fine day. He remembered that they had not yet exchanged nips, as they often did, when they met on their respective beats. It would happen after he called in; before the wagon gets here... He smacked his lips in anticipation.

Chapter 22

Isabella had her priorities straight today. From Nino's she phoned home, the four-party line not busy. She knew she had awakened her lazy no-good grandson Gaetano, for she heard low cursing as he picked up the phone. "You come get me in twenty minoots," she instructed him sharply.

"Where the fuck are you?" he muttered, still half asleep.

"Where do you tink, at dis hour? At Nino's to clean da ousa."

And then Isabella switched to a more familiar language:

"Alzati, poltrone, e lavati la bocca con un pezzo di sapone forte! Non Non si parla a la tua vecchia nonna cosi!"

Gaetano – Longcoat – winced at the scolding, and her very explicit instructions to wash his mouth out with a bar of strong soap. She was his old grandmother, she said, he shouldn't talk to her that way. But shit, it was so fu-ah-damn early!

"Sorry, Grandma," he mumbled, "I didn't tink it was you. Gimme tirty minutes and ah'll be dere."

"Bene." She slammed the receiver down, licked her lips, and headed for the cellar door. Opening it, she groped for the round button switch, pushed it in. No light appeared. She tried again, several times, shook her head, and went to a kitchen cupboard drawer, where she pulled out a long flashlight. She descended the cellar stairs carefully, shining the light directly in front of her. Falling and breaking a leg in this forbidden territory would be a disaster. She grunted happily as she reached the cool cement floor, and shone the beam around the cellar for the items she sought. Instead, she saw the shambles of the recent struggle. She gasped, a wrinkled hand going to her mouth. Then she lost her breath as the powerful smells of crushed foods and herbs and spilled wine assailed her nostrils. A jagged piece of glass tinkled and rattled away, pushed by the tip of one of her black Red Cross shoes.

The flashlight beam moved and held. A thin wet trail... of red it seemed... led away from her, towards the wine barrels. As if hypnotized, she followed the trail, taking small steps, avoiding puddles of wine and shards of glass. She slowed, close to two upright barrels which emitted heady fragrance of fermenting juice. The red trail ended at one of the barrels.

Gingerly, with shaking hands, she lifted the cloth cover over the barrel.

"God in Heaven protect us! What is this! Oimeh! Aheeee! Aheeee!"

Isabella screamed and screamed, staring in fixed, fascinated horror at the wide, unseeing eyes of a man, jack-knifed into the barrel. The liquid bubbled around his face, frozen in a mask of hate. His hands stretched for Isabella, two claws ready to tear at her throat. His own throat was slashed, and slices of flesh erupted like the petals of a blossoming crimson flower from the wine-soaked wounds.

Isabella shrank back, screaming in short bursts, her own throat raw. She ran up the steps with a vigor born of terror; and out of the house, hands flailing above her head, her screams now dull rasps.

Longcoat, coming along in his Ford saw her, and stopped the car.

"What's da matter? Yor acting nuts!"

Sobbing hysterically, Isabella managed to tell him what she had seen.

Longcoat's first thought was to TAKE OFF!

But he was in the doghouse with Natale... He could redeem himself by calling Natale, before anyone else found out about the murder. Natale would know what to do. Longcoat fairly drooled; he would be a fucking hero, and out of the doghouse. He helped his grandmother into the car. Gravel flew and the car lurched forward. He paid no heed to Isabella's cries of protest.

"Natale?" Breathless, excited.

"Yeah?"

"It's me. Longcoat."

"Whadda ya want?" Gruff, angry.

Longcoat ignored the rebuff. "Look, I'm at Nino's

house. Ya know, my grandma cleans dere. She wanned me ta pick her up. But when I went ta get her, I saw her runnin' down da road, screamin'." Oh, how he relished this!

"Yeah? Why?" Natale's voice perked up.

"Because she saw what I just did." Longcoat paused, waited.

"Awright, awright, what did you bote see?" Just a bit worried! Good!

"A dead man. In a wine barrel. His trote cut... all over his neck. And bullet holes in him, too."

"Stay dere! I'll be right out! Could ya tell who da guy was?"

"Yeah, Natale." Again Longcoat paused for effect, and boomed, "Nino!"

"WHAT!" An explosive sound; curses, followed by erratic breathing.

* * * *

"Yeah, dis is where Champ shot my friend. Right here!" Sandiewicz said. "I saw him do it. Then I ran like hell."

The ranting and screaming from his jail cell that he could take the cops to where his friend had been shot had convinced a bored Captain Hennessey (Homicide) to check Sandiewicz's story more thoroughly, Officer O'Day and the railroad cop had found nothing, though they admitted their search had been minimal. O'Day had said that when he arrested the hobo he was yelling wildly about his friend being killed by a guy called 'Champ'.

Hoboes don't usually act up like that. "Pizzuta," Captain Hennessey had said, "this time you got a legitimate reason to go to the neighborhood. Check out Sandiewicz's story... thoroughly. Something smells!"

Now, Pizzuta, following Sandiewicz who was guarded by Officer Terry O'Day, inspected the side of the road where Sandiewicz pointed.

"Why didn't you help your friend?" O'Day asked, swelling importantly.

"And be shot? No siree! I cut out... fast!" Sandiewicz spoke with perfect logic, deflating O'Day, and ending his questioning.

"Humpf... yes, I see," he said, finally.

"Here!" cried Pizzuta, "under this pile of debris." He cleared away branches, leaves, small rocks and dirt, his hands digging like a dog's paws.

"Your friend?" He glanced at Sandiewicz, returned his gaze to the body.

"Yeah," said Sandiewicz, who seemed about to be sick.

The black Cadillac, rolling slowly down the hill from Nino's house, interrupted the little drama. The car stopped near Pizzuta. The driver, Natale, got out.

"What are you doing here?" Natale tried to smile, but instead glared.

"Oh, hello Natale. Sunday driving, eh?" Pizzuta did smile. "A murder. Bad blood between some hoboes, looks like. This one saw it all." He shrugged, and then his eyes narrowed. "Funny though, you showing up. Now, why did you say you were here?"

Natale stood stiff and straight. No words came from his tight lips.

"He didn't say." Di Anello, his long fingers curled around the car's door post, stepped out of the back seat and cracked a crooked smile.

"On the job, eh Sam? Dat's what I like to see, Italian boys wit important jobs." Di Anello's smile widened, but his voice betrayed him.

"Mr. Di Anello... what a surprise!"

"No surprise, Sam, no surprise. Ah, and how is your wonderful mama and papa? Dey must be proud of you. Tell dem I asked about dem. Good people, good people." He punctuated his words with slow, affirmative nods.

"They're fine, fine. Yeah, they talk about the old days and how you shoveled horseshit behind the trolley. But now, about this–"

Di Anello held up a hand, blanched, began to turn purple, and caught himself in time... "Sam, I tink I can help you," he said, his suave, imperious manner now back. "I had business wit Nino. He says dere will be anudda world war soon. I do not know of such tings," he shrugged, "but I am an importer, and business, as the *managia patate* say, is business. So I came to listen." He pulled out a long black stogie, Natale jumped forward and lit it. Di Anello nodded, and waved him away. "Nino wanted to work out plans for buying and selling. None of dat happened. You see, Sam, Nino is dead. Murdered." Not a word about Longcoat and Isabella.

Thunderous silence, all around as Di Anello's words sunk in.

Then: "You don't say! And who, may I ask, did it?" said officer O'Day, his eyebrows dancing up and down.

Sam Pizzuta shot a cutting look at O'Day. "Why didn't you report it, Mr. Di Anello? There's a phone in there, right?"

"Sure dere is. But the line was cut by whoever did it. We were heading for a phone when we saw you." Natale averted his eyes, stuck both hands in his pockets. Sam Pizzuta understood the clumsy move. *Natale, you transparent thug, you cut the line!* he told himself. But why the hell would he do that? Something... isn't right!

"What's dis all about?" Di Anello continued, pointing to Sandiewicz and the body. The detective told him with little self-aggrandizing comments from O'Day.

"Well," said Di Anello, "I can answer officer O'Day's question now, as to who killed Nino. A tird hobo killed dis one," his hand swept the general area where Stracco lay, "and he killed Nino, too. Go, Sammy, see da mess in da cellar. I tink da tree of dem hoboes plotted to rob Nino, but the missing hobo, da killer, got greedy. Killed dat one," he pointed to Stracco's body, "dis one ran," he nodded at Sandiewicz, "and the coast was clear for da killer. But Nino surprised him, and got taken out."

"Yeah, sounds reasonable," Pizzuta said, with a touch of grudging respect in his voice. "Let's go up there and take a look. O'Day, call the coroner and take Sandiewicz back to jail."

Chapter 23

Massimo Di Anello sat at the court warehouse meeting table alone, hands folded on the polished oak, seemingly lost in deep thought. On the other side of the wall he heard the faint click of pool balls, and now and then the muffled voices of the card players. The boys in the Italian-American World War Veterans Social Hall had their orders-directly from him this time. He had also phoned Sebastiano Martello, and told him he wanted to talk to him later, and in the meantime to stay home. Yes, Di Anello admitted to a worried, sputtering Sebastiano, things have happened. No, you have done nothing wrong, Sebastiano. Enough now, eh? Details will be revealed when we have our talk. And listen, this chat stays with us. *Capito?* Sebastiano had said he understood; he would wait at home to be summoned.

After the events of the day, Di Anello was convinced that Natale would not be moving up in the new organization. His niche was the Front Street bookie joint, and there he would remain. He had frozen when Pizzuta asked a simple question – that was the clincher. Not executive material, Natale! But he is loyal, street smart, and that has value. After Longcoat had phoned him about Nino's murder, Natale had told Longcoat to get out of Nino's place fast, and come to the Front Street office. From there, as Di Anello recalled Natale saying, all three, Natale, Longcoat, and Isabella, headed for the court warehouse, and advice.

And all three, talking at once, had told Di Anello of Nino's murder. Isabella put on a one-act play, screaming at the top of her lungs, pulling her hair, pounding her bony breast, and imploring the help of all the saints in heaven. Di Anello winced at the recollection, but old age was to be respected, and he let her rant on until she fainted...

He had suspected Timothy Hoyt at first. The road construction projects were under way, and either Nino or Hoyt may have listened to the voice of the devil, got greedy, and Nino ended up killed, somehow. But then, Di Anello thought of Vito. The devastation in the cellar strengthened his suspicions. Only a lunatic could be capable of such destruction and violence. And Vito knew where Nino lived. So if Vito killed Nino it must not be known outside these walls. It is, after all, our affair – to be resolved by us. We will find Vito. When we do... Di Anello slapped the table with an open hand, leaving a sweaty imprint.

Fortunately, the murder of the hobo will help us, Di Anello mused, and his concocted story of Nino's murder by the same unknown drifter fell into place neatly. Di Anello thought himself quick-witted, his acumen timely, for Pizzuta seemed to believe, albeit reluctantly. Di Anello chuckled, deep in his throat, got up, stretched, then found and lit a stogie. He had bought some time. Before Pizzuta got wise, the Vito thing would be over. Now, get the boys going! He started for the door...

The phone rang, brash and insistent. Di Anello, nettled, answered it. "Doctor Priore is dead! Strangled with his own stethoscope! oh, oh oh! Vito, Vito–" followed by deep, uncontrolled sobbing.

"*Calmate, per l'amor di Dio!*" Di Anello urged Annette, 'Priore's nurse. Now... what happened?"

Annette calmed down. "Dr. Priore called me into the examining room, for an emergency. I went in and... ohhh..."

"Annette! Please – go on!"

"He... Vito, came out from behind a cabinet, holding a gun. 'Annette, stay. Okay, Doc, fix me up.' He must have sneaked in the back door, and... and, he was in pain. Doctor Priore asked me to help him. I didn't want to, but that gun...

"I helped tape Vito's ribs – the doctor said he should go to a hospital; that he could have internal injuries. But Vito shook his head, said he was going west after he took care of something. The doctor asked if Vito had been in an accident, but Vito didn't answer. He... he seemed to be in another world. Terrible, Mr. Di Anello, just terrible!" She stopped, sobbing, unable to continue.

"Annette, get hold of yourself! You have my protection! Go on, please!"

"Sorry, but... but..." She took a deep breath. "He turned into an animal." Her words tumbled out, high-pitched, as if she wanted to excise a malignancy from her soul. "He threw me down, and oh! he wrapped the stethoscope around the doctor's neck and he squeezed and squeezed and stared, bug-eyed...

"He lowered the doctor slow like, still staring at him. I got up and ran out, real fast! He must have come after me, but two men were helping a boy with a broken arm into the waiting room. I screamed 'killer!'-and went out the front door. Vito turned around, and ran out the back. I found out later that he jumped into a black 1935 Chevrolet sedan and tore out."

"Nino's car," Di Anello murmured. And then a thunderbolt struck him.

"I'm lucky to be alive," Annette was saying, from far, far away.

Di Anello barely heard her; he slammed the phone down into its cradle.

Vito had told Annette that he was going to 'take care of something'...

Something! Guido and his friend Phil were at the lake!

"Little Angelo!" roared Di Anello. "Go get Guido... now! *Fa presto!*"

Chapter 24

Vito had counted on more time. No witnesses if he had croaked Annette! Time to hide under a big tree on Holly Hill, wait for the punk kid, Phil. Now he had to work fast, before she squealed her fucking head off, and people would be after him. He should have paid attention to Annette when he squeezed the doc's rubber thing around his neck. How his eyes popped out behind those cockeyed glasses he wore! And how that mole on his nose got redder and redder as he croaked... Vito chortled and snorted.

"But I tink I blacked out, dat's why Annette got away. It's all Sammy Constantino's fault, yeah, and dat punk kid's, too." Vito slammed the dashboard of the Chevrolet with both hands and groaned with pain as electric shocks bit into his ribs. He was at the turn in the road that led to the lake drive now. Worth a shot, he thought. Hot day, why not? Could be, could be. And, if it paid off... he'd save time, wouldn't have to go to Holly Hill, take big risks. He patted the gun on the seat beside him.

Vito, cruising and turning back and forth on the lake road, hadn't counted on Little Angelo, who, alerted by Di Anello, spotted the Chevrolet. Vito turned for another sweep, churned his Chevrolet to a stop on the lip of the hill, which screened Phil, Guido, Vic, and the three girls.

"It's Vito!" Little Angelo yelled, again, above the screams of the girls in the Buick. "He killed Doc Priore and Nino," Little Angelo blurted. "He's got Nino's car, and he's afta you!" He nodded at Guido and Phil, and gulped. He wasn't supposed to say anything about the murders.

Rapid-fire questions from everyone.

"All I know is what I tolja," Little Angelo said. "Right now, I gotta get ya ta da boss's house." He leaned over the big steering wheel, gunned the straight-eight chunk of iron, and swept around a curve.

Marjorie, stunned, held Phil's arm in both of hers and looked at him, green eyes moist, her lips moving wordlessly.

"Come on, all of you, relax." Phil heard himself saying. "Even if he's loose, we're safe. He hasn't seen us, and won't, the half-blind idiot."

Carmela and Lucy stopped sobbing. Vic and Guido, tense, eyes riveted on the road behind them, blinked, then seemed to relax. In a show of bravado Guido said, "We can take care of ourselves. He'd better not show up. We'll paste him!" He took Lucy's hand. She smiled weakly at him.

"Murderize him!" Vic piped up. He tossed a brave look out the car window as it rounded another curve and slowed. "Oh shit!" Vic's mouth moved but nothing came. He pointed – at glittering, crazed eyes, and a contorted face. The Chevrolet had pulled up behind them and their bumpers almost touched.

"It's him!" Guido cried, his bravado stripped away. He dived for the floor, taking Lucy with him. The Buick's tires spun and grabbed. Phil, seated next to Vic, grasped the door handle with one hand and held Marjorie's shoulder against the back seat with the other. No bugles, no sabres flashing in the sun! But, with a cool detachment, he saw a hand holding a gun stretch out of the Chevrolet's driver-side window... The Buick swerved, and the wind, tires, and engine combined with the pop of a shot in a jangling cacophony.

Moments later, the pursuing car screeched to a stop, turned, kicked up dust, and disappeared rapidly in the lengthening shadows of tall trees.

Phil tapped Little Angelo on the shoulder. "Look! He turned back!"

"Yeah!" He knows where I'm goin'! He ain't dat lonney – ta follow me!"

Phil looked at Guido, who got up, a sheepish look on his face.

The Buick headed for East Hawthorne Road, and a safe haven. Anyhow, Vito would never have caught the Buick, once Little Angelo opened her up, Phil thought. And Vito probably knew it! But Phil saw that Vito had nevertheless left a calling card... a groove, carved in the left front fender and apron of the Buick... made by his single frustrated shot. Phil gulped. What if the shot had been higher? Marjorie grasped his hand and squeezed it.

The Buick pulled into the driveway under the cold gaze of the stone lions, and two steely-eyed, stocky men Phil had never seen before. The iron gate clanged shut behind the car, and Phil saw that both men had snub-barreled shotguns slung over their shoulders. He felt a cold damp chill inside him, but his mouth was desert-dry...

"If he goes west, as Annette said," Di Anello contin-ued talking to his wife, "we have seen the last of him. If his warped mind causes him to double back, he will be caught, by us or the police. He will have no sanctuary here." He smiled sardonically. "Not even in the railroad yard, our esteemed *paisano* Sergeant Pizzuta, will see to that." He switched to English, looked at the silent young people in the den. "Julia, lemonade for da kids. Den Angelo, you take dem home. Not you Phil; you stay... keep Guido company."

Julia Di Anello, a diminutive woman with large, ex-pressive dark eyes, took her arm from around Guido's shoulder, and went into the kitchen.

Wonder what the real reason is for his wanting me to stay? Phil thought. Di Anello gave no clue. Just like when they had piled out of the Buick... there he had been, calm as a cucumber, and shepherded them into the house. He had given each girl a pat on the head. Marjorie got two. Strange! And then, after Guido asked why Vito had killed Nino – and Little Angelo suddenly found things to do under the Buick's hood – Di Anello sighed and said that the police were searching for Vito, and that Sam Pizzuta, a darn good detective – why, he grew up right around here! – was on the case. Di Anello said he had met with Pizzuta at Nino's, and the detective be-came convinced, as Di Anello had (after a wrong guess as to Nino's killer) that Vito had indeed killed Nino, as well as Doctor Priore. The break had come when Vito let Annette, Priore's nurse escape unharmed, and she had identified him as Priore's killer. Why was Nino killed? Who knows how crazy people think!

Di Anello realized that if Little Angelo had kept his mouth shut he wouldn't be explaining to a bunch of kids. But then hadn't he, in the heat of the moment, told Little Angelo what had happened? Yes! So he himself had to be more careful, and begin choosing subordinates with more brains!

Despite his concern, Sebastiano Martello was pleased when Little Angelo, after driving the girls home, came for him. If anyone saw he would certainly make *una bella figura*, being chauffeured in such a fine car.

"I must leave quickly," he told Rosa. "Di Anello has asked me to come to his house. Important matters about my job, I am sure." He tried to sound low-key, tried to impress his wife. Rosa gave the wrong feedback. She screwed up her face, gave a disapproving shake of her head, and disappeared into her sanctuary, her pantry, and soon loud metallic clanks emanated.

Sebastiano, at the Di Anello mansion now was whisked upstairs by one of the guards, getting only a brief glimpse of Phil and Guido in the den.

Di Anello, short on ceremony, launched into the events of the day. Sebastiano listened. His boss, Nino, dead! Vito loose... thirsting for Filippo's blood! It was more than Sebastiano could absorb. He stood, ramrod straight.

"No need to be concerned." Di Anello said, helping Sebastiano to a chair. "You see, when Vito turned away from the Buick he drove to the highway intersecting the lake road, turned west, and forced two cars off the road. His erratic driving was reported to the police... I was informed." Di Anello smiled, knowingly. He stretched, then rubbed the back of his neck. "Sebastiano, please close the door. It is time for our talk."

"But not yet! Don't you remember? I have to go to the church hall tonight." Julia Di Anello stood in the open doorway. "I am chairman of the drive to raise money for our new church. *Ti ricordi adesso?*"

Di Anello remembered, and it would make him look good. But tonight, of all nights! "All right, go, but take one of the men outside with you. He will wait for you. Best way... just for tonight. Now, no objections!"

Phil heard. Boy, he's careful, leaves little to chance! No wonder he's the Big Boss of the Black Hand!

A few minutes later, Julia Di Anello, in jewelry and furs, left.

"She's always going somewhere," Guido whispered to Phil.

"Your mother is an important lady," Phil answered, though he wasn't thinking of Julia Di Anello. His mind was locked on the two men now behind closed doors upstairs, seated in front of an ornately carved gun cabinet. *What does Di Anello want? Why does it involve my father? And where do I fit in?* Phil drifted away, his pondering deep and serious.

"Hey, wake up, guy! Come here, and help me finish this SE-5. I just have to glue on the wings." Guido held up the smoothly tissued fulelage and wings of the flying scale model of the famous British pursuit plane.

"Huh? Oh, sure." Phil joined Guido half-heartedly, and rummaged for a tube of Comet cement.

Twenty minutes later, Guido held the two-winger over his head. "Great job," he said. "Just the right amount of dihedral on the wings. She'll fly like an eagle!" He swooped the SE-5 low over the floor, brought it up over his head, and dipped and turned with it. "Gotta get away from Baron Richtofen's Fokkers," he said.

Like Guido, Phil should have felt the vicarious excitement of being in that open cockpit and fingering the two Vickers machine guns and the Lewis wing gun as he came out of the sun, smack on the tail of a Fokker D-7.

He didn't feel like that at all anymore. Instead, his mind raced on fast forward; the two men upstairs, talking talking; Vito, somewhere, licking his wounds like an animal, still plotting, loading his gun; Mona, and her jerk of a brother, Nick; the fight in the park, and his own escape; Marjorie's dog Fritz, and... Marjorie herself. Quite a girl, and smart, too!

God! a lot had happened to him since he moved to the neighborhood. He shook his head, and felt caught up in events he had tried to control, but now couldn't. Cripes! Would one of the three Fates, Atropos, cut his thread of life soon?

"No, dammit, no!" He whirled at Guido, who, startled, dropped the SE-5, which did a falling-leaf flutter to the floor. "Guido, I'm gonna phone Marjorie, now. She left so fast, I didn't even have a chance to say good-bye to her. Besides, we gotta learn to dance, right?"

Guido came back from the 1917 skies over no-man's-land, the transition complete. He grinned, Phil's cue registering. "Call Marjorie," he said. "We'll start tomorrow, in my den." His smile lit up the den like a morning summer sun.

In the Di Anello's office the conversation was coming to an end.

"*Dunque, cosa dite?*" asked Di Anello. He looked squarely at Sebastiano.

"I say I am overwhelmed!" Sebastiano replied. He felt pleasure, pride, confusion, a tinge of fear; each emotion tumbled over the other, fighting for ascendancy.

Di Anello took out a long stogie, cut it in half with a penknife, and put the two pieces on the table. He struck a match, picked up one of the halves, and lit it. He pointed to the other half of the stogie.

"Si!" Sebastiano said. He picked it up. Di Anello leaned over the table, to light it. Sebastiano took one puff, and his words rushed out, his voice quavering. "I accept your offer with great humility, sir. It is my hope that I will be worthy of the honor you are so generously bestowing on me."

"*Benissimo!*" Di Anello replied. He wheeled around to a side cabinet, came back with a bottle of wine and two glasses. He filled both glasses.

"A rare Chianti I save for special occasions." He lifted his glass high. Sebastiano did likewise.

"*Salute!*" Di Anello said, raising his glass in a time-honored toast.

"*Per cent' anni!*" responded Sebastiano.

They sipped the wine, looked at each other, and drained the glasses.

I hope my health lasts for a hundred years, Di Anello thought, *and yours too, my eager Sebastiano, if you never forget what it will take – ubbidienza, rispetto, e silenzio.* (Obedience, respect, and silence.)

"Boys, meet my new top manager, Sebastiano

Martello. He will..." Phil emitted a loud gasp; Guido a loud "Yay!"

Di Anello held up both hands, quieting both Phil and Guido.

"He will," Di Anello repeated, "replace Nino in running the Columbus Street market and the warehouses, for now. Later, we shall see. I... must attend to much other pressing business. What do you say, Filippo?"

Phil, still in a happy daze after his phone conversation with a delighted Marjorie, couldn't switch mental gears fast enough. His tongue did not move, but Guido came to his rescue: "He thinks it's great, like I do!"

"Yeah, I think it's great," Phil mouthed, but his face said otherwise.

"I will be managing legitimate business for Di Anello," Sebastiano said to his family, arrayed closely around the kitchen table, listening intently. "Tonight he told me he has much to attend to, and with Nino gone, wants a reliable, intelligent man to manage the market and warehouses. I am that man." He looked around; no visible pro or con from anyone. "Look, if you are concerned about rumors you may have heard about Di Anello, do not be. He may have certain other business interests – in which I am not involved – that is clear, but what are they compared to that which the venal scoundrels who run our city do? They – bleed us dry! And the greedy landlords – like Barney – Rosa... Filippo... Alfredo... remember him? He who takes the last penny from poor widows! I won't forget him!"

Still no reaction from the three musketeers. Ah! a sniffle; Rosa!

"And the cheating big companies," Sebastiano sounded angry, "with their thumbs on the scales. And we all pay and pay. Well, no more! The Depression is over for us! In a few days Di Anello will introduce me to key members of the export-import companies he deals with. Di Anello put it well, when he said that what we have is truly... '*una cosa nostra.*'"

Phil clenched his teeth to control the sudden visceral anger boiling inside him, and so he spoke slowly, carefully, in English. "Sure, Pop, 'our thing' all right. It's nothing but a euphemism for all kinds of crooked rackets... that's what it really means." And then he exploded. "Oo-fa! Don't you know what you are getting into? You ought to know better. 'Una cosa nostra' – my foot! It's just a new way of spelling T-H-E M-O-B." Phil sounded out the letters, slowly and savagely. He was livid, and he leaned across the kitchen table, his facial muscles tight.

"Yeah, Mob! Heh, heh! The Shadow knows!" Al wasn't about to be outdone.

"Shut appa, all a you! You fadda knows what he is doing. Eh, and you no try foola me wid da big American words, Filippo. Talk Italian to you fadda when you wanna say somating *importante*. Now, no more talk. *Finito!*"

Sebastiano's broken English became strained and brittle as he spoke. The words felt like the snap of a lash to Phil, ordering him to behave and mind his place. Phil knew he had touched a sensitive nerve, and he knew that his father was miffed. *Well... frig it! It's going to be his tough luck if he isn't careful, and he just might get a hell of a lot more cut off than the tips of that ridiculous mustache.*

"I'm going down to Vic's," Phil said testily. He bounded out and slammed the back door.

While the Martello family sat squabbling round the kitchen table, Di Anello sat in his study alone, hands clasped under his chin, his two long fingers extended upwards, touching the tip of his nose. His thin lips curved downward, his brow deeply furrowed. He looked funereal. As if he realized it, he unclasped his hands, slapped the desk top with both of them, and a thin smile played his lips. *So,* he thought, *soon perhaps, you will deal with our Mr. Hoyt, Sebastiano. For the moment, it will have to be Natale.* He shrugged. Natale wouldn't make a move unless he checked first. *That... is good. And Fulvia, thank you for your warning last month of possible trouble with Hoyt. Your last hurrah, so to speak!*

But Di Anello's informers were aware that something was in the wind. They whisper from every corner of Hoyt's unholy domain. Di Anello thought it could involve fingering him as a racketeer; blackmail, jail, or worse. Hoyt has legal power! Di Anello knew he would know of Hoyt's plans to snare him as soon as they were hatched, for Hoyt's inner cabal was not inviolate. Di Anello would personally speed up Irish whiskey deliveries and add crisp fifty dollar bills here and there. And he would be ready when Hoyt moved on him.

"*Assolutamente!*" Di Anello cried hoarsely, coming out of his dark musings of duplicity and counter-deceit. He looked malevolently across the darkness to the ledge, up where Hoyt's house sat. Slowly, his eyes turned to his gun cabinet...

Enough of Hoyt! He recalled his terse phone calls to New York and Miami, during the August heat wave, right after Fulvia tried to brush him off. He had found out Mary Coyne was a drunkard, but she wasn't leaving City Hall. Ah, Fulvia! Anyway, how handsomely his long distance calls had worked out! Oreste – may he rot in hell! Oreste's godchild, Gennaro, had arrived in New York from Catania, as scheduled, towards the end of August. He had been whisked off to Miami to join his vacationing godfather, who was supposed to be waiting for him with open arms. Nino, on one of his trips to New York, had confirmed that Gennaro would not be coming back.

Di Anello shrugged. Relatives in Sicily were paid a handsome sum in memory of the dearly departed Gennaro, who, filled with joy to be in America, and thinking only of his beloved godfather, had neglected to heed a red light and stepped in front of a passing truck despite the frantic attempts of two friends accompanying him to pull him back out of the way. Nino had personally talked to the two friends; they had tears in their eyes when they took the fat envelopes Nino handed them. Di Anello remembered counting out the money for Nino, just before he left for New York...

He would miss Nino, Di Anello reflected. Together they had given birth to a strictly American business enterprise. If only Nino hadn't been so obsessed with Mussolini's stupid little war, and his fear of another world war, he wouldn't have made so many trips to Boston and New York, 'to be prepared' he would say. Well, Di Anello thought, he was warned. He should have paid more attention to the immediate needs of building *la cosa nostra*. But the business will prosper and Di Anello will be its legitimate head. *There will be regions, districts, offices, just like all the other big corporations. America, is, after all land of opportunity!*

He again thought of Fulvia. He had phoned her again, three times. Twice there were excuses: work, her daughter's needs, women's problems. The third time, her daughter had answered the phone. Now that wasn't supposed to happen. He had quickly hung up, deciding that ties to the past must be eliminated! Fulvia had no place in his grand scheme of building a new American-style organization. Fulvia would become, sadly, a lovely memory.

Chapter 25

Fulvia laughed gaily. She had not done so in a long time. She was in the opulent Palace Theater watching an MGM double feature and she thought of her daughter Marjorie, and how happy she had been when the nice-looking man sitting next to her had come to take her out – openly. It was good to see Marjorie smiling and hear her say, "Bye bye-have a good time!"

In the film the gorgeous lady in the flowing gown swayed provocatively towards her paramour, all decked out in fancy clothes and a top hat. Fulvia thought her escort better looking, and younger – perhaps even younger than she by a couple of years. See! it didn't matter. He took her cool hand in his warm one. He was tall and broad of shoulder, but slender with dark hair, and smiled easily with his sensitive mouth. He had a cute, quizzical look about him that she liked. She stole a sideways glance at him, and he looked at her, his eyes luminous and soft in the flickering light of the silver screen. His fingers moved gently over her hand, in tiny circles. She turned away quickly, her heart pounding dangerously, and eased her hand out of his. "Good movie," she whispered.

"Oh, yeah," Detective Sergeant Sam Pizzuta grinned, "great movie." He took her hand again. But no circles. Fulvia didn't mind. She hadn't minded the circles, either. But they had created disturbances in her body she hadn't experienced in years. Thrills she thought were gone for all time, and she didn't want Sam to notice, not on their first date. With Di Anello lovemaking had been a duty... an obligation to be paid off. And it had been! No longer would she surrender to him, nor would she be a spy for him!

Marjorie had asked veiled questions, and Fulvia had finally responded that she had been forced to have a relationship with Di Anello, but it was over. She had instructed Marjorie that if he called tonight, she was to tell him she had gone to a movie with Detective Pizzuta. That, she was sure, would cause Di Anello never to bother her again!

As for Sam Pizzuta, he felt jubilant. He sensed Fulvia's tremor when he stroked her hand, and knew she had tried to cover it up. What a beauty! And maybe, after thirty-three years, he had finally found...

A dark picture jarred his musings of love, and a sting of... what bit into him. Sam Pizzuta sank lower in the plush seat. He stared at the thick ornate fringed purple curtains on each side of the screen. Does Di Anello own her? He wondered. Hmm, box seats on the side over there, just like a fancy opera house... Damn it! how close is she to him? Phew, sure is hot sitting down here! Maybe we should have gone upstairs to the balcony. Oh shit! Quit dodging and ducking, Pizzuta silently castigated himself. You are falling for her, and can't do a thing about it, even though she may be... Pizzuta forced himself to look at the screen... Oh, what nonsense! Nobody goes to bed dressed up like that!

And his mind suddenly blotted out the screen. He moistened his lips. How the hell had he gotten from there to here?

"So Nino wasn't killed by a hobo, after all," Sam Pizzuta remembered saying to himself, back then...

He had been sitting at his desk mulling Di Anello's glib rescue of Natale, who was unable to respond to what he was doing at the site of the hobo Stracco's murder. Pizzuta had wondered about Di Anello's story of visiting Nino, and his cool response to Officer O'Day that another hobo had killed Nino. But with the nurse, Annette, identifying Vito as Doctor Priore's murder, the pretense ended. Di Anello, covering his ass Pizzuta thought, reported Priore's murder, changed his story, and said he was sure now that Vito had also killed Nino. Vito had been seen in Nino's car, driving off the lake road, heading west. Lake road? Strange detour for a guy in a hurry! Strange too, that Di Anello knew so quickly. New assignment for Luke Peris: Find Di Anello's spy in Traffic!

Pizzuta had scoured the lake road area asking questions, looking for clues. He found a gold-mine. A dairy farmer, looking for a lost calf, said he had seen a 'race' between a black Chevy and a blue Buick filled with young people. The Buick was winning. Two sharp-eyed boys, fishing for carp and perch at a little pond not far from the lake, thought they heard a shot. They looked up and saw the Buick swerving from side to side, and then the smaller black car tried around and raced away. Yes, the Buick had some people in it, young guys and girls, one a red-head.

It made sense because it made no sense. But it had to be so! Lake, Vito, Buick, red-head, and... Phil? Guido? Has to be! Probably Little Angelo driving. Pizzuta would try something on for size, at Sforza's Diner...

"Hey Sam, have a coffee on me! What are you up to these days? Heard you're gettin' a transfer, that right? Things are tough all over, yeah!"

"Any of you guys have any idea who Vito was chasing before he took off out of town in Nino's Chevy? He was chasing a big blue Buick." Very loud.

"Nobody knows nuttin' about dat. Da dumb shit was chasin' a Buick, hah? In Nino's Chevy? When was it supposed ta have happened? Sure it was him?" Sforza himself spoke, looking pointedly around the diner and wiping his hands nervously on his apron. Sam noticed that they were clean. The congenital liar! Sam also saw several heads duck into coffee mugs, averting his inquiring gaze. Two heads were particularly low, their owners studying their coffee, a vacant-eyed nobody in a dark coat – Longcoat – and a husky slow one. Let's see, yeah! Little Angelo. Sam couldn't help chuckling at the sobriquets. The neighborhood couldn't survive without them!

But one young man, the one with the crew-cut and heavy tan, stared meaningfully at him before he too lowered his head and slowly dunked a huge, leaking jelly doughnut into his coffee. It was Luke Peris, now a board boy and occasional driver for Di Anello. He was also Sam Pizzuta's implant in Di Anello's crooked gut. Luke had been across the street seeing Jimmy; the pretext a club sandwich. After checking with each other, Jimmy, tight-lipped, slapping more mortadella into Luke's sandwich, had hissed that Luke should tell Sam Pizzuta what he knew, today. But hell, Luke didn't know he could see Pizzuta today. Not a regular day; of course, he could leave a message... And then, what fucking luck! Here comes Pizzuta into da diner. Yeah, so what? No way ta get ta Pizzuta in here! Hey! Sure dere is!...

Fulvia's husky, sexy laugh broke into Sam's ruminations. He looked at her, her eyes riveted on the screen, face rapt, absorbed in the movie. The scene was supposed to be one of steamy lovemaking, but the heroine's coiffure looked like she had just stepped out of a beauty parlor. And the seducing hero? Gawd! Not a hair of his carefully parted-in-the-middle and pomaded-perfect haircut out of place! The two kissed carefully, being sure not to bend million-dollar noses out of place.

Sam exhaled a quick exasperated breath. Unrealistic, he thought. Her hair should be mussed up, and she shouldn't have those fancy clothes on. Matter of fact, she shouldn't have any on at all. Hmm, neither would I, if I were with her! He glanced at Fulvia, felt guilty for his digression, and snapped back. *Damn these big, dark, baroque movie palaces. They spirit one away to a never-never land of dreams and escape – and why not? What's outside is no paradise. Now don't get bitter!* Sam told himself. With a silent sigh, he closed his eyes and went back to his reflections – where he had left off at Sforza's Diner – and the dangerous informant's game with Luke Peris. The scene came to life behind his closed lids...

Luke took a big bite from his jelly doughnut; thick, sticky jelly oozed like red lava down his receding chin and formed bright globules in the crease where the chin melded into his neck. "Hey Sam," he said affably, "Jimmy says yor a lousy Morra player." He wiped the goo away with a skimpy napkin. "How about a game? I'll skahnk ya!" Luke's eyes implored Pizzuta.

Pizzuta looked at his wrist watch. "Some other time Luke," he said in a loud voice. He added impatiently, "I got lots I gotta do today."

"Whatsa matter Sam? Afraid da kid'll cream ya?" Sforza's shrill voice mocked, and he made sure everyone heard.

Pizzuta played along: "All right! just a few points. Let's go," he said peevishly, getting up and heading for the door, "you're wasting time." It was a natural move. *La Morra* was a game the boys from the diner played on the sidewalk in front of the diner, in the park – any-where, anytime. At the diner, Sam joined in once in a while, and everyone knew it. Shit! he grew up in the neighborhood, and some things just don't go away, even if you end up as a lousy cop.

This time, Luke's challenge for a game of *La Morra* was a signal, Pizzuta thought. Luke had something important to say that couldn't wait. Beautiful, right in front of Di Anello's cruds! And they'll never suspect a fucking thing... if all goes well.

On the sidewalk they stood toe to toe, a foot apart. Luke positioned with his back to the diner, Sam facing it. Their bodies leaned in, close, closer. Grinning thugs jammed against the center windows of the diner, wait-ing for the action to start.

"Ready to get beat?" Sam asked, his voice a bellow.

"Screw you!" Luke replied. "Yor da one dat's gonna get beat." He pointed a finger at Pizzuta. His apprecia-tive audience roared its approval. Great sport, baiting the detective, and Luke made the most of the distrac-tion.

Sam raised his right arm, and bent his elbow, so that his closed fist was by his right ear. Luke had his right arm by his side, palm out, fist clenched. Simulta-neously, Sam's arm came down vigorously, with three fingers extended, and Luke's arm snaked out from his side in a lightning thrust. He also extended three fin-gers.

"*Cinque!*" bellowed Sam. "Five!"

"*Sei!*" screamed Johnny. "Tree and tree is six. My point!" He bent his head, and whispered, "Little Angelo was driving dat Buick!" He backed away, smiled over his shoulder, and shrugged an "ain't-I-great?" shrug.

Sam nodded, imperceptibly. So, he thought, he had guessed right on that one! "I'll get him next point, don't worry," he said, feigning anger, and addressing the guf-fawing multitude in the diner. And too much! Luke was bowing, sending the hoods into a delighted frenzy.

Again the two gladiators faced off, eyes blazing. Sam mopped his mouth, said in a barely audible voice, "Five fingers, number eight.

"*Otto!*" Sam banged out the word, stringing out the

'o' confidently.

He flicked out five fingers. "Eight!"

"Morra!" cried Luke, also showing five fingers. "Five and five is Morra! My point! You lose again!" And then, quickly, "Di Anello's kid Guido was in da Buick wid some udda guys and broads." He turned to his gallery and bowed again. Right again, Sam Pizzuta thought. That dam Phil... has to be!

No one won the next throwout of hands as the total fingers of both hands did not add up to the numbers each man yelled at the top of his lungs. And as *La morra* progressed, faster, louder, with tempers rising and gestures getting wilder (in the Italian manner) Sam found out that Luke could beat him at the game of Morra, fair and square. But it was worth it, for Sam Pizzuta added intriguing facts to his store of information on Di Anello. The name 'Mrs. Fleming' kept coming up. First, Luke had mentioned picking Phil up at her house back in August on Di Anello's orders, after Phil had escaped from Vito. Second, Phil's girl, the redhead, was Marjorie Fleming, and Little Angelo had driven her back to ledge country from Di Anello's mansion, hadn't he? After Vito had given up his chase of the Buick at the lake? Right! Could be a connection between Mrs. Fleming and Di Anello... With Phil Martello mixed up in it, anything is possible! And weren't there rumors about Di Anello's amorous dalliances? He wondered.

"You win, Luke, I really gotta go," Sam said, finally. He glanced at the diner hangers – on, now starting to come out to get a closer look at the shellacking he was taking from Luke.

"What happens now?" Luke whispered.

"Sit tight. Don't tell Little Angelo you told me what he told you."

"Are you kidding? We're pals, and I wanna stay dat way. If he tells me more, want me ta reach ya?"

"No. Leave the rest to me. But let's meet as usual."

They had sauntered away from the diner. Luke gave Sam a playful punch to the stomach. Sam countered with a light jab, and walked away, rapidly. He could hear the hoots of the crowd behind him. The score had been nine to nothing, in favor of Luke. As far as Sam was concerned, the score was a million to zilch, his favor. In his mind he thanked Jimmy, Luke, and the tenement dwellers who kept secrets as well as a colander held hot spaghetti water. He chuckled. And of course, indirectly, thanks to Little Angelo, slow but with a big mouth. Pizzuta turned serious, for his keen detective nose sniffed something ripe and rotten...

"Hello, young lady. Marjorie, right?" Sam smiled at Marjorie's startled look. "I'm Detective Sergeant Sam Pizzuta... Is your mother in? Now don't look so frightened, Marjorie. My visit it purely routine. And oh, it is my job to know names, yours included."

"I'll... I'll get her Mister – I mean – Sergeant Pizzuta."

And she came, her dark hair cascading in soft waves down her shoulders, her cheeks slightly flushed, her voluptuousness evident through the blue satin robe she had hurriedly put on. She was still tying the wide belt in front. She was barelegged, had matching blue puff slippers on her feet, and no make-up an her face. She was beautiful, and for a moment Sam gaped.

"I'm Fulvia Fleming, Sergeant. What can I do for you?" Just a short time ago she had stepped out of a warm tub. Her voice was silky smooth, low and relaxed. "Excuse my appearance," she said, "but it was a rough day at City Hall. I do much work on construction projects. And the boss's secretary..." she caught herself, cut her sentence short.

And the lights popped bright in Sam Pizzuta's memory. The pleasant accent triggered it. A dozen or so years ago, maybe more. The big trolley car accident-the Irish conductor killed-leaving a pretty young Italian wife and a small child seemingly destitute. There had been rumors of lawsuits, and then a blanket of silence. Cover-up and payoff, the cynics had sneered. But the unbelievable concatenation of events – Prohibition, gang wars, the cacophony of the roaring twenties, the Wall Street crash, and the pain of the Big Depression – blotted out the past. Until now. And the lights burned brighter still for Sam. He was convinced Fulvia Fleming was the beauty he had seen in the City Hall corridors, the one he had told Jimmy he would find – when he had the time. Well, here she was!

"You're, ah, Italian, aren't you, Mrs. Fleming? And you work... let's see now, in Tim Hoyt's office." Sam recovered his composure as he spoke.

"Yes... twice. I'm Italian... Sicilian really, and I work for Mary Coyne, Mr. Hoyt's–"

"Yes, of course," Sam interrupted, "the queen bee – when she comes to work, which isn't often, I understand. Sorry," he added, hastily. Then slow and distinct, "You've been there many years now, ever since your husband was killed in an accident. Am I right?" How he wanted her to say he was!

"Why yes, how did you know?" Wide-eyed, with a slight, sad smile.

He contained himself, shrugged. "My job, Mrs. Fleming, my job." So it was the usual deviousness, he told himself. Promise her a lifetime job, then when things cool off, dump her. But she must be doing something right to have lasted this long – a good worker maybe – like the drunk Coyne once was. Could be she's a workhorse for Coyne. That's it! Rotten deal!

"Why did you come to see me, Sergeant Pizzuta?" She pronounced his name perfectly, the two z's sounding like 'tz' he noted. Detective details!

"Murder investigation. Now," Sam held up a hand, "no need to be frightened. Just routine as far as you are concerned." He paused. "Have you known Massimo Di Anello long?" He hadn't intended to say that. The words just came out. Now you've blown it, he told himself.

"Yes," came the even answer," for some time. There were some favors... in Old Country - Why do you ask? What has my knowing Di Anello have to do with your murder investigation?"

"Filling in some background, Mrs. Fleming. You see," his mind whirred, and he had it, "I am investigating Doctor Priore's murder. Di Anello phoned me after his nurse told him she had seen Vito Amorusi kill Priore. We know he has killed others, and he may kill again. He's gone over the edge – took a lot of punches to the head in the ring."

"But what has all this to do with me?" Fulvia stood quietly, seemingly genuinely puzzled. Her eyes ran up and down Pizzuta's face.

Pizzuta's felt his toes curling, but he held his gaze level on her. "Mrs. Fleming, I know that one night last month you helped Phil Martello here after he escaped from Vito. And later that same night, Di Anello sent a car to take Phil home. You see, you and your daughter could be in danger. Vito is still loose; he doesn't care much for Di Anello, and–"

"Oh, Mama, see? That man is no good for–"

"Mr. Di Anello means nothing to me, Marjorie. We owe him nothing!" Fulvia's voice was hard and icy.

"Great! Let's go to a movie tonight, and after, we'll have a big banana split at the candy store." Marjorie bubbled with happy energy.

Pizzuta didn't need a ring through his nose to take him through that one. "I won't cut into your movie time. I like movies too," he lied.

Fulvia escorted him across the small porch. "Thank you for trying to help, Sergeant," she said. She smiled. He felt light-headed.

"Oh, we're not through yet. There's more we need to talk about." And there he stood, like a freekin' dummy! Do something! "Say," he blurted, his tongue running away from his brain, "maybe we can take in a movie together soon... and talk on the way."

"Great, Sergeant! Just call anytime," Marjorie said, beaming.

Fulvia darted an odd look at her daughter, her full mouth open, but no words came. She looked back at Sam, flustered. Marjorie disappeared.

"Bye," Sam grinned. "I'll call." He took one porch step down.

Fulvia followed. "*A domani*," she said. (Till tomorrow)

"*A domani*," Sam Pizzuta replied, gallantly. And he meant it. His job demanded it. Of course. She needed protection!

Horse manure! Face it, Pizzuta, he told himself, *you acted like a love-sick bumpkin, you threw out logic in questioning her, and you could have fucked-up the case royally.* Yet, he hadn't... Matter of fact, he had come up smelling like the proverbial rose. *Sometimes you have to throw the book out the window-especially when your brain short-circuits over a gorgeous Sicilian widow, conned into spying for Di Anello – and God knows what else, over the years.*

But, obviously, she's through with him, and Detective Sergeant Sam Pizzuta will see that things stay that way! Madonna mia! He was half-Sicilian and half-Udinese, wasn't he? Sure! The Teutonic stubborness of northeastern Italy, and the patience and craftiness of Sicily was in his blood. How could he lose?

Morra!

Chapter 26

The crescendo of the movie background music soared and climaxed in a blast of brass and whining strings, accentuated by the exclamation points of drums and clashing cymbals timed with each ardent screen kiss.

"Oh, Sam, isn't it a wonderful picture!" Fulvia squeezed Sam Pizzuta's knee, and impulsively rested her head on his shoulder. Now that caused Sam to snap out of his mental rambling in time to see that in these final screen kisses, noses did bend. Crazy thought! He became acutely aware of Fulvia's nearness, and her touch. His blood rushed to his head, and in a sudden reflex action he put his arm around her shoulders. She straightened, but didn't remove his arm. In the dark, Sam saw her looking at him.

"Sam, the picture," she whispered, "did you like it?"

"Huh? Oh yeah, great," he said. *What picture?*

Fulvia studied him as the lights went on. He glanced at her, still recovering from his fast mental trip from there to here. Her eyes were laughing at him, but with a tenderness he had never seen in a woman before... and he had seen a few in his time.

"Banana splits?" she asked, slipping out of his arm. He nodded.

Later, Sam pulled up past Fulvia's house and parked his car under the overhang of two huge pines bracketing a near-bare birch. He put his arm around Fulvia's shoulders, loosely.

"The weather is changing, Sam," she said, looking at the birch, her breath forming a circle of fog on the car's window. She shivered. Sam patted the space between them. With a whimsical smile she came closer and kissed him on the cheek.

"I had a wonderful time, Sam," she said, her voice husky, emotional.

Impulsively, he put both arms around her and kissed her hard. She returned his kiss, eyes closed. Sam, his heart pounding, body now aflame, rained ardent kisses on her eyes, ears, neck. "Fulvia," he said, his voice hoarse and trembling, "I'm in love with you!"

"*Caro! caro mio!*" he heard her say, as she collapsed back on the seat, holding him tight, breathing quick and hard, her body writhing against him, her face contorted in pain... Pain? Impossible! A wave of intense heat washed over him. He reached down into the yoke of her dress, worked his hand under her light bra, and began stroking her full breasts. Raising them, his lips found her nipples. Crazily, he somehow saw that he couldn't see out the windows of the car now – totally fogged up. Not that he wanted to see out. He was on her now, her softness yielding and inviting, and he worked at removing her clothes and his. But... she wasn't helping him! He felt her pushing him away, even as her lips devoured him. What the-?

"No! No, darling! Not like this! Please, no! Not like a common..." She caught her breath, her bosom heaving with a now leashed passion.

Sam eased back, a mixture of puzzlement and anger on his face.

"Take me to the door, Sam, now, please!"

Mechanically, in an uncomprehending stupor, he did so, the cool night air having no visible effect on him.

"Sam," Fulvia whispered in a low, emotion-laden voice, "I... I love you too! Good-night, Sam. Call me!" she entered the darkened house.

What in the world got into her? Sam thought, his feelings a mess.

At his car his hand tightened on the cold metal of the door handle. He bent over. Something, wet and sticky, sloshed against his cheek and two soft weights pressed into his back, pushing him forward against the car. Frightened half out of his skull, he spun around, brushing his arm and elbow violently out and away. A yelp came out of a furry mass, and the dark shadow of an animal scuttled away.

"I'm sorry, Sergeant Pizzuta. I tried to stop him. He... he just got away. He's big, but he's still a puppy. Gee, did he scare you?"

"S-scare me? Why, no! My hair just turned white naturally, and I can't keep from shaking, is all." Pizzuta caught his breath. He didn't like dogs, particularly big ones who jumped him in the middle of the night. And Marjorie! staring at him, brow furrowed. Why? Steady now, he thought.

"Marjorie, what are you doing out at this hour?" Take the offensive!

"I waited for my mother. Fritz wanted to go out, so we took a short walk. When we got back, Fritz saw you at the car." She sighed. "He likes people, Sergeant Pizzuta, and besides, he probably smelled my mother. That's why he was so friendly."

Friendly? A debatable point! "Why yes," he said, "I had just said good-night to your mother." Wonder how much this savvy chick saw?

"I figured that," Marjorie said, with a merry twinkle in her eye.

"Uh huh," Pizzuta said meekly. "We went to the Palace. Good movie."

"I know. Did you have a banana split, after?" With the little finger of her right hand, Marjorie drew little hearts on the car's fogged-up windshield. The pine trees stirred, the birch's delicate branches rustled, clouds parted, and a dull moon, showing wide rings around itself, spilled dim light. Marjorie slouched, as if carrying a heavy burden. She seemed worried.

"Yeah, I had a triple scoop, the works. Your mother had two scoops."

"Let's see, she had one scoop of strawberry ice cream and one of vanilla, right, Sergeant?" Marjorie spoke absently, her thoughts seemingly on other matters.

"That's right." Pizzuta put a finger under Marjorie's chin, lifted it. "Marjorie, what's come over you? All of a sudden you're somewhere else. What's bothering you? Is it something about me? Trouble with Phil Martello, maybe? Say, I can fix that! Come on now, out with it! Detective Sam just might be able to help you." He smiled, reassuringly, he hoped.

"It's not Phil," her eyes glinted, "although sometimes..." she moistened her lips, "and it's not you, Sergeant..."

"Call me Sam."

"...Sam," Marjorie flashed a quick smile. "I guess you like my mother," she glanced at the house, "and I know she likes you a lot, an awful lot. You should have seen how excited she got when she told me you were taking her to the movies. I hadn't seen her that happy in years! But..."

The pines sighed as the cool night wind whistled through them. Marjorie pulled her light jacket tightly around her, the sound of pine needles thrashing and swishing intensified, and Sam truly felt the tension building in Marjorie. She stared at the ground.

"Marjorie," Sam said, "I'm here to stay. You see, honey," he gulped and took a deep breath, "I'm in love with your mother, and intend to marry her, if she'll have me." Pizzuta steeled himself, and waited.

Silence. Thunderous and shattering.

Marjorie pulled at a paper-thin sheet of curled white birch bark. Sam thought he heard muffled sobs. She came to him quickly then, her heavy mane of red hair swinging, a slice of bark in one fist. She cried, she laughed, all at the same time.

"I'm so glad! I know she'll say 'yes' Sam, I just know it."

"Hey, take it easy! You almost knocked me over! You're quite an armful, young lady, and look at that, you're almost as tall as I am. I'll bet the guys are crazy about you! Uh oh! Did I say something wrong?"

"No, but sometimes I wonder... about one guy – if..."

"Hmm, I see! Work on him, Marjorie. You're a beautiful girl! I can't see any young fella passing you up."

"Thanks, Sam. He... Phil... will be taking me to a school dance soon."

"Great. Just as I figured, Phil Martello. I know him well, yes sir!"

"Say! How did you know about Phil... and... and me?"

"Don't be so surprised, Marjorie. I'm a detective, remember?" He took her hand, and they strolled towards the house. "Now, about what's worrying you... Di Anello, isn't it? No other possibilities left, now." Terse, low.

She stopped, and pulled him into the darkness of the pines, but not before the moonlight had played across her terror-stricken face.

"You know about that too?" Marjorie asked.

"I don't know what 'that' means, Marjorie. But you

and your mother were very transparent when I told you I knew about Di Anello sending a car to your house to pick up Phil. It was clear to me that you both didn't care for the Di Anello name. Why? I don't really know. But Marjorie," Sam cracked a rueful smile, "I tell you there are rumors, about Di Anello and women." He almost said 'a woman' ...and changed his mind at the last moment. "And," he went on, "Di Anello isn't the honest man he tries to make everyone think he is.

"Marjorie," he said, taking both her hands in his, "Di Anello is a crook, a *capo grosso* of the underworld, in our city and the surrounding towns."

"Then, for goodness sakes, he should be–"

"I know," Pizzuta cut in, "he should be in jail. And why don't I put him there? Marjorie, witnesses clam up, evidence disappears, and you have no case, at least one that will hold up in court. He is lavish with his money, and corrupts the right people." Pizzuta paused, turned solemn, then said, "Marjorie, does Di Anello control your mother? Is she afraid of him because of whatever happened in the Old Country?" He regarded Marjorie, tightened his grip on her hands. "Your mother could be in grave danger."

Marjorie's teeth chattered; her shoulders shook, her hands turned cold as Arctic ice. Sam felt her torment and it hurt, but he had to know!

"Sam," Marjorie said, "don't blame my mother! Yes, yes, yes! He... the lousy bastard... controls her life, or did, for a long time. But no more, no more!" She stamped her foot and seemed to collapse inside.

She told him, in word bursts punctuated by sighs. She told him of eavesdropping on her mother's night phone call, when her mother thought she was safely out of the house. It had been Di Anello! She realized why her mother made excuses for late hours 'at the office' ...And why a black car came for her late one night and dropped her off later that same night.

"But Sam, she really wanted to end it but was too frightened, I know. I could tell when I questioned her, hinted that I knew what was going on. Finally she made excuses so she wouldn't see him. And then you came along, and she wasn't afraid anymore. Earlier tonight,

Di Anello phoned for her. She knew he would call, but didn't care. I took the call. He hung up... hard... when I said she wasn't home. I didn't have a chance to tell him she was out with a man... you Sam. Now, I'm scared, Sam! My mother has sloughed Di Anello off so much! I don't think she has gone beyond the pleasure of that, and thought of the possible consequences. Oh, Sam, I'm so worried... about her... what Di Anello could do to her, and me... and about what you might think of her when you knew."

What I think of her? What in the hell should I think?

Sam felt a raw, red rage welling inside him – directed at Di Anello, at himself, and at her. Particularly at her, damn her! Why did she–

A cold hand passed over his eyes. Marjorie was on his shoulder, sobbing.

"Don't condemn her Sam. Don't leave her now. You said you loved her!"

The pleading voice, the coolness against his closed eyelids calmed the anger in him, and he remembered what Fulvia had said just a few minutes ago... in his car... before she had asked him to take her to her door:

"... No!... Sam! Not like this... like a common–"

Like a common... whore... Sam thought, bitterly. But she said she loved him, so wasn't it... different? Then why had she stopped him? And it suddenly dawned on Pizzuta that just maybe... Fulvia wanted their relationship to be untainted with the past. She couldn't love him, not in a car, not yet...

"Don't worry, Marjorie," he said. He raised her head up from his shoulder, and felt his own body quiver. "Your mother goes with me! Tell that to the big crook if he calls again!" He nodded reassuringly, chucked her under the chin. "Good-night, Marjorie. Take Fritz into the house quietly. And oh, what we talked about stays with us, okay?"

"I already knew that!" Marjorie said. "I'm not a kid, you know."

"Guess I asked for that," Pizzuta said, grimacing. He turned to his car and whimsically drew an arrow through the hearts Marjorie had traced on the windshield. From the doorway Marjorie tried to smile, but her chin wouldn't let her...

Pizzuta drove away slowly, feeling unhappy, and the voice in his skull pounded him: *See! you had it all figured out but didn't want to believe it! He controlled her, all right – anytime he wanted to – in the back seat of his car, pumping the hell out of her!* Suddenly, Sam swerved his car and missed a deep ditch. Cool off, hot-head! That's over, in the past, before your time. What the hell could she have done-lose her life? She had a small daughter too, remember? She was trapped, a slave! So get the fuck off that trip! This is today, and she loves *you* – remember? The thought comforted Sam, and the hammering in his head slowly subsided...

Frowning, he thought of what he should do. Why not? He would let the boys at the diner know he had a girl, City Hall secretary... from the mayor's office, no less. Italian too – a widow – Fulvia Fleming. Di Anello would surely find out. He could blow his fuses, or panic and make mistakes. Any which way, Pizzuta planned to puncture the *Mano Nera* chief's aloof outward veneer. *But protect Fulvia! It is my number one priority.*

Also put heat on Longcoat, Little Angelo... and about time to have a heart to heart talk with Phil Martello. Funny, neither he nor his crowd reported Vito's attack on Mona Noci at the lake last month. Di Anello's kid Guido was mixed up in that. Hmm, so was Marjorie. But what the hell, he could understand the closed mouths – Marjorie's loyalty to Mona, her budding love for Phil, Mona scared shitless about a beating from her mother if she knew, and Guido, not wanting to upset his father, or whatever. Anyhow, Pizzuta thought, he *knew*, despite the impediments, and that was important. Now he had to put the pieces together, huddle with Jimmy and Luke, and get things moving. Something, his cop's sixth sense told him time was short.

Sam grunted, turning on the windshield wipers. A light rain slanted into the half-open driver's side window of the car. Cursing New England's changeable weather he closed the window, hard. One thing wasn't changing: the trail of deaths linked one way of the other with Di Anello. Pizzuta thought of Oreste Straniero, business partner of Di Anello, drunk and dead in a burned out car in the Berkshires. *Now that was no accident! And the other pillar-of-the-community partner, Nino whatever his last name was-getting pickled in a wine barrel by Vito. And Doctor Priore, and that hobo, also dead. All of them killed in such a short space of time. And all connected in some way with Di Anello! Who is next? Fulvia? Me? Phil? Or does Di Anello have future plans for bright young fellas like Phil? And what of Phil's father, Sebastiano? Intere and most discouraging!*

Sam Pizzuta wanted no more front page accident items, particularly those he could no longer see!

He who rides the tiger finds himself inside!

Even detectives! Accidents could be arranged; from the court warehouse, the Front Street bookie joint, or even the sanctuary of East Hawthorne Road, and he-Massimo Di Anello would be clean, untouched by the sordid affair. He would be free, free to expand the rackets of the *Mano Nera*, the Black Hand.

Pizzuta would heed the cautionary words of Detective John Fong, oldest detective on the force, and stay the hell off the tiger's back!

Naturally, Fong was known as Charlie Chan.

Sam grinned, his inner tenseness easing. He wheeled onto Columbus Street and headed for the diner, a blaze of interior light and garish colored outdoor lights announcing its location. Peering upwards he saw that it was no longer raining, but that the moon was nevertheless losing its battle to send pale streaks of light through a front of black clouds. Sam parked in front of the diner, put up the collar of his jacket, and sauntered into the diner.

"Coffee half-and-half," he said, rubbing and blowing on his hands, and sweeping the diner with a practiced gaze.

It was late, but the diner was full. Its denizens, arrayed along the stools of the long serving counter or hunched together in small groups along a narrow counter on the opposite wall where they could view the street through the large plate glass windows, were talking business: a horse that should have won today; or, about the upcoming morning trek to the racetracks, where a sure thing would come in for them in this or that race-a sly wink, acknowledged with a nod, was the tip-off-a fix, Sam knew. And others openly cursed their lousy luck at the wide-open gambling joint, a white two-decker, a block behind the diner on a dark side street.

One of these days... comes the big raid, Sam thought, sipping his steaming coffee mixed with cream. For now, he'd work on trapping the tiger-before it got to someone else. He blew lightly along the edge of his mug.

"Tinkin' hard, eh? Guess you ain't caught Vito yet." Luke Peris pushed in next to Pizzuta, nudged him. So, Vito is still loose... Sam thought, and Di Anello is worried. Good! "No, we haven't captured him yet. But we will. Say, Luke, you beat the shit out of me the other day in that Morra game. Rematch, now. Outside. Let's go!"

* * * *

Jimmy had planned to go to the diner to join Luke in a cup of coffee, but he was having second thoughts. Luke was a small-time crook, and Jimmy didn't trust him. Hell, he could easily play both sides against the middle, and whichever way the wind blew he would go with either with Pizzuta or Di Anello, or both at the same time. Jimmy felt it in his aching bones. He would not tell Pizzuta that. Pizzuta was too wrapped up in the game, probably knew it anyway, and took precautions.

But what about Jimmy! Out there in the cold, like a chunk of meat thrown to a hungry dog. Who would protect him? He had gone over the top in the war, dodged bullets, bigger stuff, and though wounded had come out alive. But now, as an older and wiser civilian, he again was 'going over the top' for Pizzuta, without arms or an army to protect his ass. As a matter of fact, the army was on the other side, and would blow him away if he crossed them. He wasn't about to be blown away. Not Jimmy!

Besides, he liked his present circumstances. Soon he'd be able to get rid of his clunker, get a newer car. His little store was a numbers outlet now, and his cut was nice. He was in with Sforza, who had suggested the deal. Yes, he had told Pizzuta about it, and Pizzuta had said "Sure, go along with it, find out all you can." Unsaid was the fact that Jimmy could keep his numbers cut. Nice deal. No hassle, so long as he kept his nose clean. And he thought he would do that. He had volunteered to help Pizzuta. Well, he could unvolunteer himself, couldn't he?

But one possible problem remained – Phil Martello. He knows too damn much! Jimmy became puzzled. Whose side is Phil on? He's in tight with Guido Di Anello, and his old man works for Nino – no, Di Anello now! What's it all mean to Jimmy? He sweated and squirmed, undecided... frustrated.

PART III

Chapter 27

The picturesque beauty and pleasant warmth of New England in the early fall contrasts sharply with its frigid winters when the valleys and glens of the countryside sleep in blankets of sleet. The fir and pine trees, their branches heavy with glistening icicles and mounds of snow, sigh their discomfort as arctic winds roar among them. Houses are buttoned up, narrow windows shuttered, and storm windows up for those that can afford them. In towns, remote villages and farms, wood cut from oak, walnut, elm or chestnut, is stacked outside or in sheds, and here and there coal is dumped down chutes for use by plump pot-bellied stoves or big basement octopus furnaces.

Vito Amorusi, in his own atavistic way, was instinctively aware of this, and aside from self-preservation, decided that the vagaries of an uncertain climate could be turned to his advantage. He had put lots of distance between himself and the Buick since he had turned Nino's Chevy around. *Little Angelo, the prick! tryin' ta trap Champ towards da boss's place! Ha! And before dat, if Champ had only stopped da Chevy at da lake and looked. Geez! dat punk Phil could a been cold meat by now. Dere'll be anudder time!*

Right now, Champ – he sure liked dat name! Champ knew that a pissed off Di Anello (and the cops) would be hot on his ass, and that his hide-outs, like the railroad yard and Nino's, were unsafe. He thought hard, and turned east on narrow country roads and lanes he knew so well. Soon he would find his way to Boston, and the labyrinths of Little Italy, where he could hide – for a while. Eventually, he knew he would be caught. Whispers and liberally distributed twenty dollar bills would see to that. The folded green stuff pressed into palm or pocket was hard to resist. Besides, he was already a dead man, so informers knew he would not be back to straighten them out, permanently.

Vito, no longer the macho Champ, shuddered as he passed an abandoned granite quarry. Good spot to dump a body. His? Geez, he felt hot! He coughed, spat hard

out the window of the Chevrolet. Then suddenly, he remembered! Cool nights – in the country – not too far
away! His hands tightened on the steering wheel, and
he scanned the road ahead through squinting eyes.
Sweating heavily, he found what he sought. A big red
barn loomed to his left. He screamed, a two-year old
finding a lost toy, and turned the car onto a narrow,
winding paved road, gunned the motor, and headed
southwest. Boston, about twenty miles away, would not
be seeing Vito Amorusi. *Screw 'em all! Vito Amorusi is a
lot smahta dan dey tink!*

"Nice guy," the tow-headed twelve-year old said, looking at the dollar bill in his hand.

"Yeah, guess so," said his companion, in knickers
and cap, his eyes fixed on his own dollar bill.

"But what's a guy dressed like that, and in a snazzy
new 1935 car, doin' in a one-horse village like this, huh?"
The first boy picked his nose and looked at the rear of
the Chevrolet disappearing around a bend of Mill Road
at the southern part of the village.

The first boy took off his cap, waving it in a south-
erly direction, "Are you deaf or somethin'? He's gonna
visit his cousin down there for a few weeks, maybe even
stay the winter."

"Yeah? Well, Donnie, if that's true, how come he had
to ask us directions to Old Man Bloom's place? Kinda
funny, I think." He picked at his nose again, and arced
the rolled, dry mucous away with a snap of his finger.

"Yuck! Don't do that, Bennie! You make me wanna
throw up! Awright! Let's sneak up there after a while..."
Donnie stopped, smiled broadly as the idea churned in
him. "I got it! We don't have to sneak at all. We'll ask the
old man for boxing lessons, with this money the guy
gave us. We can look around. Maybe we'll run into
somethin' juicy. Boy, wouldn't that be great?" Donnie
jammed his cap onto his head, and both boys walked
away, talking softly, smiling, and looking over their shoulders...

Vito peered intently ahead, mindful that it would
soon be dark. The days were getting shorter, and as soon

as the sun went down... There! the street sign, obscured by the big maple tree, just as the two cruddy village boys had said: EPHRAIM STREET, Private Street, Dangerous.

Turning left into the unpaved street, Vito slowed the Chevrolet. Jagged rocks were everywhere, some jutting threateningly into the two cart tracks that served as the roadway. He maneuvered around the obstacles, the car jouncing, tossing and vibrating. Careful! we don't wanna bust open the oil pan or wreck the tires! Vito saw but one farmhouse on the way to Bloom's, and he examined it carefully as he drove past.

Then he thought of Eyes Bloom, and the past came back in bits and pieces. He took off his hat and wiped his brow. In the old days, Bloom had been a fight trainer. His eyes were the keenest in the fight game, and he could spot an opponent's weakness better than anybody. He had worked Vito's camp several times, and Vito had won many fights under his tutelage. But Eyes ran through money like water through a broken pipe... Booze, dames, and gambling. To get more do-re-mi he got into peddling reefers, and smoking them himself. Then the dope dealer suggested that Eyes arrange to throw a couple of fights. Owing the crook a bundle, and cocksure of himself, Eyes did, with a few shady fight-game types he knew could be approached, for a price. And it worked a few times. Feeling he could do no wrong, he tried to enlarge his scheme to include Di Anello's stable of pugs and turkeys. It didn't work. Di Anello found out, and Eyes was headed for permanent cold storage. Vito, one of Di Anello's few good boxers, and on his way up at the time, pleaded for Eyes Bloom's life.

"For you, this one time," Di Anello had said, not willing to upset a fighter with promise. "But the Jew has ta get lost. No more fight game fa him, *capito*?" Vito had nodded, found Eyes, and told him. Eyes needed no prompting, and he faded from sight, like an invisible man.

About six months later, after a successful fight in Rhode Island, Vito got a phone call from Eyes: "I just had to see you fight tonight, Champ! Great win! Listen, I'll never forget what you did for me. If you ever need a favor, check in with me. I'm buying a place in this little

hick town – Stonebridge – near here. But don't tell anybody, you know why. Get it?"

Vito had understood, and had forgotten all about
Eyes until now. He needed that favor! He had found the
sparsely settled village easily enough, and the two kids
had busted their asses telling how to get to Bloom's place
when he tucked dollar bills in their dirty shirt pockets.

Money talks! No money no music! As always! He
patted the front seat. Nino's 'just in case' wad was wedged
under the springs... where Vito had put it after relieving
Nino's body of it. Knowledge of the money relaxed Vito.
Nevertheless, he glared hard at the cover of dark pine
ahead, searching... The tree line ended, giving way to
ground studded with rocks left by an ancient glacier.
Stone walls, some crumbling, covered with thorny rose
bushes and wild grape, gave stark testimony to the hard
work of early settlers.

"Poor basteds," Vito mumbled, remembering bits of
his sixth grade geography and history lessons – before
he dropped out at age sixteen, "all dem dumb Puritans
got for dere work was more rocks." He shook his head
and carefully drove the Chevrolet through the shallow
overflow of a meandering brook which bounced and
glided over a series of low cascades as it headed for a
deep, wooded chasm off to the right of the road.

The old man came out the back end of the farmhouse, stretched, put his thumbs under the straps of
his bib overalls, hitched them up a notch over his shoulders, and rubbed his back and left leg.

"Damn rheumatism," he grumbled. "How much
longer can I take this?" He swept an arm from left to
right, covering a rocky pasture which ended at the tree
line a few hundred feet away. Mumbling still, he shuffled to the front of the long house, a pail dangling from
an arm. Though he had cricks, the chickens had to be
fed, two hogs slopped, and Betsy, his mare, looked after.
Soon, he knew, his Model A Ford would be blocked up
for the winter. Snow would pile up, and the road to his
place would become impassable to cars. He'd have to
repair the old sleigh pretty quick and get it ready for
Betsy. Damn, how the grand old lady loved to pull and

strut!

Jacob "Eyes" Bloom tugged his battered straw lower over his brow against the glare of dusk. Someone coming to see him? If so, that hadn't happened for some time. The Depression had dried up the few bucks he made training local yokels with big ideas about the fight ring. They didn't show anymore; nobody had cash these days! Something had better come up soon, he thought unhappily. Only got enough to last a year, at most, and he only sixty-six years old. Frig! No poorhouse for him! He had to figure an angle, work some deal... Anything!

He stared hard at the approaching car. "Hmm, it's a sedan," he said softly. "New 1935 model," he added. He knuckled his eyes and said, "And with no eyeglasses!" Guess there's part of me that's not falling apart, he told himself silently and smugly.

Vito stopped the car, got out, and grinned at the thin, sharp-nosed man. The man leaned heavily on one leg and wisps of gray hair curled out from under his Farmer John straw. Clear, piercing blue eyes raked Vito, and a quick uncertain smile jerked his lips upwards.

"It's me, Eyes... Vito – Champ! I need dat favor ya owe me." He stuck out his right hand. Eyes Bloom took it, his eyes on Vito's scraped knuckles. "For the luvva Mike, how the hell are you, Vito? Fatter, I see, and dressed to kill... Ha ha! Hey, tell old Bloom here what's up. Come on in, let's talk. We got a lot of catching up to do." He threw and arm around Vito, pressing hard. Vito winced and tried to cover up his rib pain.

They talked. In the sparsely furnished parlor with the stone fireplace on one side, in the big kitchen, and in the barn, now an attached part of the farmhouse.

"Too cold in the winters here, Vito. I got the idea from old farms scattered around. For a few hundred bucks two local yokels, a couple of years back, connected the barn up to the house-glad to get the work they were. Depression pretty bad in these parts. Anyway, now I can walk in comfort from the parlor to the barn, even if a blizzard is blowing outside. Brought electricity in, too. Not bad, eh? Does wonders for my rheumatism."

Vito barely listened. He looked around and his mind

worked hard. Spades, shovels, adzes, forks and chains, grindstones, and an old moldboard, used for generations by previous owners of Bloom's farmhouse were piled in a heap in one dim corner near the livestock stalls. The center of the barn was clear, tarps pegged tightly into the ground, forming a square. Two big bare electric light bulbs hung down on chains from the rafters.

"It's in my blood, Vito. I'll never shake it, not as long as I'm alive," Bloom said, wistfully. "Yeah, Vito, I see you notice! I used this space as a makeshift ring, gave boxing lessons, even had a few illegal fights a few years back." He grinned owlishly. "Needed the money – still do. But the town's dry as an old maid's cunt now. Depression's flattened it." Angry now, he relived the 'old days' – and he recalled how some crum-bum had squealed on him when he tried to make a few bucks on the side, and he had to disappear fast... or else.

"I took my dough and left. Alive, thanks to you, Champ!"

Bloom's country-farmer demeanor melted away. His blue eyes blazed and glinted, and he told Vito of how he had locked up his farmhouse, and wandered around the states, haunting fight rings, picking up a few bucks. Then, he went to Puerto Rico and did all right training a few good prospects.

"Never lost my eyes, and they paid off for me," he said. "But I got tired of runnin', got homesick... believe it! So I came back here to try to figure things out. See, I'm close to the action, yet far away; know what I mean? But who the hell knows, maybe someday–"

"Ta hell wit someday, Eyes! Train me, hear? First, fix me up good." Vito ran a hand over his body, his face. "By next spring, ah'll be ready for a comeback. We kin do it, bote of us, workin' wid each udder."

Bloom's lips compressed. Vito didn't tell him why he was banged up and Bloom wasn't about to ask, knowing Vito's short fuse... *The guy's running,* he thought, *maybe from Di Anello, the police, or both. Shit! I don't need this, not at my age! How do I get him to blow... now, not next spring?*

"Here!" Vito pulled out a roll of bills, licked off four fifties... handed them to Bloom. "On account. Let's start by fixin' me up. Den, soon–" he jerked a thumb at the ring, cackled, and his eyes gleamed.

Bloom missed Vito's crazy look. Flabbergasted, he stared at the two hundred bucks. Sure, he'd make adjustments for that! Even train this punch drunk nit-wit – gain some time, figure on how to glom on to the rest of the big roll of bills Vito carried... Must be thousands! Hot damn!

"We need some supplies, Champ," Bloom said cheerily. "I'll pick up what we need in the morning with this dough. And... thanks!"

"Sure ting. I'll go witcha."

"You don't have to, Champ. Sleep late, rest."

"Naw, I'll come too. I wanna pay fa everyting. From now until spring, where you go, I go. Pals, right?"

"Yeah, sure... pals, Champ." Bloom didn't like the tenor of the conversation, nor the bulge in Vito's sports coat – no tailoring mistake that – and he didn't like the wild gleam that came into Vito's eyes from time to time. *He's no nit-wit! He's plumb crazy!*

"Before da snow comes, dere are a few tings I gotta do," Vito said, as if talking to himself. "A coupla lousy punks gotta be taken care of... Who knows, maybe even da boss. Den, in da spring, Champ makes a comeback."

Bloom sensed an opening and worked it, "What kind of trouble you in, Champ? The boys? Police? I'm your trainer, and I gotta know before you go straight to the top... Middleweight Champ Vito!" He slathered the butter on thick, smiled, and thought: *Twenty years in pen, or straight to the chair. That's where you're headed!*

Vito dropped his guard and answered, "Yeah, I got problems wit bote dem good people." He caught himself. "Tell ya da story later. Got a phone?"

"No."

"Where's da nearest one?"

"Oh... in the village, near the First National grocery store. Going in tonight?" Bloom went over to quiet Betsy, who was snorting and whinnying.

"Tanks. Yeah, gotta call someone."

"Sure, Champ. Go ahead. I'll wait for you in the barn – calm my nervous lady." He patted Betsy, spoke soothingly to her.

A warning light snapped on in Vito's head and paranoia gripped him. He knew there was a phone nearby – at the farmhouse, down the road – not far from Bloom's. So! Bloom too was out to get him, turn him in to the cops, or worse, bring in a couple of hoods to cream him while he slept.

I saw da phone lines, ya crooked lyin' bastid! Shoulda let'em cut ya trote back in dem dere years...

"See ya in an hour." Vito smiled benignly, and headed for his car.

"It's a once in a lifetime opportunity, Betsy," Bloom chortled. "I'll play dumb, call the city – yeah – the diner... from Lester's place, tell'em Vito just popped up and that he's all banged up. I'll ask if he's in trouble, innocent like. I'll tell'em I'm straight now, and don't want to get involved in a mess. They're sure to tell me what's up, and ask where he is. I'll tell'em, and they'll come for him. I'll be home free Betsy, back in the fight game!"

That's worth more than the dough the nut is carrying, Bloom mused. *But hmm, where he's going, he'll need a pitchfork – not dough. So, gotta figure a way!* He followed the departing Chevrolet with a hungry look. *But... what if the cops also want him?* Bloom quieted his inner voice with the thought that they'd never know a thing. Vito would just disappear. Period. With that cheery thought, he patted Betsy who was still nervous, and cautiously drove his Model A out of the barn.

No sign of Vito, but in the distance he made out a pinpoint of light – Lester's place, where he would make his million dollar phone call. He had found out about the diner and its occupants when he got back from Puerto Rico, and his desire to re-enter the professional fight game in the states at the time was almost irresistible. But the boys were thicker now than flies on a pile of manure. He marveled at how well things were going for Di Anello, and decided to continue the facade of gentleman farmer, for he valued life; specifically his.

Bloom now slowed to turn off the rutted road towards Lester's old weather-beaten place. The grass and gravel path to the house, lined with bush and tree, was just wide enough for the Model A. Soon – he licked his dry lips – he would be at that phone, making the call of his life...

What the-? A dark shape materialized out of the darkness, and landed with a thud on the Model A's running board.

Against the curtain of the country night, Bloom saw, knew, and gasped.

The Model A's glass shattered. A shard slit Bloom's cheek, and a gun jammed into his temple.

"Turn dis ting around... now! Do what I tell ya!" The voice was hollow, without feeling. A zombie could do no worse. Trembling, Bloom complied.

Bloom fought: "Hey, take it easy, Champ! I'm your trainer, remember? What the fuck's got into you, anyway? Get in here, let's go home. I'll drop by to see my sick friend later, and-"

"Shut ya mouth!" The gun pressed harder, the pain terrible.

"Turn off, right here," Vito ordered.

A few moments later two muffled shots stung the night. Vito jumped off the running board just as the Model A began its death dive into the chasm, its short journey masked by the sound of gurgling, splashing water below.

Vito produced a flashlight and fixed the beam on the Model A. "Rat fink!" he said.

The car lay on its right side, half-submerged in the stream, its left front wheel turning lazily. A bloody, limp hand protruded from the window. Satisfied, Vito spat into the stream, turned, and ran to his own car, hidden near the road. He got in and didn't know what to do. Should he head west? Go back to Bloom's place? As he cooled down his body ached, and he decided to stay until morning, rest up. He'd leave at dawn, that's it!

Meantime he'd check the house, get his mitts on all the dough he could find. He'd need it out west. And yeah! that fight ring was in the barn. He sat in his car, on hold, and his warped brain stripped away the years... 1934, 1933, 1932, 1930, 1929-

He stood, trim and hard, in the center of the ring, dancing, shadow boxing. He raised a gloved hand, acknowledging the roar of the crowd at Lakeside Arena. His first fight with Sammy Constantino! If he won he'd be on his way to the big time. CLANG! The fight was on! Round after round Vito bobbed and weaved, jabbed, threw his favorite punch, a crunching left uppercut, and he could see Sammy tiring. *Sammy! yor on da way ta da meat wagon!* But Sammy fought back viciously, lefts and rights to the head! Body chops! Vito felt his knees buckle. The bell!

Hecklers! Vito didn't like that, particularly one big one who screamed at him. Vito leaned over and grabbed the heckler by his long hair...

"Dat ain't nice," he said, and chopped the shape on its big nose.

Snap! Vito heard the sound in his head. He blinked, looked around... getting his bearings. A frightened blood-in-the-eye Betsy! rearing, kicking, slamming her huge body into the side of the stall. *She – the heckler?* Geez!

"Hey, take it easy dere, you nut." Vito snarled at her, not quite out of his twisted dream-world. A flailing hoof came within inches of his face and he stepped back, lost his balance, and fell into the pile of ancient tools. The rope holding Besty frayed. In a moment she'd bust loose. Shit! Vito realized he had to get out fast. If she got him with a hoof, he'd be washed up before his come-back, not even good enough for the meat wagon; a has been pug filling in as a substitute, or set up to make others look good.

With an agility he didn't realize he had, he leaped to his feet with an old adze held protectively in his hands. She's almost loose! He bolted to his car, looked once over his shoulder, and lunged inside.

Moments later, as the farmhouse receded behind him, Vito panicked. Where could he go? He needed time to heal before heading west. *Dere was still dat punk Martello!* The Chevrolet bounced over the ruts and rocks, and soon Vito heard the sound of water. A chasm around here, someplace? He thought of Bloom and the old days. Sure! *Dat's it! Where no one from da neighborhood goes – da ledge!* Bloom had mentioned some of the old-time fighters. Where were they now? Well, Fred 'Glass-jaw' Wray lives up on the ledge...

Ever see him? Bloom had asked... *At da races, some-times. Ya see, Eyes, da ledge is territory we stay da hell away from!*

"But not dis time!" Vito cried. "Wray's a turkey, and kin use da dough." He curled one hand under the seat and turned the steering wheel hard right with the other. The car, off Ephraim Street, quit jouncing. Vito hit the accelerator. Hard.

* * * *

The following morning, wrestling, jostling, picking up small flat stones and throwing them at likely targets. Donnie and Bennie went to Bloom's, ostensibly to ask for boxing lessons but also to snoop around. There was something about that city slicker–

No one answered their knock at the front door. They went around to the barn. "Hey look," Donnie said, taking off his cap and scratching his head, "Betsy's rope is broken, and she ain't anywhere around. Boy, she sure busted up her stall! Funny, huh? Let's look around!"

"Gee, I don't know," Bennie said. He began to pick his nose, his index finger probing nervously. He walked slowly past Donnie and kicked at a broken stall board, fastened to the back wall. It and other splintered wood fell away and clattered to the floor with a hollow dry wood sound.

Odd, choking, constricted sounds spewed from Bennies gaping mouth. His eyes threatened to pop out of his skull. The finger in his nose froze in place. He wigwagged the fingers of his other hand at the wall. Up and down he jumped, jabbing at the wall and struggling to speak coherently.

"You nuts or something?" Donnie asked, nettled. But his eyes followed Bennies fluttering hand. He screeched, and fell on his hands and knees, struck dumb, but not for long. Both boys stirred, looked at each other, and ran to the wall, knowing what they had stumbled upon - Blooms' wooden cash box, built into the wall and concealed by a small upward sliding door, part of Betsy's stall.

Donnie scooped up bills from the straw-littered floor. He drooled, he jabbered, he missed his pockets.

"Use your cap!" Bennie yelled, suddenly cool. He slapped Donnie, who seemed dazed but said, "Bennie, we're rich, we're rich! All right, okay!"

The cap filled quickly. On tiptoes, necks tight, the boys went to the barn door. No sign of Bloom or the city slicker. "Let's go, quick!" And they sped away at breakneck speed, Donnie's cap clutched tightly by both.

"Oh no!" Donnie yelled, with an all-is-lost look. "Someone's following us," he gasped. "I... I..." his grip loosened on the cap.

Bennie, breathing hard, glanced over his shoulder, shook his head, and pulled Donnie aside, as a big brown shape galloped by – Betsy! She curved left towards the chasm and whinnied piteously.

"Wonder what she'd doing over there?" Bennie asked. "The old man never lets her run loose. And look, her tether rope is broken. Gee, I wonder?"

The boys squinted at each other, at Betsy, and they sprinted for the chasm. Betsy followed, tossing her mane, pawing the ground.

Puzzled at what looked like fresh tire tracks in the wet ground by the chasm, Donnie and Bennie climbed down into it and looked into the Model A.

They screamed. Terrified, they clambered out and ran. Then, as if by some secret signal, they stopped, and looked at each other.

"I guess we'd better hide this," Bennie said, looking at the cap.

"Yeah! Poor Bloom! That city slicker was sure a bastard!"

"Sure was," Bennie said. "How much did he steal?"

"Huh? Oh. I get it! Let's count it." They did. "Gee, seven hundred bucks!" Donnie said, awe-struck.

"Now listen!" Bennie said. "After we hide the money we'd better go to the village and tell the cops we found Bloom."

"Are we gonna tell them that the city slicker took seven hundred bucks?"

"No, you idiot! Come here, sit down, and listen!" Bennie shook Donnie.

About an hour later, the boys, their childhood a thing of the past, neared the village. Heels kicking up dirt, they yelled, "Murder! Murder! Old man Bloom! Old man Bloom!"

Donnie's cap was nowhere in sight.

Chapter 28

Friday morning, October 11. The Columbus Day holiday weekend began! The mothers streamed out of their tenement kitchens, ants from an anthill, towards a large open Dodge truck protected from wind and rain by a red parasol canopy. The rusty truck sagged under its load of boxes and ice, and smelled of old seaweed.

"*Oo pesh, oo pesh!*" wailed the fishmonger, in dialect everyone knew. *Merlootz', anguil', calamaroo, tutto fresch', oo pesh, oo pesh!*"

The mothers, in a colorful splash of blue, green, pink, and yellow chenille robes, faded oft-washed smocks and aprons, swirled about the truck. They touched, smelled, chattered, and frowned when told what the price of the plump mackerel was, or the ostriche, plucked from their beds 'this very morning'

"*Aprile, stringi un po di sugo di limone... e poi...ahhh... inghiotile!*"

Fats Baldoni's eyes rolled behind his thick glasses, and, in pantomime, he pretended to open the oyster he held in his pudgy hand, squirted imaginary lemon juice on it, raised his head, and swallowed. He brought tightly held fingers of one hand to his mouth, kissed them with a loud smack, and flung the hand out in a theatrical wave. It worked.

Amid cries of *"Bravo Baldoni, bravo!"* ...he sold out his supply of oysters, and most everything else.

"Move it, Fats! Show's over, you clown!" The loud voice came from the tarp-covered ice truck, driven by the Lantini brothers, both decked out in their rubber shoulder and back capes. The mothers had put their ice cards in the front room windows, with the numbers '20 cents' or '25 cents' showing at the top. The three-day holiday required big pieces of ice in the ice boxes, and the brothers were anxious to please. Fats moved to the next tenement.

Swearing lustily at Fats, each brother muscled a cube of ice onto his back with a set of iron tongs and began his delivery, climbing many flights of stairs in the process. No big thing, just part of the job!

Next came Abie in his fat brown van. The mothers flocked to him.

"I got the best Florida oranges for you, Lena! And for you, Grace, the California persimmons you'd die for. Nellie...oy! For you, choice broccoli!"

Abie Goldberg knew his customers by name; their likes and dislikes. He weighed nothing, carried no pen, pencil or paper. Everything happened in his head. No matter how fast the orders came at him he remembered who gave them, and the quantity. Ducking into his truck (nothing was displayed), he emerged with the most delicious fresh fruit and produce east of the Mississippi. Accurate change came from his striped railroad engineer overalls. He knew who had given him the quarter, the fifty cents, or the two dollar bill.

"Where you get dis wondafoola stuff?" was an oft-asked question.

"Oy, better you don't ask!" was the standard reply.

Nobody pushed. The mothers knew a good deal when they saw it!

Two nights a week Abie worked a night card gam for Natale at the big stakes table in a private room in Natale's Front Street bookie joint. On two other nights a week he ran the fast and furious Barboot dice games... a new Di Anello enterprise, imported from Lebanon, at a new location – near the Yankee part of town, the west side.

Fruits and vegetables, though, were Abie's legitimate business. Di Anello had so decreed. Furthermore, he would peddle only top quality, fancy produce. It would give him a reputation as a solid, honest businessman who could never be suspected of doing anything crooked. Abie, king of the produce peddlers!

Phil, casually dressed in a blue short sleeve sport shirt, light gabardine slacks and black, polished loafers stopped and watched. He stood near the front street-level entryway of the tenement. He glanced at his wrist watch – some time to kill. He enjoyed what he saw: Mothers, bent on picking out the freshest fish, submerged Baldoni's truck. And Baldoni himself – geez – what a fake! Abie? A human adding machine. Phil wished he had that talent for school. Ugh!

But today was a sparkling tonic for Phil. He was part of this teeming, scheming, life-loving neighborhood, where *la famiglia* reigned supreme, and *non me ne frega* was the attitude-glue that kept everyone insulated and secure against the outside world of *mangia patate*.

Phil put on his light jacket, zipped it up, and looked apprehensively at the sky. Unexpectedly a cloud of lint and dust settled on his hair and shoulders. His new jacket! Quickly, he brushed at what he thought was soot from the railroad yard. It wasn't.

"Hi, big boy! Long time not see!" Mona, on the front porch above, again shook the dust-mop she held.

Phil sidestepped the debris. "Oh, hi Mona. Guess so."

"You're pretty spruced up for so early in the morning. Going somewhere special?" Mona knew darn well where he was going. The phones still worked.

"Maybe." He glanced at his watch. "Gotta go. See ya, Mona."

She blew him a kiss. Nice guy, she thought. I can get him back from that skinny Marjorie anytime. But tonight Mona knew she had a heavy date with a young chase and Sandborn coffee salesman. He wanted to show her some samples he had. Well he wouldn't if she could help it. Then again, he was so handsome! *So many nice men, and just one of me.* She shook her head sadly and gave the dust mop one final shake.

Phil walked briskly up Holly Hill. After about a mile he would be at Marjorie's house for the fourth and last dance lesson. The big dance was tonight! For now that's what he would think about, although he couldn't help but wonder what had happened to Vito. Two Stonebridge boys had found an ex-boxing trainer named Bloom dead, two bullets in his skull. And they described a 'city slicker' who had come to visit Bloom the day before. Their description of him fit Vito. And the new 1935 Chevrolet? Nino's! Oh! how the newspapers had played that up: 'Murderer at large! Will he kill again?'

Massimo Di Anello, interviewed by the press, humbly acknowledged that he should have paid more attention to the deteriorating state of his ex-boxer's mind. Where is he? Who knows? Even though he's nuts, he's smart enough not to stay around here. He's probably out west by now, laying low...

Phil wondered. Di Anello could have given the press – and cops – a bum steer, so he could deal with Vito himself, here, quietly. Oh, shit!

And what about Jimmy? Phil recalled how Jimmy, a week or so ago, had refused to take back his Silver Star. "You hold on to it a while longer, Phil." Strange! And strange too, were the number of diner characters hanging around Jimmy's store. What the heck was that about?

The days slid by, September became October, news of Vito disappeared from the papers, and school homework and the dance lessons fully occupied Phil. Gee! He had even taken Marjorie to the candy store for a banana split. Now that had been nice... And she had told him that Sergeant Pizzuta was dating her mother. Wow! Really something... all right!

Phil kicked at a pile of dank oak leaves, their color faded. Was his war with *them* – the Black Hand, fading too; a quick splash, and then gone? And Pizzuta, what of him? Would his courting of beautiful Mrs. Fleming so turn his senses that his determination to nail Di Anello would crumble?

Phil thought not, on both counts. Right now though, it was time for fun... and Marjorie. *Oh yeah?* that damned little voice in a corner of his skull mocked him. *That's what you think! You're in the eye of a hurricane Phil Martello! So watch it!*

Phil grimaced. "Aw shit!" he said aloud. Funny though, how things had worked out... Dance practice was supposed to have been in Guido's den, but Di Anello told Guido it wasn't possible. Something about painting and remodeling. And... Mrs. Fleming would not drive a Di Anello car, as Guido had promised. Repairs... business developments... An unhappy Guido told Phil, who promptly phoned Marjorie. She burst into tears and told her mother of the horrible turn of events, from which she obviously would never recover.

Marjorie recovered quickly though, for dance practice took place in Mrs. Fleming's little front parlor and, Marjorie said, a car large enough for them all was available. Her mother would chaperone as planned. She would drive Phil and Marjorie, Vic and Carmela, and Guido and Lucy to the school dance in Tim Hoyt's personal City Hall car, a new Chrysler made available by Mary Coyne.

Mary had assumed Fulvia, when Fulvia told Mary how Di Anello had vetoed his son's promise to furnish transportation, that Hoyt wouldn't be needing his car. He had other plans for the evening; and the weekend. A clambake and other things. Fulvia hadn't pressed for clarification of 'other things'. Why should she... anymore?

But Mary Coyne, well lubricated at the time, decided to needle Mr. Big Eye-talian, so she phoned the East Side Export-Import Company. Di Anello picked up the phone in the court warehouse: "Hello, Di Anello here."

"My, how fortunate! You are just the man I wanted to talk to," Coyne said in an affected, dulcet voice. "Mary Coyne, Mr. Hoyt's secretary?"

"Yeah?" His voice exuded suspicion. *No dame sounded like that! What's she up to? What does she want? Rather, what's that bastard Hoyt up to?*

"Well, I just wanted to thank you anyway for your offer to help our sister school by letting us borrow one of your cars... For the dance? I know how awful you must feel now that events way beyond your control have simply forced you to renege." She paused for a quick breath and a hiccup. "But don't fret, now, Mr. Dallo, we'll manage. You see... Mr. Hoyt is letting the left-out-in-the-cold driver, Fully Fleming – she works for me you know – borrow his brand new Chrysler Airflow. Isn't it awful that some nitwits have had the nerve to call the car a bathtub turned upside down? Mr. Zallon... are you there?"

Di Anello wasn't. Red with rage, he had hung up somewhere between 'nerve' and 'bathtub'. He had been insulted, his honor sullied. No! not by a drunken Coyne, but by the betrayer, Fulvia Avellini Fleming, who obviously was to blame for the phone call. She would live to regret her perfidity...

"No, she will not live!" He calmed down and lit a stogie. Her death had to be accelerated, and Detective Sam Pizzuta, her lover, must also die. Alive, he would be dangerous, a relentless avenger. Done!

Di Anello dialed his Front Street operation. "Natale,

come to the court warehouse. We have an important piece of business to discuss. Think of someone to fill the fountain pen and not mess up, eh? One of our boys with moxie." Di Anello hung up. If Natale was good at something, this was it! Natale understood. *But who? Longcoat? Redeemed himself... telling us of Nino's murder, and keeping his mouth shut. No. I still don't trust him. Ah, Little Angelo? No... his cylinders are weak. Skinny? No, not his line. Who then? Natale screwed up his face, and it came to him. The new boy! He's quick, takes orders well. He would make a good addition to... what does the boss call his organization now? La Cosa Nostra, yeah, that's it.*

Natale put out the word: "Get Luke Peris here... fast!"

Phil of course wasn't aware of these machinations. He approached Marjorie's house cautiously. All clear! Guido and Lucy would meet him at Marjorie's, but not Vic and Carmela. They were at Vespucci Park, helping with arrangements to put up two greased poles. The poles would be crowned with loaded baskets of goods donated by neighborhood stores, and teams of young men would strive to shimmy to the top to claim them. This was to occur after the band concert, speeches, and before the first of two evenings of fireworks signaled that indeed the *festa del Gran Scopritore, Cristoforo Colombo,* was in full swing.

Phil, lost in thoughts of the all-out festivities, was startled by the familiar sound of a joyous bark. Fritz! At the door Phil knocked, and heard rapid footsteps approaching it inside. It opened. Marjorie! in a snazzy white sweater and skirt, her hair flaming red, catching and intensifying the weak rays of the sun. Her big green eyes smiled a relieved welcome.

"Phil, you came! I wondered whether you would. Oh–!" She threw both arms around his neck and kissed him on both cheeks. And Phil, impulsively, did something he had never done before to Marjorie, or any other grown girl, for that matter. He pulled her into his arms and kissed her hard, full on the mouth. Fritz, puppy ears crossed over his head, sat on his haunches, and yipped.

From inside, "Hey, let's get started – practice dancing I mean."

Chapter 29

Forty girls, giggling and whispering, lined up with their escorts at the entrance to the assembly hall. When they filed in each received an orchid corsage donated by Tim Hoyt, who had also supplied a seven-piece band composed of musicians from the Parks and Recreation and the Sewer Departments. Each boy received a carnation to pin on his sweater or wear as a boutonniere in his jacket. Again, Hoyt. Sweaters were a concession to the times-many boys did not own jackets – but each boy had to wear a clean shirt and tie. Not that the event was formal. It wasn't, nor was it even semi-formal under the usual connotation of the term.

The dance was the first in years for the sister school. But now, in late 1935, parishioners were returning to work. The mills, shops, foundries stirred again; many open two, three days a week. The hopelessness of the earlier thirties diminished somewhat as pay envelopes, however meager, came home again.

Perhaps because of this happy fact, tight-fisted parents relented. Then too, it was a night out for parent chaperones, and Sister Agnes, the school principal, assured everyone that none of her demure girls would dare appear in plunging necklines or bare backs.

She was wrong.

The band played a slow fox-trot now, and the young couples circled the oak hardwood floor stiffly, for it was their first dance. Sister Agnes surveyed the scene happily. She had done it! She was sure the enrollment in the parochial high school would now increase, for this was a notable first, and her notoriety for having, of all things! a dance, would surely spread. And the girls, half-naked! is what narrow-minds would whisper... Ex-flapper Sister Agnes smiled a sweet, saintly smile. Then her eyes caught and held a tall, strikingly attractive young red-head – Marjorie – and her handsome young man, frowning and obviously concentrating hard.

Phil was concentrating: *One, two, side, together; Forward, forward, side, together. Repeat! Repeat! Oh my gosh, there's the wall! What do I do now?* The trombone player got up for a solo and stumbled; Phil remembered! *Forward, back, and turn; forward, forward, side together! Phew!* His sigh of relief was matched by Sister Agnes. It wouldn't do to have still another couple against the wall, marking time wondering what to do next.

Phil guided Marjorie past Sister Agnes and smiled. See, she somehow telegraphed in her smile, you did it! I know, Phil smiled back.

"Phil, why did you kiss me so hard this morning?" Marjorie asked, dreamily.

"I did?"

"Yes," Marjorie said. "Were you thinking of Mona?"

"No." He remembered he had told Marjorie about the dry-mop incident.

"Do you like her?"

"I guess so."

"Do you know she goes out with older guys now? And that awful brother of hers is trying to fix her up with a creep he hangs around with?"

"Yeah, I know she likes older guys... I hardly ever see her anymore." *One, two, side, together. Repeat! Repeat! So, Nick is back with the diner gang now. Wonder who's he's latched onto this time? Wonder if its Longcoat... again. Hmmm, Gotta look into that. Naw, its none of my business.*

"Phil?" Pause. "Do you like me?"

"Yes." *Watch it! The wall, again.*

"As much as Mona?"

"More." *There, got by the wall! Guess I got the step down fine.*

"Then," Marjorie sighed deeply, put her head on his shoulder, "are you my boyfriend?"

Her light perfume... she was so close... that red hair. "Yes," he said.

The trombone player, a burly sewer worker, set his instrument down and sang, his deep voice coming from somewhere under the polished floor: "I'm forever blowing bubbles... Pretty b-u-b-b-les in the air."

"Ta-ra... ra-rump; ta-ra... ra-rump..." The band replied, in rhythmic counterpoint. The sewer worker had tears in his eyes.

Marjorie nestled closer to Phil and he didn't mind

her defeating him, for bubbles exploded in joyous rainbow colors all around him.

"Tsk, tsk," clucked a bald-headed male chaperon, taking his eyes off Fulvia, whom he had ogled all evening, much to the chagrin of his wife.

She had poked him in the ribs with sharp elbows: "She's not the one you are supposed to watch, Jack the Ripper!" And she glanced enviously at Fulvia, in a modest but clinging black silk dress.

The bald-headed voyeur addressed Phil and Marjorie, "More space between you two." He held his hands a foot apart. He meant to redeem himself. He was ignored. Angry now, his face reddening, he reached out–

At that moment, Sister Agnes whispered to the musicians. The music abruptly stopped. The dancers, Phil and Marjorie too, unclasped and opened towards the band, as dancers do when the music stops.

Fulvia Fleming sighed, her hand coming back up from her shoe. She had been about to throw a stylish black pump at the bald-headed lecher's head. Uncomfortable with his ogling, she became furious at his intrusion into her baby's world of dreams. She looked at Sister Agnes who, surprisingly, looked back with dancing eyes, a shadow of a smile crossing her angelic face. Fulvia crossed herself. The good sister knew all!

Music... again. Phil and Marjorie, eyes only for each other, had missed the antics of the self-proclaimed keeper of the chastity belts, and Fulvia's near explosion. Fulvia observed and understood. Her baby had grown up, and she was in love. With Phil. Phil? Gudio's friend. And Massimo Di Anello, Guido's father! Would the grasping fingers of the *Mano Nera* wreck Marjorie's life, as it had her own? She shuddered at the thought.

But it need not happen! Sam Pizzuta wouldn't let it. Oh, how she ached for him! Perhaps tomorrow night he would finally ask her to marry him! Marjorie had hinted that she thought he would ask her – soon.

Fulvia's attention was drawn to Sister Agnes, who was extolling the virtues of brotherly love and neighborliness, for many young people from below the ledge (and on it) were here tonight. Fulvia's mind drifted. Tomorrow night she would dress stylishly for Sam

Pizzuta, and she thought of the moment when he must surely ask her to marry him, and they would be together – forever.

* * * *

Unknown to Fulvia Fleming, plans had already been made for her to be together with Detective Sam Pizzutta – in a cold eternal embrace.

"You understand, Natale?" Di Anello folded the diagram he had sketched, on a sheet of paper, tore it up, put the pieces in an ash tray, struck a match, and tossed it into the paper. It flared instantly.

"And you, Luke? Remember, after da transaction is complete," Di Anello mouthed the words slowly, his teeth gleaming behind his stretched mouth, "we will talk, together with each other, about your big future."

"I understand perfect," Luke said, staring at the smoldering ashes. Moments before they had been a sketch of a road, a house, pine trees, and vegetation across a narrow gravel street. The house was Fulvia Fleming's place! No turning back now! Luke felt trapped and he could see no way out alive for himself unless Fulvia Fleming and Sam Pizzuta died.

"We have something big ta talk about," surrogate Natale had said when they entered the court warehouse office an hour ago. "Before we start, you tella us whedda you wanna be in on it. If you say 'no,' itsa awright, no problem. But ifa you say 'yes', and we tella you of dis big ting, you cannot back out. Why you fa dis job, eh? You got, as we say, *lu spiritu*. Da boss here tinks you can go far wid us. So, whadda you say?"

"Count me in for sure," Luke had said. Something big! A heist, bribery, extortion, cars to be stolen. Maybe even a kidnap. God, when he warned Sam, and these gangsters were in jail, he would be a free man, his job done.

Then he was told what the job was, and he felt as if an ax had split his head. He controlled his shaking, but not the sweat suddenly running down his forehead into his eyes.

"Don't worry, Luke," Di Anello said, "you stay close

ta Natale. Go over da plan good wid him, and do what he says. All right, go now."

Snared by those damn long fingers! Sam and Mrs. Fleming... Oh God! But... there had to be a way out. Wasn't there always? Even this time? Luke, for once in his life, wasn't so sure. He hadn't prayed since he was a little kid.

He did now.

Chapter 30

The court warehouse door slammed behind Luke Peris. Geez! he felt lower than a... than a snake's belly in a wagon rut! How in the hell was he to get out of the mess he was in?

"Come on, we walk," said Natale.

"Yeah? Where to?"

"Don'tcha know what day dis is?"

"No."

"You young pricks! Dis is da day Sforza makes his special dish at da diner, *pasta fazool'*, and I'm hungry. I love da stuff." Natale pushed Luke.

Pasta fazool, dialect for *pasta e fagiuoli,* marcaroni and beans, Luke knew. The beans were soaked overnight to de-gas them, later cooked in olive oil, garlic, onion and tomatoes, and then mixed and simmered with macaroni which had been boiled separately. A ubiquitous Depression meal. No in-between on *pasta fazool'* – one either loved them or hated them.

"Hey, I love 'em too!" Luke piped up. He hated the dish! But a thin glimmer of hope warmed his cold despondency. Jimmy's store was across the street, near the diner...

In the diner a short time later Natale shoveled in his third huge platter of the horrible stuff, to Luke's way of thinking. Then, finished, Natale shoved his empty plate along the counter, and smiled. Actually smiled! Well, if you called it a smile. It would scare the shit out of a houseful of little kids, Luke thought.

Then a soft flat burble erupted from the stool Natale sat on, and a pained, bloated expression grew on Natale's face. His discomfort continued, and the ripe stench emanating from his pants reminded Luke of the stink bomb he had thrown in the Majestic theater when he was a kid.

Luke turned his face away. God! if a couple of dead skunks were thrown into an empty-can bin filled to the top for a week, the smell wouldn't be as bad as this... Ah! the smell... Prayers are answered in different ways!

"I'm stepping outside," Luke said, "ta get some air.

Tink I'll go ta Jimmy's and get an Eskimo Pie. Want one, Natale?"

Natale, still having digestive pain, said with tight teeth, "You ain't goin' nowhere, Stay where–"

"Hey, let him go, fa chrissake," Sforza, standing a safe distance away, said. "Jimmy's all right. He's with us. Luke, take this box ta him for me, will ya? Saves me a trip over dere. He'll need the slips tomorrow."

"Sure, glad to." Luke took the old cigar box, tied with twine.

Natale grumbled under his breath, said nothing.

"I'll be right back," Luke said. No sense in pushing the advantage!

Luke handed Jimmy the box with the numbers slips. "Hey Jimmy, let's take a look at your hand. Finger healed up okay?" He leaned over, examined the hand, turned it over and back, and whispered rapidly.

Jimmy stiffened, paled, but he said in a loud confident voice, "Yeah, everything's gonna be fine – with my hand – count on it, Luke."

Luke left, but he gave Jimmy a grateful over-the-shoulder look as he closed the door behind him.

His store closed, Jimmy fought a terrible battle with himself. He was doing fine now, no problems. With Pizzuta gone, he would be off the meat hook, home free. No risks any more. And he'd be in the chips.

Yeah, so what happened to your noble thought of helping clean up the neighborhood of the likes of Di Anello? Didn't you fight a war, almost got deep-sixed, to save the world from the Kaiser? And you did. So what the hell's gotten into you now? Where's the difference?

And what about Pizzuta? He ain't just after a promotion, you know that! The asshole reminded Jimmy of Woodrow Wilson: Make the world – check that! The neighborhood – safe for democracy, and for smart young guys like Phil Martello who could be an honest leader in the neighborhood and out. But no chance of that with Di Anello around, tempting 'em, scaring 'em. Oo-fa!

And now with Pizzuta blinded by that... that Widow of Death... what chance does he have? Di Anello is really pissed!

So, Jimmy, what are you gonna do?

Shit! I don't know!

Hey, remember the war? You went on patrol a few times? Looked for the enemy? Took a few prisoners? Ambushed one of the Hun patrols? Well?

Jimmy's argument with himself came down to that. He would scout Fulvia Fleming's place, look for some brush on the side of the road in which to hide his car – not too far, not too close to the house. Then, starting tonight, he would wait in his car for the hunched creeping figure of Luke Peris to make his move. What Jimmy would do about it he did not know, for Luke would be backed by Natale. Of course, Jimmy thought, he could do nothing. And let Luke down? But conditions could change, the murders could be called off...

Wouldn't that be great? Jittery, upset and confused, Jimmy limped to his car, started it up, and jerked away. His destination was the outer edge of the ledge settlement. Fulvia's place.

Chapter 31

When, on Friday morning, Phil walked to Marjorie's house, Luke Peris sat behind the wheel of Di Anello's black Cadillac, tooling the car expertly round the curves of the Berkshires. Di Anello, in the back seat, smoked a stogie. He flicked an ash from his dark pin-striped suit, adjusted his expensive Dobbs fedora, and gazed admiringly at his gray spats over shiny black shoes, and then at the two-carat diamond ring in a massive gold setting on his right ring finger. Sebastiano Martello, dressed well in a dark blue serge suit, also wearing a Dobbs felt hat (but no spats on his shoes) sat next to Di Anello. His face was creased with worry. Natale, sitting stiff and straight next to Luke, stared straight ahead, a sullen look frozen on his face. *He's an escapee from a wax museum,* Luke thought with heavy scorn.

Ahead, Little Angelo drove the blue Buick, newly waxed and dentless. Next to him sat an unhappy Longcoat. Abie Goldberg rested against the rear seat cushions, his mind in overdrive, calculating furiously.

"We are ready to expand," Di Anello had said earlier to Sebastiano, Natale, and Abie. "All of us will meet, before Columbus Day, with friends of mine. They are independent, and not connected with anyone in trouble with the law or the tax people." He had paused to let that sink in. "When they join us – and they will – we will control business in eastern New York state from Troy to the Canadian border. After that we go south, beyond Washington, D. C. Then... we will be ready for our first big fish, Miami.

"We will slowly surround the big cities of the east coast. And we will be a monopoly, like a big American corporation. Natale, you talk about your operations; Sebastiano, the warehouses and store operations. Abie – you follow me when I talk Italian?" Abie nodded. "All right. So, Abie, you bring the books in your head, eh? I will cover the rest of our enterprises." Di Anello had looked at Abie, who had nodded again.

"Pretty country," Luke now said, to break the silence. "We passed da big mountain back dere a while, off ta da right. Mount Greylock, I tink. We should be turnin' nort soon."

No movement or sound from the Wax Museum. Sebastiano? Off somewhere in his thoughts. Di Anello leaned forward and tapped Luke on the shoulder with a long finger. "Good, Luke, you turn north near Pittsfield." Satisfied, he leaned back, blowing enormous smoke rings.

Creepy fuckin' trip, Luke thought... *But better'n stayin' with Charlie McCarthy!* He nodded imperceptibly towards Natale. *Maybe somethin' will come up, and we won't get back in time for Columbus Day. That'd be great!*

The others had their own thoughts: *What does he think he's doing?* Sebastiano shuddered involuntarily. *Di Anello is corrupted beyond redemption! His success in the neighborhood and nearby towns does not mean he can do the same elsewhere. He is so blind! When the Big Ones awake to his scheme he will be squashed like an unwanted spider in the kitchen. His lust for power will be his downfall, and perhaps mine! And yet, his plan could work...*

Natale's thoughts weren't on the trip. Old business occupied his mind, the business he had entrusted to Longcoat. After the Nino killing incident Natale had given Longcoat his old numbers route again. "You did good," he had said. "Tanks. Now, don't go fucking up." But something was wrong...

Too much variation in Longcoat's take, and one irate customer phoned in asking where the hell his fifty bucks in winnings were. Longcoat hadn't shown up with them. Natale had been furious.

After collections, Longcoat had gone home for a short nap. Afterwards he would turn in the take. So when Natale phoned and asked for Longcoat, a volley of colorful invectives streamed at him over a line that seemed to sizzle. Grandmother Isabella was disgusted with her no good grandson! He had been sleeping for hours. He was still dead in bed, *un vero poltrone!*

Natale let Longcoat live, thanks to Isabella's innocent intervention, and Longcoat was so informed, coldly. Longcoat had sobbed his thanks.

Now Natale watched the car ahead. For the next several days someone else would take Longcoat's numbers route, and collections would be compared. Natale had asked that Longcoat come along on the trip: 'Good experience'.

Di Anello had shrugged. "Fine. We can use another man... to watch."

Now Natale grunted loudly as the Buick disappeared around a sharp curve. Luke glanced quickly at Natale and cringed. *What's with him*, he thought? *I'd hate to be on da wrong side a him!* But, Luke knew he would be. Geez!

In the Buick, Longcoat thought about the fifty bucks Natale had forced him to cough up to pay off the irate bettor. Unhappy about that, he also chafed at being away from the neighborhood. He wanted to pin Nick Noci down: When are ya gonna fix me up wit yor sister? Longcoat had done Nick favors, but Nick never brought Mona around.

Since he had been back together with Nick, Longcoat had cut Nick in on the skim from his collections, and the easy dough from peddling reefers. And soon he would be dealing in stronger stuff. His out of town 'relatives' – ha! were set to supply him! Sure, he knew Natale and Di Anello didn't go for drugs, but others did. So he'd be his own boss, and Mona his girl. When he got back, Fat Nick would come through, or else.

Back in the Cadillac, Di Anello scanned a copy of Il *Progresso Italo-Americano*, a New York City Italian language newspaper, but his mind was elsewhere – on Vito Amorusi. The neighborhood and the railroad yard had been methodically searched, for Vito could have doubled back. No luck. In Boston's *Piccola Italia* Di Anello's money sang. Shadowy figures combed the brick buildings of Prince Street, cobblestone alleys, and the multistory tenements of Fleet Street with their awning-draped street-level shops. In Italian restaurants on historic Hanover Street keen eyes examined customers. Nothing. Questions were asked. Again, nothing. Boston's Little Italy had apparently not been graced by Vito's presence.

Di Anello's thoughts turned to the two kids from Stonebridge. He recalled their pictures in the papers, astride new racing bikes. They had gone to Bloom's for boxing lessons with the money the 'city slicker' gave them, found the place empty, and left only to find Bloom dead in his Model A in a chasm, and the 'city slicker' gone in his 1935 Chevrolet. So the story went...

Smart kids, Di Anello mused. New bikes eh? He knew no money had been found in Nino's house. And Bloom? Probably had a bundle stashed. The kids had probably found it, or stolen from Vito. He would look'em up one of these days soon. Too hot to handle right now. They could give him a clue as to Vito's whereabouts... Little punks! He could use them though, in a few years – in his new organization – his *Cosa Nostra*!

A fresh look without Nino, Oreste, Doc Priore, and even Vito. Too bad, in a way... And two dangerous obstacles to his success would soon be removed: Fulvia Avellini Fleming, and the fool, the dreamer detective – Sam Pizzuta. Their pattern of dates was established, and their lust for each other increasing. He would turn this to his advantage, weather permitting.

The white farmhouse, straddling the New York-Massachusetts border, appeared over the hood of the Buick. Little Angelo, emboldened by his new status as driver and aspiring bodyguard, decided that once this trip was over he'd warn Longcoat to stay the hell away from Mona. Shit... all da boys knew he wanted to make her. If he tried, Mona would surely tell the bug-eyed no-chin prick to get lost. He could easy flip his lid and hurt her. Little Angelo could not permit that to happen. Nosiree!

The Buick ground to a stop. Abie Goldberg took off his round, steel-rimmed glasses, and wiped his brow and his partially bald head. At forty-six he felt too old for intrigue. Short, stocky, and flabby, he missed the comfort of the card tables, and even his produce van. Now that was for him!

He didn't like the boss's expansion ideas. Too dangerous! But it could happen, and with it new people; maybe some wanting to look at his books. Well, he could not permit that! Not that the boss wasn't doing well... But, after Oreste's death, and then Nino's, the boss had relied more and more on Abie Goldberg in financial matters. And Abie knew... he had fudged, a little. In business, the word was 'embezzlement'. And the artist who did it would get a slap on the wrist and lots of admiration. In the Black Hand, Abie knew he would get bound wrists, a slashed throat, and no admiration.

Abie made a decision. It was time for him to move on.

Di Anello's Cadillac pulled up beside the Buick. Two men, Di Anello's age emerged from the farmhouse. Luke etched their faces into his brain: the heavier one, round face, dark hard eyes, long nose. The other-thin, almond-shaped blue eyes, delicate features. Dangerous! Luke thought. Behind them, at a respectful distance were two husky bodyguards, their eyes never resting, their hands dangling loosely by their sides. Killers!

Luke heard Di Anello say the trip was fine, and it was good to see his friends again. The group sauntered towards the farmhouse door. The New Yorkers nodded to their men, and Natale spoke briefly to Little Angelo and Longcoat. The latter-day Praetorian Guard took their posts, the New Yorkers by the door, Little Angelo and Longcoat by their cars.

"You come with us inside," Di Anello said.

Luke looked over his shoulder.

"I mean you, Luke!" Di Anello turned and walked inside, arm in arm with his two friends. Natale, Sebastiano, and Abie Goldberg followed. Trailing behind them came Luke Peris, his head whirling, his heart pounding.

Three hours later Di Anello, standing in the sparsely furnished parlor, said in Italian, "We agree." Heads nodded and glasses filled with anisette clinked. "*Va bene!*" Di Anello continued: "Sebastiano, after Columbus Day, you return with Luke and begin working out the details of meshing our friends' warehouse operations with ours."

"*Sì!* Sebastiano replied, "it will be a great honor for me." *He doesn't sound very enthusiastic,* Luke thought.

"And I," said the heavy friend, Sylvio, he of the hard eyes, "will visit Natale to learn all about his splendid enterprises." Natale sat, impassive. His left cheek twitched slightly. Luke couldn't help smiling. Bastard to bastard!

"*Magnifico!*" piped up Aldo, the second New Yorker, in a contralto voice, "I will arrange review of our joint finances with Goldberg." His fingered his mustache then switched to English. "Next week, Goldberg. I bring my man. We compare books." He gave Abie an ice-cold stare.

"Sure. Of course. I'll be ready," Abie said. But mentally, he had already packed his bags.

"And so, we go now," Luke heard Di Anello say. "We get a good night's sleep. Tomorrow I sit in the lead parade car wid da mayor fa da parade."

Luke was in a daze. He had been inside! Seen the inner workings of the Black Hand, and was part of it! Geez! Suddenly his legs trembled, for he realized he and Natale's lethal meeting with Sam Pizzuta and his girl was still on, probably for tomorrow! Di Anello had seen to it that he was tied in with the Black Hand – with no room to wiggle.

Luke's eyes flew around the room. Perhaps by so doing he could find a way out of the terrible trap he was in. No way – unless Jimmy – Natale's cold eyes were on him. Luke's shoulders sagged.

Outside, Aldo put his hand on Di Anello's shoulder in a farewell gesture. One of the guards watched closely, his lips a tight knife-slit. Di Anello frowned, staring him down.

The doors of the Buick and the Cadillac closed. The cars roared away. Back to the neighborhood and the jolly festivities of Columbus Day!

Massimo Di Anello felt he had accomplished much.

At the farmhouse so did his new partners, but for very different reasons. Slowly, they went back into the house.

Chapter 32

Columbus Day, October 12, 1935!

The tenements pulsed with activity. At five a.m. mothers began their day. The sweet aroma of baking bread stirred the drowsy. Garlic simmered in olive oil, and soon would merge with tomatoes and tomato paste in a glory of flavors and spices to make sauce for spaghetti. Ambitious mothers were already forming the meat mix for meatballs.

In spare moments sewing machines hummed as mothers and older daughters put the finishing touches to uniforms for the big parade, when each *societa di mutuo socorso* (mutual benefit society) would do its best to outdo in pomp and flash the country bumpkins from neighboring towns and villages in the Old Country. *Fare figura*-cutting a fine figure, to the immigrant, was an important part of life, as vital as breathing... Fragmentation and petty jealousy among the neighborhood communities was endemic. It was a miracle Italy was ever united into one country, some said 'Is it?' was a typical laconic response.

Phil turned in his sleep, sniffed, and wet his lips. His eyes opened slowly; the delicious fragrance of baking bread stirred him. He ran his gaze across the ceiling, looked out the window, and thought of a fragrance of a different kind, more delicate, more – It was last night:

"Good night, Phil," Marjorie had said at the front door of the tenement, after the dance. "I had a wonderful time." He had kissed her, held her close, closer... Mrs. Fleming had gunned the engine, a quick short signal, and they had reluctantly parted. Marjorie had run back to the waiting car, stopped, and blown him a kiss.

Wow! Phil tossed and turned, pulling a bedsheet over his head. Thoughts of meeting Marjorie again later in the day (and the out-of-this world aromas) caused him to throw off the sheet and bounce out of bed.

"Morning, Mama." He poured himself a cup of hot cocoa from the pot Rosa had prepared. He moved about the kitchen in fast springy steps, sampling Rosa's polenta with two fingers and dipping a hot chunk of crusty newly-baked bread into a pan of simmering sauce.

"So, you had a good time wid la ghella, eh?"

"Yeah, I did. Everyone else had a good time too."

"Datsa good." Rosa's flat, spiritless voice belied her words.

"Papa still sleeping?" Phil asked, eyeing his mother closely.

"Yesee. He come home later dan you." Rosa bit her lip. "You fadda worry lots, Filippo. I no like it."

So, Phil thought, secret meetings somewhere with a bunch of gangsters! He just won't listen! Heck, even the annual rite of wine-making had been forgotten this year. He shrugged, what can I do? and gave his mother an encouraging hug.

"Bye, Mama, gotta go. See you later." Phil reached for his jacket.

"Where you go so elly? See da ghella?"

"Heck no, Mama! This is Columbus Day, remember?"

"Yesee," Rosa lost her dour expression. "I know dat. *Un momento*," she said. She reached into an apron pocket, took out a pair of two dollar bills, and handed them to Phil. "For day of Cristofero Colombo," she said. "No get inta trouble, eh?" She wagged a finger in motherly admonitions.

"Aw, Ma! You know me!"

"Yesee, I do!" she said at Phil's retreating back. "Eh beh!" she murmured, returning to her cooking. The ways of the *Nuovo Mondo* were hard for her to understand, even on the day her famous countryman was honored!

Sforza's Diner was jammed. A round neon clock announced that it was seven-thirty. Bleary all-night card players slurped coffee; some cursed as they swallowed. Members of the *Banda Reale Italiana*, resplendent in round collar, red military-cut uniforms with gold-braid bordered shoulder epaulets, tuned up wind instruments.

Phil, sipping coffee, felt the undercurrent of excitement. He took a jelly doughnut from his plate of four and gave it to Vic, who sat by him. "Look Vic, at the end of the counter," Phil said. "Turn around slow!"

"Gee, it's Longcoat and Nick! And they don't look

too happy"'

"And now look near the door," Phil urged. "See? Little Angelo."

"Wow! Looks like he wants to kill them," Vic whispered.

"Wonder what's got Little Angelo so mad?" Phil whispered back. Nothing the two dumb shits did would bother Little Angelo. Longcoat and Nick, Phil knew, had learned a very hard lesson with their park shenanigans.

"I think I know," Vic smirked. "Last night Carmela told me Nick tried to fix Mona up with Longcoat. He's got... hard nuts for her." He lowered his voice. "Mona told Carmela about it. Mona – boy was she mad at Nick! Carmela said Mona tried to throw Nick down the back steps, head first!"

"I believe it!" Phil said, with a twinkle in his eye. *Longcoat with Mona? Never in a million years! But the guy seemed to be in the dough now; maybe he figured he could impress Mona. Ah–!*

"Watch me, Vic! I'm going to discombobulate a few things."

"Huh?" But Phil was gone, moving through the jostling crowd of men.

Phil elbowed past an elderly clarinet player of the *Banda Reale*, who had his tongue on the reed of his ebony clarinet. Then he moved to a knot of 'da boys' who blocked his path to Little Angelo. They were nose to nose, and bellowing at each other. Phil had no choice but to listen. They were arguing but not about Hitler, Mussolini, or President Roosevelt's programs, nor anything else so esoteric or of such *minor* importance.

Holy mackerel! Baseball! The argument was about baseball, and how the Boston Red Sox would cream the New York Yankees next year. The bitter rivalry had begun. But... no one knew at the time, that with the SECOND COMING in 1936, the advent of Joe Di Maggio, the neighborhood would go berserk and riot squads would be brought in to quell the 'celebrations' when the Yankees beat the Red Sox.

Finally Phil sidled next to Little Angelo, and tapped him on the shoulder. Little Angelo turned, an annoyed look on his face.

Phil put his finger to his lips. "Know what those two cement-heads are cooking up? If you don't, I do."

Little Angelo, about to curse, didn't. Instead he said meekly, "What, Phil?" *So, being a friend of Guido Di Anello has advantages,* Phil thought.

"Nick is gonna fix up Longcoat with his sister Mona," Phil said. "They will all probably meet tonight after the greased pole climb and band concert. I'll bet Mona doesn't want to be fixed up with Longcoat, though." Phil made a clucking sound.

"Yeah? Well, she ain't gonna be!" Little Angelo's chest swelled. The corners of his mouth turned down. His big hands opened and closed...

"Hey, I gotta go. See ya!" Phil went back to Vic, and both eased out of the diner. A short distance down Columbus Street, not far from the entrance to the park near a Socony gas station, the parade was forming. Guido would be there with news of when the three girls were to join them.

Lucy had spoken for all three girls at the dance. They would be 'busy' on Columbus Day. But if Guido phoned in the morning, she could tell him when all three would be 'free'. It would probably be towards the end of the day, she had said with measured coquetry, motioning to Marjorie to be still.

Back in the diner, Little Angelo knew what he had to do. "Shoulda done it dat time in da park," he grumbled, ominously. Controlling his fury, he managed to get close to Longcoat and Nick. "Hey, fancy seein' you guys heah! Kin I getcha anudda cup of coffee?" he said.

* * * *

Di Anello, dressed in a dark suit, tried on a black homburg, looked out his study window at Tim Hoyt's distant house atop the ledge, and glowered. Abruptly he turned and went to the phone on his desk.

"Hello, Natale?" Pause. "Is your helper there?" Another pause. "*Bene!* The weather should be right for planting tonight. Wait for my call. I'll let you and your helper know in plenty of time when the plants will arrive at the garden. You be ready to put them in the ground.

Capito? ...Benissimo! Oh, by the way, about the time of the planting you'll see a marvelous display of fireworks. Enjoy them! You see, I supplied them."

* * * *

Tim Hoyt woke up with a big head. He groaned and staggered to the kitchen. A swallow of Irish nectar helped. The whiskey was wearing out his liver, his doctor had told him. Hoyt didn't believe such nonsense. By all the saints, he was a big man, and the smile of Ireland in a bottle never did anyone in. *Work! That's the culprit! And the crazy Protestant Yankees, with their work ethic and blue noses – killing themselves, and infecting everyone else with the disease.*

But wasn't last night's clambake a classic? He nodded, thinking of his boys, full of whiskey and blarney, dancing up a fast Kerry set around a bonfire someone lit. He stretched. *Now, where is the wife this day?* He remembered. She said she would leave the house early... help Sister Agnes decorate a float the sister school would trundle along in the Columbus Day parade.

Hoyt glanced disdainfully 'down below'. Not only did he have to worry about the Yankees now, but also a bunch of dirty, illiterate foreigners cutting into his territory. As if he didn't know that Di Anello was telling Natale when to crap and when to get off the pot. Natale's a goon; no business sense like Nino had – poor dead sonofabitch! Now Natale wants to bring in his 'manager' to talk about the road construction deal. Guy by the name of... name of Sebastiano something-or-other. No deal! Di Anello better come out and play himself, and quit his shell game with Hoyt! And the nerve of the guy, going behind my back to the mayor, working out deals for new gambling joints around town. Well! Dear corrupt father-in-law would be dealt with!

Then it will be Mayor Timothy Hoyt!
After that – why not? Governor Hoyt!

Hoyt's frown, which had become tighter and deeper as his thoughts wandered, melted away. "Tonight," he growled aloud to himself, "we put the fear of God into Mr. Di Anello. At just about the time of the fireworks."

He scowled anew. How appropriate, he thought.

Tomorrow Hoyt meant to discuss the divvying up of the construction pie with Natale, and his much too high gambling debts, which so far had not been erased. When Natale stalled, Hoyt would say point blank that a vice-squad would soon be set up in the city. Information on where and when it could strike, he was sure, would be much appreciated. And, Hoyt would say, he would only talk to Mr. Di Anello about that.

He chuckled, a deep, bottom-of-the-barrel sound, as he pictured Natale's consternation. Satisfied, he left hurriedly, for he had to pick up the mayor and drive him to the Columbus Day parade.

Then he would watch the parade, cheer the bands, the marchers, and Christopher Columbus...

The Bastard!

Chapter 33

"Hi!" Guido said, coming up behind Phil and Vic, his voice muffled by a mouthful of cream-filled pastry. He swallowed and licked his fingers. "Where the heck did you get that chunk of mountain?" Vic asked, awed.

"Dante's bakery, next to the Socony gas station. Columbus Day special... didn't have breakfast." Guido took an oozing bite. "My mother dropped me off."

"She going somewhere?" Phil looked at Guido's cream-lathered face.

"Yeah. All day and most of the night. She's got plenty going on, church building fund, women's clubs... My father'll be tied up, too. Cripes! We're becoming a house of strangers. So I'll eat at the diner today."

"No! You'll eat with me! My mother has enough food cooked up to feed an army," Phil said.

"Mine, too," added Vic. "Homemade ravioli. You can have some."

"Thanks, guys! And hey, do I have an idea about what we can do tonight!"

Boom! The bass drum, followed by the tat-a-ta-tat of snare drums, and bugle calls. The mayor arrived, waving, bowing, smiling, his mass of iron-gray hair over a large, florid face easily identified. He liked the adulation. The neighborhood dwellers liked the mayor. When the city trucks came by to fill up pot-holes in the street, who walked behind the trucks, waving at his tenement constituency? Why, the mayor, of course! And who opened the folding chairs for old ladies at neighborhood weddings and funerals? The mayor! Irish, but a good man, and *Catolico!*

The mayor got into the lead car, an open Packard. Another car, driven by Luke Peris drove up. Beside him sat Natale, impassive. In the back seat, Di Anello. He got out, shook hands heartily with the mayor, and climbed into the Packard beside him. A neighborhood aspirant for the city council and one for alderman also climbed in. The crowd roared its approval. More *prominenti*, dignitaries from the societies, bankers, jewelers, funeral directors, were in other cars. The *maresciallo* of the parade, selected by lot-no other method worked-raised his baton. The police motorcycle escort roared and rolled, and the honored *Banda Reale*, leading the parade, struck up a stirring march. Hundreds of arms, feet and bodies picked up the beat. Capes undulated, plumes rustled, and standard-bearers grunted and raised their emblems; multi-colored breast sashes shimmered and dozens of American and Italian flags began waving in a riot of color...

Members of religious groups, intermingled with the bands, reverently formed around the statue of a praying Madonna on a flower-decorated truck, or hoisted statues of favorite local patron saints onto small platforms carried by four men, and all stepped forth as a collective cheer broke out.

The parade was under way! It was a stirring sight. Or so Phil thought – the noise, the color, and the smell from Dante's bakery! "Great, just great!" he exclaimed to Guido and Vic. They nodded and said something Phil didn't hear, for his mind was on tonight, and Guido's idea. Phil knew what it was now... maybe, just maybe, his luck in the neighborhood was changing, and everything would work out. The statue of the Madonna startled Phil as it passed slowly by him... She seemed to be looking at him! And, was that a tear in her eye? Hey,... forget it! You are seeing things! Now, watch the parade!

Sam Pizzuta mingled with the crowd, enjoying the festive mood. But there – now that doesn't fit, he thought. Spiffed up Di Anello, sure, but not the rest: A somber, tight-lipped Luke Peris driving, and next to him in the front seat of the Cadillac, Natale, arms folded, looking like a jailer. Pizzuta sensed trouble. Quickly, he headed for the Cadillac.

"Great parade, eh Sam?" The voice, heavy with sarcasm, stopped Sam. He turned around to face his questioner.

"Oh, hello Tim, slumming?" *The crooked asshole!* Pizzuta thought.

"Ha, ha! No, but very funny. You see, I just dropped the mayor off." *Damn the mayor!* Hoyt thought, bitterly.

He's giving away my store to that gangster, Di Anello. My dear brother-in-law has to go! "Keeping your eyes open for trouble, detective?" Hoyt, now free of the mayor for the day, mouthed the words mechanically as dark thoughts clouded his mind.

"Not today, Tim." Nodding to the arch-manipulator, Pizzuta walked away. The Packard, full of big-wigs, now led the parade. Luke Peris and Natale in the Cadillac had disappeared, as if swallowed up by the crowd. Damn! Oh, what the hell, he could check with Luke later. Maybe Jimmy could have told him what, if anything, bugged Luke. But Jimmy wasn't around this morning. Funny, he's open 365 days a year! But this being a holiday, maybe he'll open his store later... *So, Pizzuta, quit being a detective – for one day?*

He thought of Fulvia, and he smiled. Tonight, about the time of the fireworks, he would take her in his arms, and... He glowed inside.

* * * *

As the proud marchers began strutting up Columbus Street, two men, Sylvio Bigli and Aldo Mandrola sat in rickety wooden chairs at an old round oak table with sturdy ball and claw legs. A stooped old crone in traditional black poured each of them a cup of hot coffee; for the third time. Both men acknowledged that the meeting with Di Anello had gone well. So why not, they reasoned, tarry in this old, secluded farm? A Calabrian owned it, and ran a small herd of dairy cattle. It was a stopping off place-a temporary refuge-depending on the circumstances, for men of the *Mano Nera*. Sylvio and Aldo had stayed overnight before and then had stopped off to pay courtesy calls on Di Anello, just before departing for their annual vacations to Italy.

The circumstances this time had been such that neither man had wanted to go back to New York state after the Di Anello meeting. When he had observed Aldo, Sylvio could see the delicate one's mustache twitching. The signal caused great pain in Sylvio's crotch. Late that night he had slipped his bulk into Aldo's room. Aldo had been waiting, naked, face down on the bed.

"You look disgusting," Aldo now said, watching Sylvio eat. Sylvio again dipped a huge piece of cold, thick pizza into his coffee, lifted it, and bit into the soggy lump as if it were expensive caviar.

"Better than those boiled eggs and toast Mafalda cooked for you. That is sissy food." Sylvio immediately regretted saying that, and added hastily, "Do you think the *commendatore* will do as he said?"

"Of course. He is carried away with his own importance," Aldo said. Sylvlio's storm-dark eyes narrowed into Oriental slits. "Then, before midnight, we should get the phone call."

"Yes." Aldo waved a hand gracefully.

"We'd better go upstairs," Sylvio said, his eyes gleaming with lust.

"Yes, we'd better. No reason to stay down here any longer, is there?"

From the kitchen the old crone, Mafalda, looked at them contemptuously. As they moved out of sight she spat, and hurled a village curse after them.

* * * *

The parade and the boring speeches, was over. At Vespucci Park the band concert blared its last, and skinny grease-spattered boys from run-down streets angling off lower Columbus Street ceremoniously ate their fill of salami and pepperoni sticks they had thrown down from the greased poles they had laboriously climbed. The crowd loved it. Phil, Vic, and Guido too.

But, hunger aroused, the three went to Phil's house for supper, to the delight of Rosa, who fussed and loaded plates to overflowing.

Sebastiano however, ate lightly and then excused himself.

"I have to go to a special meeting tonight. Business," he said.

"And I take Alberto to da fireworks tonight. Later, we eat a big banana split. What you say Alberto?" Rosa jutted her chin out defiantly. Little brother Al? Phil had never seen a smile so wide.

And, obviously, Phil and Guido couldn't leave the

tenement without accepting Vic's invitation to sample homemade ravioli. That they did.

Walking to the park, cleaned up, hair carefully combed, feeling on top of the world, Phil, Vic and Guido passed Dom De Prospo's closed market and then Jimmy's store, also dark and closed. Hmm, he is always open, Phil mused. But he thought, Jimmy probably was open earlier. Sure, now he wants to watch the fireworks. And Phil's mind turned to the expected delights of tonight...

As Phil reasoned, an old Ford stopped at the court warehouse. A thin weasel of a man with shifty eyes got out. His dark clothes made him difficult to discern from the darkness around him. He went to a back door and knocked. It opened slightly. He was recognized and motioned in by a long-fingered hand.

"Well?" said Di Anello.

"Boss, they left the house at six in his car and went to the Oak Park theater. They should be out by nine if they stay for the double feature."

"Good, Quaio, good! For you." He handed Quaio an envelope.

"Tanks a lot, Boss." He switched language, *"Grazie, grazie!"*

Di Anello waved Quaio away. He blew on his cold hands, looked at the somber sky, put on his warm jacket, and smiled.

He walked out of his office and over to a poker game in progress.

"Deal me in, Skinny," he said. "What's the bet?"

Later Di Anello lifted a starched shirt cuff held together with gold links and looked at his wrist watch. It's late," he said. "Got business to take care of at da house. Now listen, I never left this game. Got it?"

Heads nodded. Di Anello left. The game continued.

At about the time Di Anello left for home, Tim Hoyt, from his locked study, dialed a number and listened.

"Hello, this is Fred Wray. Who's calling?"

"Cousin Mike," Hoyt hissed. "Is our friend ready for the last round?"

"Absolutely!" It will be a glorious night, and–"

"Shut up! Just go ahead, and don't screw it up!"

"Yes sir!" The line went dead. Fred Wray wondered whether he had done the wise thing to check with Hoyt when Vito had showed up. Vito was a wanted man! But Hoyt said no cops – he had other ideas – and then too, Glass Jaw liked money. Hoyt had given him lots of it, for the caper Wray would lead on Columbus Day for Hoyt and for hiding that nut, Vito. Now, thanks to Hoyt, Vito was part of the caper... Glass Jaw Wray didn't like that at all!

Chapter 34

Little Angelo cursed. He knew that Nick and Longcoat were at the park – away from the crowd awaiting the fireworks – in brush near the bocce court probably, their favorite haunt. And soon Mona would show up! He couldn't do anything about it, not yet. Right now he was driving the three giggling girls in the back seat to Guido and his pals, waiting at the entrance to the park. Then he had to drive them all to Guido's house. Guido had come back to the diner, caught him as he was leaving, and that was that. Little Angelo obeyed his future boss! But there still could be time afterwards to do what he must do, he hoped.

At the park, Guido and Vic got into the back seat of the car with Carmela and Lucy. Phil looking rather solemn, Little Angelo thought, considering the helluva good time he was gonna have with the gorgeous redhead – got into the front seat with her.

Not long afterwards, having unloaded his young passengers at the big white house, Little Angelo sped back to the park. He would return the car he had borrowed from one of the boys first, and then–

No! He wouldn't return the car... not yet! He parked it in an alley, as close to the park as he could get, leaped out, and ran towards the bocce court. And there they were! Longcoat, limp as overdone spaghetti, eyes bulging and vacant, drooling, laughing crazily. And Nick, talking, "Here, take anudda one. It'll make ya feel even betta." Longcoat reached for and missed the offered reefer. Nick lit it and put it in Longcoat's mouth. Longcoat grasped it with both hands, and inhaled deeply.

"Disgustin'," Little Angelo mumbled. He looked around quickly, a puzzled frown on his face. Then, he smacked an open palm on his forehead, hurled himself between Longcoat and Nick, pushed a stoned Longcoat to the ground, and grabbed Nick by the shoulders. Nick's belly heaved and rolled in terror.

"Where is she, hah? What's he done wit her?" Little Angelo moved his right hand back, fist clenched.

"Who? What, whata ya talkin' about? Ow! Ya hurtin'

me!" Nick cried.

"Mona, dat's who. Where is she? What did dat crum do ta her?"

Nick understood! *So dis moron has da hots for Mona too!* He leaned into Little Angelo, a sly look on his face, and his lips quivered. "She ain't here, and she ain't comin' neither, Little Ang. She hates him!" He jerked his head towards a blissful Longcoat. "She'd spit in his eye if she ever sawr him. Dat's right! She... has udder ideas about guys. She tole me she likes you." *Dere*, Nick thought, *dat'll get the clumsy ox off my case.*

Little Angelo gave Nick a swift kick in the ass. "Get outa here," he said, "unless ya want ya arms busted."

"No, Little Ang, no!" Holding his aching butt with both hands, Nick took the advice with unusual alacrity.

Little Angelo turned to Longcoat. He grasped an arm and began twisting. He stopped. His mind worked furiously! He blinked. He had it!

"C'mere, you prick," he said, hoisting a humming Longcoat across his shoulders and back. As fast and as stealthily as he could, Little Angelo went to his car and dumped Longcoat in the back seat.

"I'm a genius!" he told the rear view mirror. He started the car.

Natale stopped abruptly and stared. He had just said "Let's go," to Luke Peris, and headed toward the door of his Front Street office, when the door opened and a perspiring Little Angelo dumped Longcoat on the carpet.

"He ain't doin' his job, Natale," Little Angelo said, wiping his brow, "he'll getcha into trouble."

"Yeah, I kin see dat. Where did ya find da doped-up turd?"

Little Angelo told him.

"Uh huh. Tanks, eh? Ya kin go now. Say nuttin' ta nobody about dis." Little Angelo nodded. "Awright," Natale continued in a sepulchral voice, "Luke and me got tings ta do now. We'll lock Longcoat up in my office – take care of him when we get back. Geez, he stinks and smells terabil!"

The look Natale gave Longcoat was not friendly.

Chapter 35

In the den, Carmela squealed, "Oh, this is so cozy, Guido! Coming here was a great idea. Come on everyone, let's move the chairs back and dance!" Phil looked for signs of painting or remodeling. There were none. "Guido, how much time do we have before someone comes home?" A feeling of foreboding gripped him, for Di Anello had lied to Guido. Why?

"Two hours or more." Guido said, and he dimmed the single light.

"Will Little Angelo remember to pick us up before someone comes home?"

"Huh? He'd better! But if he doesn't, we can walk the girls back. Maybe we'll even see some of the last fireworks." Guido smiled.

"Oh, Phil, you worry too much," Carmela said. "Come on Vic," she led him to Guido's record player, cranked it, and put on a record, "let's dance!"

"Phil?" Marjorie, quiet up to now, opened her arms. He led her slowly around the den. Her warmth through her soft white sweater felt good to Phil. He held her closer. No hare-brained chaperone with a tape measure here!

Ten minutes... twenty minutes. The three young couples danced on, their bodies seeming to merge, swaying with the soft music; their shadows long, dark, and shapeless. The scrape of a shoe and the swish of a skirt or dress were the only sounds besides the music.

Then quietly, Lucy, her blue eyes averted, took Guido by the hand, and firmly led him out of the den and up the stairway. Phil did not see Guido object. He went rather willingly.

Marjorie stroked Phil's neck. Impulsively, Phil kissed her...

"Ohhhhhh! " The purple tranquillity shattered by Carmela's cry. Pain? Joy? Bewildered, Phil stared as Carmela jumped up and wrapped her legs around Vic's waist. "Oh my!" Carmela moaned, and she let out several strange sounds. She pulled Vic's head down by the hair and ran her mouth over the back of his neck... many times.

"What the-?" Phil started to move towards them.

"Phil, no!" Marjorie's command was sharp. "It's all right, really!"

He froze and watched Vic stumble back, propelled by the writhing force around him. His heels hit the step up to the marble entryway, and his arms around Carmela, he stepped up, backwards. Before he disappeared around the corner towards the front door he looked at Phil. It was a frightened look Phil thought, yet... exultant too. A moment later a door opened quietly, then closed with a muffled sound.

The closet! The large entryway closet! Vic had taken Carmela there? Guido, and now Vic! There was no precedent here. None of Phil's pulp heroes ever faced this situation! His forehead wet, Phil sat down heavily on the den couch. Marjorie quickly sat next to him, her eyes shining.

Cathedral-like silence settled on the den. Then, from the direction of the closet, faint thumping sounds. Marjorie rested her head on Phil's shoulder, ran her hand lightly over his cheek.

"Phil?"

"Uh huh?"

"Do you like me a little bit?"

Coming out somewhat from his trance-like state, he responded, "Yes, I like you a lot of bits." What? Geez!

Marjorie tilted her head towards him. "Then prove it!" He did, and it took her breath away.

"I love you, Phil!" she said, reclining backwards, taking him with her.

"Marjorie, I... I love you too!" He was on her now, his hand moving under her skirt. "But... but; I... I-"

"But what, honey? You can tell me." She helped him work her panties.

"I'm afraid," he blurted out, raising himself on his elbows.

"Afraid? Afraid of what? Ohhhhh! I think I understand," she said, in a grown-up voice. "Come back down here," he obeyed. Marjorie put her lips to his ear and whispered earnestly, head bobbing in emphasis.

Phil's eyes widened – two new moons. "I didn't know that!" he confessed in a suppressed whisper. *Rhythm, huh?* he thought. His mind raced. And Carmela... just like guys... ready to– "Wow!" he said, in a loud voice.

"Shhhh!" Marjorie put a finger on Phil's lips, and giggled.

Slowly, unafraid now, Phil descended on her. With a strong pull Marjorie yanked her panties off and tossed them behind the couch. That caused a surge of passion in Phil. He fumbled to open his pants; Marjorie helped, and they touched. He pushed. She bit her lip, but nevertheless rotated her hips upwards.

The front door! Both heard it being flung open! The quick click of leather heels of hard marble! Too late to react... to do anything! Frozen in place, unable to move. They'd be caught, lying on the couch, key parts of their anatomy bare. The thought raced through Phil's mortified mind.

It didn't happen. Di Anello, head down, moving rapidly, went straight to the stairway. Back! Sooner than expected. Oh shit!

Phil looked at Marjorie. She didn't seem to be upset at all. But she did say, "What will we do now?"

"Leave!" Phil rolled off her.

Click! Phil listened, nerves on edge, body taut.

And another sound, a slight squeak. The front door? being opened... Yes! So very cautiously, by someone! Someone, who doesn't want to be heard, or seen.

But, Phil thought, he and Marjorie would be seen by an alert intruder! He grasped Marjorie, and both slid off the couch. Silently, they crawled behind it. By now Marjorie seemed scared stiff.

Phil saw the gun first, with a long cylinder attached. A silencer! Then the owner of the gun... slender, dark-skinned. He moved with an easy animal grace, his black leather jacket tightly buttoned. Thick soft-soled shoes made no sound on the marble. He swept the den with savage, deep-set eyes. Satisfied, he moved towards the stairway, taking short, sure steps, his gun thrust forward.

To kill Di Anello, the voice inside Phil's skull screamed. *Not a bad idea,* Phil answered silently. But what about Guido and Carmela? If the assassin sees them he'll kill them too! Phil didn't want that! Raw fear gnawed at him, and he felt twangs of panic tightening his throat.

"Phil, let's get out of here, now!" Marjorie, fully dressed, lips at his ear, pleaded in a strained little voice.

But Phil couldn't abandon his friends... up there, in danger. A strange calm came over him. He'd warn them and they would sneak out, safely. It had to be done! But first, Marjorie. He took Marjorie's hand and led her to the front door. No one in sight. Good! Oh! the entryway closet! He had almost forgotten. Two sets of eyes peeked out at him, terror-stricken. Arms and legs struggled silently to put on clothes. Phil pushed Marjorie into the closet, and went in after her. He whispered to Vic, who nodded, and replied, "We'll do it!"

Phil opened the closet door a crack. "All clear," he said. "Now go, all of you! I'll hide outside with Guido and Lucy until help comes."

"Phil, I'm staying with you!"

"No, Marjorie. Go with them. Honest, I'll be all right." He forcibly removed her arms from his neck. Reluctantly, Marjorie joined Vic and Carmela, who were tip-toeing out the door. In a moment, Marjorie was gone.

Phil felt a cold chill grip him. Escape! Join Marjorie! Go, now! He forced himself away from the door. Damn it, get hold of yourself! Grimly hugging the wall, he pushed up the stairway... What was that smell? Himself! The stink of fear! He stopped, took a deep breath, and he heard the murmur of voices, a steady low indistinct hum.

At the top of the stairway he flattened himself on the carpet. The voices came from the far end of the corridor – Di Anello's study. Phil glanced at the bedroom on his left-empty, as the next one was. He crawled on. A bathroom on the right, its door ajar, was also empty. Beyond the bathroom would be Guido's room, and beyond that the corridor made a left turn, to Di'Anello's study. Study? Den of thieves, Phil thought bitterly.

He made his way to Guido's room, inhaling carpet dust. He heard nothing. Good! The two are safe, he thought. He crawled into the room and came face to face with Lucy, half-dressed, cowering in a corner, her pretty face drawn into a mask of terror. Phil quickly put his hand over her mouth, quelling the scream that rose in her throat. Then she recognized him. Phil gulped, swallowing his own terror. What if she had screamed? He let that one pass.

"Guido?" Phil tenderly smoothed Lucy's disheveled blonde hair. She seemed to regain some composure, nodded, rolled her eyes towards the study, and said in a frightened little voice, "He went there – same way you came in here.

Phil breathed a sigh of relief. "The guy with the gun..."

"He didn't see us," Lucy said. She blushed, "we... we were in the shower, about to turn the water on. Guido heard a strange rustling noise, came out and saw his back and gun... We sneaked back here, and–"

"I get it," Phil interrupted. He Pointed to the stairway and jabbed a finger at Lucy. "Go," he said. "Run down East Hawthorne. Maybe you'll catch up to Vic and the girls." He looked out the bedroom door. He motioned to Lucy. She crouched low, gave him a grateful look, and scampered out barefooted, carrying a bunched up skirt, blouse and sweater in one hand, shoes and stockings in the other. *She'd better put the rest of her clothes on. She'll catch cold with so little on.*

The whimsical thought aside, he inched his way to the study, flat on his stomach, as Guido had done. In his left hand he carried two of Guido's new baseballs. He could throw them... hard... in quick succession... at the assassin... if that seemed possible. Di Anello had guns, Phil knew that. A distraction might give him time to reach for one. Phil would do this... for Guido. Beyond that, he dared not think. But Guido, would not have gone in there unless he had seen an opening. Maybe by now he's been nabbed by the killer! If that turned out to be true Phil decided he would back off, save his own hide, and hope help arrived in time for Guido...

When Phil entered the entryway closet with Marjorie to ask Vic to sneak out with Carmela and Marjorie and run for help, the intruder walked silently into Di Anello's office. Seated behind his desk, head down, Di Anello sensed a malevolent presence and reached for the center drawer of the desk.

"No!" the intruder wheezed. His gun leaped forward. Di Anello fell back, and his lean faced paled.

"Get up! Move to that window!" The gun waved, and Di Anello obeyed. "Now open it! *Bene!* Turn around, face me. No, don't move. Stay where you are."

"Who are you? Who–" Di Anello checked himself. *"Chi sei?"*

The intruder spoke good Italian. Educated... and well trained! Di Anello felt a strange uneasiness. Had he seen the man before?

"Chi sono? You will see! Don't move! Oreste... remember him? And Nino? And of course you know Sylvio Bigli and Aldo Mandrola. I come because of all these men."

"I don't understand," Di Anello said. Though perplexed, his mind was working and his feral instincts alerted him to danger and treachery.

"Ah, *signore!*" the intruder said caustically, "I work for Bigli and Mandrola. I was at the farmhouse when you met with them."

"Sì, sì, Ricordo!" Di Anello remembered now. The guard who had raked him with hate-filled eyes as he was getting into his car. He hadn't given it any thought. Now he knew he should have!

"What do you want of me? Your employers are my partners, my friends."

"Are they?"

The sharp words sent icy needles up and down Di Anello's spine. He calmed himself with effort.

"Yes," he said, in a patronizing voice, "they are. Now, control yourself young man. You are making a very big mistake."

"No!" screamed the intruder, "there has been no mistake, *signore!* I come to avenge the death of Oreste! You know you had him killed. You must die! At the hands of his godchild!"

"Gennaro?" Di Anello gasped. Knuckles white, dizzy, he held onto the window sill with both hands. "But, but..."

"Zitto! (Silence!). I did not die in the 'accident' you planned. Nino was too kind-hearted. He saved me and lied to you. He recommended me to Bigli and exacted a promise from me that there would be no vendetta. But

Nino is dead. My promise is canceled. It is I who will call New York tonight to report your death." Gennaro seemed to be enjoying himself. "You see, you are too dangerous for your partners, you arrogant fool. Your telling them of your plan to kill the woman and the detective convinced them. No, you will make no phone call tonight to tell them it is done. I will avenge my dear godfather!" Gennaro snarled, and aimed the gun.

The door to the office was open, and Phil, flat on his belly, arrived in time to hear Gennaro snarl and aim his gun. The scene before him was etched into his brain. By the open window, under the gable... Di Anello. Crouched in front of him, Gennaro, his gun raised. He took two steps towards Di Anello, and stopped.

Phil's eyes swept the room in a frantic search. Guido! Where is he?

Gennaro lifted his gun high. *"Basta! e finito!"* he cried. (Enough, it is finished!) Then he lunged, and the gun, in his right hand, came down towards Di Anello's skull. His left shoulder jutted out, like a football blocking back. In that split-second, Phil knew! Di Anello was to topple out the window to his death below, victim of an unfortunate accident.

Suddenly the sky erupted in bursts of color – green, blue, yellow – followed by booming, artillery-like detonations. Skyrockets, fired from Vespucci Park below, announced the final Columbus Day pyrotechnic display.

A sharp, thunderous explosion reverberated in the room. An errant rocket? Phil dropped the baseballs and buried his head in the carpet. Another report, and another, building on the first two. Different from the fireworks! The thought skidded through Phil's mind. He raised his head. At the window, staggering, his neck erupting blood, two neat dark holes in the back of his leather jacket was Gennaro. Knees buckling, he turned, raised his pistol, and dropped forward, a floppy blob of bleeding flesh. He fell and lay still, next to Di Anello, on his hands and knees. Both hands covered his face and head, and rivulets of red circled the hands, seeped between his fingers, and ran onto the carpet.

A gagging sound caused Phil to snap his head left.

Behind Di Anello's desk, apparently kneeling, teeth clenched, his elbows firmly propped on it, Guido! Held firmly in both hands was a .38 revolver. His father's – from the desk drawer! So that's what he was up to! The acrid smell of powder filled Phil's nostrils. Guido didn't move, his eyes a stone stare.

"Guido–" Phil, his mind struggling, got no further. Sounds! from downstairs – of splintering wood, and sharp metal on metal sounds. Startled, without thinking, Phil got up, ran to top of the stairway, and looked down. The front door was smashed inwards, off its hinges. And men, many men, in dark clothes streamed in!

Clubs, axes! Swinging! He would be seen! On hands and knees, Phil scrambled back to the carnage in the office. His mouth moved, but no words came. His head throbbed and pounded horribly.

"Phil what is it?" Guido's cry shocked Phil back from the edge–

"Men! With clubs... and everything! Tearing up the house! They'll be coming up here, I know they will. Oh, Jesus, Mary and Joseph!"

A bloody head lifted, and Di Anello's mouth opened. "Guido, da cabinet, da metal box... desk." Di Anello dropped two keys on the floor. "Open – da guns! Tommy!" His fell on his side, unconscious. Phil dove across the room, scooped up the keys and tossed them to Guido, who stared at them. The noise of the destruction below intensified. The invaders, whoever they were, would soon be coming hell-bent up the stairway, destroying everything in their path. *Their blood lust up, that could include me!* Phil thought, his mind whirling. There was a way to prevent that.

"Guido, open the cabinet," he screamed. "What your father tried to tell us. The Tommy guns, get them!" A skyrocket burst, close to the house. It painted the office in a sickly, reddish hue.

Phil ran to Di Anello and quickly tied a handkerchief around his head.

"Hurry up, Guido!" he thundered, leaping to the desk and pulling out a locked metal box from the center drawer. Guido fumbled with the cabinet doors. Phil yanked the second key away from him. He opened the metal boxes. Guido glanced back, seeing the loaded drums. His eyes glinted, and a strange cold smile played his lips. He had the doors of the cabinet open now, and picked up the two Tommy guns.

"Give me those," he said, pointing to the ammunition. A few moments later, he handed Phil one of the Tommy guns.

Without saying another word, both pointed their weapons at the open door... and waited.

Chapter 36

Jimmy wasn't out watching the parade as Phil had thought when he passed Jimmy's closed store. Jimmy was in the store's small back room, sweating...

The night before, on the way to scout Fulvia's place, he had stopped at Eddie Abdow's Atlantic gas station, and as Eddie cranked in five gallons Jimmy phoned Pizzuta's apartment. No answer. Jimmy tried downtown, Homicide.

Sergeant Pizzuta? Not here right now. Yeah, of course he's on duty. Crime doesn't take a holiday you know, heh, heh! Jimmy thanked the desk man, and hung up, relieved. Sam wouldn't be seeing his damn widow – the Widow of Death – tonight! And Jimmy figured Di Anello also knew that. So Luke had a day of grace; and, Jimmy thought, so did Jimmy!

Jimmy had found an acceptable hiding place for his car. Off the gravel road, behind the brush and overhanging branches of tall oak. At night the car would be difficult to see, but Jimmy had an unobstructed view of Fulvia's house, some sixty feet ahead, and the oak and birch trees nearby where Pizzuta was supposed to park and make out with the damn woman. And across the narrow road, heavy brush. An ideal ambush spot! Jimmy had winced.

And he winced now as he thought of it. But shit! He had faced German machine guns in the war and come out alive. Why the hell was he worrying about an ambush by someone with a pea shooter? Hell, he might let things ride, couldn't he? He just might do that. All the same...

Jimmy blew the dust off his Army foot locker, opened it, and took out a package in an oil cloth. He unwrapped it and picked up the contents, a Luger pistol he had brought back from France. He pressed the trigger, once, twice. Perfect working order. The action was smooth, and the top toggle opened with a metallic click. From another locker compartment Jimmy removed a magazine loaded with powerful Parabellum rounds. He pushed the magazine into the butt of the pistol. He was ready... for what, he wasn't sure.

* * * *

"We are very European tonight, Sam." Fulvia cracked a lobster claw and delicately extracted the succulent flesh with a tiny fork.

"Oh?" Pizzuta, hands on his chin, happily watched her sensuous enjoyment – sucking, cracking, seeking – and listened to her small cry of joy at discovering a shell-encased morsel she had overlooked.

"Eating so late," she said, nibbling a white shred from a fingertip. "It is the civilized way to eat. In America, everything is so rushed! All the food goes on the plate at one time! No talk between courses; just eat fast, get up and leave." She shook her head in mock dismay.

"Yeah?" Sam asked. "And who does all the dishes after all those courses?"

"Why, the women, of course... Ah! I see! You make a good point. Less time in the kitchen for American women!"

"Right!"

"And if you marry," she teased, "what will you expect of your poor wife?"

"Quite a lot!" he teased back. He paused dramatically, and said, "But not in the kitchen!" He reached over and touched her arm.

"Sam," Fulvia said, delighted, her dark eyes flashing, "I... I... it's been a wonderful evening. The movie... the wine; dinner... you!"

"Well, I'm glad someone besides my mother and my boss recognize my sterling qualities." Tonight he would ask this gorgeous lady to be his. How she had turned heads when they walked regally into the Eden Garden Restaurant: black silk dress, pearl choker, matching pendant earrings, an heirloom cameo, platform high-heel pumps over sheer silk stockings, and a beautiful embroidered white sweater draped over her shoulders. Elegance! And touches of perfume and make-up added a Mediterranean flair to her dark beauty. Pizzuta had never seen her so beautiful...

They had watched the feature picture at the Oak Park theater and then left for dinner. Sam had parked in a No Parking zone in front of the restaurant, and being so close, Fulvia's coat was left in the car, as Sam had deviously planned. Her entering with a coat on would take away from the first impression he wanted her to make. Sam had many friends at the restaurant, and he wanted to show them he had an eye for a beautiful woman.

That... he did! When Demetre Sotanopulous, the proprietor, found out Fulvia liked lobster, he had beamed happily. He just happened to have...

Quaio had been wrong when he told Di Anello that the detective and the woman would be out of the theater around nine-thirty if they saw the double feature. He wasn't too far wrong about the time however, for at nine forty-five a happy Pizzuta and a radiant Fulvia left the restaurant. They drove through the neighborhood and up the gravel road to her little house by the pine and birch trees. They parked. The engine ran. No car door opened...

From behind the brush opposite from Fulvia's house, Luke Peris watched Sam's 1934 Pontiac sedan approach and park. Get out! His mind screamed, as if by magic thought transference Pizzuta and Fulvia would hear and obey.

They didn't. The car stood silent and dark under the trees.

Luke didn't feel the chill, though he and Natale had waited an hour, like a couple of bushwhackers. Waiting... for the car to complete its studied pattern and routine, for Quaio was a competent spy. One variable couldn't be controlled: the weather. But tonight it was ideal. It fit the pattern, and Luke had silently screamed. Now, though the night was cold, he was bathed in nervous sweat.

"Awright, now go! Do da job! Don't screw up. I'll be watchin'." Natale waved his gun. Luke nodded and picked his way through brush on the bank by the side of the road. Moments later he had climbed a small granite outcrop and was in darkness, away from the spill of light from the double lamps on Fulvia's porch across the road. He would come down here, sneak to the other side of the road, creep up behind the car, and–

Luke lost his footing. Pebbles and ground dust on the smooth boulder gave way, and he slid five feet down the hard sloping rock to the ground.

"Ouch!" he said, landing hard in a pile of rock. Then he cursed in two languages. Gingerly, he tested his ankles. Stinging pain from scratches and scrapes, but no breaks. He knew baleful eyes were on him, and quickly he scurried across the road, stopped, and listened. Nothing... from the Pontiac. They hadn't heard his fall. Stealthily, he made his way to the rear of the Pontiac. All windows were fogged, the engine idling...

Luke blinked rapidly. A way out! There had to be! Something in him stirred. And it came to him. The rocks! It could work! Did he have the guts to try? He had to! No other choice...

Damn Di Anello, Natale, Sforza, and the whole rotten bunch! And most of all, that dirty, double-crosser Jimmy! Where the hell is he?

Full of anger, and little hope, Luke bent down next to the tailpipe. He reached into his jacket pocket...

Sitting in the darkness of his car, watching the parked Pontiac, Jimmy hoped that the plot to do in Pizzuta and his woman had been called off. What the heck, nothing had happened. Looks like Di Anello came to his senses. Killing a cop! Geez! But then Jimmy saw rocks tumble twenty or so feet ahead of him, across the road, and a dark figure land heavily.

Luke, damn him! It's on! Jimmy reached for the door handle. Careful! Natale is up ahead somewhere, gun in hand. And the bastard can shoot! Jimmy saw Luke quickly cross to his side of the road, go to the Pontiac, bend over and then kneel by the tailpipe. With mounting horror, Jimmy watched shredded rags being stuffed into the tailpipe, and then something mashed against the opening. It stuck. Clay? Jimmy thought.

That done, Luke doubled back, picked up a large rock from a pile near where he had fallen, and clambered back up the slope.

Jimmy swiveled his head from the spot where Luke had disappeared to the car – sitting there – engine idling. Jimmy tried to figure out likely spots ahead where Natale might be hiding. Shit! It's war... again!

Zero hour, Jimmy! What... are... you... going... to do?
Jimmy squirmed. The car ahead kept speaking its message of death.

*Whistles! Cries! Men cursing, climbing out of trenches.
Flares bursting overhead. The boom and glare of exploding shells. Jimmy was in the lead, running, weaving, towards that damn Hun machine gun nest!* But the pain in his gimpy leg, the dim wash of porch lamps, and bullets kicking up dust around him brought Jimmy back to 1935. He didn't remember leaving his car, but he had, somehow! Above, to his right, the fireworks continued their rainbow display. Why had he hesitated this long? He should have tried harder to find Pizzuta and warn him!

Jimmy slithered to the tailpipe, aware that in the dim wash of the porch lamps he made a perfect backlit target. He aimed his Luger where he thought Natale's shots were coming from and sprayed five rounds. He reached for the tailpipe and swept away the goo. Now the rags! No, dammit! Get Sam out first! He got up and his gimpy leg gave way. A pain he recognized almost paralyzed him. He was hit! He dragged himself behind the car, and pulled himself up to the windows.

"Sam, Sam!" he screamed, and yanked at the front door handle! Locked! He couldn't see inside. Muttering incoherently, he wrapped his jacket around his right arm and smashed it against the window. It exploded. Reaching in, he opened the front door. He brushed glass away, and lifted the still form of Fulvia Fleming off the seat and lowered her to the ground.

Sam! Had he moved? Yes! He was groaning. Shots zinged into and out of the car, past Jimmy's head. With great effort he dragged himself to the hood of the car and blazed off the three remaining rounds in the Luger at the moving brush opposite him. He reached for another magazine and in so doing lifted his head. He felt a sledgehammer blow in his left shoulder. Then another. Somehow he managed to insert the second magazine into the Luger.

Through a deepening haze he saw a burly form emerge from the brush diagonally across from him. The form staggered, its face a bizarre red mask in the light of a popping multi-color starburst. Natale! And behind him, a hand held firmly on Natale's left leg, was Luke, his nose at a grotesque angle. Natale tried to kick free, and raised his pistol towards Jimmy. Jimmy swore at the oblivion closing in on him, and with a mighty effort raised what seemed to be a two-ton Luger. He fired.

At the same time Natale also fired, and a split-second later Luke's rock came down on Natale's head with a loud hollow thump. Natale fell heavily and rolled to the center of the road, gathering a coat of gravel over (and in) his crushed skull. He lay still, bleeding.

"Got him dis time!" Luke yelled. He sprinted to Jimmy's side.

Jimmy raised his head from the hood of the car, "Luke," he croaked, "get Sam out!" He struggled to raise his upper body off the hood, failed, fell forward face down, and passed out.

Luke leaped into the car, turned off the ignition, and dragged Pizzuta out. Somewhat revived by the rush of air into the car when Jimmy broke the car window, Pizzuta shook his head, stood up unsteadily, and took several breaths of fresh cold air. He saw Luke's battered face, and Jimmy.

"Luke! What... what happened?"

"Dey tried to kill you and yor girl. As... Asfixinate you!

"Who?" Pizzuta seemed more alert.

"Di Anello. Natale. I got roped into da deal. But I got out of it Sam. Honest! I went for Natale when he shot at Jimmy, hit him wid a rock. But he slugged me. See?" He touched his nose. "But he didn't cold cock me like he tot. Den we wrestled. And I got him da second time, wid da same rock. Jimmy must a got a good shot in dere too, I tink."

Sam was alert now. He saw Fulvia. "Fulvia," he screamed, his warm breath a cloud of despair in the cold air. He went to her, turned her gently on her stomach, and frantically began the Danish method of artificial respiration. She began to breathe regularly. But in another few minutes – sons of bitches!

"Here Luke." Sam threw Fulvia's purse at him. "Get

the house key. Open the front door." He looked at Fulvia. She'll be okay," he said. When the door opened, Pizzuta guided a dazed Fulvia into the house.

"Watch her, Luke," he said. He went to the phone. "Hello, this is Sergeant Sam Pizzuta... Yeah, its been a really great Columbus Day... Uh huh. Now SHUT UP, and listen good!"

A few minutes later both Jimmy and Natale were on the floor of the little living room, covered with blankets. "Isn't much more we can do," Pizzuta said, looking at Jimmy, worried. "The ambulances will be here in a few minutes." He added... "Luke, tell me more."

And Luke did, including the trip to the New York border with Di Anello.

"Thanks, Luke," Pizzuta said. "Starting tonight there's going to be the biggest round-up of hoods this fucking planet has ever seen!"

Sergeant Sam Pizzuta finally riveted his eyes on Luke. "God, Luke! You look like you just went ten rounds with Joe Louis."

"Didn't you know?" Luke said, grimacing, finally feeling pain, "I did!"

Though he didn't much feel like it, Pizzuta cracked a wan smile.

Chapter 37

Vic, Marjorie, and Carmela ran past the stone lions guarding the entrance to Di Anello's house, and darted hard left down East Hawthorne Road. Speed, more speed! Supple bodies strained and pushed. Suddenly, behind them, Marjorie heard a familiar sound – noise from a broken vehicle muffler. She slowed and looked over her shoulder.

Vic had already turned, and was in the middle of the road. "We can hitch a ride," he said, hope in his voice. "I'll flag the car down."

"You come back here quick!" Marjorie hissed.

Vic obeyed instantly, returning to her side. "What's wrong, Marjorie?"

"Look!" she whispered, pointing.

The driver of the vehicle, a pick-up truck, had turned off its lights, killed the engine, and was rolling it up to the stone lions. The dark shapes of men piled out of the cab and off the back of the truck. They huddled quietly around someone who seemed to be the leader, and then single file, they moved into the Di Anello driveway.

"They... ss-ta! they're carrying clubs and things!" Vic said, his voice shaking. "Who... who–"

"I know who they are," Marjorie said. "Oh, I knew this was going happen someday! Vic, those thugs belong to Tim Hoyt. He hates Di Anello. Oh, poor Phil! He'll be caught between that monster with a gun and these brutes!"

Carmela began shaking violently. "What can we do? What can we do?"

Marjorie didn't answer, but with the leap of a startled deer she surged past Carmela and Vic. She had to reach help! Faster, Marjorie, faster, she urged herself on. Phil could be either shot or pummeled to death!

She zoomed ahead, her long limbs pale blurs in the night. She felt an intense burning pain in her chest. She sucked in oceans of air. She gasped. Still five minutes before she reached the bottom of the hill.

Tears welled in her eyes. She would be too late! Her promising world... coming to and end. Feeling more and more desperate, fighting to save the one she loved, Marjorie commanded her legs to go faster. They didn't respond. They felt as if they had suddenly changed into lead weights.

She was finished; Or was she?

The car bathed her in its headlights. It braked to a stop, and Little Angelo jumped out.

"Gee, Marjorie, I diden mean ta be late. I... I... almost fugut I was supposed ta pick all ye guys up. Where are da udders?"

Marjorie shrieked, threw her arms around him, and gave him a resounding kiss, flush on the mouth. Startled but pleased, he took two steps back.

Vic and Carmela arrived, panting. "Let's go, turn around," Vic wheezed. "Get to... a phone, quick! Phil and Guido are in trouble. Even Di Anello." Vic gave no indication that he had ever stuttered.

Marjorie jumped into the car. Carmela followed, shoved in by Vic, and lastly came Vic who barely made it inside, for Little Angelo had already tromped on the accelerator. He spun the car around expertly, and Carmela grabbed at Vic to keep him from falling out. Mouth gaping, Vic managed a "Thanks!" Marjorie quickly filled Little Angelo in.

"I'll getcha to a phone in less than a minute," Little Angelo promised. Boy, she's no banana-head, he thought, throwing her a quick, appreciative glance. She was leaning out the window, her red hair flying, searching for the first glimmer of a house or store light at the bottom of the hill.

* * * *

The tall gables glimmered in the bath of light from the fireworks below, which exploded in an increasing crescendo of noise and color. Inside Di Anello's office, the Tomy guns, loaded with full drums of fifty rounds each, sagged in Phil's and Guido's trembling hands.

"Listen!" Phil said, his voice rising, "they're not coming up!" Necks craned, heads angled and two sets of ears strained to verify the words. The clop of footsteps on the stairway receded, followed by the sound of breaking glass and a braying voice: "Whiskey, cognac, and lookee here, champagne! Now ain't he a gentleman! Drink up boys!"

Loud, strident voices; curses, hoarse laughter. A few minutes later the sound of exploding bottles against walls... And heads?

"They found the liquor cabinet my father has downstairs," Guido said in a quiet confession-box voice. "Now maybe they'll get whacked out and leave," he added in a barely audible voice.

Phil thought differently. He saw alcohol fumes pickling the wastelands that passed for brains in the thugs below; and greater danger... The men could linger, work themselves up into a frenzy, and come upstairs.

"Guido," Phil said, "I gotta take a quick look... see what our chances are of getting out of this."

"Okay. Be careful! I'll get Gennaro's gun. In case my Tommy gun here jams." Guido tried to look brave. The look disappeared when he peered at his father. "I really gotta phone for help. I don't care if they hear me!" He started to cry but stopped when Phil put an arm around his shoulders and squeezed.

"Go ahead, phone," Phil said. "With the racket those bastards are making they'll never hear you. Just hope they haven't cut the phone lines." He set his Tommy gun down carefully, and hugging the wall crawled to a point two feet from the top stairs. Nothing up ahead but the gaping hole where the front door used to be. In the den and kitchen, that's where they are, boozing it up. *Maybe we can make it by them unseen!*

No! At the bottom of the long staircase, sitting, their backs to him, were two hunched men, one in a Navy pea jacket, the other in a soiled pullover sweater. Both had caps pulled low on their heads. One held a bottle of whiskey high over his head. *What cruds!*

"My turn, ya pig!" the one without the bottle snarled.

"Suck on it!" said the man with the bottle. He didn't mean the whiskey.

The revelry in the kitchen and den continued, and the two dregs on the stairway seemed to stir. *To join their fellow cruds?* Phil's heart pounded.

No! to fight over the bottle. Mesmerized, Phil saw

the bottle careen over both men's heads. Up, up... towards him! It smashed on the wall next to him, and splashed him with a few remaining fingers of sour mash whiskey.

"Aaaak!" The cry exploded from Phil, and he rolled away from tinkling shards of glass. Two capped heads turned at the sound of Phil's voice.

"Look!" The man in the pea jacket pointed a limp finger. "Someone's watching us! Aw shit! You should a gone up right away."

"Don't worry, Glass Jaw, I'll get da punk!" said the one in the dirty sweater. He stumbled against his partner. Both tottered and grabbed. Arms and legs tangled and they fell to the floor, cursing each other's entire ancestry.

Phil didn't wait to see the outcome of the drunken tableau. He scrambled back to the ofice. The Tommy gun! where is it? He didn't see it. There! Guido... mumbling, sitting on his ass against the desk holding a Tommy gun tight in the crook of each arm, barrels down. Gennaro's gun, a .32 semi-automatic rested next to his left foot. In his hands he held the silencer. He turned it over and over, as if inspecting it. His eyes seemed glassy and unfocused.

"Guido! Let go! Please! He's coming!" Phil tugged at a Tommy gun without success. "Oh my God, we're dead!" he wailed. "Guido, believe me! One of the bastards is–"

The fall of heavy footsteps and a loud voice cut him off: "Not the kid, you idiot! Bust up Di Anello... he's up there, hiding somewhere!"

Phil swept up the .32. In a nightmare fright, he slapped Guido's face hard. He swung the gun around, towards the voice. Glass Jaw's, Phil thought, the crud in the pea coat who had spotted him. He began firing wildly.

The sound echoed and intensified in the room, and the gun bucked in Phil's unfamiliar hands. Undaunted, he kept firing. With each rapid shot, ceiling plaster shredded and flew, and ripped pieces of wood from the door frame rained down into the corridor, along with ricocheting slugs.

"Back, back! He's got a fucking gat!" roared Glass

Jaw. Bodies collided, and then fell back, screaming and scrambling in the bedlam. Phil kept firing until the gun clicked on empty.

"He's out of ammo!" Phil heard Glass Jaw's voice. "Drink up boys!" And then a slurred command, "Come on now, we rush him. Fuck Hoyt! Use your gat on 'em all, Vito. Anybody else got a gat? C'mon, speak up!"

Overwrought, choking, his mouth dry, Phil felt he was coming apart. A firm long-fingered hand grasped his shoulder.

"Phil, take this, and thanks!" Guido handed Phil a Tommy gun. "I'm all right now. You see, my father is a gangster. He's a murderer too, and now he wants to kill a detective and a woman. I overheard Gennaro... before I had to kill him."

Phil's eyes locked on Guido's tired, drawn face. *So, the mask is off!* "Yeah, I've been dumb," Guido said, reading Phil accurately.

And it hit Phil. A detective? A woman? His brain cells fired skyrockets of their own. Sergeant Pizzuta, and Mrs. Fleming... Marjorie's mother, slated for death... by *them!* He had to get out, sound the alarm! But first he had to face a zombie back from the grave – Vito – and the pack of jackals egging him on.

Phil dropped to one knee beside Guido, submachine gun ready.

"This time, *nobody* gets away," Guido said, in a super-calm voice that chilled Phil. In the momentary stillness his mind worked overtime. Would he ever see Marjorie again? If he died, who would she go with? Who would claim her for his very own? That red hair! Those green eyes! Oh–!

"Here they come!" Guido's voice broke through Phil's self-flagellation.

Mad howling, and "We're gonna cut yor hearts out, we are, and feed them to the swine!" Slobbering agreement, and... pistol shots! A black cloud of bodies surged and skidded around the angle of the hallway, and rushed the office. Clubs, blackjacks, and pistols waved their promise of mayhem and death. Leading the pack... Vito!

Oh! what a glorious one-sided Donnybrook Fair of a night it will be! Vito saw, recognized, and didn't think so! His .45 boomed twice; he fell flat as a worm and frantically pushed backwards as fast as he could.

Amidst the din of drunken excess, rapid bursts of automatic fire, gouts of flame, and cries of terror, pain, and panic rent the night.

Pandemonium! Vito's frantic backward scrabbling stopped the mob's forward momentum, and legs gave way like struck candle pins. Bodies rolled and shoved to get back around the corner, down the stairs, out the gash that used to be the front door and away from the wall of flame and rattling death.

Prone on the floor, where he had dropped when Vito got off his two rounds, Phil stopped firing. The short corridor outside the door was clear, except for blood stains on the carpet. Phil wet his lips. He hadn't tried to hit anyone, not even Vito. He had aimed in front of thudding feet and over heads. But not Guido. His lips curled in hatred, he had aimed waist and head high, and he still fired short bursts from the ample drum.

Now there was another sound; high pitched, wailing. Sirens! Lots of them, coming closer, followed by the screeching of brakes, and the sound of new, clear voices: "Freeze! Hands up. Over here... slowly!"

"Guido, it's all over! Quit shooting! Hear? Now!"

Guido obeyed reluctantly but he caressed the Mistress of the Roaring '20's lovingly with his long piano-concerto fingers.

"We're alive because of him," he said, nodding to his father. "He was afraid Vito would come back and he was ready. Too bad. Too bad he..."

He left the sentence unfinished, and Phil understood. But he didn't know what had happened to Vito. Dead? Alive? He had to find out... End it, once and for all!

"Wait here for the cops, Guido. I'll check on Vito."

Guido nodded mechanically, and Phil ran to the doorway. He stopped, came back, and picked up the Tommy gun. The wall of the short corridor opposite the doorway resembled Swiss cheese. Phil turned the corner into the long hallway leading to the stairs. Two sprawled bodies on the bloody carpet moaned, and Phil looked at them. No, not Vito.

"Hang on," he whispered to the wounded duo,

"medics are on the way."

He hurried down the dark stairway and saw several men, four he thought, being herded by gun-toting cops. None resembled Vito – too tall, thin... But there! on the ground, a trail of blood, heading back to the rear of the house, the stone wall, the woods, and escape! Only Vito would know that – he had done it before... And disappeared.

Déjà vu! No, it couldn't happen again! Phil had to rid himself of his terrible nemesis. He crouched, hugged the shadow of the house and a line of shrubs, and turned the corner to the stone wall. A girl's scream? No, it had to be his imagination.

Flat on the stone wall Vito Amorusi panted, sweater ripped and bloody, little sunken pig eyes darting back and forth, his .45 gripped tightly in his right fist.

"Drop the gun, Vito," Phil heard himself saying. He raised the Tommy gun menacingly. Vito's neck swiveled, a cobra seeking and opening...

"Don't shoot, kid, don't shoot! Look, I'm hurt bad, real bad." Phil had never heard such a whine. The .45 clattered on the wall and fell behind it. "See," Vito said, "I won't hurtcha." *Of course you won't, you missing link, not while I've got this Tomy gun on you!*

"Gimme a hand, will ya? Help me to da ambulance back dere."

Phil hesitated. But shit! he couldn't let a human being bleed to death, even Vito. He approached cautiously, and Vito seemed to go limp. Phil lowered his submachine gun to take a closer look.

It happened! Thin steel glinted and arched up fast towards Phil's gut. The barrel of the Tommy gun came up faster. It caught the underside of Vito's wrist, flinging it up and out but not before the knife ripped through Phil's jacket and nicked his skin. He felt warm blood ooze in his left side. Reacting angrily, he brought the gun down, squeezed the trigger, and fired... at old stone. Vito, screaming in pain, but still ring wise, had rolled into the woods, in time to avoid being stitched to the wall.

Phil leaned over the wall, peered in the darkness, and let go a long volley. Nothing except the heavy swish of someone moving through brush.

"I'm gonna get ya, punk!" Phil yelled, savoring the words, and he vaulted over the wall. Another volley, in the air this time. He moved through the trees quickly, seeking his quarry. Soon, dead ahead, he heard the sound of a heavy body crashing through brush.

Phil fired another burst, in the air again. "I'm almost on ya, punk!" he taunted. "Stop and give up!" He moved faster, ignoring his bleeding side and the whip of branches in his face. Suddenly he stopped short. He knew where he was.

"Vito!" he cried, as loud as he could, "watch out for the—"

"Aiiiii!" the terrified cry froze Phil into silence. He heard the sickening thud of a body falling and rolling through rock and brush. He trembled, for he knew what had happened. Vito had stumbled and fallen into that rocky hole; the one Phil himself had barely missed when he had fled Guido's den pursued by Vito such a long time ago.

Carefully Phil threaded his way to the bottom of the drop...

Emotionally exhausted, Phil swung back over the stone wall, around the house, and into the glare of spotlights. His head sagged onto his chest. He dropped the Tommy gun. He didn't need it any more. Vito was dead, his face shattered by his head first fall, his neck broken. Too much! All feeling left Phil, and he swayed forward, as if in a drunken stupor.

"Are you all right?" Two husky policemen in blue coats approached.

Phil looked at them blankly.

A girl's scream? Again? Dully, Phil looked about.

"Let me through!"

That voice! Marjorie's?

Marjorie scrambled like a wildcat, making her way past ambulance attendants and pushing past the two startled husky policemen. Sobbing, she hurled her full weight wildly at Phil. He staggered back. She kept him from falling, embraced him, and salty wetness touched his lips. He knew she was crying, and he realized so was he. He didn't care!

A loud hollow pop erupted in the sky, followed by ear-shattering blasts, each preceded by bursts of color, shooting out in all directions. The pyrotechnic finale was under way, a glorious salute to another fun-filled Columbus Day.

"Cripes, a scene out of Romeo and Juliet," said a thin ambulance attendant, pausing to look at Phil and Marjorie.

"Yeah," said his rotund partner. Both lowered the stretcher holding Gennaro. "No rush on this one," said the first attendant, "he's bought it."

Two other stretcher-bearers hurried past. "That's the boss man," the thin attendant said. "He'll make it."

"And look at that!" said his partner, cupping his hands. The last series of skyrockets began bursting.

"The redhead and her guy got sound effects!"

"Yeah, and special lighting!"

Phil and Marjorie didn't hear the bemused ambulance attendants, nor did they see the tall detective hurrying towards them. He alternately frowned and smiled, and he carried a white first aid kit, which he opened as he approached. In the glare of spotlights on the ground and the shimmering light and shadow cast by fireworks bursting above, he knelt by Phil's side and yanked up his jacket.

The fury and spectacle of the fireworks intensified.

Everyone later agreed they had been the most ambitious, loud, and spectacular Vespucci Park had ever seen... and would probably ever see for a long time.

Made one forget the Depression, *veramente!*

Chapter 38

Vespucci Park was quiet and dark. The fireworks were over and another Columbus Day was history. But, high above the park, in a gabled white house, lights glowed, flashlights flickered, and spotlights glared.

Inside, among the wreckage and clutter of the entryway, Sergeant Sam Pizzuta talked quietly with other detectives and a State police official. In the shambles of what was once the den, huddled together, were Guido, Carmela, Vic, Lucy, and Little Angelo. Luke Peris, his jacket held in front of his pants, stood stiffly beside them. A handcuffed sullen man in a Navy pea coat sat just outside the den on the blood-stained brecciated marble of the entryway.

Pizzuta glanced at Luke, whose pained expression was a message.

"Just a minute," Pizzuta said. "I'll be right back." The men nodded.

Pizzuta led Luke upstairs to Guido's room. He opened a closet door, then eyed the contents and then Luke. "Here, these should fit." He tossed Luke a new pair of gray slacks.

"Thanks!" Luke said gratefully. He ripped off his own urine-stained pants and shorts. As he did so, he gave Pizzuta a sheepish grin.

"You were great tonight, Luke!" Pizzuta soothed. And don't worry about it," he nodded to the limp pile of clothes on the floor, "in your shoes many people would have done worse, maybe even me."

Luke sighed, relieved, tried a lopsided grin, went to a bureau, pulled out a drawer, then another, and came up with a pair of boxer shorts. Pizzuta watched the delicate drama, and he vividly recalled what had brought him here.

Two patrol cars and an ambulance had answered Pizzuta's call from Fulvia's house. She had shaken her head. "I'm all right; no ambulance, Sam, please!"

Pizzuta acceded to her stubbornness and helped put Jimmy in the ambulance. Jimmy's eyes flickered. "Sam," he whispered, "My Silver Star..."

"What?" He's out of it, Pizzuta thought. Poor guy!

A look of annoyance creased Jimmy's face. "The kid... Phil... has it. Tell him... to keep it." Mumbling. Pizzuta put his ear to Jimmy's mouth.

"...honest ...it'll keep him honest..." Jimmy managed, and he sank back into unconsciousness.

Natale's inert body slid into the ambulance. Pizzuta didn't give a shit whether he lived or died, but Jimmy–!

"Sergeant!" Pizzuta didn't need the alert, he had heard the crackle of the patrol car's radio.

Ordering an officer to stand guard at Fulvia's, Pizzuta had jumped into one of the patrol cars, taking Luke with him, and siren wailing, the car roared away. The Di Anello house! A near-hysterical girl had called in. She and her friends had run from the house... Assassin with a gun! Stalking Di Anello! And a truck full of men with clubs... Other subjects in the house in danger!

"Other subjects?" Pizzuta had translated that! Guido and Phil. What else? That fella Phil – in the middle of big trouble again. Geez, will he ever learn? But Pizzuta was worried. Obviously something was very wrong with Di Anello's unholy empire, and Phil might not escape this time.

He had asked the cop driving the patrol car to go faster. The car had screeched into the Di Anello driveway in time to see three dark-clothed men, bleeding from wounds in legs, side, and shoulders, come limping out the open front doorway and surrender to cops with guns drawn. Then he had seen a Buick pull up (obviously it had followed the police cars), and a group of young people cascade out of it. One girl, for crying out loud, was still struggling to get a dress on... Another girl, a redhead. Marjorie! She had screamed and tried to tear herself away from a restraining cop. Pizzuta had sprinted to her side, followed by her friends, all talking at once.

"Calm down, everyone," he had shouted. "Whatever was gonna happen already has! No, Marjorie! you can't go in yet. Phil and Guido are fine, I'm sure. Wait here."

He had taken two steps toward the house when he heard machine gun fire from behind the house. Everyone had flattened, and waited. More machine gun bursts. "Move in, slowly," Pizzuta had said. "Train the lights on the side of the house. Careful now!"

The few cops, their numbers bolstered by men from several more patrol cars, moved in, arrayed like a skirmish line of combat troops.

"Hold your fire!" Pizzuta had cried. Phil had appeared... A scream, a blur of motion, and Marjorie had joined him.

A few minutes later, Pizzuta had shepherded Phil and Marjorie to a patrol car. "Wait here, Marjorie," he said. "I'm taking you home. Your mother needs you. Don't worry, I'll be back in a little bit. I want to talk to a few people first. Tell you what, have one of those medics over there check out the patch job I did on Phil's side." He knew she would go for that, and she did.

But Luke Peris' problem with his plumbing prevented Sam Pizzuta from coming back 'in a little bit'.

"Sam, aren't we going back downstairs?" Luke now said. "I'm ready."

"Huh? Oh sure, Luke." Sam replied with a deep sigh. "Let's go."

Officer Patrick McHugh, his huge bulk squeezed into a long blue coat, smiled at Pizzuta at the bottom of the stairway and then glared at the manacled, black-haired, lantern-jawed man in the Navy pea coat.

"You were caught red-handed this time, Glass Jaw Wray. We don't need the likes of you and your trouble-making ways running loose. A disgrace you are to the good people of the ledge. The back of me hand to ye!" It was a lyrical brogue; his threatening gesture wasn't.

"Just following orders," Wray cringed at the raised ham of a hand," you don't say no to Tim Hoyt, honest!" Glass Jaw Wray tucked his neck deep into the coat. Shocked sober, he had talked. A grim detective told him there had been a murder upstairs, plus other infractions that could put him and his hired thugs away for twenty years. Why, Glass Jaw could even sit in that famous chair that roasted butts and brains!

His memory dimmed by alcohol fumes, Glass Jaw had tried desperately to remember the events of the evening, but blank spots kept appearing in his memory. He vaguely recalled goading Vito and his men to charge. And hadn't they fired off pistols? Is that when the murder took place? After that he remembered nothing except for hammering noise and swirling shadows – until cold fresh air scraped some of the barnacle-like numbness from his mind – and he heard screams and sirens. Cops and lights; lots of both!

Seeing his men taken away, and hearing the accusation of murder, he blamed a trigger-happy Vito and a couple of his drunken fools. He, Glass Jaw, wasn't anywhere near the room where the killing took place. Hoyt had ordered him to bust up Di Anello's place, using Vito, that's all. Hey! who knows, maybe Hoyt secretly planned things to work out the way they did. He could have set it up with Vito and a couple of the bully boys. Yeah, sure! Everyone knows Vito hated Di Anello. Perfect, right? See? Glass Jaw Wray ain't no murderer!

"You were 'Just following orders' were you, eh?" Officer Patrick McHugh now mimicked Glass Jaw. "You can be sure we will 'take it up' with himself, Mr. Hoyt, by all that's holy!" He wished he was closer to the two detectives, who, he could see, were now talking in low tones to Sergeant Pizzuta. They looked upstairs, and then at Guido, who still sat quietly in the den.

"Yeah, the kid freaked out, shot everything up," a young detective said.

"I'd say it was self-defense," Pizzuta replied. "Lucky he didn't kill anyone. What's happening on Hoyt?"

An old leather-faced detective from Traffic, Sergeant Thomas Riley, answered, "Your Captain Ferguson may pick him up. I hear he just checked in with the chief. A delicate matter, don't you know."

"Yeah, I know. By the way, do we know where the mayor stands in all this?" Pizzuta asked, not really expecting an answer.

Riley grinned. "We'll know soon."

A uniformed cop trotted up. "Radio for you Sarge... On the mayor."

A few minutes later Riley returned to the entryway. "Good to have contacts," he beamed. "Well! His Honor has spoken." He slapped his thigh and burst out laughing. "I can retire happy now!" he added.

"All right, Riley, so you're a comic! Now, what did

His Honor say?"

"Sam, you won't believe this." Riley said, his hoary face swathed in wrinkles, "His Honor laughed like hell he did! Then he told the chief 'Sure, lock him up. I'll get around to tending to it in the mornin'."

"I'll be go-to-hell!" Sam said, nonplused.

* * * *

His Honor, wide awake now, still chortled. In a rich virgin wool Seymour Flannel, an exclusive STATE-O-MAINE lounging robe, he rubbed his ample belly. What was he to do with his conniving fart of a son-in-law? Jail? His daughter wouldn't stand for that. *What then? Certain legal moves for appearances sake, a fine perhaps, and fire his ass out of his cushy City Hall job... Afterwards... hmm, ah, why not? A nostalgic trip to Ireland, to visit relatives. And then, to France, Italy, Germany, and beyond, for an extended cultural tour... of at least eighteen months. By all the saints, what a capital idea!*

And, of course, by the end of that time, I shall no longer be mayor.

No, I shall be... the governor... of this fair state!

Timothy Hoyt, you shrewd son of a bitch, you will not stab me in the back! You have lost, dear son-in-law! Of course I knew of your ambitions. City Hall is a sieve! And, I admit, I was a wee mite worried, 'tis true. But, no longer! No longer! You really outdid yourself, this time!

Laughing heartily, His Honor toasted himself in the full length mirror before which he always practiced speeches and gestures.

* * * *

Back at the shambles of the Di Anello house the night was not yet over.

"Just got word," said the State police official, dressed in civilian clothes, ambling up to Pizzuta. He spat and made a sour face. "We acted fast on your call, Sam. Troopers in unmarked cars went to the farmhouse you described. It was too darn easy!" He shook his head, continued. "A dried-up old bitch in a black dress opened the door for us. How she knew we were coming I'll never know. Our men flashed their badges. She put a finger to her lips, pointed upstairs, stuck up two fingers, and made a funny motion with her hips. I swear, it looked like a burlesque grind." He smiled oddly and switched a tooth-pick from one side of his mouth to the other. "Gotta quit eating those damn sticky jelly doughnuts," he said, out of the corner of his mouth.

"You were saying?" said Sam, a bit impatiently.

"Yeah," the State man said. "We went up quietly to the second bedroom, figuring that's what she meant, and we found 'em all right. Just like the old gal tried to tell us with that little hip movement. Geez, what a galdern sight! The big ugly guy had it jammed up the arse of pretty boy from here to Christmas. Never heard us coming until we snapped the cuffs on 'em. Now we got 'em for attempted murder... and sodomy, among other things."

Pizzuta smiled sardonically. The roundup of hoods he had promised Luke had gone faster and farther than he had expected. But before he could respond, a big shiny black Cadillac rolled up, and Julia Di Anello, resplend-ent in furs and jewellery, got out, saw Pizzuta, and walked quickly to him, her quizzical look changing to one of fear.

"Guido is fine, Julia," he said, "and Massimo will be. He's been taken to City Hospital. Come on, let's go in. I'll tell you what happened here tonight." Pizzuta told her quickly. She showed no emotion, except when she saw Guido, who ran to her and said, "Mama, I had to shoot Gennaro! He was gonna kill Papa! And Vito was after me and my friend Phil."

"I know," she said, her voice hoarse, her arms around him, "I know..."

Chapter 39

Marjorie leaped out of the police car taking Phil with her before Pizzuta had brought it to a complete stop. The patrolman standing guard got out of her way quickly when he saw Pizzuta give a let-them-by-wave and an affirmative nod. The cop scratched his head as the red-head dynamo whizzed by him, pulling that big husky fella like he was a toy.

"Mama, Mama, Mama!" Marjorie screamed once she cleared the policeman and was in her house. Fulvia came quickly, and mother and daughter embraced.

"I'm all right, Marjorie! I'm all right!" Fulvia insisted in a soothing voice. Finally they separated and gazed at each other tenderly and with tear-filled eyes.

"Marjorie is a heroine, Fulvia," Pizzuta said, breaking the awkward silence. "She phoned in the alarm, got the police to Di Anello's, and–"

"Oh, don't thank me," Marjorie said. "Thank Little Angelo; he drove to the candy store like... like Barney Oldfield and Tazio Nuvolari combined!"

"Well, I have to go," Pizzuta said, "continue with the investigation at Di Anello's," he took both of Fulvia's hands in his,"and answer questions and fill out lots of paper... on what almost happened to us." He pulled her to him, held her a moment, and kissed her good-by. Fulvia flushed, murmured something no one but Pizzuta heard, and pulled away. Marjorie dried her tears, and smiled at Phil.

"Get plenty of rest, Fulvia," Pizzuta said, sternly. He turned to Phil. "Wait here. I'll either come back for you or send someone for you. Now, don't you think you'd better phone home?" With that, Sergeant Pizzuta left.

Phil phoned home. Sebastiano answered. He wasn't surprised. He already knew what had happened at the gabled house; a detective had told him. He was still at the tenement, drinking Rosa's strong coffee when Phil called.

He told his father he would be home soon. A tired, hollow-voiced Sebastiano said he and Rosa would wait, and had the phone snatched from his hands by Rosa.

She wanted to hear for herself, she said, in a biting tone. The detective poured himself another cup of coffee...

"Mama," Marjorie said, when the door closed behind Sergeant Pizzuta, "your make-up is all smudged, and your dress," she slipped behind Fulvia, and began buttoning, "is a mess... There, I'm finished." She came around and eyed her mother, eyes twinkling. *That was no brother-sister kiss Sam gave you!* She asked in a sweet little voice, "Mama, why were you in the car so long? Why didn't you take him into the house? It was cold outside, and–"

"Marjorie," Fulvia interrupted, and she sighed, "I know we should have, and I did reach for the door handle. But Sam said he'd keep the car heater on for me. He said he wanted to ask me something, *cara*." She placed a hand gently on Marjorie's cheek. Her eyes glittered. Her face glowed. "Cara," she repeated, "Sam... asked me to marry him. I said 'yes' and, we both get happy, and well," she shrugged magnificently, "we talk and talk." She paused briefly, threw a look around the room and finished rapidly, "You know the rest!" *No she doesn't! We could have gotten out. We were so happy, we make the love... And after a while I no remember anything!*

Marjorie's happy shriek cut off Fulvia's thoughts: "Oh, that's wonderful Mama!" She clapped her hands in childish delight. "Isn't it Phil?" She threw her arms around him and kissed him several times. This time Fulvia raised an eyebrow at them, Phil mumbled, embarrassed, "Y-yeah, it is."

Marjorie continued to bubble. "And Mama! Phil and I are going to get married too. Oh, Mama!" She hugged Phil.

"What! What did you two children do?" Fulvia looked worried now and glared accusingly at Phil, who was bewildered and struck dumb by it all.

"Oh, Mama, it's not like that at all, Phil hasn't done... *that*... to me." She smiled sweetly at Phil. All he could do was gulp and shake his head back and forth, for the mother-daughter exchange had become very, very clear to him! Suddenly he realized he was honor-bound to marry Marjorie. After all, he *had* done it to her, though

Marjorie had just lied about it. For only a moment, sure, but it had happened, there in the den. So he had to marry her, didn't he?

"We won't get married for a few years, Mama. We'll go steady first, then we'll get engaged. We will, won't we Phil?"

Phil felt his head moving up and down... up and down... moved by some invisible force reaching out from that redhead! The redhead took his hand and kissed him on the nose with very wet lips.

And Fulvia wondered if it would really happen. Her beautiful, impetuous, fiery daughter, blooming suddenly into womanhood, seemed certain of it. And Phil? She glanced at the uncomfortable, perspiring young man, whose eyes seemed to be glazed. Fulvia rubbed her forehead, moistened her lips and sighed, a sigh of knowledge, a sigh of the vicissitudes of life.

They are so young, she thought. But, she decided, she would not interfere. Time will pass... They will mature, meet others, and perhaps slowly grow apart. *Chi sa?* She shrugged her shoulders, brightened, Who knows?

And she moved on to important matters of the moment.

"Marjorie," she said, "Sergeant Sam Pizzuta and I will be married soon. Perhaps as early as November. Perhaps on November 16, his birthday."

Again Marjorie shrieked.

She was joined by a big "Wow!" from Phil.

Chapter 40

Carpenters hammered and sawed, the noise a rhythm of renewal. Repairs to the Di Anello mansion commenced less than twenty-four hours after it had been savagely torn apart. Someone had clout.

Upstairs, in Di Anello's office, a woman's voice commanded, "Close the door, Abie. The men still have some work to do before they quit for the day."

Julia Di Anello had wasted no time. The night of the attack, after assuring herself that Guido was not hurt, she had visited her husband in the hospital. Learning that he would recover but would be hospitalized for up to a week and then jailed, she got busy. Rousing Harvey Lane from his sleep, she informed the distinguished criminal attorney that his services were needed. His mental cash register ringing despite the hour, he accepted the case with charm and alacrity. Julia then awakened Sforza, talked to him for half and hour, and gave him several orders. One order was that she wanted her house repaired promptly. Sforza assured her it would be.

Now Abie Goldberg closed the office door. He sat down and fiddled nervously with the straps of his striped overalls, his working clothes for the day. He looked what he was, a defeated runt of a man. Sitting next to him, back stiff, hands folded in his lap, his face set in a grim, determined look was Sebastiano Martello,

"Please, relax," Julia Di Anello began in a soft ingratiating contralto. "What I have to say will not take long." She spoke in virtually accent-less English, and she knew she had both Sebastiano's and Abie's strict attention, which was her intent.

"I called you here because you are two very lucky men, unlike my husband, who, when he recovers, faces an uncertain future. Perhaps he will go to prison for a very long time." She leaned forward. Sebastiano wasn't sure whether he saw look of sadness or a smile on her face. The slanting light from a fast-sinking sun made it difficult. *Sadness, I am sure,* Sebastiano reasoned to himself.

Someone knocked on the door.

"Come in, come in," Julia said. "It isn't locked, Isabella."

In came Grandma Isabella, a flowery apron over her black dress. She set a tray of espresso and rich pastries on the desk and waddled away after giving the two men a withering look.

"Help yourselves," Julia urged, turning a palm-up, gracefully pointing hand at the tray.

"*Grazie!*" said Sebastiano, never one to refuse good espresso, or so the aroma told him, and mouth-watering *pasticceria*. He helped himself; so did Abie Goldberg, who now looked more upbeat about the proceedings.

"The vicissitudes of life are unpredictable," Julia Di Anello began, sipping and savoring slowly. Her heavy perfume mixed with the espresso aroma, reminding Sebastiano of the lingering, not unpleasant smell of a fall burn of leaves and vines. She was dressed to kill, too! Fancy blue dress, diamond necklace, heavy earrings and make-up. Her dark hair, upswept, reminded him of that movie star, what's her name? Ah yes, Joan Crawford. *Madonna!* But Julia Di Anello is no movie star. She... she looks more like the Madam of an expensive bordello!

"Do not mind Isabella's seeming grouchiness," Julia said. "It is really sadness, for she was poor Nino's housekeeper. She will help keep this house in order now. And her grandson... a strange one called Longcoat... worked for Natale." She shrugged. "Natale died this morning. Two bullets in his chest and a crushed skull. Serves him right, trying to kill that detective and his *puttana*. And my innocent husband is accused of planning it."

Her dark eyes flashed dangerously. Her carefully lacquered fingernails dug into the desk top. "*Che disgrazia!*" she muttered. (What misfortune!)

She recovered her composure quickly. "But this Longcoat was found asleep in Natale's locked office by Sforza. He said he was waiting for Natale. When told that he had a long wait, that Natale was dead, he burst out laughing." Julia Di Anello pursed her lips, nodded, and in a musing tone said, "I shall have a long talk with Isabella's grandson..." She paused, lost in thought.

Abruptly she said, "Well, shall we continue, gentlemen?"

Watch out! Sebastiano thought. *Do not get enmeshed in her web. She will eat you!* But his face did not betray his thoughts.

She had already said something, and Sebastiano tuned her in "...and as you know, the police have not implicated either of you with the murder intrigue, and you are free. Luke Peris was believed, and the dying words of that little Columbus Street storekeeper – I don't remember his name – to Sergeant Pizzuta, helped keep you both clean," she looked at Abie, "in their eyes."

Abie, relieved, missed Julia's nuance. He sighed, "Had I known, I would have had no part of it," he said.

"Luke Peris and Jimmy wanted no part of it either," Sebastiano said softly, "and look what they both went through, one died."

"Massimo Di Anello," Julia said, ignoring the two, "was ambitious, and his ambition corrupted him. Evil men turned against him. Consider the cowardly assassination attempt by one supposedly dead Gennaro. And for what reason? Who knows? May those faggots who planned it rot in hell, where Gennaro now roasts with his scheming godfather, Oreste."

Sebastiano tightened inside. The truth came to him, iceberg cold. *Oreste was killed by order of Di Anello! And Gennero came back to avenge Oreste, courtesy of the two New York Black Hand faggots, with an agenda of their own... What deadly Sicilian currents!*

Abie came to life. "Hell comes later for Bigli and Mandrola," he said. "Jail for the next twenty years would be a good beginning for those two miserable queers."

And a new great beginning for Abie Goldberg! Faggot Aldo Mandrola, the effeminate one with the twitchy mustache and cold stare, would not be visiting Abie Goldberg 'next week' to review 'finances of our joint ventures'. Not next week, not ever! Abie's belly jiggled with glee under his overalls. He looked like a condemned man who was saved from the gallows seconds before the trap under his feet was sprung. Hot mist from his sweaty forehead blanked out the glass on his steel-rimmed eyeglasses. It was a moment to relish.

"Yes," Julia Di Anello said venomously, cutting Abie's

silent rejoicing short. "At least twenty years for those betrayers and arch-deceivers. And after that, if Mandrola and Bigli are still alive–"

She caught herself in mid-death sentence. "But enough of this," she said, her tone all business. "Now, we look to the future!"

"Sebastiano!"

"Sì, signora!

"You have done well with us. Now, I want you to stay on. You will be in complete charge of all warehouses and the Columbus Street market. Later, in good time, I will talk to you about new warehouses, here and in New York state."

"New York? Isn't there danger? I thought..." His voice trailed off.

"There is no danger, Sebastiano. That is settled. I want you to build and buy. There will be a war – a big war. No, I do not mean Mussolini's little pavan against the helpless Ethiopians, I mean," she lowered her voice. "Another World War. And we must be ready for it."

"Ma, signora! Non so..." Sebastiano's doubts and hesitation was an obvious statement as he lapsed into his native tongue.

"Non mi hai capito! Per piacere, ascoltami!" Julia tried to hide her impatience, but not her scolding tone.

Sebastiano nodded. He would certainly listen, and he would do his best to understand what this woman really wanted.

"Your part of the business will be most legitimate." Back to English. "For the next few years I want you to work Guido hard; train him after school, weekends, and during school vacations. Assuming," she added, sotto voce, "he can break away from that sexpot blonde he's been seeing." She sipped delicately. "Your son too, must learn the business, Sebastiano. Under the tutelage of a subordinate manager of your own choosing. It would be better for both of you that way. Sons do not take easily to their father's directions!"

She paused momentarily, and a wry smile crossed her face. "Also," she added, pointing a jeweled finger at Sebastiano, "considering the delicate situation my reckless husband is in, my son's work, and your son's, like Caesar's wife, must be above reproach. *Capito?"*

"*Sì!*" A wonderful opportunity for Filippo to escape the Depression!"

"Then, you accept?"

"*Sì, accetto!*" How quickly the words came out!

"You will report directly to me. I will be your boss. All right?"

"Of course."

"Good! It is done. And now you, Abie! You have come a long way, haven't you?"

Abie wasn't sure he liked the way she said that.

"I mean... from the time you delivered fish and dandelion greens to me, and I noticed how quick you were with figures. And not much later I mentioned your name to Massimo, and you went to work for him."

Abie chewed a hunk of pastry slowly, It tasted sour.

"You were good with records too, weren't you?" Julia looked out the window at some distant object. "Funny, so was I. I still am! All those nights I was gone – on church affairs? True, but not all those long hours. Lately, I've taken an active hand in Massimo's enterprises. The financial condition of the escort houses, for example. Not good, Abie, not good. So, as of a few nights ago, I run them. The old manager? Retired."

Ah, thought Sebastiano, things are not always what they appear to be! She is a she-devil! The power behind the throne!

"While you all were in New York, and the night of the unfortunate attempt on Massimo's life, I was busy reviewing records at the court warehouse. I had done this before, but not thoroughly. A few things piqued my interest. Are you following me, Abie?"

"Ah... yes, I am." Abie began choking. "I... can explain," he wheezed.

"Not necessary, Abie." Julia said as Sebastiano pounded Abie's back. "Here, sip this," Julia said. She handed him his cup of espresso. "I wouldn't want you to choke to death – not yet, and not in my office!" She ran her long-nailed index finger across the back of his neck, her lips pursed.

Lights of understanding flared in Sebastiano's head. Skimming! Abie!

"What you've done, I suppose, is understandable. But now, little Julia is in charge. Though I have some misgivings I need your experience. Of course, you will be scrupulously honest, and work for me, only me. Abie... do we understand each other?"

Sebastiano pounded harder, and Abie spewed up a chunk of pastry. He straightened, his face the color of an unripe lemon. He cleared his throat once, twice, and spoke with a rasp, "I... understand! Betray your confidence in me? Oy! never. Not me!"

"Thank you! That's wonderful!" And Julia purred, "Now, until some time in the future you will work without pay. We need not touch on the reasons for this, of course, don't you agree? Hmm? Ah, good, I see you do! And whenever I ask, we will go over the books together, see how we are doing. Don't you think that's a good idea?"

"Yes!" Old Abie almost snapped to attention and saluted.

"All right. We are finished. Now clean up the mess you made and wait."

Julia Di Anello got up and went to the window. She would next enlighten the dear mayor. *While he suspects, he has no idea of the size of the road construction deals his cunning brother-in-law, Tim Hoyt worked out with Massimo's people. Now the dear mayor wants to poke his snout into the biggest pork barrel of all, the governorship! Well, little Julia can help him get there, provided he is malleable – which he will be – once he knows that little Julia, and only she, can now provide him with the big neighborhood bucks he needs. Not Massimo, not Hoyt anymore, and certainly, not the dead ones...*

She turned and her slight form was silhouetted against the window. She threw back her head and laughed heartily, startling Abie and Sebastiano.

"What did Massimo call this new organization of his? Oh yes, let's see, *La Cosa Nostra*, wasn't it?" She giggled like a little girl.

"La Cosa Nostra!" she repeated.

Julia Di Anello put a finger on her lips, sat down and crossed her legs.

"To think," she said, chuckling heartily, "that this thing of his... now has to depend on a woman, a non-Sicilian and a Jew, to stay afloat. Ridiculous, isn't it?"

Neither Abie Goldberg nor Sebastiano Martello said a word.

PART IV

Chapter 41

Columbus Day, 1943.

In Europe, in the Pacific, World War II raged. Cannon roared, warplanes flew, and bomb and shell fell, raining indiscriminate death and destruction. Like all soil in America, the soil of the Holly Hill neighborhood bore no scars of battle, but tell-tale signs of its results abounded. The few men of military age seen on the streets were in uniform, walking alone or in the company of women, children, or old men. Women, in small groups, tucked into cloth coats, hurried along to work, to shop, to church... Rust-scarred cars coughed and banged on worn tires, using their 'A' sticker three-gallons a week gasoline ration only when necessary. Newspaper headlines screamed and radios blared their incessant litany of sacrifice and misery.

The neighborhood tenements, their paint faded and peeling, stood huddled, row on row; wooden soldiers, stoically accepting their lot 'for the duration'. They were covered with soot from the railroad yard, busy around the clock hauling war materiel or draftees to infantry training camps. The tenements looked like senescent, arthritic dowagers, tottering on the brink of extinction.

But... not so! At least one window of each flat was polished and bright, the curtain or draperies open, displaying a service flag with a big blue star. The neighborhood youth had really gone to war, unlike the self-serving inane Lucky Strike cigarette ad that bleated: 'Lucky Strike Green Has Gone To War!' And from a few windows, a gold star peered solemnly, for this tenement family had lost a son.

From the bedroom window across the tracks, in what once was Nino's house the tall girl with rumpled red hair and glittering green eyes stretched luxuriantly as she gazed out at the neighborhood. She tightened the blue satin robe around her body. She looked at the deep green tunic of an Army officer carelessly folded on a chair near the bed and then at the colorful contrast of the two top-row ribbons on the left breast of the tunic, the Purple Heart and the Silver Star. Her gaze was drawn to the mahogany chest-on-chest opposite the bed, and to a wood-framed picture on it. A slight, slim, smiling young soldier in a tight-fitting World War I khaki uniform smiled through the cracked glass. Two medals dangled from his left breast – the Purple Heart and the Silver Star. Mechanically the girl looked at the smaller gilt-edged frame next to the picture. They contained the actual medals the young soldier wore in the faded picture.

Jimmy's medals! Jimmy's 1918 photo!

She sighed and again moved her gaze to the sleeping Army officer's tunic and the small hair's on the back of her neck tingled and rippled. Quickly, she turned and fixed her eyes on Jimmy's picture.

Why, the image had moved! Wasn't that a smile on Jimmy's face?

The girl shook her head rapidly several times, and said in a quiet voice, "Your imagination is running away with you!" Satisfied, she blew the sleeping soldier a kiss. She wouldn't disturb him... She knew she had done enough of that throughout the long passion-filled night!

She tucked her robe tightly around her body and her eyes wandered across the drabness of the neighborhood. She thought of what had happened to those wonderful people, and some not so wonderful people, of 1935. She picked up a dainty cookie from a nearby tray, nibbled slowly, abstemiously, and paraded what she knew before her mind's eye.

Mona! Oh, how she had tried to take Phil away from Marjorie! She was about to succeed too, until in 1937 she was swept off her feet by a Wisconsin cheese salesman and whisked off to help run a large dairy herd near Eue Claire. Mona was now in North Africa, a WAC no less, and surrounded by soldiers of all nations. Her marital status? Unclear.

And that drip of a brother of hers, Nick! Drafted, under strenuous protest. Assigned to an infantry company in Louisiana as a latrine orderly. Rumor has it he has found a home there.

And oh! Nick's sidekick, Longcoat. After his grandmother Isabella died in 1939, he became a cocaine runner. In 1940 he was found wrapped in a burlap sack on the banks of the Blackstone River, dead, six slugs in his head.

Luke Peris. Dead too, but a hero! Went down with his ship in the Pacific. That saddened a lot of people, particularly detective Sam Pizzuta.

Little Angelo, proved to be a late bloomer. Joined the Marines. Wounded at Guadalcanal, medical discharge, got many medals... The girl selected another cookie... Let's see, oh yes! he's Julia Di Anello's chauffeur now. Julia is one busy lady! Funny, she never seems to run out of gas for her cars. Lots of charity work and morale boosting for the boys in uniform, she says. Wonder when her husband gets out of State prison?

Carmela? Now she knows about morale boosting! 'Tis said she works for Julia... has a fancy suite at the Williams Hotel, and entertains only high-ranking officers. My, oh my! Vic certainly awakened something in her way back then in 1935!

And Vic, what about him? Somewhere in the South Pacific, with the Sea Bees. We think New Guinea. Gee! hope he makes it out alive, and not hurt – like him – she nodded to the sleeping officer. *But Vic and Carmela? Finished, long ago!*

Guido? Managing Guido's Diner with his wife Lucy. Wasn't the diner called Sforza's some years back? Think so. Big changes after Di Anello got sent up, oo-fa! And Guido will help Sebastiano run those new-type stores he's planning... where you help yourself, put the stuff into carts you push around yourself. Supermarkets... that's what they are called! Come to think of it, Guido and Lucy should both be at the diner today.

And finally, what about Marjorie? the girl thought. The screams of toddlers in trouble interrupted her ruminations. The spell broke, and it was once again October, 1943.

Across the room Little Anthony, twenty months old, was doing his best to unscrew twin brother Bryan's head from his neck. He seemed to be succeeding. The girl lunged for the twins, her robe flying open.

"No, no!" she cried, and stumbled over a toy dump truck. Hastily, her big toe throbbing, she regained her balance.

Too late. The young officer, startled by what seemed

to him to be a battery of air raid sirens, had rolled off the bed, limped to the twins, and separated them. Happy for the attention, they gurgled. The officer saw the flustered girl, slipped his arms under her robe, encircled her, and pulled her back to the bed.

"No!" she said, not too firmly, "my toe hurts... We have to dress... now." They were at the edge of the bed. "Your leg!" No visible impact. "We have a breakfast date. Don't you remember?"

"We've got time," the young officer said, pulling her down on the bed. "We have business, dedicated business to finish. Guido's den, 1935. Don't you remember?" He mimicked her words. Her eyes widened. She smiled and surrendered.

The twins eyed each other suspiciously.

"You two are almost an hour late. Trouble getting the twins ready?" the distinguished looking gray-haired Captain of Detectives, Homicide, said.

"Come, sit down with us, we've kept the coffee hot," the plump, attractive lady with him said. "The others will join us in a few minutes. Now don't fuss! Grandma and Grandpa will take the twins. See how they want to come to us!" She held out her arms, and poked Grandpa.

"Thanks Sam, Fulvia," the Army 1st Lieutenant, Infantry, said. He scratched his nose and added, "Yes, our being late had something to do with the twins."

Marjorie looked at her husband of just under three years, 1st Lieutenant Phil Martello, her eyes wide and shining, "Yes Sam, as Phil said, I guess you could say it had something to do with the twins."

The long look she gave him said it all.

Captain of Detectives Sam Pizzuta coughed and took a big swallow of hot coffee.

THE END

About The Author

Flavio Joseph "Joe" Rosati was born in Massachusetts and educated at Cornell and Clark Universities. His 40 year career included tours with the U.S. Army as an infantry officer, private industry, local, state and federal governments. In 1971 he was appointed Chief of Intergovernmental Personnel Programs for the San Francisco Region, U.S. Civil Service Commission. He worked with the governors of four western states, mayors, Pacific Rim jurisdictions, and Indian tribal governments to improve their management capacity. He and his staff wrote and published dozens of special technical studies in organization, pay, classification, and training.

Of special significance was Joe's on-site work with the Trust Territory of the Pacific Islands (Micronesia) in the '70's when the islands broke up and other countries sought to influence or take over these strategic isles. The Northern Marianas chain which includes Saipan opted to become the Commonwealth of the Northern Marianas under the United States.

Joe was also immersed in curriculum development for the dozens of courses offered by the San Francisco Region's Training Center and managed the editing and publication of the course catalog and course schedule, a major undertaking covering 340,000 federal employees. He has been published in a professional journal, was editor-in-chief of a house organ, and in the Jurassic period (or so it seems!) he was editor of a prize-winning high school paper.

Joe holds the prestigious State of California Senate Rules Committee Resolution of Commendation, and special proclamations of appreciation signed by the governors of Arizona, Nevada, and Diane Feinstein, then mayor of San Francisco. She now serves in Washington D.C. as one of two female California senators.

Joe and his wife Sue have five children and seven grandchildren. They live in Lafayette, part of the San Francisco Bay Area. They are expert ballroom dancers, and Joe has been jogging for years. He has competed in several 10 K runs and finished them all. He now is immersed in a new career, the writing of novels, both fiction and nonfiction.